T0268684

The Chandelier

ALSO BY CLARICE LISPECTOR

Água Viva

The Besieged City

A Breath of Life

The Complete Stories

The Foreign Legion

The Hour of the Star

Near to the Wild Heart

The Passion According to G. H.

Selected Crônicas

Soulstorm

THE CHANDELIER

Clarice Lispector

Translated from the Portuguese by Benjamin Moser
and Magdalena Edwards

Edited by Benjamin Moser

A NEW DIRECTIONS BOOK

Originally published as *O lustre*. Published by arrangement with the Heirs
of Clarice Lispector and Agencia Literaria Carmen Balcells, Barcelona.

New Directions gratefully acknowledges the support of

N𝕭 MINISTÉRIO DA CULTURA
Fundação BIBLIOTECA NACIONAL

First published clothbound by New Directions in 2018 and as New Directions
Paperbook 1446 in 2019 (ISBN 978-0-8112-2871-8)
Manufactured in the United States of America
New Directions Books are printed on acid-free paper
Design by Erik Rieselbach

Library of Congress Cataloging-in-Publication Data
Names: Lispector, Clarice, author. | Moser, Benjamin, translator. |
Edwards, Magdalena, translator.
Title: The chandelier / Clarice Lispector ; translated by Benjamin Moser
and Magdalena Edwards.
Other titles: Lustre. English
Description: First edition. |
Portuguese editions published in 1946, 1967, and 1982.
Identifiers: LCCN 2017051736 | ISBN 9780811223133 (alk. paper)
Subjects: LCSH: Women—Fiction. | Social isolation—Fiction. |
Creation (Literary, artistic, etc.)—Fiction.
Classification: LCC PQ9697.L585 L813 2018 | DDC 869.3/42—dc23
LC record available at https://lccn.loc.gov/2017051736

10 9 8 7 6 5 4 3 2 1

New Directions Books are published for James Laughlin
by New Directions Publishing Corporation
80 Eighth Avenue, New York 10011

For my sister Tania

The Chandelier

SHE'D BE FLOWING ALL HER LIFE. BUT WHAT HAD DOM-
inated her edges and attracted them toward a center, what
had illuminated her against the world and given her intimate
power was the secret. She'd never know how to think of it
in clear terms afraid to invade and dissolve its image. Yet it
had formed in her interior a far-off and living nucleus and
had never lost the magic—it sustained her in her unsolvable
vagueness like the single reality that for her should always be
the lost one. The two of them were leaning over the fragile
bridge and Virgínia was feeling her bare feet falter insecurely
as if they were dangling atop the calm whirl of the waters. It
was a violent and dry day, in broad fixed colors; the trees were
creaking beneath the warm wind wrinkled by swift cool drafts.
The thin and torn girlish dress was pierced by shivers of coolness. With her serious mouth pressed against the dead branch
of the bridge, Virgínia was plunging her distracted eyes into
the waters. Suddenly she'd frozen tense and light:
   "Look!"

Daniel had turned his head quickly—stuck on a rock was a wet hat, heavy and dark with water. The running river was tugging it with brutality and it was putting up a fight. Until losing its final strength it was taken by the light current and in leaps disappeared into the foam almost happy. They hesitated surprised.

"We can't tell anyone," whispered Virgínia finally, her voice distant and dizzy.

"Yes ...,"—even Daniel had been frightened and was agreeing ... the waters kept flowing—"Not even if they ask us about the drow—"

"Yes!" Virgínia almost shouted ... both fell silent with strength, their eyes bulging and ferocious.

"Virgínia ...," her brother said slowly with a rawness that left his face all angles, "I will swear."

"Yes ... my God, but one always swears ..."

Daniel was thinking while looking at her and she wasn't moving her face waiting for him to find in her the answer.

"For example ... that everything that we are ... turns to nothing ... if we speak of this to anyone."

He had spoken so seriously, he had spoken so beautifully, the river was rolling, the river was rolling. The leaves covered in dust, the thick and moist leaves along the banks, the river was rolling. She wanted to respond and say that yes, yes! hotly, almost happy, laughing with dry lips ... but she couldn't speak, she didn't know how to breathe; how it unsettled her. With dilated eyes, her face suddenly small and colorless, she cautiously assented with her head. Daniel moved off, Daniel was moving off. No! she wanted to shout and tell him to wait, not to leave her alone above the river; but he kept going. Her heart beating in a body suddenly empty of blood, her heart skipping, falling furiously, the waters rushing, she tried to open her lips, blow out any pale word. Like the impossible cry in a nightmare, no sound was heard and the clouds were sliding quickly in the sky toward a destination. Beneath her feet the waters were murmuring—in a bright hallucination she was thinking: ah yes, so she'd fall and drown, ah yes. Some intense and livid thing like terror but triumphant, a certain mad and bristling happiness was now filling her body and she was waiting to die, her hand closed as if for all time on the branch of the bridge. Daniel turned around right then.

"Come," he said surprised.

She looked at him from the quiet depth of her silence.

"Come on, you idiot," he repeated angrily.

A dead instant extended things lengthily. She and Daniel were two points forever hushed and immobile. But I already died, she seemed to think as she was letting go of the bridge as if being cut from it with a scythe. I already died, she was still thinking and on strange feet her white face was running heavily toward Daniel.

Walking down the road, blood had started beating with rhythm in her veins again, they were advancing quickly, together. In the dust could be seen the hesitant mark of the only car in Upper Marsh. Beneath the brilliant sky the day was vibrating in its last moment before night, in the paths and in the trees silence was gathering heavy with sultriness—she was feeling the last warm rays of the sun on her back, the thick clouds tensely gilded. It was nevertheless vaguely cold, as if coming from the shady forest. They were looking ahead with keen bodies—there was a threat of transition in the air being breathed ... the next instant would bring a cry and something puzzlingly would destroy itself, or the light night would suddenly soften that excessive, rude, and solitary existence. They were walking quickly. There was a perfume that was swelling the heart. The shadows were slowly covering the road and when Daniel pushed the heavy garden gate night was falling. The fireflies were opening livid dots in the half-light. They stopped for a moment indecisive in the darkness before mingling with the ones who didn't know, looking at each other as if for the last time.

"Daniel …," Virgínia murmured, "I can't even speak to you?"

"No," he said surprised by his own response.

They hesitated for a moment, restrained, quiet. No, no! …, she was denying the fear that was nearing, as if to buy time before rushing ahead. No, no, she was saying avoiding looking around. Night had fallen, night had fallen. Don't rush! but suddenly something couldn't contain itself and started to happen … Yes, right there the vapors would arise of the sickly, pale dawn that was like the end of a pain—Virgínia was suddenly seeing calm, submissive, and absorbed. Each dry branch would hide beneath the brightness of a cave. That land beyond the trees, castrated in the bud by the fire, would be seen through the soft mist, blackened and difficult as if through a past—she was now seeing quiet and inexpressive as if without memory. The dead man would slip for the last time among the frozen and sleeping trees. Like bells ringing from afar, Virgínia would feel in her body the touch of his presence, would get out of bed slowly, wise and blind as a sleepwalker, and inside her heart a spot would beat weakly, almost fainting. She would raise the window, her lungs enveloped by the cold mist. Plunging her eyes into the blindness of the dark, her senses beating in the frozen and sharp space; she would perceive nothing but the shady quiet, the twisted and motionless branches … the long

expanse losing its limits in sudden and unfathomable mist—
there was the limit of the possible world! Then, fragile like a
memory, she would make out the tired stain of the drowned
man moving away, disappearing and reappearing among the
haze, plunging at last into whiteness. Forever! the wide wind
would blow in the trees. She would call almost mutely: man,
but man!, in order to keep him, to bring him back! But it was
forever, Virgínia, listen, forever and even if Quiet Farm with-
ers and new lands emerge indefinably never would the man
return. Virgínia, never, never, Virgínia. Never. She shook herself out of the sleep into which she'd slid, her eyes had gained
a shining and shrewd life, contained exclamations were aching
inside her narrow chest; the hard and suffocating incomprehension was hastening her heart into the dark of the night. I
don't want the owl to cry, she shouted at herself in a soundless
sob. And the owl immediately cried blackly on a branch. She
jumped—or had it cried before her thought? or at the exact
same time? I don't want to hear the trees, she was saying to
herself fumbling within herself, moving forward stunned. And
the trees upon a sudden wind were rustling in a slow murmur
of strange and tall life. Or hadn't it been a foreboding? she
was begging herself. I don't want Daniel to move. And Daniel
was moving. Her breath light, her hearing new and surprised,
she seemed to be able to penetrate and flee things in silence
like a shadow; weak and blind, she was feeling the color and
the sound of whatever was almost happening. She was tremulously moving ahead of herself, flying with her senses ahead
crossing the tense and perfumed air of the new night. I don't
want the bird to fly, she was saying to herself now almost a
light in her chest despite the terror, and in a tired and difficult
perception was presaging the future movements of things an

instant before they ring out. And if she wanted to she'd say: I don't want to hear the rolling of the river, and there was no nearby river but she would hear its deaf wail over small stones ... and now ... now ... yes ...!

"Virgínia! Daniel!"

In confusion everything was hurrying scared and dark, their mother's call was sprouting from the depths of the mansion and bursting between them in a new presence. The voice had not altered the silence of the night but had split its darkness as if the cry were white lightning. Before she was aware of her movements, Virgínia found herself inside the house, behind the closed door. The parlor, the stairs were stretching in indistinct and somber silence. The lit lamps were flickering on their wires under the wind in a prolonged mute movement. Beside her was Daniel, his lips bloodless, hard, and ironic. In the quiet of the Farm some unbridled horse was slowly moving the grass with thin legs. In the kitchen they were rummaging through silverware, a sudden sound of a bell and Esmeralda's steps quickly crossed a bedroom ... the lit lamp flickering calmly, the sleeping stairs breathing. Then—neither from relief nor from the end of a fright, but in itself inexplicable, alive, and mysterious—then she felt a long, bright, high instant open inside her. Stroking with cold fingers the old latch of the door, she narrowed her eyes smiling with mischief and deep satisfaction.

Quiet Farm and its lands extended some miles from the houses clustered around the school and the health clinic, keeping a distance from the center of the municipality of Upper Marsh, to which they belonged. The mansion belonged to their grand-mother; her children had married and lived far away. The youngest son had brought his wife there and in Quiet Farm Esmeralda, Daniel, and Virgínia had been born. Little by lit-tle the furniture had defected, sold, broken, or grown old and the bedrooms were emptying palely. Virgínia's, cold, light, and square, had nothing more than a bed. On the headboard she'd deposit her dress before going to sleep and sheathed in her thin petticoat, her feet dirty with earth, hide beneath the enor-mous queen-size sheets with extended pleasure.

"It'd be preferable to have more furniture and fewer bed-rooms," Esmeralda would complain lowering her eyes with rage and annoyance, her big feet bare.

"Quite the contrary," her father would answer when she wouldn't shut up. The stairs meanwhile were covered with a thick carpet of purple velvet, dating from the time of her grandmother's wedding, branching out through the hallways to the rooms in a sudden luxury, safe and serious. The doors would open and instead of the cozy wealth that the carpet an-nounced you found emptiness, silence, and shadow, the wind communicating with the world through windows without cur-tains. From the high windowpanes you saw besides the garden of tangled plants and dry twigs the long stretch of land of a sad and whispered silence. The dining room itself, the larg-est room in the mansion, extended below in long damp shad-ows, almost deserted: the heavy oak table, the light and gilded chairs of an old set of furniture, a console with thin twisted legs, the quick air on the shining latches, and a long sideboard where a few glass and crystal pieces were shimmering trans-lucently in smothered cries, asleep in dust. On the shelf of that fixture lay the washbasin of pink china, the cold water

9

in the half-light refreshing the bottom where a fat, crooked, and sensual angel was struggling, captive. Tall murals were rising from the walls scratching vertical and silent shadows over the floor. On afternoons when wind would roll through the Farm—the women in the rooms, her father at work, Daniel in the forest—on smooth afternoons when a wind full of sun would blow as if over ruins, stripping the walls eaten in the rubble, Virgínia would roam in abandoned brightness. She'd walk while looking, in a serious distraction. It was daytime, the fields were stretching out brightly, without stains and she'd go ahead wakefully. She felt a diffuse nausea in her calm nerves— small and thin, her legs marked by mosquitoes and falls, she'd stop next to the staircase looking. The steps rising sinuously would achieve a firm loveliness so light that Virgínia would lose her perception almost upon grasping it and stop short just ahead seeing only dusty wood and incarnadine velvet, step, step, dry angles. Without knowing why, she'd nonetheless halt, fanning her bare thin arms; she lived on the verge of things. The parlor. The parlor filled with neutral spots. The smell of an empty house. But the chandelier! There was the chandelier. The great spider would glow. She'd look at it immobile, uneasy, seeming to foresee a terrible life. That icy existence. Once! once in a flash—the chandelier would scatter in chrysanthemums and joy. Another time—while she was running through the parlor—it was a chaste seed. The chandelier. She'd skip off without looking back.

At night the parlor was lit up in a flickering and sweet brightness. Two lamps were resting on the buffet available for anyone ready to retire. Before entering the bedroom the light should be put out. At dawn a rooster would sing a clean cross in the dark space—the humid scratch was spreading a cold smell all around, the sound of a little bird was scraping the surface of the half-light without piercing it. Virgínia would hoist her dull senses, her closed eyes. The bloody young cries of the roosters were repeated throughout the neighborhood of Upper Marsh. A red crest would shake in a shiver, while delicate and decided legs were advancing slow steps on the pale floor, the cry was released—and far off like the flight of an arrow another tough and living rooster was opening his ferocious beak and responding—while the still-sleeping ears were awaiting with vague attention. The enraptured and weak morning was radiating outward like a bit of news. Virgínia was getting up, getting into her short dress, pushing open the tall windows of the bedroom, the mist penetrating slow and oppressed; she was dunking her head, her face sweet like that of an animal eating from your hand. Her damp nose was moving, her cold cheek sharpened in brightness was moving forward in a searching, free, and frightened thrust. She could only make out a couple of metal posts from the garden fence. The barbed wire was pointing dryly from inside the frozen fog; the trees were emerging blackly, with hidden roots. She was opening wide eyes. There was the stone streaming with dew. And beyond the garden the land disappearing abruptly. The whole house was floating, floating in clouds, disconnected from Upper Marsh. Even the unkempt brush was moving off pale and still and in vain Virgínia was seeking in her immobility the familiar line; the loose kindling beneath the window, near the ruined entryway arch, was resting neat and lifeless. But then only seconds later the sun was coming out bleached like a moon. Then only seconds later the mists were disappearing with the speed of a scattered dream and the whole garden, the mansion, the plains, the forest were shining even brighter setting off small thin, brittle, still-tired sounds. An intelligent, clear, and dry cold was traversing the garden, blowing itself into the flesh of the body. A cry of fresh coffee was rising from the kitchen mixed with the smooth and breathless smell of wet grass. Her heart was beating in a painful and moist flutter as if pierced by an impossible desire. And the life of the day was beginning puzzled. Her cheek tender and frozen as a hare's, her lips hard from the cold, Virgínia lingered for a vacant second at the window listening with some spot of her body to the space before her. She was hesitating between disappointment and a difficult charm—like a madwoman the night would lie during the day…

Like a madwoman the night would lie, like a madwoman the night would lie—she'd go down the dusty stairs barefoot, her steps warmed by the velvet. They were sitting at the table for breakfast and if Virgínia didn't eat enough she'd get slapped right then—how nice it was, his flattened hand would quickly fly and crack with a joyful sound on one of her cheeks cooling the somber parlor with the lightness of a sneeze. Her face would awake like an anthill in the sun and then she'd ask for more cornbread, filled with a lie of hunger. Her father would keep chewing, his lips wet with milk, while along with the wind a certain joy was lingering in the air; a fresh sound from the back of the mansion was filling the parlor softly. But Esmeralda always got away, her back upright, her chest raised. Because Mother would stand up pale and stuttering and say—while a bit of cold was coming through the bright emptiness of the window and looking at Daniel's hard and beloved face a desire to escape with him and run made Virgínia's heart swell dizzy and

light in a forward thrust—while her mother would say:
"I don't even have the right to a son?"

"To a daughter, she should say"—Virgínia would think without raising her eyes from the cup because in those very moments the neigh of some horse in the pasture would hurt like a sad and thoughtful daring. Esmeralda and Mother would talk at length in the bedroom, their eyes shining with quick understandings. Every once in a while the two would work on the cut of a dress as if defying the world. Father never spoke to Esmeralda and nobody ever mentioned what had happened to her except from a distance. Not even Virgínia had ever asked about it; she could live with an unrevealed secret in her hands without anxiety as if that were the true life of things. Esmeralda would clasp the long skirt she wore at home, climb the stairs, burn an angry, insistent, and solemn perfume in her room; you couldn't stay in her room for more than a few minutes, suddenly the smell cloyed and stunned in a chapel-like queasiness. But she herself would stay absorbed before the bowl that served as a vase, seem to inhale the hot flame with her strong, feminine, and hypocritical eyes. All her underwear was embroidered by hand; Father didn't look at Esmeralda as if she were dead. The last time he'd touched her had been precisely when she'd spoken once again of the journey that Daniel and Virgínia would one day make to the city in order to study languages, business, and piano—Daniel who had such a good ear and practiced sometimes on a piano in Upper Marsh. With the other daughter, he'd say, he wouldn't do the same because "you only set loose a toothless animal." Esmeralda would sit with Mother at mealtimes; she'd always come down a bit late and slow, but Father wouldn't say anything. And she could also turn up pale and with bags under her eyes because she'd gone dancing in the house of a family in Upper Marsh. Mother would then come down invigorated by exhaustion, her body frightened, such was the excitement that would overtake her when she started going to parties again. Her eyes would go blank and she'd envision the salon again as she chewed. Sweet and shining the girls once again would spread across the balconies, the parlor, in calm and contained poses, waiting their turn to be entwined; then they'd dance, their faces almost serious; the more immoral ones would heave their bosoms with innocence, all of them coiffed and content, in their eyes a single and indecipherable thought; but the men, as always, were inferior, pale, and dashing; they'd sweat a lot; since they were few in number, some girls would end up dancing with other girls, excited, laughing, jumping, their eyes surprised. She was chewing, her gaze fixed, feeling the incomprehensible reality of the dance floating like a lie. Father would stare at them in silence. Before starting to eat and letting everyone begin, he'd agree with a certain sadness:

"Well then."

Virgínia loved him so much at times like this that she'd want to weep into her plate out of hope and confusion. Mother would sigh with thoughtful eyes:

"Who knows, my God."

But she'd spend the days like a guest in her own house, she wouldn't give orders, taking care of nothing. Her flowery, worn-out dress would cover her floppily, allow a glimpse of her long breasts, fat and bored. She'd once been alive, with small decisions every minute—her tired and angry eye would shine. That's how she'd lived, married, and caused Esmeralda to be born. And then a slow loss had supervened, she didn't encompass her own life with her gaze, though her body kept living, separate from other bodies. She was lazy, tired, and vague, Daniel had been born and then Virgínia, shaped in the lower part of her body, uncontrollable—a little skinny, hairy, their eyes actually even beautiful. She was clinging to Esmeralda as to the remains of her final existence, from that time when she'd breathe forward telling herself: I'm going to have a daughter, my husband's going to buy an upholstered living room set, today is Monday ... From the days before she married she lovingly kept a nightgown thin from use as if the days without a husband or children were glorious. That's how she'd protect herself from her husband, from Virgínia, and from Daniel— her eyes blinking. Her husband bit by bit had imposed a certain kind of silence with his cunning and still body. And bit by bit, after the heyday of prohibiting purchases and spending, she had found out with brooding joy, in one of the greatest urges of her life, that she wasn't living in her own home, but in her husband's, in her old mother-in-law's. Yes, yes; before she'd connect with joyful threads to whatever was going on and now the threads were fattening stickily or breaking and she'd bump abruptly into things. Everything was so irremediable, and she was living so cut off, but so cut off, Maria—she'd turn her thoughts to one of her little schoolmates, one she'd lost touch with. She was simply going on, Maria. She'd look at Daniel and Virgínia, calmly surprised and haughty; they'd been born. Even the birth had been easy, she couldn't even remember the pain, her lower parts were nice and healthy, she'd think while confusedly glancing quickly at herself; they weren't connected to her past. She'd say meekly: eat, Virgínia ...—and come up short. Virgínia ... She hadn't even been the one who chose the name, Maria. She liked names shiny and ironic like someone waving a fan to turn something away: Esmeralda, two waves, Rosicler, three quick waves ... And the girl, like a branch, was growing without her having decorated her previous features, always young, strange, and serious, scratching her dirty head, being tired, not much of an eater, drawing silly things on pieces of paper. Yes, Mother didn't eat much but her abandoned way of being at the table gave the impression she was wallowing in food. She did almost nothing but somehow, she seemed to feel so wrapped up in her own life that she could hardly even shake loose an arm and gesture. Seeing her stranded atop the table; her father chewing with staring eyes; Esmeralda sharp, rigid, and keen saying: where am I supposed to walk?! through those swamps?!; Daniel darkening proud and almost stupidi-fied by so much contained power; and, when she closed her eyes, seeing inside herself a small dense feeling, full of joy, firm, mysterious, and undefined, Virgínia would never know that people wondered whether one quality in a person excluded the possibility of others, if whatever there was inside the body was alive and strange enough that it was also its opposite. As for herself she couldn't even guess what she could do and what she couldn't, what she'd manage to get just by batting her eye-lids and what she'd never obtain, even by giving up her life. But to herself she granted the privilege of not demanding gestures and words in order to show herself. She was feeling that even without a thought, a desire, or a memory, she was imponder-ably whatever she was and that consisted in God knows what.

The days on Quiet Farm were breathing as long and empty as the mansion. The family didn't receive guests all together.

Mother would rarely cheer up for the arrival of two neighbor ladies, she'd whisk them to her own bedroom as if trying to protect them from the long hallways. And Esmeralda
would brighten with excitement and a certain brutality when
her girlfriends, pale and tall under corn-colored hats, came
to see her. She'd quickly put on shoes and, flushed, lead them
to her room locking the door, time passing. And sometimes
some member of the paternal family came from the south to
visit Grandmother and Father. Uncle would sit at the table,
smile at everyone with his deafness and eat. And also Aunt
Margarida, skinny, her skin flaccid, her sharp dry bird face
but her lips always pink and moist like a liver; she'd wear on
a single finger the two rings of widowhood and three more
with stones. Father would be reborn on those days and Virgínia would watch him frightened, with a worried disgust. He
himself wanted to serve the table, he excused the black servant
from the kitchen — Virgínia would look at him restless and
mute, her mouth full of a water of nausea and attention. With
wet eyes he'd bring Grandmother up to the table, saying:
    "The lady of the house must dine with her children, the
lady of the house must dine with her children ..." — and you
hardly noticed that this was a joke. Virgínia would laugh. Aunt
Margarida's gaze was hasty and in the fraction of a second it
lasted she seemed to smile. When it was over, however, and
her face was already turned the other way, something would
float in the air like the aftermath of a revealed fear. With her
head like a little bird's with combed feathers, slanted to the
plate, she'd eat almost without speaking. You could tell she'd
die someday, you could tell. Uncle was saying with a profound
and calm mien:

"But this is so tasty."

"Have some more!" her father was shouting blinking with joy.

Uncle was looking her father right in the eye with an unmoving smile. He was kneading a ball of bread and answering with tact and bonhomie as if needing to mollify his own deafness:

"Well then, well then."

Father was looking for a moment with surpassing astonishment. He was suddenly grabbing his brother's plate, filling it with food and pushing it back, emotive and happy:

"Go on, eat it all at once."

Uncle was slightly gesturing by jerking his hand in front of his own head in a military salute. Father was watching him with his arms outstretched like a doll's, overstating his happiness.

"Ah what a sad life, what a sad life," he was saying laughing a lot.

When after a few days the guests would depart, life in the mansion was once again sucked up by the country air and the flies would buzz louder, shining in the light. Father would resume his solitude without sadness, push away his tablecloth and silverware, bring over a lamp, read the paper and never open his book. He'd later go up to sleep, climbing the stairs slowly as if in order to hear the whinny of the steps, a dark and calm hope, almost a lack of desire. On occasion, in his rolled long johns—he'd suddenly transform into a funny man and Virginia had trouble falling asleep on those nights—in his rolled long johns he'd go about living and stay until two, three in the morning watching the birds lay their small, small eggs. With his body covered in chicken lice he'd then get into a tub full of water and kerosene placed in the courtyard and, lit weakly by the lamp, wash himself, rinse himself silently, the darkness was sprinkled by wet and abrupt noises, he'd go to sleep. Mother would ask amidst the forgetfulness of the dinner, in the heart of the mansion:

"How's the stationer's?"

"Fine," responded her father.

Virgínia would walk past her grandmother's door, stop happily for a second to listen to her snoring. She didn't snore in a straight sharp line but on a pair of wings. The sound would start off broadly, gather in a narrow center and flare out again. Her satisfied and strange snore was a flying wing. Virgínia would enter her room with closed eyes, feel surrounded by a flutter of tender, hoarse, and rapid wings, as if the old lady were releasing a scared little bird with each breath. And when she'd awaken—she'd always awaken suddenly, look around terrorized as if they could have transported her to another world while she was sleeping, and look at Virgínia with spite—when she'd awaken the sound would snap in a straight line, a little bird half-free in a mouth would hesitate trembling and luminous and was swallowed in a murmur. Grandmother no longer left the bedroom where the black servant she'd raised would bring her meals. She only came down when the relatives from the south were visiting. Esmeralda, Daniel, and Virgínia were required to go into her room at least once a day to receive her blessing and give her a sort of quick kiss on the face. And they'd never visit her more than that one time. When the black servant would get sick they'd send Virgínia to stay in her room and attend to her. She'd go in good spirits. Her seated grandmother wouldn't speak, wouldn't laugh, would hardly even look as if now living was enough for her. Sometimes she'd be reborn in a quick expression of a cunning and indecent face. Virgínia would speak to her in a low voice so she wouldn't hear and get annoyed. Her greatest gesture of rage or contempt was spitting to the side; with her dry mouth, she had trouble mustering enough saliva; and by then, distracted from her anger, all she tried to do was spit—propped against the door, her face deeply still and thin, Virgínia would peek. The old lady would seem to meditate for a second, her head bent to the side, in the position to which her rage had brought her; then she'd back down with a satisfied and agile look as if she'd saved up enough saliva for everyone; she'd freeze up again, her shining eyes blinking in their slits every once in a while. Virgínia would shake from distaste and fear. She'd watch her move her hand leisurely and with a shaky slowness scratch her dry nose. "Don't you die, damned old woman," she'd repeat the servant's phrase angrily to herself. But her grandmother would suddenly let out a sneeze of a cat in the sun and something would mix with Virgínia's fear, an ashamed and irritated pity would weigh on her chest. "Don't die, darling little old lady," she'd repeat. The bedroom would darken in her open and staring eyes while she'd press her whole body against the door. And suddenly a movement of life would seem to hurry and fall onto the same level—the feeling of falling when you go to sleep. Immutable, immutable.

But sometimes her life was so fast. Lights wander around, Virgínia peers at the sky, colors shine beneath the air. Virgínia wanders around, the brightness is the air, Virgínia breathes brightness, leaves shake unawares, Virgínia isn't thinking, the lights wander around, Virgínia peers at the sky ... Sometimes her life was so fast. Her small girlish head was dizzy, she was staring at the field in front of her, peering at Quiet Farm already lost in the distance and looking without trying to understand. In Upper Marsh there was no sea, yet a person could look quickly at the broad meadow, then close her eyes, clutch her own heart and like a child, like a child being born, smell the sweetly rotten odor of the sea. And even if just then the day were hard and new, the plants dry with dust, red and hot summer clouds, the rough sunflowers shaking against space at the end of their thick stalks, even without the happy moistness of the lands beside the waters ... once a bird blossomed from the meadow to the air in sudden flight, made her heart beat quickly in a pale fright. And that was free and light as if someone were walking along the beach. She had never been near the sea but knew what the sea was like, neither would she force her life to express it in thoughts, she knew, that was enough. When you least expected it night arrived, the owl would cry, Daniel could at any moment call her to take a walk, someone could show up at the door delivering some message, she and Daniel would run to find out what it was about, the servant could fall ill, she herself might wake up once a bit later—she was so finely simple during that time. The unexpected didn't exist and the miracle was the revealed movement of things; had a rose blossomed in her body, Virgínia would have plucked it with care and with it adorned her hair without smiling. There was a certain amazed and tenuous joy without comic notes—where? ah, a color, the cold plants that seemed to give off small, vacant, and bright sounds in the air, tiny breaths, tremulously alive. Her life was painstaking but at the same time she was living just a single streak sketched without strength and without end, flat and terrified like the trace of another life; and the most she could do was cautiously follow her glimpses of it. Could everyone know what I know? she would wonder with the stubborn and unintelligent look that was a shared characteristic of the family, her head drooping. She'd stop for an instant at the edge of the field and grow still lying in wait paying close attention to her own possibilities. A long minute would unfurl, of the same color and on the same level as a point emerging from itself in a straight and sluggish line. As long as it lasted everything that existed outside of her was seen only by her eyes in a clean and curious realization. But from one moment to the next, without any warning, she'd shudder delicately gathering all at once the movements contained in the things around her. She'd instantaneously transmit her own movements outside of her mixed with the load received; before long in the country air there was one more element that she was creating by emitting with small mute smiles her own strength. She'd move ahead and freely penetrate the wet grass, her narrow legs would get wet. Everything would spin lightly around itself, the wind on the leaves of the courtyard. Every once in a while, like a little almost inaudible cry and then silence denying it, she'd quickly gain the feeling of being able to live and then she'd lose it forever in a dizzy surprise: what happened? Though the feeling was fleeting as a perfume while you run, almost a lie, it had been exactly that, being able to live ... She said to Daniel:

"What's good and what scares us is that ... for example, I can do my things ... that I've got ahead of me a thing that still doesn't exist, you know?"

Daniel looked straight ahead inflexible:

"And then what? the future ..."

"Yes, but it's horrible, isn't it?" she'd say fiery and smiling.

Profoundly ignorant she'd do little exercises and comprehensions involving things like walking, looking at tall trees, waiting on a bright morning for the end of the day but just waiting for an instant, picking out one ant just like all the rest from many, strolling slowly, paying attention to silence by almost grabbing on to a slight sound with her ears, breathing quickly, placing an expectant hand over the heart that didn't stop, looking emphatically at a stone, at a bird, at her own foot, swinging about with her eyes closed, laughing out loud when she was alone and then listening, dropping her body onto the bed without the least strength almost aching all over from such an effort to annihilate herself, trying coffee without sugar, looking at the sun until she cried without pain—space would then turn woozy as before a terrible rain—, carrying in the palm of her hand a little bit of river without spilling it, placing herself beneath a flagpole in order to look up and grow dizzy with herself—changing with care the way she lived. The things that would inspire her were so brief. Vaguely, vaguely, if she'd been born, plunged her hands in the water and died, she'd exhaust her strength and her forward movement would have been complete—that was her impression without thoughts.

In the afternoon the palm trees had been knocked down for some reason and great palm leaves hard and verdant were covering themselves nervously with ants that went up and went down mysteriously carrying out a mission or having fun for a reason. Virgínia kneeled down peering at them. She lifted her eyes and saw white smoke rising in the distance, amidst the black kindling. A quick kaleidoscope movement and a still image was taking shape, insoluble and nothing beyond: grasses standing in the sun, hot and calm sun, warm rows of ants, thick stalks of palm, the earth pricking her knees, her hair falling in her eyes, the wind piercing through the rip in her dress and coolly brightening her arm, veiled smoke dissolving in the air and all this connected by the same mysterious interval—an instant after she raised her head and made out the smoke in the distance, an instant before she lowered her head and felt new things. And she also knew vaguely, almost as if she were making it up, that inside that interval there was yet another instant, small, pallid, and placid, without having inside her any of the things she was seeing, like that, like that. And how poor and free were she and Daniel. The whole world could laugh at both of them and they wouldn't do anything, wouldn't find out a thing. People said they were sad but they were happy. Sometimes Daniel would come talk to her about running away someday—both knew that they didn't quite want that. She'd lift her head from the ground and see above her lips trembling from nascent imagination a badly drawn arc of already-dried coffee-with-milk! She'd turn aside eyes suddenly wounded in the most tender spot in her heart and haughty, frightened, stumble amidst repugnance, tears, and contempt, at wit's end, living, living. She'd finally fall into a deep and intolerable devotion, brutal with herself and that eventually drove her to a kind of intimate glory, a bit miserable too. During that time she'd feel quite sorry for herself, with an almost voluptuous violence, feeling in her mouth a flashing taste of blood. In secret, she felt sorry for everything, for the most powerful things. Sometimes, terrified by a scream from her father, her eyes low and frightened would light on those thick boots where a gray shoestring was hesitating to be of use. And suddenly, without warning, all her flesh hurting as if a sweet acid were covering her all at once, she'd slide toward a martyrdom of understanding and her eyes would be covered with moist tenderness. People were so ridiculous!, she felt like crying from joy and shame at being alive. That was her impression. Father was coming in the wagon, asking:

"What's going on? Virgínia's crying?"

"No, singing," the black woman would answer. "She's been singing loud, loud ballads for hours, it's awful."

She was skinny and dirty, the long veins of her neck were trembling—she'd sing awfully, pure sound screaming, going beyond things on their own terms. What mattered were the realms her voice was reaching. First of all, she was still small while standing on the doorstep; meanwhile the notes were rising like soap bubbles, shining and full, and wander off into the brightness of the air; and meanwhile, those soap bubbles belonged to her, to her who was small while standing on the doorstep. That's how it was. And it was also in her nature to know how to imitate the cries of animals, sometimes of animals that didn't exist but could exist. They were guarded voices, round in the throat, howling, crazy, and rather small. She could also make sharp and sweet calls like those of lost animals. But suddenly things were rushing into a resistant reality. One day Father found her crying; she was almost a big girl looking distractedly at the clouds that were moving past. Stupefied he'd asked:

"But why? Why?"

Everything had grown difficult then, he'd come and was boring her. And since she didn't know how to answer she made something up:

"Daniel and I can't live here forever ..."

Terrified her father heard this as if hearing a tree speak. And then in a strange and sudden understanding that scared her because she hadn't understood a thing, he was filled with a rage that turned him red and tense, in an almost dangerous outrage.

"That's a lie, fool! fool! fool!"

Since she looked at him surprised, her young face already shining without tears, he stared at her with furrowed brows, concluded more calmly shrugging almost with indifference:

"Fool."

Daniel was a strange boy, sensitive and proud, hard to love. He didn't know how to make an excuse for hiding. Even when he'd fall into fantasies these were cautious, familiar; he didn't have the courage to make things up and she was always the one who with a surprising facility would lie for both of them; he was sincere and harsh, hating whatever he couldn't see. With his clean and dry eyes he was living as if with Virgínia alone at the Farm. Ever since his sister was born he'd taken her and secretly she was his alone. When she was still very small, her long and dirty hair falling in her eyes, her short legs hesitating above her bare feet, she would grab with one of her hands the hem of Daniel's pants and her brother, his face sunburned and without sweetness, his eyes sure of themselves, would climb the slopes of the mountains, with stubborn movements as if not feeling Virgínia's weight, the resistant incline of the hills, the wind that was blowing firm and cold against his body. He didn't even love her, but she was sweet and simple, easy to lead toward any idea. And even in the periods when he'd shut down severe and rude giving her orders, she'd obey because she felt him near her, paying attention to her—he was the most perfect creature she'd ever know. She would then spend days in a strange euphoria, like the wind, high, calm, and silent. My God, she didn't even know that she was thinking, all she had was ardor, nothing more, not even a point. And he—all he had was fury, nothing more, not even a point. Despite everything Daniel would tread lightly, allow that unwieldy and watchful despair of his to live inside her, a sharp weakness, the possibility of perceiving with the nose, of foreseeing inside of silence, of living deeply without carrying out a movement. And of being shut inside a room while in danger. Yes, yes, little by little, softly, from her ignorance the idea was being born that she possessed a life. It was a feeling with neither fore- nor afterthoughts, sudden, complete, and united, which could neither be increased nor altered by age or wisdom. It wasn't like living, living and then knowing that you possessed a life, but it was like looking and seeing all at once. The feeling didn't come from facts present or past but from her own self like a movement. And if she died young or took the veil, the warning that she had a life was just as good as having lived a lot. That's another reason she was a little tired perhaps, for as long as she could remember; sometimes only with an imperceptible effort did she manage to keep afloat. And above all else, she'd always been serious and false.

In the afternoon they put on clean clothes, wet and combed their hair and went with Father to the stationer's. It was a good place to hang around, with a door and a window, almost dark and pleasant inside. They sold books, notebooks, saints, and religious medallions. For every birthday at Quiet Farm the present was a little medallion with a different saint, generally the one least sought after by the clientele of Upper Marsh.

They also sold postcards with kissing lovers, angels and cupids, snowy landscapes. Esmeralda had brought one with a young man offering a flower to a girl who was thinking with a hand on her forehead, her elbow loose in space. The most popular items however were religious articles. The street where the stationer's was rose narrowly and with effort to the Bom Jesus Church, with a white courtyard encircled by rusty fencing. People leaving church bought little medallions. Daniel and Virgínia, while they were waiting for their father, went into the church. It was squat and clean, dark; the exterior had been whitewashed. Inside the oil lamp was lit and a purplish and solitary stain was muffled in old carpets. "Pray for us," they said quickly, peering at the small font of holy water and left hurriedly stepping without violence on the floor of damp tiles. A thunderclap was heard in the distance. It was already growing dark but Father's store was full of men talking business. Virgínia and Daniel left again walking through the almost-dark streets; they'd look through the odd window someone had forgotten to close at the dusty interiors of the houses; the furniture, the bits of old and squat crockery seemed to be made of matter alive and expectant like trees. The tight streets went up or down lightly along with them. Between the stones the City Hall had forgotten weeds. Things at a certain point intensely took on some imprecise color, perhaps bluish without the air that was bathing them in tone and transparency appearing to exist and touch them. Their arms were translucent and wild, their faces vacant and softly awake. The low houses gave directly onto the sidewalk, one stuck to the next, with small iron balconies that didn't stick out. The pink multi-story houses were wide and flat, the windows colored. They walked to the park, tired and hungry. They sat together on a bench. Through the slight fog in the park the lampposts were already turning on round lights, yellow and frightened. Across the calm and treeless expanse that surprising silence, a simple and roaring sound blinking serenely. Another thunderclap rolled, muffled, distant. A frog was jumping from the shadows, gilding itself for an instant in the brightness and plunging into the darkness of the shrubbery. Suddenly Daniel looking at her, got tired of Virgínia sharply, while she was nodding off from fatigue. He stood and sat on another bench without her protesting. There the fountain was spilling water that was always new and soft, noisy. The smell of the creeping plants was carried by the wind, the cold of the water was spreading through the air in drops. He started thinking with violence about nothing. A desire to kill, to conquer, while the slow and reddish ant was moving atop long legs across the cement of the bench. Daniel didn't know what to do and the wet noise of the water was refreshing his enormous spirit. A great wish as if ironically was seizing him and he was already even almost fifteen. He grabbed a tall piece of grass, pulled it, chewed it, and in defiance swallowed it. But that wasn't much. It seemed to him that he should die as an answer, yes as an answer. He needed wrath to live, it gave him an eloquence. He breathed with eagerness feeling the hard and inflexible greenness of life in his heart—the new vitality slipped a thought into him, he'd frighten her, tell her he was going to die! The little notion gave him a more hurried life as his eyes were rejoicing. He returned to the bench where a seated Virgínia was plunging her sleepy eyes into the ground. A thin woolen shawl was protecting her thin shoulders from the cold.

"You're hunchbacked," he said as an opening.

She straightened her back for a second and went back to her old position with weakness. He was annoyed; but was wisely transforming his urge into the slow strength of patience. He said:

"Let's walk."

He made her run almost. Quickly a kind of joy overtook her, her drowsiness disappeared.

"I'm going to die," he said in a blasé tone because he could no longer contain himself.

She blanched.

"No."

Virgínia never disappointed him ... He scrutinized her with curiosity, noted that she was moved, laughed out loud with disdain and vehemence, shimmied as if splashing in the water.

"I'll die like ..."—he made a face of a dead man but observed that right then his violence had fallen away and without interest he was looking at the garden. She wasn't frightened. And he started getting tired as they walked. They remained quiet but maybe both were thinking slightly about the same thing. Could it be that everyone knows what I know? Virgínia was reflecting. Because she'd just thought almost certainly, without astonishment, about dying.

Daniel also knew about a game that started off calm and bright but then got scary for some reason or another. He'd dig into the ground, resistant and dried by the sun, until finding humid soil, new, crumbly but quite amenable to being gathered into a single mass. He'd dig a trench, Virgínia would get in. It was with a face of serious and painstaking pleasure that she'd feel the warm coolness of the earth on her body, that smooth, delicate, and heavy shelter. Through the soles of her feet a shudder of fear was climbing, the whisper that the earth could deepen itself. And from within certain butterflies were arising beating their wings through her whole body.

"You're closed off," Daniel was saying to her rudely, but she was laughing softly without feeling afraid. Slowly however, she did get scared, the wind bending weeds, scattering leaves. And they didn't mention it again, they tried to forget and forgot forever without a sign. He was making a small feint forward as if about to jump: look, Virgínia, I'm going to jump off! Off the world is what he meant—and it had been hard to make her understand. When it had sunk in, a white and quavering dread had appeared on her suddenly diminished face as if it were shrinking backwards. Daniel's eyes were shining in a hot, dark, and terribly exciting pleasure: look, Virgínia, I'm going to jump off! He feinted the jump that would fling him off the earth. No, no—she was saying hoarsely, the palms of her hands quickly becoming damp, she was grabbing her brother's clothes with frozen fingers, feeling her own stiff movements on the rough cloth. He never kept going with the game, as if sparing Virgínia for another time. She'd open her dry lips in the difficulty of a smile of relief.

Back then Father would go early to the stationer's. As soon as he'd headed to town the house would become less pinched, a large space with a few walls because they didn't have to pay attention to their mother and Esmeralda would only come out of her room at lunchtime. She and Daniel. But she wasn't like Daniel, so filled with thoughts you couldn't guess at, so proud. He'd never apologized, he knew that was the sign of a power. Between son and father floated a cautious and disturbed sincerity. And he was so stubborn that, even when he was small, he wouldn't speak a single word after the sun set, even breaking off a sentence or a laugh. He'd sit in a nook, his eyes glassy with fury and sadness. He'd only settle down the next day. They'd ask him with annoyance why and he'd say as if offended by someone:

"I like when it's daylight."

Yes, he'd always been manly in a way that irritated the family. I don't want to be a boy, he'd say quietly while shaking his body briskly while his eyes would sharpen dark and ferocious. Virgínia wouldn't answer, they both knew that he was screaming from emotion, he'd have to wait so long, with eyes squinting, his face mobile as if in response to an approaching murmur, that's how long he'd have to wait to grow up. His anger was also directed at the family that would watch his development with pleasure and pride, making this into a domestic celebration and since he wanted to grow up alone, watchful. He had a collection of downy gray spiders, caught in the forest.

"Papa can't know."

"Why?" inquired Virgínia, curious.

"He might think they're poisonous, you idiot."

"But are they?"

"How should I know? how should I?" his useless hands.

"But I'm scared …"

"So?" he'd answer.

He'd threaten to open the box of spiders if she ever disobeyed him. And suddenly, without her knowing why, he called her over, his eyes intense, showing her the little box:

"Just look …"

She refused, nauseated. But she ended up sticking an eye into the hole of the little box and seeing nothing but slow movements in the darkness. She was saying:

"I saw, I saw it, I saw it all!"

He'd laugh:

"You'd almost be less idiotic if you weren't so idiotic."

One day the little box of spiders drowned in the rainwater that invaded the hiding place. A sharp smell, purple and nauseous, was coming from inside it. Suffering, tough and calm, Daniel ordered Virgínia to throw it away.

"No, don't push it with your feet. Grab it with both hands and put it outside."

The eye with which she'd peered at the spiders was hurting. For days it had watered, droopy and askew and in the morning she couldn't open it until the heat of the sun and her own movements would awake it. It swelled later, numb and bloodless. When it was all over, it was no longer the same, it had become imperceptibly squinty and less alive, slower and more moist, more deadened than the other. And if she hid the healthy eye with her hand, she'd see things separated from the places where they lay, loose in space as in an apparition.

"The spider didn't spit on you, you always liked to lie. What happened with your eye was foolishness. You and Aunt Margarida are made of almost nothing, a sneeze and that's it! you two ache all over, crippled, so just drop dead."

She was feeling a certain fear in his voice. It wasn't the fear of being told on, he knew his sister would never tell. Regret?— that was making her love him with a love full of crazy joy, an excited willingness for the two of them to run off, to ramble, hearts glowing. Her noble ardor was growing in mystery and seriousness when Father was saying:

"The Bay was spooked today on the way home."

Nobody was saying a word. Sometimes he'd go silent as if the phrase already said it all. Sometimes he'd go on:

"And there was nothing on the road to scare the animal. The weather was clear, the only noise the wagon wheels. I had to say: quiet down, Bay, God is with us. He quieted down."

And when night arrived, in the middle of dinner, he breathed, said:

"Daniel."

Daniel lifted his head, paused and stared at him with resistance and disdain. Bemused and scared everyone was waiting. Father said slowly looking him straight in the eye, as if taking his son's strength:

"You are forbidden to stand in the road making disgraceful ... gestures at passing ladies"—a deep pallor was making his face shapeless and opaque. Daniel seemed stuck in his own body. Everyone was waiting, contrite, interrupted for a long moment that would never culminate. Then Daniel looked away. Mother sank into her chair, softening her eyelids in a fainting of relief. Their father added, hoarse and low, as if exhausted:

"They complained to me."

The next morning a leaf came loose from a tall tree and for enormous minutes glided in the air until coming to rest on the ground. Virgínia did not understand where the sweetness came from: the ground was black and covered with dry leaves, so where did the sweetness come from? a desire was taking shape in the air, fluttering about intently, dissolving and had never existed. She cleared off the leaves and with a stick wrote in crooked letters Empire of the Rising Sun. Then she erased them with her foot and wrote Virgínia. She sharpened her being as you sharpen a pencil and made a light scratch on the ground with the stick. She erased it again and wanted to draw a thing with greater intensity, with a seriousness full of fire. She concentrated and a nervous wave ran through her like an omen. In an extraordinary serenity, eyes closed, she drew roughly as if screaming intently—then opened her eyes and saw a simple, strong, rough, common circle. (Today I fell apart)—that was the impression and she'd known it since she was little. I am unhappy, she thought slowly, almost stunned— she was almost a big girl. She let herself slide down the big rock in the middle of the garden. Just a second to reach the ground. But while that second lasted, eyes closed, her face cautious and moving, she scrutinized it at length, longer than the second itself, feeling that it was empty then, big as an unpopulated world. Suddenly she reached the ground with a crash. She opened her eyes and from the darkness to the light her heart opened toward the morning. The sun, the icy sun. And certain places in the garden were so secret, so almost with your eyes closed, secret as if they had hidden water. The air was humidly shining like almost shining dust. And anyone who ran forward without strength would feel invisible, fragile, and frigid arrows breaking imperceptibly, and the air was vibrating in their ears low, nervous, inaudibly sonorous. She was trying to close her eyes again and grasp the surprise once more. But the vision from the morning had only wanted to sparkle inside her and it would be useless to try to make out the emptiness of another moment. Yet if Daniel would agree they could speak a difficult language. The two had grown used to speaking.

"Ten is like Sunday. People think Sunday's the end of the last week, right? but it's already the start of the next. People think it's the end of nine, right? but it's already the start of eleven."

"No, I think ten's like Sunday because they're both round, they're not broken."

"But Sunday's not round, only ten is."

"Well I think Sunday's round. I think it and see it."

They were laughing because they knew it was all wrong, wrong in a veiled way. She, more than he, liked being wrong. And faced with Mother's almost repulsed gaze, Daniel said to her: poor lady …—Daniel sort of liked reading. Nobody understood them and that was as exciting as escape. Daniel had told her:

"Why are you eating?"

She listened with surprise and one day asked him:

"Why are you going to sleep?"—both laughed a lot.

Daniel said to her:

"Think of the most beautiful color in the world."

She was looking at him lit up by the liberty he was giving her. In a fleeting and nearly audible mixture she was making out heavy colors, shining and dizzying, everything moving, running away, turning off before she could grasp a single one and describe it to Daniel.

"But in the whole, whole world?" she was making sure.

"Y-yes," Daniel conceded with stinginess.

Then, closing with difficulty her overly radiant eyes, she was searching so deeply that a nonexistent, invented, crazy color was rising to her lips: hm!, she was exclaiming sharply and immediately her voice was falling with disappointment.

"What?" Daniel was asking, intrigued.

She couldn't explain. To bridge the moment she'd say quickly: purple that's yellowish at the edges.

"That's a nice color," Daniel would agree, "but not the nicest."

For Virgínia, however, anything you could say after that cry would be poor and worn out. Hm, hm, she was repeating without results. Hm, she'd say in a softer voice as if in order to surprise. Yet it was a word bursting with understanding as if from one moment to the next it would start to sing out its own meaning. Truly Mother was looking at them as if she'd nursed them without realizing it. Avoiding a suffocating feeling that she should call Mother over so that she might understand, Virgínia without words was trying to tell herself that after all she had a husband, the odd guest; when evening would fall she'd comb her thin womanly hair, live more slowly, look straight through the window. She wasn't ugly, but her powerless features never wavered, warned of nothing, in a calm vulgarity that would hide even the unhappy and vital moments. Virgínia and Daniel were quickly delighted to avoid her:

"What's keeping on buying, buying and putting things away and opening everything one day and peeking at it?"

Virgínia didn't know: so hard to take the things born deep inside someone else and think them. She even had a certain kind of difficulty with reasoning. Sometimes it wasn't by starting with any thought at all that she'd reach a thought. Sometimes it was enough to wait a little and she'd grasp it all. Until Daniel would say, victorious, his voice cold:

"It's collecting things, you grazing mare!"

Virgínia would retort:

"What's keeping on walking, walking and then saying: oh, forget it, let's take a stroll, shall we?"

He'd guess immediately, offhand but deep down thrilled:

"Why, it's not going to school, who wouldn't know that?"

And then she'd said to him with serious ardor:

"Look, someday, you know ..."

And he'd given her a look, accepting something she herself didn't understand. But he'd rarely praise Virgínia's discoveries, rarely be fascinated by her cleverness. When that would happen he'd usually say as if speaking to some absent person who might understand him better, as Virgínia attentive and curious would listen:

"She's so dumb that everything's easy for her."

One time though—her face was swollen because of a toothache—they were leaning over the guest room balcony and looking at the night. Down below the darkness was stretching out uniformly and when the wind blew the bushes seemed to move in a sea. Fleeting waves of fireflies were lighting up faintly and going out.

"Look, Daniel," Virgínia had said, "look what I saw: the firefly disappears."

He looked at her, saw her swollen red chin through the sad light of the oil lamp placed in the room.

"What? ...," he asked without pleasure.

"It's like this: when you see a firefly you don't think it appeared, but that it disappeared. As if someone died and that were the first thing about them because they hadn't even been born or lived, you know? You wonder: what's the firefly really like? Answer: it disappears."

Daniel understood and they stayed silent and satisfied. She could sometimes tie a thing with one hand far from the other and make them dance startled, mad, sweet, dragging. Trusting and serene, she went on:

"Would you want to be like that, kid?"

"Like how?"

"Like a firefly is for us ... Without anyone knowing what you're like, if you're appearing or disappearing, without anyone's knowing for sure, but you think we're not living in the meantime? living, going about our business and everything like the firefly."

"For the first time you're saying something that I think too: it would be good," said Daniel and again they fell silent watching.

When the afternoon was ending and the whispering and blurry serenity of dusk arrived Virgínia's heart would fill with an expressionless sadness while her face would calm, deepen. Quiet, their souls maddened, taut, terrified, they seemed to enter irremediably into eternity. She and Daniel would lean more intimately on the guest room balcony and sit for a long while looking out at the purplish expanse of the farm, the black blue of the forest, the motionless dryness of the branches.

"What do you like more: eating or sleeping?" she'd ask pensively.

He'd hesitate.

"Eating."

"Why?"

"Because you fill your stomach. What about you?"

"Sleeping ... because you sleep, sleep, sleep ..."

A cold wind was rising from the ground and making the small plants fragrant mixed with the still-hot earth. Though the day had been joyful and busy it was then seeming to begin anew.

"Rain is coming ... look at the smell," Daniel was saying.

"I'd like to have an odd and sad life, you know," Virgínia was saying.

There was an impossible sliding in her truth, she was like her own error. She was feeling strange and precious, so voluptuously hesitant and strange as if today were tomorrow. And she couldn't correct herself, every morning she'd let her error be reborn through an urge that would find its balance in an imponderable inevitability.

"Well I'd like to be able to say what I think, the world would be amazed," Daniel was saying. "Only if I could, but it wasn't any trouble to find out!" he'd finish in despair.

"I don't want to sleep by myself, I'm scared."

"Bedtime isn't for a long time," he'd answer calmer and drier.

"It feels like it's soon."

He was aware she was asking for help. In a horrible act of kindness, as if feeling sorry for himself, he didn't make his sister wait:

"Then I'll sit and read with the lamp on the stairs."

Sometimes he'd push her rudely, in a game that would give her the painful and surprised feeling of being hated. But that was just his strength. Playing with Daniel always wore her out, because she had to take care not to displease him. They'd grown too subtle and Daniel was strict, he didn't allow a single stumble. Her answers had to be fast and he was smarter than she was. Until once he woke up in a good mood and first thing in the morning said:

"Good morning, human …"

The illuminated surprise of seeing him start the day by letting her in, made her freeze for an instant, delight gave her excessive confidence and in a sharp and happy cry she answered:

"Good morning, so-and-so …"

He turned around surprised, almost ashamed, while inside her the smile was quickly dying. He stared with disgust as if she'd ruined everything, all his life:

"You always have to say something stupid."

Because sometimes she'd think such slender thoughts that

they'd suddenly break halfway before reaching the end. And since they were so thin, even without completing them she understood them all at once. Though she could never think them again, even point to them with a single word. Since she couldn't transmit them to Daniel, he'd always win their conversations. In some mysterious way her fainting spells were connected to this: sometimes she'd feel a thin thought that was so intense that she herself was the thought and since it broke, she'd interrupt herself in a faint.

"But there's ab-so-lute-ly nothing wrong with her!" the old doctor of Upper Marsh was saying containing his impatience under his eyeglasses.

In fact she'd never suffered. Yet her head would sometimes spin, though rarely. Suddenly the ground would threaten to rise to her eyes, without violence, without hurry. She'd wait for it quietly but before she could understand, the floor had already sunk to somewhere she couldn't make out, falling to the bottom of an abyss, far off like a stone thrown from a height into the sea. Her feet would dissolve into air and the space would be crossed by luminous threads, by a cold and nervous sound like violent wind escaping through a crack. Then great calm would envelop the light world. And then there was no world. And then, in a final and fresh reduction, there was no her. Just air without strength and without color. She'd think about a long shaky line — I'm fainting. A pause would be born without color, without light, without strength, she was waiting. The end of the pause would find her abandoned on the floor, the bright wind piercing the motionless window, the sun staining her feet. And that weightless silence, buzzing and smiling, of a summer afternoon in the country. She'd get off the ground, vaguely start taking shape, everything was waiting around her meekly inorganic; then she'd walk and keep living, spending hours and hours drawing straight lines without the help of a ruler, just with the weight of her hand, sometimes as if only with the spur of her thought; she'd slowly manage to trace pure and plain lines, deeply amused. It was such refreshing, such serious work; it would smooth her face and open her eyes.

Sitting in the shade of a tree, she'd soon be surrounded by empty instants because nothing had happened for a while and future seconds would bring nothing—she'd foresee. She'd calm down—she couldn't quite disguise the broad inexplicable well-being that would sink her deep into her own pensive body, the being leaning toward a delicate and difficult sensation—but she'd hide herself for some reason trying to see the stones on the ground, her eyebrows furrowed, deceitful, all of her sly and stupid. Some curious and cold thing was happening to her, something a bit smiling with contempt but careful to go to the end, making her almost think in a futile and ironic urge: if thou art as thou sayest a living creature, bestir thyself ... and she'd almost want to stand and pluck a slightly tender bright weed. Within her face notions were whispering liquefying in decomposition—she was a girl resting. She was looking, looking. She'd close her eyes observing all the impenetrable points of her narrow body, thinking all over herself without words, recopying existence itself. She was looking, looking. Slowly, from the silence, her being was starting to live more, an abandoned instrument that started making sound all by itself, her eyes discerning because the first matter of the eyes was looking. Nothing would inspire her, she was isolated inside her capacity, existing through the same weak energy that had caused her to be born. She was thinking simply and clearly. She was thinking small and clear music that was stretching a single thread and unfurling bright, fluorescent and moist, water in water, meditating a silly arpeggio. She was thinking untranslatable sensations distracting herself secretly as if humming, profoundly unaware and stubborn, she was thinking a single swift streak: in order to be born things must have life, for birth is a movement—if they said that movement is necessary only for the thing giving birth and not for the thing that is born that's not right because the thing that gives birth cannot give birth to something outside its nature and thus always gives birth to a thing of its own kind and so it is with movements too—in this way stones were born that have no power of their own but were once alive otherwise they wouldn't have been born and now they're dead because they don't have movement in order to give birth to another stone. No thought was extraordinary, words are what would be. She was thinking without intelligence about her own reality as if discerning and could never use what she was feeling, her meditation was a way of living. It was coming to her without a shape of its own yet at the same time within it was chiming some precise and delicate quality like thin numbers entangled with thin numbers and suddenly a new light number ringing polished and dry—while the true sensation of her whole body was expectant. And finally something was happening so far away, ah so far away and maybe reduced to a yes that she was growing tired to the point of annihilation, thinking now in words: I am very, very tired, you know. Go, go, something profoundly satiated and already known in her body was murmuring with a certain anguish, go, go. But where? The wind, the wind was blowing. Barely hushed and on the lookout, as if facing the north or the east she seemed to be headed toward some true thing through the great incessant taking-shape of tiny dead events, leading the delicateness of being in the direction of an almost exterior feeling as if by touching the earth with her bare and watchful foot she might feel inaccessible water flowing. She was traversing long distances simply by assigning herself a direction, immobile, sincere. But she couldn't quite be sucked in, as if it were her own fault. She'd help herself by feeling a vague notion of travel, of the day she'd leave for the city with Daniel, a bit of hunger and fatigue, barely touching her lunch. Sometimes she'd almost approach a thought but she never reached it though everything around was breathing its beginning to her; she'd look with astonishment at the space devoid of mystery, the breeze would raise shivers of understanding on her skin; an instant would yet penetrate the silence seeking in its depths a thread to grab on to. And if a bird were flying or the cry of a winged creature gushing from the nearby forest, she was wrapped by a cold whirl, the wind spinning dry leaves and dust, vague unfinished beginnings, in a vortex of her and of whatever no longer was her. The moment had arrived to let climb to her outermost nerves the wave that was taking shape on the near side of her weakness and that could die of its own urging. From particle to particle, however, the indistinct thought was coming down violently mute until opening in the middle of her body, on her lips, complete, perfect, incomprehensible because it was so free from its own shaping—I need to eat. She took from it then nothing more than its softness, barely alighting on her being; she could go forward without being pushed, without being called, going along simply because moving was the quality of her body. That was her impression and her stomach was plunging deeper, joyful, famished. But she was still seated. She didn't seem to know how to stand up and actually guide herself, distressingly she was lacking a direction. She stretched into the distance as if slowly she could lose her shape—she thought she could hear the voices and the sounds from the mansion and leaned forward to try to make them out. She leaned back against the tree, rubbing one of her dusty feet, going beyond her understanding and with a kind of irrepressible force attaining misunderstanding like a discovery. Now unsettled, motionless, reality seemed to bother her. She was thinking with her mother's languid voice: I'm nervous. In a misgiving without sweetness, she was fluttering aridly in the fanciful and hysterical immobility. Until the tautest rope would snap, as if a presence were abandoning her body and she was getting closer to her own ordinary existence. Pushed, extraordinarily indifferent and no longer very hungry, she was forgetting everything forever like a person who's forgotten.

But what she loved more than anything was making clay figurines, which no one had taught her. She'd work on a small cement path in the shade, next to the last window of the basement. When she wanted to with great strength she'd go down the road to the river. On one of its banks, which was slippery but scalable, she found the best clay that one could desire: white, supple, sticky, cold. Just by touching it, feeling its deliciously joyful and blind delicateness, those timidly alive bits, a person's heart would warm and soften, almost ridiculous. Virgínia would dig with her fingers that pale and washed earth— in the can tied to her waist the amorphous segments would be collected. The river in small gestures wet her bare feet and she'd wiggle her damp toes with excitement and brightness. With her hands free, then, she'd carefully leap over the bank to the flat surface. In the small cement courtyard she would deposit her riches. She would mix the clay with water her eyelids fluttering at attention—concentrated, her body on the lookout, she could obtain an exact and nervous proportion of clay and water with a wisdom that would be born in that same instant, fresh and progressively created. She'd get a clear and tender material from which she could shape a world. How, how to explain the miracle ... She'd grow scared, thoughtful. She said nothing, she didn't move but inside without any words she repeated: I am nothing, I have no pride, anything can happen to me, if - - - they want they can stop me from mixing the clay, - - - if they want they can crush me, ruin me entirely, I know that I am nothing. - - - it was less than a vision, it was a sensation in the body, a frightened thought about whatever let her accomplish so much with the clay and the water and before which she had to humble herself with seriousness. She would thank it with a difficult joy, fragile and tense, she felt in - - - some thing like one you cannot see with closed eyes— but one you cannot see with closed eyes has an existence and a power, like darkness, like darkness, like absence, she would contain herself consenting, ferocious and mute with her head. But she knew nothing of herself, she would travel innocent and distracted through her reality without recognizing it, like a child, like a person.

After obtaining the material, in a slump of exhaustion she could lose her desire to make figurines. Then she'd go on living forward like a girl.

One day however she was feeling her open and thin body and deep down a serenity that couldn't hold itself back, alternating between not recognizing itself and breathing in joy, things incomplete. She herself sleepless like light—wild, fleeting, empty, but deep down an ardor that was a desire to head toward one thing only, an interest that would make her heart speed up without rhythm ... suddenly how vague it was to live. All this could pass too, night falling suddenly, the darkness upon the warm day. But sometimes she'd remember the wet clay, run fearful out to the courtyard—plunge her fingers into that mixture, cold, mute, constant as waiting, kneading, kneading, slowly extracting forms. She'd make children, horses, a mother with a child, a mother alone, a girl making things out of clay, a boy at rest, a happy girl, a girl seeing if it would rain, a flower, a comet with a tail sprinkled with washed and sparkling sand, a wilted flower beneath the sun, the cemetery of Upper Marsh, a girl looking ... Much more, much more. Little shapes that meant nothing but that were in fact mysterious and calm. Sometimes tall like a tall tree, but they weren't trees, they weren't anything ... Sometimes like a little running river, but they weren't a river, they weren't anything ... Sometimes a little object in an almost starry shape but tired like a person. A task that would never end, that was the most beautiful and careful thing she'd ever known: since she could make anything that existed and anything that did not!

After they were ready the figurines were placed in the sun. Nobody had taught her but she would deposit them in the patches of sun on the ground, patches with neither wind nor heat. The clay would dry gently, keeping its light tone, not wrinkling, not cracking. Even when it was dry it seemed delicate, evanescent, and moist. And she herself could mistake it for the sticky clay. Those little figures seemed quick almost as if about to move. She was looking at the immobile figurine. Out of love or merely going on with the work she'd close her eyes and gather herself into a live and luminous force with the quality of danger and of hope, into a silky power that would run through her body quickly with an urging that was destined for the figure. When at last she let go, her fresh and tired well-being would come because she could send something away though she didn't know what. - - - maybe. Yes, she sometimes had a taste inside her body, a high and distressing taste that would tremble between power and fatigue—it was a thought like heard sounds, a color in her heart. Before it smoothly dissolved quick in her inner air, forever fleeting, she'd touch an object with her fingers, surrendering. And when she wanted to say something that came subtly, dark, and smooth and that could be dangerous, she'd rest just one finger, a pale, polished, and transparent finger—a trembling finger pointing. In the slenderest and most hurt part of her feeling she would think: I will be happy. In fact she already was in that instant and if instead of thinking "I am happy" she sought out the future that was because she was darkly choosing a forward movement that would serve as a form for her feeling.

Thus she had gathered a procession of tiny things. They sat almost unnoticed in her bedroom. They were figurines as skinny and tall as she was herself. Detailed, slightly disproportionate, joyful, a bit surprised—sometimes they looked like a lame man laughing! Even her most mellow figures had a watchful immobility like a saint's. And they'd seem to lean toward whoever was looking at them like saints. Virgínia could stare at them all morning long and her love and her surprise would not decrease.

"Pretty ... pretty as a little wet thing!" she'd say surpassing herself in a sweet rush.

She was watching: even when nicely finished they were rough as if they could still be worked on. But she would vaguely think that neither she nor anybody could try to perfect them without destroying the thread of their birth. It was as if they could only perfect themselves by themselves, if that were possible.

And the difficulties would arise like a life as it grows. Her figurines, thanks to the light clay, were pale. If she wanted to darken them she couldn't do it with the help of colors and because of that shortcoming she even learned to give them shadows through their shapes. Then she invented a freedom: with a little dry leaf beneath a thin smudge of clay she achieved a vague coloring, sad and frightened, almost entirely dead. Mixing clay with earth she'd obtain another less plastic material, though more severe and solemn. But how to make the sky? She couldn't even start. She didn't want clouds—which she could obtain at least crudely—but the sky, the sky itself, with its inexistence, loose color, lack of color. She discovered that she needed to use lighter materials that couldn't be so much as touched, felt, perhaps only seen, who knows. She understood that this could be achieved with dyes.

And sometimes with a crash, as if everything were purifying itself—she'd settle for making a smooth, serene, united surface, in a delicate and tranquil simplicity.

She also liked to supply herself with stones, stones, and stones and then throw them one by one far, far as an echoless scream. And sometimes she'd just sit with her head down, her eyes squinting until the trembling and confused ground would near her face and lazily back off merging with the heat. In the summer sky a fluttering of wings would rapidly whisper. She was thinking about whether it was worth lifting her head and looking. And when she finally made up her mind, the sky was already hovering clean and blue, without the bird, without expression, eyes barely open. She'd move her head in a slow search. Sleeping, a few dry branches were growing motionless against space, splintered sounds dangling in the air like clouds. In a tenuous awakening she would feel that in that same instant many things were existing beyond the ones she saw. So she made herself firm and subtle wanting to inhale all these things into her center after a brief pause. Nothing was coming, she was looking at things gently gilded with light—without thought she was getting satiated, satiated, satiated like the ever sharper and faster sound of water filling a canister. She would stand and walk, walk until passing through the school from which was sweetly born a smell of children mixed with that of new varnish and bread with butter. Some girl was crying suddenly giving an odd happiness to the air, the teacher's voice was rising, rising until falling and the whispers would return docile, sniffing. Nearby the new and flavorless houses were lying under the sun exposing their small gardens, shining and poor. A woman was outside speaking to someone inside the house, giving orders. There was little old Cecília, who had told them with goggling eyes, while they'd covered their mouths in order not to laugh: violent death, kids, be careful, both of you will meet violent deaths, as she looked at the dirty and empty palms of their hands. Cecília yelled with a voice that always hovered a tone above her stature—and she'd stand on her toes as if to reach it:

"How's Mama ...? ..."

Virgínia straightened her body, in an inspired and free moment, released the answer in a voice as joyful as clothes fluttering on the line:

"Fine ... thank you ...!"

Old Cecília would wag her thin arm, her head, showing that she'd heard, had heard, a great breeze was shushing everything, carrying far away the murmurs of the place where they'd halted, slipping among the leaves of the trees, making a person stop and smile feeling her skirts, her hair flying coldly. Yes, the impression that some thing was then going ahead. She kept going until leaving behind the houses and the school. She was once again entering open country. As the long walk went on, her waist, her legs, her arms were being reborn lightly, asking for movement. She was running and through her half-closed eyes the green would muddle into a single bright and moving stain, with flashes of flowing water. Until she'd stop tired and panting, holding back her laughter for some reason. She'd look around, there were the thin weeds hiding the nakedness of the ground, the mountain covered by new grass, and near her body a sparkling beetle bending the stalk of a shrub—then, as if something were missing in all that and she could supply it, she'd cup her hands around her mouth, close her eyes, and her heart beating furiously, scream with strength beyond the mountains:

"I! ... Daniel! ... World! ... I! ..."

The first scream was difficult like a first boldness and was shattering the air in every direction. She was waiting thrilled, her heart hurrying, scared. But then it was the countryside itself that was screaming: "I! ... Things! ... Daniel! ..." She'd stop. What? some quick thought, a spark that flees. She wanted to say and though she didn't know what, the only reason she didn't say it was because she didn't dare. She'd murmur quietly with a deaf violence: arrh, arrh. She'd forget the need to scream and sit on a still-burning rock, waiting for some thing inside herself. Slowly she'd tilt her head back, her eyelids lowered and trembling in a smile, in a shudder as if someone had touched her. Her face would brighten, flower in an almost charmed half-laugh, fluttering atop her skin, almost repugnant, intimate. She'd let herself remain in a calm celebration, gently excited; the confusion made her eyes damp and hesitant like a woman's. "Ah, so that's what happened? but I didn't know ... Ah, ah, ah ... As the saying goes, that's very funny ...," she was rehearsing with a small and affected voice. Thus she'd hover until nothing was happening, her heart slowly cooling, she'd awake disappointed and dry, opening her eyes, hurting them in the violence of the light. She'd peek for an instant, lips open, serious. Little by little, deeply offended, she'd bring her head toward her body and her face would gather in shadows.

In the winter life would become focused on itself, understanding and intimate. The smell would grow gentler, mud would pacify the countryside. Her voice which was silent for hours sounded hoarse and dull. The air was humid, the things in her bedroom were isolating themselves through the cold and only darkness would melt the furniture. Outside rain was falling without power, without pause. The lowered glass of the window was weakly lit by the sleeping light of the courtyard. Drops were running trembling, sparkling, secret, down the windowpane. But the leaves were letting go of the trees and dragged by the wind thrashing against it with an almost imperceptible whisper. She would have liked to tell or hear a long story made only of words, but Daniel at such times would stay silent and difficult, almost inexistent in the mansion. She'd grow more and more alone, watching the rain. She'd feel purplish and cold inside, in her body a little bird was slowly asphyxiated. But it was so much living that the hours would roll by happy and distant as if already marked by longing. From her wide bed she could make out the ceiling lost in the shadows, the walls fusing in half-light. Only the window was calmly shining, only the wet incessant noise. In the air a pent-up breathing was hovering in the dark like the continuous beating of a butterfly's wings. She'd turn her back to the window, move slowly in her grandmother's double bed. The existence of the butterfly kept gasping with its eyes fixed on her. A wind of screams was coming from inside the forest like souls fleeing in despair. It was a mixture of the voices of the owl and of the waters, of the chafing of the leaves, of the last dry cracking before the moisture, all united in the same sharp wild flight, a wind of screams piercing the mansion like a breath. Virgínia would pull the hot and thick bedspread with a slight smell of ash. Underneath it, her body and the narrow space that her body was occupying would become a familiar world. She'd then let fear finally flow, now that she was sheltered. She'd even try not to fall asleep in order to feel everything until everything got along by itself and transformed itself into something else besides fear. In that way she'd miss nothing of the silence of the winter night. The days were of a perfect sadness that ended up overtaking itself and sliding toward a limitless stillness. The branches were bending nervously in the wind, water was flowing quickly and sparkling through the leaves, a push without direction would torture the trees and from the murmur without rhythm was being born like a great fresh wind the hope of loving and living.

She'd go to the back of the mansion with the old cape over her body. For an instant more she would stop to look at the half brightness of the rain flowing and then go on. She couldn't see much in front of her, her eyes would bump up against the rain that seemed to rise from the earth in a thick smoke. With a cold face she'd move ahead and something was pungent, high, and indecisive in her heart. She'd part her lips receiving the frozen mist in the warm center of her body. She'd walk pushing off the branches that were heavy with water, painful, trembling. She'd look back and could no longer see the mansion, rain, only rain. Then she'd say out loud in a voice that sounded strange and daring amidst the murmur of the dripping water: "I am alone."

As if she'd said more than she could she'd bow her head for an instant, scared, happy, wondering. She lifted her wet face and needed to say some thing more than herself, more than everything.

"I'm alone, I'm alone," she was repeating like a small rooster singing.

Then she went back. She'd put on dry clothes, smooth her wet and limp hair, taking care of herself with seriousness. Her image was reflected in the old yellowing mirror among the shadows of the guest room and there she was hesitant and damp like the brightness of a rainy dawn on a travel day. The white face floating above the thick blouse was strange and young, her eyes were hiding in warm light and her lips were breathing calm, innocent. Some thing in her was sweetly shining in the glory of ignorance as in a god with an exposed heart, there was in her existence the afterlife of martyrdom but she hadn't been martyred, she'd been created many times. She was looking at herself quietly hearing the rain fall in a single canticle. There she was flickering like light slow flames, her shapes in shadow and light animating the mirror.

"I," she said to the frozen mirror in a silky and hoarse voice. And her body dissolved with the sound in the dark air of the room.

The end of the year was approaching, classes were coming to a close and Virgínia was attending the lessons sitting among the truants. The school's glee club was strained and shaky, Virgínia would sing with squinting eyes without hearing her own voice, her fingers would wander distractedly across the nearby wall. She knew how to fake a concentrated face while checking out in an instant. Sometimes the teacher would join the choir, vigorous, ardent. And sometimes in a fleeting moment that would long ring in the body the voices would join in a full and fast line, in a single vibration, drawn and tense, as if being born from the cave into the light. Virgínia would open her eyes astonished, the instant that followed was new and bristly, she was peering at the world with its smooth surface, the sun more pale and happy, the girls' dresses with white, red trappings, moist mouths opening, flickering in a breath of light. Sharp as if to surprise all things into confessing that same moment, she would point her head in a second, without prior notice, toward a piece of furniture—toward the inside of the school—toward the students' feet ... In the sky, through the window, white clouds were coming undone, running loose from the calm blue. The windowpane isolated itself from the classroom and the courtyard, sparkling with steely light. A cone of brightness was lighting a whirlwind of dusts that were dancing with hallucinatory slowness … Virgínia awake in the hurried instant was turning back, lightly in order not to destroy anything, and yes, there was the slate half burning alive under the heat of the sun, half coolly black … dead and morose, a lake in the forest. Virgínia was breathing, her face mobile, loose. Without seeing, she could nonetheless surprise the shady field behind the school, the long weeds vibrating nervous and green in the wind. A moment later, in a tiny and silent crash, things were rushing into their true color. The classroom, the sky, the girls, communicated amongst themselves with distances already established, fixed colors and sounds—the unfurling of an oft-rehearsed scene. Virgínia was understanding, disappointed, that everything had been seen years before. In order to distinguish once again what she'd seen and which had now fled as if forever, she was trying to start from the end of the feeling: she'd open her eyes very wide with surprise. But in vain: she wouldn't make the same mistake again and would see nothing more than reality. She was drawing back. Now the sheaf of voices was separating into fragile shafts and these were breaking an instant before they reached the center of the sounds; the other things too now were slack and nothing was touching any longer the living point of itself. Virgínia would be quiet for the rest of the afternoon, vague, misty, distant, slightly tired as if something had actually happened. There were days like that, when she'd understand so well and see so much that she'd end up in a gentle and dizzy drunkenness, almost anxious, as if her perceptions without thoughts were dragging her in a shiny and sweet swirl to where, to where.

Slowly, looking, fainting, grasping, breathing, waiting, she would start connecting more deeply with whatever existed and having pleasure. Slowly without words she was subcomprehending things. Without knowing why, she was understanding; and the intimate sensation was one of contact, of existence looking and being looked at. It was from that time that something of an indecipherable brightness would survive. And where was it coming from that perhaps everything deserved the perfection of itself? And where was that inclination coming from that was almost like: connecting yourself to the next day through a desire. Where had it arisen? but she almost didn't have desires ... She almost didn't have desires, she almost didn't possess strength, she was living at the end of herself and at the beginning of something that already no longer was, finding her balance in the indistinct. In her state of weak resistance she was receiving in herself something that would be excessively fragile in order to fight and conquer any power of body or soul. She was too dumb to have difficulties, Daniel would repeat.

Then the lost time—he would move away, moving through mists and returning more elongated, more brutish, more sad and more innocent, yet impassable. His life was getting more and more stubborn. She had also isolated herself through fatigue, a bit of insomnia but had soon shown herself even and calm again, her skin taut, her legs scratched by branches, one eye more tired than the other. That was the time that Daniel had said to her for the first time, almost for no particular reason:

"By God and the Devil ..."

She'd stopped short. A great silence had followed. She'd looked at him and discovered in his trembling victory the same disturbance. He had timidly brought her a scream. They stared at each other for an instant and everything was indecisive, fragile, so new and nascent. And everything was so dangerous and agitated that both looked away almost abruptly. But there was some enchanted thing between them at that moment. Though she never truly worried about God and rarely prayed. Before the idea of Him she would stay surprisingly calm and innocent, without so much as a thought. Daniel was moving off. Around that time he had started to think and say difficult things with zest and love. She would listen uneasy. He'd pace back and forth through the shadowy hallways of the mansion with his arms crossed, engrossed. Virgínia would uselessly scrutinize his face with his closed mouth, his dark indecisive eyes, that near-ugliness that was getting worse with age, suffering, and pride.

"What are you thinking?" she couldn't contain herself sweetening her voice, effacing herself with humility.

"Nothing," he'd answer.

And if she would dare ask again she'd get an answer that disturbed her even more because of its mystery and because of the jealousy it would awake in her.

"I'm thinking about God."

"But what about God?" she'd inquire with effort, in a low and ingratiating voice.

"I don't know!" he'd scream with brutality, irritated as if she were accusing him. "Even you are so stupid that you'd die before you understood"—and he'd keep pacing through the hallways, as if walking cleared his thoughts. The most she could manage was for him to let her accompany him back and forth, back and forth, hurrying if he was hurrying, staying anxious and quiet at a certain distance if he would halt. Daniel would talk too much about his own future. She didn't want, didn't want ... as if advancing to the middle of the world would mean losing his own footsteps. But out of love she wanted to understand him, falsely happy she invented that new intelligence of Daniel's that was changing him as much as it would change someone's life to know how to handle lace-making needles. She'd persist in treating him like an equal, respect him as if he were made of the soft dough of flowers. Though he was sometimes so rude that with one gesture he could wipe out a girl. She'd grow pale and giddy among the offended instants. And loving him as much as she could ever love.

Had it been because of the drowned man that the Society of Shadows was born? They had foreseen the charmed and dangerous beginning of the unknown, the momentum that came from fear. Daniel said to her:

"Let us create the Society of Shadows."

Even before learning what it was about Virgínia had already confusedly understood with her body and consented. The Society of Shadows had strange and undefined objectives. They themselves did not know them and mixed its commands with an almost desperate ignorance. The Society of Shadows must explore the forest. Yes, yes. But why? Near the mansion there was an almost-closed path and along it you could reach the darkness. Yes, the darkness, but why?

"Because solitude ... Solitude—is the motto of the Society," Daniel ordered.

"What?" Virgínia was having trouble understanding.

"Everything that frightens because it leaves us alone is what we must seek," he was hesitating.

He would hover for an instant, drifting, his thinking intersecting with hers like the bow over the violin string, light sparks of insight and surprise unmaking themselves in the air. Days would go by without a single word being added about the Society, without either daring to touch that living, shapeless matter. But they hadn't forgotten: they had to be quiet in order to create a pause in the dread that was already dominating them. And in the happiness that would make Virgínia shake, her eyes undemonstrative. The Society of Shadows was bringing her so close to Daniel! he would allow her to be with him every day. Even she loved secrets with ferocity as if they were of her own kind.

"And truth?" she was asking.

"What truth?"

"Another motto should be: Truth."

"Yes," Daniel would get annoyed, it was so hard for him to be directed even a single time by Virgínia.

In the beginning they'd agreed that there would be a meeting on Saturdays, in the first clearing on the path that branched off from the fence. It was a stopping place where everything that had to happen in somebody's life hurried up and happened, they'd figured out. If you have to die in girlhood, you go there and die, Daniel was explaining. It was really the worst clearing, damp, shaded, closed in by tall, thin trees; among odorless parasites and dangling vines the branches would sway; dark, large swallows would fly vertically as if they'd never dare free themselves. The earth was black and wet; between rains the small puddles would mirror branches and shadows without the sun exhausting them.

Fever didn't allow them so much time between meetings. They started to meet daily as soon as the sun had set. They were supposed to, according to the rules, take different paths to the clearing and return from there alone. As the days passed they couldn't stand the solitary return. In the almost night terror gathered speed. The little birds were flying like blind men and hitting them in the cheeks. The leaves of the tall trees were thin and wide, the clearing's trapped air was spinning, spinning, hitting the leaves and some thing like a breeze against glass bells was sounding in the same tone, lengthily, tranquilly. No, they wouldn't be able to stand going back alone … They'd return together, falsely calm, pale. Nobody at home had noticed the anxiety in which they lived. And that was as if both were alone in the world. How scary and secret it was to belong to the Society of Shadows. Daniel, at its helm, was growing in power. Virgínia was plunging dangerously into her weak and rapt nature. And when Daniel would find her standing in the middle of the clearing, waiting with cold hands, with wide and blackened eyes, and ask her obeying one of the rules of the Society: what was the strongest thought she'd had today? she would go silent, scared, unable to explain to him that she'd lived a day of excessive inspiration, impossible to be directed by a single thought, just as the excess of light could impede vision—her soul exhausted, she was breathing in pure pleasure without a solution and feeling so alive that she could have died without realizing it. Daniel was getting angry, pushing her as he squeezed her arm, calling her a fool, threatening to dissolve the Society of Shadows, which terrorized her, more than his physical brutality. Daniel was worrying her: it was as if he'd degraded with the power acquired in the Society of Shadows; he'd hardened and never forgave. Virgínia was scared of him, yet it would never occur to her to escape his dominion. Even because she herself realized she was dumb and incapable. Daniel was strong. Before realizing what he wanted she'd already agreed, since:

"Virgínia, every day when you see milk and coffee you like milk and coffee. When you see Father you respect Father. When you scrape your leg you feel pain in your leg, do you see what I'm saying? You are common and stupid." — Yes, by God she was — "So the Society of Shadows must perfect its members and orders you to do everything backwards. The Society of Shadows knows that you are common because you don't think, as the saying goes, deeply, because you only know how to follow what you were taught, get it? The Society of Shadows commands you to go into the basement tomorrow, sit down and think a lot, a lot in order to figure out what is your own and what is stuff you've been taught. Tomorrow don't bother with the family or the world! The Society of Shadows has spoken."

She was secretly rejoicing: despite what Daniel had thought, she loved the basement and had never feared it. She said nothing however because if she confessed then the location for *thinking deeply* would be moved. She was trembling at the thought that Daniel could send her to think in the middle of the forest at nightfall. Not having a difficult task for the next day was like getting a holiday. Daniel scrutinized her a bit surprised that night, seeing her happy, talking almost by herself at the dinner table, and receiving without sadness a wallop from Father. Beyond the clearing though they couldn't speak of the Society of Shadows and that way she was free, observing almost mischievous and happy Daniel's uneasiness.

The next morning, since she wasn't supposed to bother with the family, she made sure the family didn't bother with her. So she didn't avoid the habit of having breakfast with everyone and answering their questions. Obedient to Daniel, however, she was clenching her heart without rage and without glory, as in a sincere task, hiding it intact in a dark and quiet region. She had to take care not to mix, not to move anything around her with her thinking in order not to be imperceptibly moved. Distracted she was guessing: thinking deeply she'd find out what was hers like water mixed with river water and what wasn't, like stones mixed with river water. Ah, she was understanding so much. She was sighing from joy and a sort of incomprehension. One day she might not show respect for her parents, the pleasure of strolling, the taste of coffee, the thought of liking blue, the pain of hurting her leg. Though that had never worried her. She walked to the basement slowly, pushed open its grate and dove into the cold smell of the half-light where washbasins, dusts, and old furniture were timidly living. She sat by the black clothes of an old bereavement. The waft of the trunks was wheezing, a smell of cemetery was rising from the slabs of the floor. She sat and waited. She clasped her thick dress against her chest every once in a while. The birds outside were singing but that was silence. In order to think deeply a person shouldn't remember anything in particular. She purified herself of memories, stayed attentive. Since for her it was always easy to desire nothing, she remained frozen without even feeling the black shadows of the basement. She moved off as if on a journey. Slowly she started getting a thought without words, an ashen and vast sky, without volume or thickness, without surface, depth, or height. Sometimes, like light clouds released from the depth, the sky was crossed by the vague consciousness of experience and of the world outside of itself. The fear of disobeying Daniel—a fear that wasn't a thought and didn't disturb her thoughts—was assailing her and also a curiosity to go forward without interruptions, that made her move above her own knowledge. Without effort, without joy—as if not to linger in any defined feeling—she was pushing away perception and the sky was becoming pure again. Could she be thinking deeply? a separate consciousness was inquiring within her. Luminous lines, dry and fast, were scratching out her inner vision, without meaning, crawled out from some mysterious crevice and then, beyond their own place of birth, weak and dizzy. She could think in every direction; closing her eyes, she would direct inside her body a thought of the kind that emerges from bottom to top or otherwise of the kind that rides running through open space— that was neither word nor content but the mode of thinking itself finding its bearings. Could that be what thinking deeply was—not having so much as a thought to bring to the surface … Silence would follow ashen and light. In the sky a hesitant clearing would open for a second, but she was confusedly discovering that the opening was that of her own concentration; and it remained dense, of a density without form or volume, the accumulation of a substance more impalpable than the air, of an element more vague than perfume through the air. For an instant she was rejoicing tenuously and sharply for having obtained—just an instant, light that goes on and off. Could she have been thinking more than deeply and already seeing nothing? she was thinking frightened. The sky was still going on monotonous, monotonous, rolling. Though it had no image on its surface, it was not immobile, its expanse-without-measure was being substituted continuously like the unfurling of the sea—always moving forward without ever leaving itself. She tried to transform it by moving the position of a body tired of existing with such brutality. She stretched out on a colorless sofa, head beneath her limbs, pale face expressionless. In an uncomfortable clairvoyance she was seeing black clothes hanging, piano bench, blackened basin, doll without legs, lamp, cup. Slowly, in a concentrated effort that was arising from the center of her body, she freed herself from the basement and could wait without sensations. The sky appeared to her again. Outside, on the weeds dried by the sun steps made a sound. They were moving off ... And since she'd allowed herself to hear steps instead of not hearing them everything would now come together suddenly in an undeniable reality. She got up and still bothered by the low position of her head tried to free herself from the basement and its smell of suitcase. She pushed the stiff grate, cleaned the slime and the rust of the cold bars from her hand. With narrowed eyes and forehead furrowed, she left the earth toward the brightness with a mildly painful jolt, her face rambling in paleness. A subtle pulsing began on her cold forehead. The hazel air of the basement was extending outside green and pink. She smiled weakly. From the darkness to the light—this was one of the events that would most delight her, delight her, delight her ... Deep down what made her happy was that the experiment hadn't succeeded. Daniel would surely make her return the next day and again holidays ... But she wasn't strong enough to be happy. She'd tired herself out.

She walked toward the field slowly. Her forehead was now burning while her hard and frozen hands weren't warming in the sun. Her head was starting to throb atop her weakness and she was shuddering at each breeze. She broke off her stroll and returned painfully home. Going up the stairs she felt someone moving on the landing, she saw Daniel spying on her; his eyes were dry, steady, they would never forgive her. What would she say to him that afternoon in the clearing? what thought would she bring him from the experiment? Fear roiled her in exhaustion. She entered the bedroom, curled up in bed. She was trembling from a cold that seemed to come from her bowels and from a tight and blackened heart, her head was still being hammered with a joyful accuracy. Am I mad? It occurred to her as if someone said it, but she couldn't stop thinking. I should go to sleep in order to stop—but she couldn't. What to say to Daniel? She no longer even knew if she'd seen the sky for herself like someone seeing something that exists or if she'd thought about sky and managed to invent it ... She'd entered an unknown and crazy world, it seemed to her vaguely that the sky was existing in every instant like something always past, always present and quiet ... and that atop it were floating her desires for things, her visions, memories, words ... her life. And it was still the one who rose and loomed in moments of silence, giving her also a silence of thoughts ... or was all that just one of her ideas, an invention? would seeing the truth be different from inventing the truth? her head was cracking, growing rocking like a cold ball of fire. Would seeing the truth be different from inventing the truth? her thought was after all so strong that it didn't seem to be surrounded by any other. In her near-delirium she kept on thinking: if that sky was a reality, she was observing, once reverting she nevertheless wouldn't know how to reach another phase, the one prior to the sky, the

higher one, through effort: her power to seek had worn itself
out. No, she couldn't. But with an inexplicable certainty of
perfections, she was thinking that if she could reach whatever
was beyond the sky then a moment would come when it would
become clear that everything was free and that one wasn't un-
avoidably connected to whatever existed. You wouldn't have to
respect Father, feel pain in your injured leg, get happy about
happiness ... Scared, in an agitation that was kindling the sen-
sitivity of her head, she stood and walked to the window. That
knowledge she was feeling, would escape undeniable reality yet
was true. Now it was becoming clear: it was true! everything
was existing so freely that she could even overturn the order
of her feelings, not be afraid of death, fear life, desire hunger,
hate happy things, laugh at tranquility ... Yes, a little touch
would be enough and with a light and easy daring she'd leap
over inertia and reinvent life instant by instant. Instant by instant! thoughts of glass and sun were trembling inside her. I
can renew everything with a gesture, she was bravely feeling,
damp like a thing being born, but confusedly she was realizing that this thought was higher than her realization and
was doing nothing perplexed and serene, no gesture. Then she
would slowly sink into the beneficent darkness of fainting and
of happy giving-up—some minutes were passing, the flies of
the warm morning were flying around the room, landing on
her calm body and leaving it in order to rest on the dry and
shining windowpane. Slowly she returned to reality emerging
peaceful and cold from the half-light.

In the clearing she told him that she'd failed. Daniel's first
movement was rage. But, as if he'd thought better of it, he suppressed it:

"Do you want to go back to the basement tomorrow?" he asked her a bit absentmindedly.

The delicateness of the question surprised her, how she loved him, how she cared for him, those thinking eyes, that neck strong and straight but gentle. And she always failing, she rebuked herself, moved. But no, now she was afraid of the basement, she'd fainted after she got out of there, Daniel, it was dangerous to think deeply, no …

"Silence, the Society of Shadows wishes you to complete another task," Daniel was finally saying, his focused eyes were pursuing a difficult idea.

Virgínia was waiting without breathing.

"Free the family from Evil."

"What evil?" she asked immediately.

"Silence, you idiot. The Society of Shadows wishes to know if you know Esmeralda. It wishes to know if you know Esmeralda's secret, her meetings in the garden with that …"

"But I'm the one who told you, don't you remember?" Virgínia was interrupting faking excitement, flattering him.

"But shut up! Do not dare interrupt me or I will finish off the Society and you too. The Society of Shadows wishes you to tell Esmeralda's father about Esmeralda's meetings in the garden."

She parted her pale lips.

"The Society of Shadows has spoken."

Now she couldn't object. The Society of Shadows always got the last word and the formula employed by Daniel meant the end of the meeting.

*　*　*

She seemed to have plunged into baseness with the Society of Shadows.

She was looking at herself in the mirror, her white and delicate face lost in the half-light, her eyes open, her lips without expression. She was enjoying herself, liking that sleek, so sinuous way about her, her shaded hair, her small and skinny shoulders. How lovely I am, she said. Who will buy me? who will buy me?—she'd give a quick smooch to the mirror—who will buy me: agile, funny, funny as if I were blonde but I'm not blonde: I have lovely, cold, extraordinary brown hair. But I want someone to buy me so much that ... that ... that ... I'll kill myself! she exclaimed and peering at her face frightened by the phrase, proud of her own ardor, she laughed a fake guffaw, low and shining. Yes, yes, she'd need a secret life in order to be able to exist. From one instant to the next she was once again serious, tired—her heart was beating in the shadow, slow and red. A new element, foreign until now, had penetrated in her body since the Society of Shadows had come to exist. Now she was learning that she was good but that her goodness would not impede her badness. This feeling was almost old, it had been discovered days ago. And a new desire was touching her heart: to free herself still more. To go beyond the limits of her life—it was a phrase without words that was rolling around her body like nothing more than a push. To go beyond the limits of my life, she didn't know what she was saying looking at herself in the mirror in the guest room. I could kill them all, she was thinking with a smile and a new freedom, staring childishly at her image. She was waiting for an instant, watchful. But no: nothing had been created inside herself with the feeling provoked, neither joy nor fear. And where had the idea been born to her?—ever since the morning she spent in the basement questions were arising easily; and at every moment she was heading in what direction? moving ahead learning things whose beginnings all her life she hadn't even felt. Where had the idea been born? from her body; and if her body was her destiny ... Or was she inhaling thoughts from the air and giving them back as if they were her own, forcing herself to follow them? ... There she was in the mirror! she screamed at herself brutish and happy. But what could she and what couldn't she do? No, she didn't want to await some condition in order to kill, if she had to kill she wished it freely without any circumstances ... that would mean going beyond the limits of her life, she didn't know what she was thinking. In a sudden exhaustion where there was a certain voluptuousness and well-being, she lay down on the guest bed. And like a door that closes hurriedly and without noise, she quickly fell asleep. And quickly dreamed. She dreamed that her strength was saying loudly and to the ends of the earth: I want to go beyond the limits of my life, without words, only the dark power guiding itself. A cruel and living impulse pushed her forward and she would have wished to die forever if dying gave her a single instant of pleasure, such was the seriousness at which her body had arrived. She would hand over her own heart to be bitten, she wanted to go beyond the limits of her own life as a supreme cruelty. Then she walked outside the house and went searching, searching with the most ferocious thing she had; she was looking for an inspiration, her nostrils sensitive as those of a thin and frightened animal, but everything around her was sweetness and sweetness was something she already knew, and now sweetness was the absence of fear and danger. She'd do something so beyond her limits that she'd never understand it—but she didn't have the strength, ah she couldn't go beyond her own powers. She had to close her eyes for an instant and pray to herself brutally with disdain until in a deep sigh, ridding herself of the final pain, forgetting at last, she headed toward the sacrifice of destiny. Because if I am free, if with a gesture I can make everything new again—she was heading through the field beneath a whitish sky—then nothing keeps me from making that gesture; that was the murky and worried sensation. While she was walking she was looking at a dog and in a gasping effort like that of emerging from closed waters, like leaving the realm of what one could do, she was deciding to kill him as she walked. He was moving his tail defenseless—she thought about killing him and the idea was cold but she was afraid she was tricking herself by telling herself that the idea was cold in order to escape it. So she led the dog with gestures to the bridge over the river and with her foot pushed him surely to his death in the waters, heard him whimpering, saw him struggling, dragged by the current and saw him die—nothing was left, not even a hat. She continued serenely. Serenely she kept searching. She saw a man, a man, a man. His long trousers were sticking to the wind, his legs, his thin legs. The man, the man was mulatto. And his hair, my God, his hair was going gray. Trembling with disgust she headed toward him between air and space—and stopped. He too halted, old eyes waiting. Nothing in her face would make him guess what was just waiting to happen. She had to speak and didn't know how to say it. She said:

"Take me."

The mulatto man's eyes opened. And before long silhouetted against the pure air and the wind, against the light and dark green of the grass and the trees, before long he was laughing, understanding. He lifted her mute, laughing, his hair graying, laughing, and beyond the prairie was stretching beneath the wind. He lifted her mute laughing, a smell of kept meat was coming from his mouth, from his stomach through his mouth, a breath of blood; from his open shirt long and dirty hairs were emerging and around the air was lively, he lifted her by the arms and the sensation of ridiculousness was hardening her with ferocity—he was dangling her in the air proving to her that she was light. She pushed him with violence and he mute laughing mute walked and dragged her and invincible kissed her. Yet he was still laughing when she stood and serenely, like the end of going beyond the limits of her life, stepped with calm power on his wrinkled face and spit on him while he mute, looking wasn't understanding and the sky was lengthening in a single blue air. She awoke immediately and when she opened her eyes she was almost standing, her face clear and anxious. Motionless she was feeling her own body all the way to the end, large, her muscles meek and happy. She wasn't feeling numbness but a possibility of moving herself with balance. What had happened? quickly she understood, for a second she was confused, she thought she'd really left the house, hesitated, returned to a vague good sense. It had been a short dream, enough to let her leave the limits of her life. Swollen and slow sensations were broadening her body. Surprised as after an act of sleepwalking, she headed toward the mirror: what was happening to her? there was a strange ambiguity in her face where her weakened eye was always dreaming, a determination in her lips as if she were obeying the fatefulness of a hallucination. She was feeling that some countless time had passed and she was remembering the house in whose center she found herself as something far away. A sweet power was weighing upon her hips, lengthening the smooth neck to which the big and irregular cleavage was giving birth. In some way she was no longer a virgin. She had lived more than she had dreamed, lived, she would swear to it sincerely though she also knew the truth and scorned it.

"Virgínia."

Father was calling her from the parlor with his voice that was never raised but could be heard throughout the house. In a difficult reminiscence she noticed that he had already called her while she was dreaming. She went down a few steps, stopped in the middle of the staircase:

"Daddy, you called me?"

Esmeralda with her face wet with tears was hesitating by his side, on her cheek the red outline of the palm of a hand— Mother was hovering on the threshold without support staring her old rat's dusky, slow gaze. Virgínia sought Daniel uselessly.

"Repeat what you ... what we heard from that person," Father said to her.

"Daddy, Daddy."

"Repeat it."

"Daddy."

"Repeat it!"

"I can't."

Father looked at everyone, victorious, old, sullen. In those moments of rage he'd seem fatter and shorter.

"Then listen and confirm it: this slut here meets a male in the garden."

Esmeralda sobbed:

"But nothing happened this time, nor ever ... I already swore!"

"God!" screamed Father with sudden eloquence, "what's a poor man done in order to receive evil spirits in his house for the second time! What's a poor man done to see his life and that of the house he made brought low by his own daughter!! Punish me, Lord, but bring down thy punishment upon my own head!"

Virgínia was watching him lucidly, her eyes mobile and cunning. Her whole body was aching in anticipation. Her father abruptly calmed down, turned toward her:

"Confirm what you said."

"She's the one who told?!" Mother screamed.

"No ... no!" groaned Virgínia, white, looking at Father.

He hesitated for an instant with clouded and hot eyes:

"It doesn't matter who it was, what matters is that this ..."

Quick thoughts were blending inside her and before anyone could expect it she let out a piercing scream and fell. Her father kept her from rolling down the stairs. Eyes closed, ears tensely on the lookout for whatever was happening, she felt carried upwards in a slow flight. She was smiling inwardly without knowing why amidst the alert terror. The effort she was making not to open her eyes and to stay lifeless was absorbing her so strongly that for several instants she stopped hearing and being aware. When she cracked open her eyes she found herself on the bed in the empty bedroom. A great silence was enveloping the house, whispering through every corner as on a Sunday. She stayed for a few moments almost distracted pulsating sweetly. In her body the blood was renewing itself. Standing in a light thrust she was at the door, searching through the air in order to find out where the people were. Nothing could be felt, the mansion vast and naked. She felt herself smiling, brought her fingers to her lips but these were still closed and narrow and the smile had only been a thought. A thought without joy but that was making her smile: her goodness wasn't preventing her badness, her goodness wasn't preventing her badness. She had committed a corrupt and vile act. Never though had she seemed to have acted so freely and with such freshness of desire. She needed to study herself in the mirror, yes, yes, she thought with urgency and hope. She was sensing that the guest room could be reached without anyone's seeing her. She crossed the hallway rapidly, the steps of her bare feet muffled by the purple carpet, her heart beating violent and pale.

So there she was. Her face for an instant as if eternal, her flesh devoutly mortal. There she was, then, her innocent eyes peering inside her own degradation. And in the meantime it would be useless to try to deter what was happening around her. And inside her it would be useless to try to awaken the understanding of her body living in that lengthily tense afternoon. She would never manage to repeat what she was thinking and what she was feeling was happening to her evanescently, light and shiny, so immaterial and fleeting that she couldn't stop on any thought. Surprised, intimidated by her own ignorance beside an immobile certainty, she was dangling for an instant, interrupting the movement of her life and looking at herself in the mirror: that shape expressing some thing without laughter but anguishingly mute and so inside itself that its meaning could never be grasped. Looking at herself she wouldn't be able to understand, only agree. She was agreeing with that deep body in shadows, with her silent smile, life as if being born from that confusion. Now her permission for herself was seeming even more ardent as if she were allowing her own future too. And she ... but yes, yes, she was seeing the future ... yes, in a glance made of seeing and hearing, in a pure instant the whole future ... Though she only knew that she was seeing and not what she was seeing, just as all she could say about blue was: I saw blue, and nothing more ... With her eyebrows raised she was awaiting the timid annunciation. What had existed in her life was an indistinct and infinite power, really infinite and pallid. But she could never have demonstrated the existence of that power as it would be difficult to prove that she felt like going on, that the color of the rose was pleasing to her, that she was feeling strength, that she was connected to the stone in the garden. What had existed in her life, untouched and never lived, had raised her through the world like the bubble that rises. But just after accomplishing some act—having one day looked one more time at the sky? having watched the man who was walking? having entered the Society of Shadows? or after a simple quiet instant?—after accomplishing some act impossible to refrain from, something fatal and mysterious, suddenly she could only henceforward this or that and her power had ceased ... Henceforward she could manage to name whatever she could do and that capacity instead of assuring her of greater power was guaranteeing her in some inexplicable way a fall and a loss. Previously her most secure movement of life had been disinterested, she'd notice things she'd never use, a leaf falling would intercept the path she had started out on, the wind would undo her thoughts forever. After the Society of Shadows however she'd steal from each gaze its value for herself and beautiful would be whatever her body thirsted and hungered for; she had taken a side. She'd also observed Daniel lately. And without awareness she was seeing that her lightest matter had been corrupted slowly, that in him the sweet suffering in which both of them were living had been annihilated; in his being something had become more serious and inflexible, a trembling brutality. Or was she seeing him for the first time? She herself, though she wouldn't deny or confirm, her eyes would automatically rise or lower before certain images and even if she strove never to choose, bemused she had already chosen. And now when she was hesitating in the dismay without pain she was aware that if later she resuscitated for joy and opened her heart in order to breathe again laughing, she was aware: lapsing and standing back up was irrepressible. The danger had ceased forever. Suddenly the words from which she lived in childhood seemed to have run out and she couldn't find any others. She set out with care. She was experiencing a worried feeling of regret for living that moment, for being almost a young woman and for being the one to whom the instant was happening—she was seeming to feel that from a deep untouchable freedom she could garner strength in order to not allow herself. She was looking at the silent and pale air of the room, an instant immobile and without destiny. How fatal it was to have lived. For the first time she had aged. For the first time she was aware of a time behind her and the restless notion of something she could never touch, of some thing that no longer belonged to her because it was complete but that she still clung to because of her incapacity to create another life and a new time. Her entire childhood had been wrinkled by the cold air that was hurting inside her nose with icy ardor; she was seeing herself as if from far away, small, the dark shape in the fog already gilded by the sun, cast down looking on the ground at something she could no longer name; now her own breath was seeming to surround her with a tepid atmosphere, her eyes were opening in wide color, her body was straightening into a human creature. With a sigh of impatience and fear her body rebelled as if possessed and again froze in the bedroom. Having experienced the sweetness of fascination with and ardent obedience to Daniel, her malleable and weak nature was now longing to hand itself over to the force of another destiny. She was feeling that the harmony between her existence and the Farm where she had been born and was living had ceased; for the first time she was thinking about the journey to the city with a nervous pleasure full of hope and confused rage. Upper Marsh, the fog in the mornings, the narrow streets, the solitude of Quiet Farm were still now in some incomprehensible way above her and if once the silence of the fields and the indecipherable noise of the forest carried forth her own sensations, now she had to move about in a cold and indifferent land; she was thinking with concern about next winter's rains as if foreseeing a new despair at remaining stuck in the mansion. Inexplicably until then she had dreamed and only now was opening her eyes, rushing into some solid and mortal thing—with a surprised disgust she was secretly guessing herself to be more known, as if recognizable. In a few years she'd leave with Daniel. Still years away. With steadfastness she was making up her mind to close her heart and traverse them closed in order only to start living again in the city—her thought left a livid resonance in the air—how many possibilities a person had if she lived in the open world, her body was trembling almost frightened by its own urging, by all the darkness there was in its power. She gave a little shout of joy and hard promise: ah! But she herself was just thinking the surface of what was happening to her in those instants and was paying attention to herself as if placing her hand atop her beating heart and not being able to touch it. She waited for an instant. Nothing was happening then … Silence surrounded her impalpable and she then calmed down, looked at the mirror somberly shining. Stubborn, she was staring at her face trying to define its fleeting magic, the softness of the movement of breathing that was lighting it and slowly putting it out. The corruption was bathing her in a sweet light. So there she was. So there she was. There was no one who could save or lose her. And that's how the moments were unfurling and dying while her quiet and mute face was floating in expectation. So there she was. Even yesterday the pleasure of laughing had made her laugh. And ahead of her stretched the entire future.

After so many days in which she hadn't left the house and not even once had seen Vicente, she was looking to Sunday for pulling herself together and not turning up at Irene's dinner pale and barely resuscitated. The open air after dragging through so many hours in the unmade bed was awakening her skin in an indefinable and strong scent, timidly harsh. The perfume that heat awakes in thick and green plants — but she was poorly alive and though the stroll was breathing a vague smile into her she was getting tired.

She climbed the hill in search of the dam where the volumes of water were being contained, imprisoned, condensed into such an intimate union that her rough whisper had the force of a prayer. Tufts of weeds were bending beneath their own weight, lying on the narrow path under her feet. She was arranging with one of her hands her little brown hat while with the other she was leaning on the long, black umbrella. She was going up the difficult slope and above herself seeing nothing more than a line of earth linking itself, new and clear, to the sky; the tall weeds were flailing against the cold pink of the air. Near the dam lived the custodian with his dry and wrinkled skin, with clean eyes—a dog was barking without approaching. And from the hill before her, when the wind would blow, a quick noise of movements would come, the peaceful singing of a cock, light and shredded laughter, the children's shouts bubbling into the Sunday—everything from the remote and disappeared beginning, one that had been forgotten and that you couldn't put your finger on and that would suddenly repeat, losing itself again. When it would fall silent it was as if someone were breathing while smiling. From afar she saw an old woman smoking, a woman carrying oranges, a man building a house; a fire was kindling and shining. Virgínia was facing forward and kept climbing the mountain; to better feel it she'd almost say to herself distracted with slight stubbornness: she's old as the earth, she's old as the earth, and try to feel fear. She'd remember at moments the letter that she'd written to the Farm—shorter every time. My health is fine, I've just had a little nausea. I eat a lot of sweets, that must be it, because I became such a glutton in the city! ... I keep fattening up, thank God, but I'm getting pretty heavy; I don't remember fainting, no one in Upper Marsh would recognize the skinny girl I was ... I already paid the rent, having made the most of everything, yes, yes, yes. Each time she found it harder to send news. When Daniel was still living with her she felt like she had to tell them that everything was fine. But now ... It would be nice to take a walk with Daniel this afternoon. Not that he could define some feeling in her; despite his invulnerable integrity he too would allow things to remain in their own nature. It would just be good to stroll with Daniel and point out to him what she was seeing with that familiar grunt that between the two of them meant something different depending on the tone. In the city the river was smooth, the coconut palms aligned, even the mountains seemed clean and trimmed, everything stretched across the surface, fulfilled. Whereas in Upper Marsh existence was more secret—and that's what she would say without speaking.

The dam was groaning without interruption, shivering in the air and shaking inside her body, leaving her somehow trembling and hot. She sat on one of the rocks still sensitive to the sun. For an instant, in a light silent whirl, she'd spent her whole life sitting on rocks; another reality is that she'd traversed her whole life looking at the darkness before going to sleep and moving around in search of some comfort while some thin and awakened thing was lurking: tomorrow. Yes, how many things she was seeing—she sighed slowly looking around her with sadness. She'd thought to find other species in the city ... Yet she still kept sitting on rocks, noticing a glance in a person, meeting a blind man, only hearing certain words ... she was seeing what she was making out for the first time and it was something that seemed to have completed the capacity of her eyes. A long empty well-being seized her, she crossed her fingers with delicateness and affection, set about looking. But the sky was fluttering so frayed, robust, so without surface ... What she was feeling was without depth ... but what she was feeling ... above all fainting without strength ... yes, swooning in the sky ... like her ... Quick thick circles were moving away from her heart—the sound of a bell unheard but heavily felt in the body in waves—the white circles were blocking her throat in a big hard bubble of air—there wasn't even a smile, her heart was withering, withering, moving off through the distance hesitating intangible, already lost in an empty and clean body whose contours were widening, moving away, moving away and all that existed was the air, so all that existed was the air, the air without knowing that it existed and in silence, in silence high as the air. When she opened her eyes things were slowly emerging from dark waters and shining wetly sonorous on the surface of her consciousness, still wavering from the faint. The water from the dam was murmuring deep in her interior, so distant that it had already surpassed her body infinitely behind. The wisdom of the cold air was awakening the flesh of her face stinging it with freshness. My God, how happy am I, she thought in a weak and luminous jolt. Waking so girlish from her faint, she was smiling exhausted, feeling as if she were too little to remain without protective thoughts or experience atop a hill hearing the other hill like another world living painstakingly on Sunday. She was feeling in silence that after a faint she was in the greatest part of life because there was neither love nor hope that could transcend that serious sensation of nascent flight. But why was that instant not calming her with the satisfaction of the attained goal ... why? it was extending her to the heights, stretching her out almost desperate with the tension of a bow full of its own movement ... as if living that way on the summit she'd feel more than the potency of her great dark body and wipe herself out in her own perception. Her heart was still beating with fatigue and she was thinking: I fainted, that's what it was, I fainted. She was looking at the red and illuminated light hovering in the half-lit forest. What did her light mean? her eyes kept demanding opening clearings in the sweet confusion of her fatigue. She couldn't understand, she could agree, just that, and only with her head, assenting, scared. She was agreeing with the afternoon, agreeing with that fragile power that would sustain her as she met the air, agreeing with her joyful fear—the fear of facing the dinner with almost strangers, Vicente's love, her own everyday fake feelings? that watchful error—she was agreeing with the living hill saying out loud, out loud inside her: ah, yes, yes! ardently united and quiet. Not however on the level of undeniable reality, only in a certain truth where you could say everything without ever making a mistake, there where there wasn't even such a thing as a mistake and where everything would live ineffably by the power of the same permission, there where she herself was living splendidly erased, vacant and thing, purely thing like the moist blinking of a bitch lying against the air and panting, agreeing deeply without knowing like a bitch. She felt almost close to fainting again, along with the desire to yield— and even in the dry present she still belonged to the previous part of her life that was getting lost in a calm distance.

After fainting everything was as if easy. She got her balance. She hadn't fainted in years. Night was now almost falling and lowering her eyelids she could feel the deadened rays of light like somber translucent music tumbling down the mountain in a supple torrent abandoned to the power of its own destiny. She was squeezing with one of her hands the rough handle of the umbrella. It would be impossible for it to rain now, she was feeling looking distracted at the cold sky of the mirror. It was confusingly seeming to her that it would also be impossible for her to free herself from her way and follow another path— she was smiling a bit serious and floating in a frightened but in itself peaceful feeling—so potent and imprisoned she and her nature were seeming to find themselves inside the tenuous balance of their lives. But there was a freedom—like a desire, like a desire—above the possibility of choosing, in her and in her nature, and from it would come the odd and tired serenity of the near-night without rain in the mountains, the laziness once again renewed inside her body.

She opened the door of her little apartment, penetrated the cold and stuffy surroundings of the living room. Slight stain was rippling in one of the corners, expanding like a light nearly erased coolness. She screamed low, sharp—but they're lovely!—the room was breathing with half-closed eyes in the silence of mute pickaxes of the construction sites. The flowers were straightening up in delicate vigor, the petals thick and tired, damp with sweat—the stalk was tall, so calm and hard. The room was breathing, oppressed, asleep. The smaller petals, like hair on the nape of your neck in summer, were stooping, wilted, blind, yet still able to live and amaze. Virgínia hurried laughing toward them, tilted her dark head yet retreated slightly scared. Because they would close hostile without the slightest perfume as if some thing in their nature secretly repelled Virgínia's nature. But I always got along well with flowers—that was her impression while she was undressing—she touched them lightly with the tips of her fingers, disappointed, discreet and already uninterested. They were trembling. Without knowing why, permission had at last been given to feel sad and she was trying without really managing it all that Sunday afternoon. Her true sensation during the stroll had been so intimate, pervaded her with such delicateness that it just remained like a hesitation, an expectation. She was wanting a thing to dress her for Irene's dinner, a calm and stable feeling, some clear certainty of defeat so that she couldn't start again irresistibly to fight and have hopes. She got ready to go out. The white dress was stretched on the bed, lighting up the small room, giving it the look of strange and forbidden excitement. Placed in the short slip and with a body with so little in the way of waistline, she looked at herself in the mirror—would she be ready to confront other people's laughter and shine? her face was wandering in shadows. Ever since she looked at Daniel's black spiders her eyes were a little squinty, they'd set a quick tone of wandering and movement to her face where some indefinable trait seemed to waver almost transforming itself—her face would sometimes recall an image reflected in water. Around the room things were living profoundly tranquilized and on the street since the day before the construction noise had ceased. The other apartments in the building at that hour on Sunday were empty: the occasional shout of a child could be heard stuck in the building's cement. With one of her hands forgotten on her face in a distracted caress she was waiting without enthusiasm. Slowly in the depth of her neglect some spot in her body started to live weakly, to pulsate accompanying the things all around ... Now she was waiting more cautious, her eyes open, her heart open, darkly open shuddering with hope. She was waiting ... But it was so unfamiliar the silence and her white slip, which suddenly as if she herself hadn't been feeling the waiting, set out and kept living in another milieu, easy and light among the quiet construction sites. When she put on her dress someone banged with a jolt on the door. She opened it and found the washerwoman and her daughter with the package of washed clothes, apologizing for not having come on Saturday, looking surprised at Virgínia's silk dress that had never been washed, Virgínia whom they always saw in poor clothes. The neckline and the fitted bodice raised her bust giving it even bigger proportions; the narrow belt was uselessly squeezing her waistline without shrinking it. The small glass buttons were trembling with every breath. The cream-white was sweetening her fine skin, making her short hair shine. She exchanged a quick look with the women, took on a worldly air while her pupils were darting around with satisfaction and pursuit:

"Now it's completely impossible, but com-ple-te-ly!" she was saying with a busy and voluptuous pleasure. "I waited yesterday and all afternoon today, you have no idea, do me a favor and come back tomorrow, a big favor ... tomorrow, I'll give you dirty clothes because I have a dinner today ... understand, I must be ready on time, the car will certainly come get me ... Unfortunately that's how these things are, you know ..."—she interrupted herself with blinking eyes in search of more words for her momentum, almost pensive. With delighted and foolish faces, the washerwomen were saying yes, yes, one pushing the other one with awe and anguish while Virgínia was also seeming to push them with fascinating excuses; they were laughing humbly with affliction, disappearing down the stairs with a white smile still on their faces. Virgínia stopped, listening for an instant to the calm silence that had followed her own rampage ... an instant more. A moment more. She was absorbed and without thoughts but it seemed to her as in an illness of will that she'd never again have strength to want to move. She asked herself for one more, one more instant. She herself was struggling against giving up. She then moved, went to comb her hair. Pensive, it occurred to her that she could never forget the offense to the washerwomen but in the same moment she thought she was late and changed course forever. Before going out, with her hand on the door latch, that prim and careful feeling of face powder and of the fragility of her appearance, she remembered and with slow coldness grabbed the scissors, cut the stem of three flowers, of the hard and opaque flowers, fastened them to the neckline of her dress, there where her large breasts and her heart were living, veiled. In a protest a green smell was rising to her nose, so acrid for her teeth, that revived her. She didn't want to go to the dinner, she was scared!—she thought for the first time clearly in a light lament, interpreting the pale rattle that was being born, dizzy, in her chest ... She didn't want to, that's what it was ... No, that wasn't it, how could she make so many mistakes? ... on the contrary ... such confusion ... she wanted to go so powerfully that ... she sighed rapidly, felt her already-sweaty waist beneath the light dress that was squeezing ... understood that the afternoon had naturally been sad and never happy ... Oh, on the contrary, on the contrary, the flowers were pushing her forward in a happy, nervous urge ... horribly desperate... and she'd see Vicente.

The construction sites had covered themselves with shadows, with long irrevocable stains—she saw crossing the deserted street. A pure smell of quicklime, angles, cement, and cold was being born from the debris where the silence of some stone chip was strongly shining. She inhaled with pleasure the fog that was seeming to rise from the damp construction and kept going in a controlled urge that would take her to the dinner but that could bring her forward ... as without end inside the luminous and bustling bus where she'd installed herself with her white dress and the resistant flowers; she was keeping her eyes firm as if to sustain the reality of those instants— with one of her hands she was clasping the white hat with its wide brim against her head, her neck stiff and prudent. And that's how from far away, jumping from the bus and walking on the polished cobblestones and most of all maintaining above whatever could happen the same reality, straightening herself like a bouquet of flowers above the crowd, she spotted Vicente with Adriano waiting for her. She spotted him so suddenly with surprise that in a movement of life and confusion the flowers were connecting to the dead smell of the construction sites, the vague lost afternoon sad or happy? to the urge that had breathed into her hope for the dinner, to the silent construction sites ... mixing herself with everything to which she was saying: yes! yes! almost irritated and she agreed intensely with the moment; yes, she was agreeing at a glance and with a wisdom of fireworks understanding the yellow and dense light that was coming from the lampposts trembling in thin rays within the noisy half-dark of the night; she was feeling behind the tender lights, traversing them, the sweet and softly sharp sounds of the wheels of the cars and of the hurried conversations, a near-scream rising and giving quick silence to the murmuring, the slabs of the sidewalk shining as if it had just rained and above all from afar, as if brought by a wide free wind, the touching almost painful and mute perception that the city was extending beyond the street, connecting to the rest, was big, living quickly, superficially. With effort she was transforming her pace into something that would mean reaching, the brim of her hat was trembling, her breasts were trembling, her big body advancing. Her serious eyes smiled, drifting forward as if she knew that upon contact with her body the air would give way; she was deeply hearing the two men and inventing a confused and cynical body as only a woman could imagine; no one could accuse her of being immoral, and she was moving ahead, offering her body to the street, meeting her lips, wetting them flirting, imagining them red like flowing blood because the instant was asking for blood flowing toward her luminosity of newborn matter. How dare I live? yet that was the persistent impression. And despite her lips being only pink—who? but who would ever notice? she gave them a strong thought like the glory of a saint and that thought was of blood flowing. And, by God and by the Devil!, Vicente's friend was seeming to understand. Yes, she and Adriano were communicating, he small, peaceful, clear, and unknown was looking and noticing and scarcely knew, oh scarcely knew that he was noticing—she didn't know what he was thinking. Vicente was staring at her slightly surprised amidst the greetings, averting his attention but coming back with almost severe eyes—since what expression could he use for that minute if the minute was invented? And he scarcely knew what he was feeling ... he would even die not knowing what had happened but maybe not forgetting ... No, there was nothing picturesque in the moment, there was something calm and old around the instant. Vicente had understood why he was addressing her or not with that look that he'd only adopt in the presence of still-unpossessed women and to whom he never could say: close the door before going out. But nothing had happened after all, just that quick confusion of smiles and greetings, that satisfied uneasiness born of the awareness that everything was happening delicately as it should be, that arrival of Virgínia's with her head held up and her wide eyes ... just that, one person feeling that her dress and lipstick are fine, above all they exist, an inexplicable attitude of pride in her own femininity itself like a woman.

"Today you are evanescent ...," Adriano said to her smiling with a cold and smooth look as if he were forced to say it. Vicente was smiling, the lights were smiling, the illuminated sidewalks were smiling, Virgínia was smiling.

"She was sick, weren't you, Virgínia?"

"You know how it is," she responded, "a little sickness here, another there ... that's how you go on living," she concluded with a too-big smile, she pursed her lips, they were watching in silence.

Although at the moment of the meeting it hadn't even existed ... "that"—what Adriano had just said—had made something unfold inside her and join the care with which she'd dressed and "that" would live for the rest of the night even after the flowers withered. It was what she was needing to get through the night of the dinner—she didn't know what she was thinking while drinking with the two men one warm glass and another cold one of alcohol, doing it again before going up, and telling herself: yes, yes. After shaking hands with all the guests and smiling she was forced by the gaze of the guests not to refuse a jaunt to Irene's *toilette*. In order to straighten out mysteriously feminine things—they were being allowed and didn't look at her as she did so that she'd feel comfortable. Timidly she was accepting, almost fat, even if Irene were quite busy to take her there herself and Irene's husband was bringing her to the bedroom down a long hallway where not a single word would sound between them. Make yourself comfortable, make yourself comfortable, the flustered man was murmuring as he hesitated between leaving or saying a few more words, maybe a joke about something. In a corner of the room a lamp was burning, white, and making flutter across the walls and ceiling circles of soft light and shadow, wispy colorless veils; above the headboard of the bed a Christ with dry wounds was hanging, tired. She took off her hat, her head looked naked and poor, her hair lifeless. Yes, she was saying with a murky ardor. She looked at herself in the mirror of the dressing table: where, where was her warm power from the instant of the meeting? she was combing her hair. But there really was—she insisted almost despondent—yes, almost fainting, glimmering from the depths of a face that was still as serious and offended as a girl's. Again the old idea attacked her, so vague and swirling, and that wasn't exactly the one that should be being born but another, small and too difficult to think:

"I hold myself back in order not to be loved by everyone."

That wasn't it! that wasn't it! the feeling that followed was as good as if she'd said what she didn't even know how to think and even feel. But with her eyes half-open and a constant desire she could see herself like veils heaped under lights before the start of a waltz—though she'd grown so much, her movements reflected, and the fear of the clean evening returning, sad or happy and a certain way of seeing returning in which she could sometimes fall not knowing how to take on a false demeanor among the unknown people, unable to steal away like dormant flowers nonetheless giving off perfume uselessly, seeing and hearing everything, mingling and wandering bemused. She mustered a little courage straightening her body and falsely giving it a quicker movement that sounded too alive in the empty room. She headed to the living room. She sliced through that dining room quietly lit by a single pale color, whitish and gold, that was existing solidly beneath the sweet cold dust. She lost her urge—she'd always felt like a prisoner of luxury, of those shining surfaces, shifting and hostile. She stopped watchful. The silence was holding itself back in the set table. Coming from a world not as clean as this one a fly or two was flying over the placid and sparkling plates. A stopped smile was settling over the entire room as if it were so stretched out that it had lost meaning and were just its own reminiscence. Virgínia was floating between the table, the air, and her own body fluttering in search—so indecipherable was that party silence. Don't forget, don't forget, she was thinking distractedly observing as if she were about to leave and needed to tell what she was seeing. Also because she was feeling that the alcohol would abbreviate the memory of those instants. She extended her lightly drunken hands in an attempt at tenderness. Without knowing why, surprised and delighted, she was feeling herself on the verge of a revelation. Don't forget ... A halo of pale excitement was shining around the ferociously blazing lights, the lamps burning themselves with pleasure, bloodless. Don't forget. In a glacial and sleek blink a glass existed for a moment and extinguished itself forever in the watchful silence of the china cabinet. She attempted once more an ordinary gesture; she managed to extend her fingers lightly, achieved nothing, retreated. Since what could she do in relation to that world? the two drinks were warming her, wrapping her in a faint bodily fatigue while her lucid eyes were noticing. She was feeling foreign to that milieu but was guessing that she was subordinated to it by fascination and humility. In a few short minutes she would enter the living room by destiny and everyone would not see her while smiling at her for a second. How to free oneself? not to free oneself from something but just free oneself because she wouldn't be able to say from what. She not-thought for an instant, her head bent. She took a napkin, a bread roll ... with an extraordinary effort, breaking in herself a stupefied resistance, deflecting destiny, she threw them out the window — and in that way kept her power. One day when she was small the teacher had sent her to get a glass of water for a visitor — she, who sat in the back row, the never-chosen one! She'd gone trembling with pride but on the way back, gripping with care her prize, not out of revenge, not out of anger, she had spit in the water keeping her own power. What else? she was seeking while smiling, her eyes shining with warm love because without assistants she was feeling harmonious and powerful in that live, calm room. What else? she was pushing her drunkenness with sweetness. A wine glass was shuddering in still sparks, its crystal connecting nervous and ardent to the light of the lamps. She stretched out her small hands, so damp, took it delicately as if it were electric in its fragility; intensely slow she let it fall out the window shattering in herself the resistance of her life; she heard its shards singing rapidly alongside the distant cement. Frightened she listened for an instant to the room where Irene's guests were gathered: nobody had heard and the cheerful murmuring kept going in a single whirl; no maid was turning up. So it had really been her?! Her own courage made her heart beat outside the subtle rhythm of the crystals. Again the un-confessable sensation that she herself was creating the moment that kept coming ... And that she could stop the flow of the other instants with a small movement all her own, controlled: don't enter the living room! Destroying the glass had nothing to do with her past, with the time that was running out, it was an instant above her own life—she was strangely noticing what she was thinking as in one of those pale and silly memories of things that don't exist. Above all because she was separated from herself by two delicate glasses of drink. But she already knew this: that it was always too late in order to not enter the room.

And what she knew within undeniable reality is that, now, sitting with everyone on the sofas, she was saying: ah yes!, I think so too, thanks, smiling, seeing Vicente tall, strong, and friendly curiously living independent of her, feeling in her legs a benevolent heat; and where, where was her sweet power? now she was feeling inside herself a metallic and harsh insect, of stinging flight. And where was her own brand on Vicente's face; one of the guests was saying while smoking:

"... and it was at that same time that I read *The Problem of* ..."

... she in vain sought some spot in her body that might attest to the reading of *The Problem of* ... And inside herself—who would have thought that that insignificant creature had just felt like someone who had to hold herself back in order not to be loved by everyone? and who would have thought that the white dress, the dinner, the flowers were a high point in her days. She was paying attention to the conversations trying now to show that she was intelligent and different. What was enriching her was knowing obscurely that by saying: "it was I who did" instead of "it was me who did" would impede intimacy, earn a certain calm way of being looked at. She was feeling indecisive among all those people who were so natural, so well-dressed, their teeth shining. Sometimes she would remember herself dressed in white and in a light stiffening she'd straighten up; that was the most intimate sensation of the party. She was also remembering the Farm, her unkempt mother walking through the middle of the house with neither pleasure nor strength. She was remembering Esmeralda with her fancy clothes, her eyes tender and impatient. Her father, silent, dominating the house and unheeded, going up the stairs. And Daniel now, how to recall him? it was darkened inside him the way she would look at him. She was remembering the days spent in the small apartment, that familiar feeling of tired and expectant misery that she in an end-point of degradation was coming to love getting emotional.

The door opened once again and Maria Clara entered.

The furniture was becoming intelligible, the arrangement of the greenish room quaked beneath the light, a vase of flowers began—even those who were still seated were headed in her direction. What was making her difficult was the crystalline part of her body: her eyes, her saliva, her hair, her teeth and dry nails that were sparkling and isolating. Maria Clara was drinking, her lips blood-red and opaque, the cold shine on her skin and her silken neck; she was greeting people with a half-smile, her pupils open without fear. In Vincent's pupils the smiling black was always mixed with a certain haste—nothing essential had been attained with his love ...—that was the impression. Yet he was laughing through his eyeglasses like a grown-up student. Maria Clara's pink camel-hair dress was reminding her of a motionless river and the motionless leaves of engravings. With a movement of her leg, with the breathing of her breasts the river would move, the leaves flutter. How clean and brushed she was. Except unlike the other women she was forgetting that she'd put on perfume and done her hair and like a child was playing without worrying about getting dirty. Her intimacy was rich and impassable, a secret life filled with details, whereas Virgínia could almost live publicly, beneath a tree. With Virgínia you'd never risk overstepping boundaries and ridiculously trespassing over what was permitted—her intimacy even if violated didn't seem to be possessed, useless to inhale her perfume, see her clean underwear, watch her bathe; only she herself would use her surroundings. Poor Esmeralda, embroidering chambray trousers, burning perfumes in her bedroom, her body exacerbated like a lemon—her femininity was almost repugnant to another woman. Whereas Maria Clara had more humid thoughts, she kept that mysterious and dry quality, clear as a number. It was horrible to feel how nice she was. Pretty, mutable, weak, intelligent, understanding, brutish, selfish, there was no point pretending she wasn't lovely, she would penetrate in your heart like a sweet knife. The thin, confident women were chatting—they seemed easy for the men and hard for the women; and why didn't they have kids? my God, how disconcerting that was. And if they did they treated them like friends, yes, like friends. She remembered that one day she'd seen Irene at the entrance to a cinema with her son, yes, yes, now she was remembering. He was a red-headed, thin boy, the kind who didn't get surprised and who'd be joyful and hapless when he was a teenager. But you aren't unlikable either, honey. She was surprised by the worn-out affection and was touched in her solitude almost to the point of crying. She was careful nevertheless with a fearful self-confidence never to go beyond certain liberties with herself because whatever there was that remained unexplored could lead her to lose her good sense forever. Maria Clara had sat down drinking and smoking in her motionless dress: it was of an ardent pink burning itself in its own color; yet in a certain light it would turn off and emerge dead, stretched, almost cold in its calm, flat tones—meanwhile Virgínia was waiting in her white dress with its little buttons and the couple's son was showing up before going to sleep, Irene shining in black silk, his watchful well-groomed lamb's face; she was leading him by the hand dressed as if by chance in pajamas of striped silk, his red hair in a tall pile above his narrow, pale, and weakly smiling face.

"Ernesto, Ernesto, come here," said the director of the newspaper's voice.

The child approached, the man seated on the armchair reached the edge, encircled the thin waist of the boy who was still smiling. The thick and hairy hand of the man was making pleats of silk on Ernesto's bent body, everyone seated was doing nothing in the green room, smiling, watching. Everyone was waiting to say something funny and didn't know what, they were waiting seated.

"Ernesto," the director of the newspaper said at last leisurely, "do you know about the importance of being Ernesto?"

The boy was smiling vaguely in reply looking at the wall behind the man, everyone laughed discreetly, a few closed their eyes, quaking. Irene was wanting somehow to thank him, was laughing louder; afraid the newspaper director would think he hadn't been understood, she said disappointed at the end of a fake and tender laugh:

"Oscar Wilde…"

The director of the newspaper fell silent but his eyes still resting on Ernesto transformed imperceptibly, froze in order to reveal nothing. Ernesto was smiling. The room was suddenly decaying like face powder toasting the skin, eyesight tiring, the lamp losing strength—Irene had a hurried movement:

"Say good night to everyone, Ernesto!"

Without pleasure everyone squeezed Ernesto's warm little hand as he was smiling and stopping in the middle of the room without knowing what to do next. His wide eyes were blinking, serious by now.

"So?" asked Irene laughing with irritation.

The boy looked at her, said inexplicably, out loud:

"Yes …"—a kind of red splotch arose around one eye, Irene slightly defenseless observed the dark stain; she was seeming to seek the most humble guest in search of support, said with a difficult smile to Virgínia:

"He's sometimes so sensitive."

"Yes, yes," said Virgínia laughing too much.

"Say good night to everyone now!" repeated Irene feeling that everything had been lost. The abandoned boy was insisting on looking at them waiting. So funny, said the fattest woman. His father, between the director of the newspaper and Vicente, tall, was watching the scene with quick and anguished eyes, Irene was looking for him for a second, the family was coming undone in front of the guests. Irene pushed the child sweetly out of the room. When Ernesto disappeared she turned around, straightened herself up by smoothing the dress over her thin and suddenly inelegant body; everyone was seeming to demand the conclusion, she laughed, said loudly in an appeal: he was tired … Ah, yes, of course, naturally, some voices said quickly. The drinks were preventing her from letting the events connect to one another by visible paths but made them follow one another in soft, oblivious, tepidly doomed jumps. She shouldn't drink, she'd fainted today, it could happen again—and as if fainting had a secret meaning, she couldn't stand passing out if she wasn't alone; and returning from the dizziness opening her eyes and not understanding. And so, all of a sudden there they were in the dining room near the ridiculous table, entirely square atop fat bow legs. And one of the women, astute, daringly alive, threw a quick arrow in her direction:

"And your brother? your nice Daniel?"

But before she could finish opening her mouth in a smile, someone replied for her and her mouth once again closed in a smile. Someone was adding: he got married so long ago, my God! with a girl from a fine family. She wasn't needing to talk much, she'd only been invited because of Vicente. Nobody was expecting anything from her body except for it to eat discreetly using the napkin, smiling. Nice Daniel. So the way she liked him surpassed her powers with difficulty and pain. What she desired with her uniform, ardent, and martyred heart was to die before he did, never to witness him losing the world, never, never, my God—she was looking at a spot on the wall with glassy and luminous eyes. And suddenly she felt frozen and brutish: and if he were dying now? why not, idiot?! can't anything happen? it can, yes it can, idiot! she stopped short stiff, squeezed her heart with both hands looking toward any spot with care and delicateness. Hearing the sounds around her she was aware that if she started suffering they would all dangerously take their distance running, eating and laughing, forever far in a warm hallucination, intangible. She was waiting. From the soft noise itself was coming a dizzy and confused feeling that present life was greater than death and each instant that went by without bringing it was laughing out of fear—almost pacified, afraid, she was drinking a bit of wine: he was alive. He was alive. And he was so brave. He wouldn't do anything but he was brave like a demon, like a conqueror. He would never bother to save, maybe, even a child but he was generous just as she would live even without bothering. And so proud … there was not one thing he didn't think he could do but by some mysterious force he wouldn't do anything. She saw across from her one of the faces of such rich vulgarity, loud lipstick on pale skin, a sensual and quick understanding. Everyone had already known one another for a long time and was talking without interruption at a medium pitch. How easy everything is with drink, Vicente—otherwise how could she be doing so well, feeling the shine of her own eyes floating between her and other objects? an almost indecent impression in her legs sweetened by wine. They were living off the knowledge they had, using whatever could be used. Irene was shimmering above the dark fabric, her husband's bald spot was happy to ask: aren't you feeling a draft?, though a bit sad, Irene was attentive, eager, lively, and tough with her short hair whereas he was more made of people. All his life he must have been a son, a brother. And now a father. All of them, including the women, had some specialty in their character, their past or their job—and it was through that specialty that they were addressing one another and laughing. They were speaking about their own difficulties with pleasure. Only Maria Clara, whose stories she would be happy to hear, wasn't referring to her job of painting flowers on clay pitchers and exhibiting them in salons where she invited friends, only Maria Clara with her slightly wide face, the broad circles of the lilac, painless bags under her eyes, was smoking even at table, damp teeth on display. Vicente, where's Vicente?! like a child who wakes up in the night sitting in the dark, calling mommy, mommy, scratching its body with sleepy hands. There he was! he was embarrassed by her not being like him, ah mystery—Vicente headed toward Irene's body and Maria Clara with that controlled reverence used with women not yet possessed: a respect, Virgínia was thinking absorbed, as if he thought that possessing them made them unworthy. But no, no: the same word that now had almost been spoken inside her, mystery, would explain it. Feminine mystery, mystery of a woman whose son in the striped pajamas was now sleeping, mystery of a woman who without such shiny lipstick might not be able to laugh out loud throwing her smooth head back in a laugh or in a fatigue—and while her head was still thrown back and her throat was shuddering in laughter, her eyes surely were starting to think about something else that certainly was far away because she would cock an almost tense ear in space. Without preventing her laughter from reaching its own conclusion:

"Oh no!" said Maria Clara shaking her head, laughing with her slightly big and pronounced teeth sparking with saliva. But Virgínia didn't want to notice them, she was heading toward a conclusion to the feeling, getting upset: not big, she thought hurting herself and observing Vicente's smiling gaze, but bright, fine. It was horrible to feel that she was so penetrating and to know that if Vicente were not attracted by her existence, she herself, Virgínia, would despise him, happy. If he fled toward that fat woman she wouldn't suffer and wouldn't take him back ... yes, she thought with a disguised surprise, yes, she'd at last be free. If he went to Maria Clara she'd wait suffering and take him back upon his return. She was feeling her unhappiness grow by the instant. At the same time she was smiling as if it were calm to endure it. With a deep feeling of irony that could never rise to her lips as a smile, through a deep feeling of irony and self-martyrdom she thought about the two of them with tenderness, delivering one to the other and at the same time despising them with a sincerity that freed her from them. She wanted to see them together and happy and her repulsion for Vicente grew as he was laughing and smoking at the dinner table—so this was the man with whom ... She drank a glass of sweet and acid needles that rose through her nose. Drunk, drunk, she was saying to herself with hot shame, smiling now. She was surprised that no wish to do foolish things was coming to her; the most she desired was to say low and mysterious, almost with fury, to all the particles of that warm, intimate, and shining air: farewell, farewell. And in that there was a captive anguish, a dark and opaque blot.

"Thank you, I'll have another glass ... ah of course ...," she said shaking her body with the politeness of someone expecting a tip.

"Virgínia," laughed Vicente, "you don't *think* it's too much ..."

He had a way of speaking with her in public ... Clear and cold, for everyone to hear, play a role in and for nothing to be settled between them. Nothing essential had been reached with her love, nothing?! Maria Clara had been possessed by many things, hence her mature and satiated appearance; she'd tried everything lightly, very full, her manner relaxed and tired. But suddenly her face was starting to grow more refined, slightly passive and desperate, very innocent as if it were trying to isolate itself inside itself. Some thought was giving her a surrendered look, her mouth was transforming into an almost-ugly and intimate expression as if she were alone. Yet you couldn't trust her and be forward because that same gesture was coming together in a calm and free woman who painted flowers on clay pitchers. Maria Clara was laughing, becoming more vulgar, older and more attractive and Virgínia, part serious and part scared, was clinging to the sound of her laughter. She was more and more afraid of growing fascinated by her as she'd been by Daniel in childhood and becoming her slave. Yet Maria Clara wouldn't even give her orders and needed Virgínia so little that she offended her. With his lips wet with butter her neighbor for the first time spoke to her:

"Beautiful dinner, don't you think?"

She looked at him fixedly, protractedly, running her eyes over his lips — asked with hardness and rough joy despite having heard:

"What ..." — but the moment dissolved and she inquired with delicateness — "What?"

Between Adriano's plate and hers was dangling isolated a green, round pea, greasy. On the lace tablecloth! before she could avoid it she looked at it: was it me or you? she immediately blushed but he, understanding? extended to her the round bread plate — was he forgiving her? but she hadn't been the one who ... the pea ...—and he said to her kindly, yes, kindly with a distant and short appearance:

"Bread?"

Vicente had told her to sit next to Adriano, she wouldn't need to talk much and she would be well looked after. He'd insisted that she go to the dinner, sent her flowers. But she knew that the insistence was Irene's or some guest of hers; everything really was going well, the dinner was a success, Irene's husband was laughing leaning over the table, though the voices sometimes freed themselves far above the harmonious noise of the cutlery and thickened unpleasantly—after the gathering they'd be friendly to each other, grateful because nobody had been offended, no piece of chicken had leapt off the plate, because nobody had eaten to the point of feeling unhappy, only that fullness that a moment longer would be uncomfortable, leaving eyes bleary and afflicted—but no, only the light dizziness nice, nice, nice. How I understand, how I understand everything, she was surprising herself passionate and confused: my God, make me sad—she was feeling her eyes and lips. And in the middle of everything Irene's power leading herself with a certain anguish above everyone, inquiring rigorously of each face whether everything was all right. That was what was connecting the dinner to the kitchen toward which quick looks from Irene were being directed and where the dinner should be simplifying itself with a yellow light bulb, smoke, a heap of dirty dishes and where the little maid in a stiff rubber apron and cap was losing her impersonality. Oh no! ... said Maria Clara laughing, one of her hands with its sparkling nails half-raised clutching a cigarette and lightly bending her sweet and ripe body. They were forming a group that understood one another. If one of them would see the drawing of a sad and tired woman with a red dress they'd say with a succinct air: it's well-drawn. And just like that those men and women were meeting for an instant in that brown room—it occurred to her with a sigh. She said with a clear and pleasant voice—she who was far from the Farm, far from her own birth, swimming in an unfamiliar liquid but swimming:

"Please pass me the olives."

That's when things became real. Who'd forced her to speak, who; she could cry scared and tired in that instant because if there were a strange phrase to say it would be: please pass me the olives. Things were fleeing her shining in the distance, the table was glittering in the silverware and the glasses, everyone was bending their heads toward their plates smiling, she exhausted from always smiling lightly without ever releasing a guffaw—her face smooth, large, and blushing. The man across from her was a great journalist, Vicente had said to her, but added: of course, he came as Irene's friend and not as the director of the newspaper; he wasn't a great journalist, she was remembering now, he was the director of the newspaper. His face like a shoelace coming undone, Vicente. If Daniel had been there, witty as he had become, was "witty" the right word? she was afraid confused …, he'd give an answer: no, it looks like a wound that still hasn't completely healed. Really, Daniel, when he laughed his features would stretch tightly and you should almost shout: careful, careful. She asked the little maid for water, suddenly life was so natural. Above all there were certain things that when they happened were so powerful that they destroyed their opposites no matter how real those were—was she making herself clear, Vicente? because she couldn't manage to remember her body before Vicente without guiding herself back to a window at night, unable to sleep. Love had come in a single surge extinguishing the wait. But the power she'd possessed when she was a virgin she'd never have again. At the same time she felt the firm awareness that nothing had changed, nothing. Not exactly that ... But that Vicente and the city were temporary like the rain that cannot last. She'd like to say it to Vicente, it would be good for him to realize that he hadn't made her happy—or had he?—and then say: but Virgínia, darling, I don't want that ... She'd reply: but I feel so happy suffering for you ... it's the most I can do for someone ... She'd suffered for Daniel, that's it. The director of the paper had fleshy and eager ears, grossly blossoming beside his face and while he was speaking was pointing his finger at the things that were most impossible to be present. But what was happening?! God Almighty! whatever it was gave her a happiness, she was feeling like a piece of tremulous light, had the deep intuition that it was good to be alive—but whatever it was would end, that sparkling and frozen instant, that moment of a successful dinner party mixed with a calm and warm pleasure in her stomach, that moment that was bringing together in a compact memory the victorious minutes ... what was happening?! so what was happening? they were offering her a cigarette and she was tapping it on her other closed hand in a gesture familiar for the others but new, balanced, tensely elegant, and careless for her. Horribly happy is how she was feeling and she was overcoming herself agonizing.

Heavy from fatigue and wine, managing to reach places and situations in stages without union, she stood from the table with the others, heavy with sadness. She looked at Vicente feeling extremely feminine and pensive. His eyes like illuminated walls were darkening but not allowing themselves to be scaled. The way of being with her in public. As if she'd forced him to do something in the past and now it was irremediable, hatefully irremediable—he was rebelling against her as against a family. In mutely violent fury she stared at him detached: what do I have to do with him anyway? don't I have my own room? don't I sleep my own nights? The director of the paper stood, the napkin fell, he bent down, stood again, his head hit the edge of the table!, he looked lightly shocked without the least joy with the napkin in his hand, his slack lips shining, everyone watched, talked about different things.

"Ridiculousness is so nice, isn't it?" she managed with sudden strength to bring herself together with the right words, discreetly elbowing Vicente's back, feeling again a disturbance that was bringing her extraordinarily close to the fact of being a woman, of having lived, a sensation of herself.—"It's so nice sometimes, isn't it?"—the wine was making her light for herself, Vicente looked at her surprised, withdrew his body with delicateness as if he needed to direct it to the chair he was leaning on, maybe she should shake him, say to him: you don't recognize me, you don't know who I am, you don't remember? but he smiled at her a little with his eyes, exactly enough to take away her strength; he'd always make sure "the thing" couldn't be used; now, after that half-smile, though both knew it was fake, she couldn't shake him, tell him who she was, not even with a glance; but ridiculousness was funny, Daniel would approve. And she knew how to walk between the beautiful dark furnishings with her white dress, she was understanding them at a glance, seeing with closed eyes her own harmony with things in a perception that was coming from outside in through a grace conceded by strange vibrations. Scanning the room with her eyes it became clear, as if it explained the whole night, it became clear that she didn't like Adriano; he awoke in her an unease and surprise like the warning you get when faced with an evil nature. He's my friend, Vicente was saying succinct and curt, interrupting some question that she was posing leaning over him, her eyes blinking in a curiosity that he detested. She didn't like him. For an amazing reason—she discovered excitedly at that very instant—because he'd been nearby when she'd met Vicente ... and that had excluded him. But ... no, no it couldn't be that ... But yes, it really was. Sometimes Adriano would help her imperceptibly to live. Across from her, for example, in some mysterious way Vicente seemed to be more interested in her. And Virgínia's attitude was a difficult understanding of that favor. She looked at him. He himself was cold and delicate—yes, his hands were cold—and was observing her with an attention that nonetheless didn't wound her. As if for that reason inexplicably when she was with him she emphasized herself rude and ironic trying with a certain astonishment and pleasure to show herself to be worse than she was, chewing with her mouth open at dinner, even like now scratching her head, with a dark joy.

"Your flowers might fall," he was saying.

"Ah ... thank you, my dear, Vicente gave them to me."

"I know. I was with him when they were bought."

Oh really? and now she was becoming aware that, without Adriano, Vicente would never remember to send flowers. Yes—and she disguised the intensity of her gaze containing herself, red—she needed to establish forever that they couldn't stand each other. Just as she and Daniel's wife mustn't tolerate each other. She stared at him without however managing to contain that bemused impulse that was coming from the little man. Small, clean, and slim he was expanding a dry light around him. He didn't seem to have come from any place in particular; when he'd say goodbye his hand with bright fingernails would cut invisible connections and when detached he didn't seem to go exactly anywhere. The little man, she called him. Without being very tall she nonetheless seemed to surpass him and that humiliated her; but he wouldn't let on that he'd noticed. Instead of sensuality like Vicente—she looked at Vicente who was laughing taking off his glasses and cleaning them with a handkerchief—instead of sensuality he seemed to have a quiet persistence. When they were sitting around a table in a bar he didn't give the impression of participating but of waiting, without leaning his thin body on the back of the chair, smiling with regular and clean teeth; he'd pay the bill, nobody ever objected, he was rich and above all had something impossible to hold back in his light and direct approaches. He didn't smoke and drank quickly. With unease Virgínia would watch Vicente let him pay, inviting him whenever they went out—placing the little man between the two tall ones. And above all Vicente's joyful and voluptuous manner, as if infantilized, when he was with Adriano, making observations and living with buoyancy near the other who would listen without ferocity, watching with that strange absence of confusion of his. What he didn't have within him was sleep.

Within her was the concern to laugh whenever it was necessary and that gave him an afflicted face like that of a deaf man's, Adriano was thinking with a painstaking look as if finding

something among the sands of the beach; but that difficulty in
following the lecture, a tendency toward a certain calm inex-
pression as if she were then thinking about nothing; the most
he could surprise in her was a certain sincerity that was unconscious but not childish; as if she'd long since understood
something, already forgotten it but still bore the mark of that
understanding; she didn't know how to talk or explain but nevertheless went around as if she did; so silly at the same time, so
in a certain way base; what you'd call a normal person right at
the beginning, affected like a silly and normal person; sometimes however a demeanor so profoundly unknown that you
barely noticed it, a diluted gesture, a movement in the depth
of the sea suspected at the surface. Who? who was thinking?
he, he himself—he shivered with a luminous smile, as if resigned, someone just barely awake. Fingernails cut too short
resting on the dry whitewash of the wall, the perfect teeth.
His fingers were colliding with the halo of the objects and the
people. God, give genius to those who need genius—there are
so few who need it; he smiled with thin lips, with his bright
and delicate health, shaking in his laughter a quality that had
never attained the loss of his own being. He was taking pleasure. He looked at Vicente and placed him with his eyes next
to Virgínia: above all the gazes of both were of a female and
a male of two different species; yet he would never speak to
Vicente, that was the quality of friendship that he was dedi-
cating to him with open eyes. His head sharpened, intelligent,
fresh, and empty: yes, he might even be able to love her despite her clear insignificance, he thought with a lively air and
again was seeking a small sea snail among the sands of the
beach. To take her from Vicente would be easy for Vicente, he

was reflecting with swiftness and interest as if about a curled and subtle problem, yet she must have the stubbornness of a child. He looked at her with a certain limpid precision as if to compare what he was thinking with the model. What turned him on about her was the vulgarity as the vice is a turn-on in a prostitute, in some way she seemed made of her resemblance to others. Staring at her for a second with wisdom he saw her profile, silly again, a little vain, her chin resting on her chest, and straightening the flowers at her cleavage with both hands. Reality was seeming to laugh at all of them. He was taking pleasure. Her clothes made her ridiculous, recalling a tree covered with fabric, a fruit pricked by a brooch. She didn't seem to be a woman but to imitate women with care and worry. And she would irritate; but not him, not him—he was laughing with silent and sharp pleasure. Reality was laughing at all of them. She was arranging the flowers with all her fingers. Her barely-present lips were hiding in shadows born from the position of her head. Her breasts were growing congested squeezed by her clothes, her hips were widening with fatigue, without beauty. He looked at her, her thin head forward, her eyes mobile and swiftly interested with coldness. He closed his lips; with a small effort as in an experiment he could feel a sincere fake cruelty toward her, a certain scorn. Virgínia turned her face and looked at him. He tensed up in his ivory color, surprised in the middle of the game. Both looked at each other for a long time, without interest; the man's heart rang out heavy, unknown.

"Have you noticed, Adriano, that a lot of people together in a room and spending a while together end up thinking the same way? at least at the outset ... Just now that fat man over there said a thing that I almost said just now … It seems that we end up guessing, right? But not always because after all" — she was seeming to get a grip on herself and after a small hesitation added with a certain force — "because after all everything's relative … I always thought everything, everything's relative, don't you think? not always because naturally there's an exception to every rule … of course, that goes without saying …"

He laughed, all his teeth appeared in silence. She turned her face in another direction looking at something new. She headed to the armchair and sat down. All night she'd watched the armchair from afar desiring undetectedly to sit on it. In truth she had always lived as if on the verge of things. The armchair was tall, narrow, and green but not a leaf green nor even an old leaf; it was a green filled with resentment and peacefulness, gathered in itself over the years; on the armrests the color had retreated with reserve and an almost brownish base was poking through sweet and martyred by the constant friction; in truth it was a fine armchair where you could have a dark, opalescent sleep — she felt fatigue and sadness. All of Irene's living room was dizzyingly greenish, pale, mortal — Vicente was laughing. She was smiling at everyone, Vicente was talking, a cynical air of someone who's been alive a long time.

"He's got something feminine about him or at least something that's very common among women. He thinks with movements, his thoughts are so primal that he acts them … You remember, Adriano" — how he pronounced the word "Adriano" … — "he came in the room that night and since he saw us all together he found himself excessive and left. All that reached him with little abstraction, a small gesture, a tiny sign came with each phase reached by thought. Daniel" —

he turned suddenly toward Virgínia frightening her and she quickly looked at everyone—"Daniel would say in that case: I can't stand people whose convulsions of intelligence I have to watch ..."

Everyone laughed, she smiled as if she were Daniel's mother and had the right to be shy. But from one moment to the next she thought that they were laughing at Daniel—she blushed violently—laughing at that very thing even though she ... no, she'd never laugh, but ... yes, a certain way Daniel had of reaching a conclusion out loud that everyone had already figured out discreetly ... was that it? he, he—why not think it all at once? she grew angry, frightened—he, she continued docilely with the thought she was already familiar with, he really had a hard and comical life.

"Thank you ..."

"But Virgínia ..."—Vicente was making his teeth shine odiously—"how many glasses have you had already ..."

She didn't smile, Vicente averted his eyes, Adriano looked at them, taking pleasure, people were talking and smoking, she was drinking. It was anise liquor. The thick liquid like something warm, anise was what she'd been given in candies in childhood. Still the same taste sticking to her tongue, to her throat like a stain, that sad taste of incense, someone swallowing a bit of burial and prayer. Oh the calm sadness of memory. Both wild and domesticated, purple, solitary, vulgar, and solemn flavor. Father was bringing anise candies from town! she'd suck on them alone in the world with her love for Daniel, one per day until she finished them, nauseated and mystical, so miserly, so miserly as she was. She drank the liquor with pleasure and melancholy—trying once again to think about her childhood and simply not knowing how to get near it, since she'd so forgotten it and since it seemed so vague and common to her—wanting to fasten the anise the way one looks at an immobile object but almost not possessing its taste because it was flowing, disappearing—and she only grasped the memory like the firefly that does nothing but disappear—she liked the notion that occurred to her: like the firefly that does nothing but disappear … and she noted that for the first time she was thinking about fireflies in her life even though she'd lived near them for so long … she reflected confusedly on the pleasure of thinking of something for the first time. That was it, the anise purple like a memory. She surreptitiously kept a mouthful in her mouth without swallowing it in order to possess the anise present with its perfume: then it inexplicably withheld its smell and taste when it was stopped, the alcohol numbing and warming her mouth. Defeated she was swallowing the now-old liquid, it was going down her throat and in a surprise she was noticing that it had been "anise" for a second while it ran down her throat or after? or before? Not "during," not "while" but shorter: it was anise for a second like a touch of the point of a needle on the skin, except the point of the needle gave an acute sensation and the fleeting taste of anise was wide, calm, still as a field, that was it, a field of anise, like looking at a field of anise. It seemed she had never tasted anise but had already tasted it, never in the present but in the past: after it happened you'd sit thinking about it and the thought … was the taste of anise. She moved in a vague victory. She was coming to understand more and more about the anise so much that she could almost no longer relate it to the liquid in the crystal bottle—the anise did not exist in that balanced mass but when that mass divided into particles and spread out as a taste inside of people. Anise, she was thinking distracted and seeing through the open door a sliver of the dining room and in that sliver a quadrilateral of the china cabinet and atop the china cabinet the plate of artificial fruit, radiant, smooth and stupid with lacquer. Now she was starting to follow an almost-silent feeling, so unstable that she carefully shouldn't be aware of it. At those same instants her body was living fully in the living room such was she divining the need to surround with solitude the beginning erected in the half-light. Beneath an appearance of calm and hard brightness she was addressing herself to nobody and abandoning herself watchful as to a dream she would forget. Behind secure movements she was trying with danger and delicateness to touch the same light and elusive, to find the nucleus made of a single instant, before the quality came to rest on things, before what really came unbalanced in tomorrow—and there's a feeling ahead and another falling away, the tenuous triumph and the defeat, perhaps nothing more than breathing. Life making itself, the evolution of the being without the destiny—the progression from the morning not aiming for the night but attaining it. Suddenly she was making an almost harsh interior gesture or was seeing Maria Clara's sleepwalking and luminous smile and everything inside her was muddled in submerging shadow, the diffuse movements resounding. She wanted to go back down her sinuous path in the darkness but had forgotten her steps with the dizziness of a white rose. She'd forgotten in what part of her body she'd arranged herself in order to wonder. An indecisive feeling lingered like a promise of revelation ... some day in which she wanted with real true strength ... ah if she had time. But when would she have in life such a potent care that it would make her grasp through desire the same thing that had come to her mysteriously spontaneous. All that had remained to her was a sensation of the past. Suddenly she was only aware that something had happened because she herself in a material proof was existing now seated in the armchair. She started living again off the fact of being seated in the armchair in front. She remained absorbed staring with an almost terrorized insistence at the beyond of a chair, it seemed impossible to be awakened from her strange dream. And as everyone fell silent for a moment in a pause at the end of a conversation, they looked around, discovered her, and smiled in an ironic surprise. She held back with an absurd look, eyes astonished, lips thickened, and her face seemed to be buzzing imperceptibly in vibration. But as if they'd looked at a strong light for an instant too long, the surroundings seemed to darken beneath a shady cloud, an error of vision, and a pale stoppage of life widened their pupils for a second.

"Virgínia's quiet tonight," said Irene smiling, awakening quickly. Her role seemed to be to nudge them. Everyone pulled themselves together with a light movement of sighing.

"Oh, it's not just today," Vicente answered in a falsely happy tone, "she is, how can I put it?, a serious creature ..."—Everyone laughed and thus he repudiated her in public extricating himself clearly from the responsibility of her existence. They made the record play in a shady corner of the living room and she felt the music unfurl above the sounds, she who never thought about music. Suddenly the sounds were rising, harmonic, high, chaste, without sadness. They were sounds so connected to themselves, they would sometimes fall into a richness almost heavy but not complex, only comparable to the smell of the sea, to the smell of dead fish—she closed her eyes stricken, tolerating something sweet, sharp, and full of joy: no, it wasn't like love, not spinning helplessly in the nausea of desire, not loving meanly its own agony. Pain, but a pain that was not the kind that would appear on those interrupted and impossible paths—how things were falling into themselves, becoming true, finally true, oh God, God, help me. That was the sensation: oh God, help me. Her despair was mysteriously going beyond the bitterness of life and her most secret joy was escaping the pleasure of the world. That intimate impression of astonishment. How new it all was, how she was freeing herself from all of them, from her own love of life, calm and without ardor.

"Now I'll put it on a second time ..."

She opened the eyes she had closed for an instant, saw herself sitting in the armchair in a quiet posture, her body closed inside itself. Several people were moving, passing one another luminous. Her back curved, she couldn't pose for a Greek sculpture but was profoundly a woman, a sensation of unreality overtook her. It suddenly seemed to her—as if she were watching something disappear in silence—it seemed to her that she was erring herself, mystified and fluctuating; and how high the error was, and unattainable, even the error. She looked with vacant eyes at a certain immobile and light life around her while her lips were parting in a scared smile—she touched with the palm of her hands the thin railing of the shelf next to her and upon the rough contact returned to the surface of the occasion and the dinner party, Maria Clara walked over to her and as if giving her a quick flower said smiling:

"Virgínia come one day to my house ... I'm not just saying

that," she repeated ... "Come ... I live alone ... We'll have a good conversation just between us girls, we'll talk about bras, menstrual cramps ... whatever you want ... all right?"

Virgínia was laughing confused, charmed, laughing too much animating her body: yes, yes ... all right ... The circle formed tight and noisy beside the door and Virgínia stayed beyond it having in front of her fat and dark backs shaken by movements of laughter that she couldn't follow. Being expelled belonged to her own nature. She tried to squeeze between two men but suddenly realized her gesture and retreated, she remained a few steps away from the noise, looked around, free. She finally slid her eyes toward the window, toward the black and shapeless night that was stretching beyond the pale and vivid light of the living room. Wherever she was she could always look at the night, there was time — the branches were hovering suspended in the frozen darkness and each leaf encrusted itself in the air as if forever. The city below was shimmering and cold, from afar it seemed motionless, calm and dangerous. And since nobody saw her she took one more glass from the tray, drank, coughed a little, nothing was noticed, things were wavering shining and suffocated. Everyone was extending a hand to a woman, she too offered hers and indeed it wasn't long before she felt it lightly crushed with a certain dampness, an unpleasant insistence and several words. Irene. The car was gliding smoothly, in the tepid interior the motor was breathing like a heart. With extreme comfort and yearning she shrank between Vicente and Adriano. With eyes shining and hard from whiskey they were talking while coming closer to Virgínia feeling the heat of her body, staring eyes dissimulating, brief words. Amid her sleepiness she felt a bit unhappy and abandoned, heavy eyelids, lips numb and cynical. In a fluctuating and fleeting crisis she wanted to be protected, for someone to defend her, consider her excessively pure to be touched like that, erring and stirring her—between the two men comfort was deepening her. From the street sounds of solitary horns were coming, her pupils dampened with sleep she was peering at the shadow. Without realizing it she dozed a little clutching with vigor in her lap the wide hat that was swimming white atop the half-light, seeing as in a dream the lights blinking in the empty city. The trip was so fast that soon she was undoing the sheets from the bed, opening her lips saying a name full of softness and darkness: vicente. The flowers were shuddering vivid in the darkness. As if she were dissolving and plunging into her own dissolved matter and in the milky and translucent darkness she herself were gliding as a pure fish swinging her serenely resplendent tail. Yes, vicente. She was moving ahead without fear and without hurry, her big limpid eyes closed through herself while the man was moving away with another man inside a taxi through the city accompanied by the way that she was missing both of them squeezing her and insulting her, leaning on her in the back of the car. The neighbor's clock, suddenly moved, struck three transparent notes on three levels of sound, the first high and scared almost solidifying her in the beginning of a vigil, the second containing itself between the first and the one to come, the last, lower, pacifying, pacifying, each separated from the next and brilliant like diamonds separated from one another and brilliant—but the three notes were liquid and diamonds would never fear breaking in a single confusion; she went on undone in a great thick sea and crossing it filled with a calm that was made of satisfaction, of the feeling in the deep car, of hope, of memories scattering—with a beating of eyelids she was changing the level of her inner existence. A little child dressed in a long nightgown and very slowly was standing like a target at the back of her sight but she was scarcely trying to see her better everything was disappearing into its own sea—she was always experiencing short visions and when she'd close her eyes over her already-closed eyes she'd see in the darkness shapes made of darkness itself. Each little wave was passing on to another like a message: vicente and with each vicente everything was much more real and it would be useless to deny. For a second she was feeling that she was atop the white bed, excessively fast since she wasn't the one who was feeling it but just a section of her arm pressed beneath the pillow—with each vicente she was sinking more and more into her own nature. And also more, more, almost to the point of seeing from the other side something dusky green lighting up like a lantern that was the immobile memory of a party lantern in Upper Marsh, ah Upper Marsh. One last vicente like a sigh before dying and sleep closed in a single unhappy rock, Virgínia held onto herself like a black stain. She could see no more through the sleep and if she dreamed she'd never know.

These were the moments when she suffered but loved her suffering. She'd go through the day, the necessity of doing little tasks, tidying the bedrooms, waiting, reality and the streets— part-serious, part-anxious, scrutinizing herself and space as if she were already mysteriously linked to Vicente through the distance. Because she'd scarcely woken and she knew that today was a day she'd see him. Perhaps it wasn't so sudden—she was offering herself the small surprise in order to give herself happiness even at the price of keeping her conscience closed and locked inside there the dark and stimulating lie. The first hours burned out difficult and slow but near ten in the clean morning time was hurrying along happy and fleeting, bright with the day and in a smile she was watching herself moving ahead easy and gentle. She was hardly having lunch, it was hard to cook just for herself and anyway today she'd have a nice dinner with Vicente—she was eating a fruit to satisfy her distant mother. And that's how she was getting ready to live-daily, eager to transform herself into what she wasn't in order to get along with things around her. If Vicente had woken up shapeless and abrasive she would keep herself in waiting, her hands delicate, not expressing herself in any direction so that he could change all by himself, free of her existence. If he stayed mute and nervous she'd try to be ample and though she couldn't quite manage it—neither her slightly absorbed eyes nor her body with little gestures would help that approach— Vicente would notice her effort to appease him; and that so often was enough for him to smile and improve with goodwill.

After lunch she'd quickly tidy the house because by the time she got back it would already be late. It had been hard to get used to the new empty apartment since Daniel had married, gone to the Farm, and she'd had to move. She tolerated a quick shower, she'd always had a certain repugnance toward taking baths; undressing, exposing herself to the jet of blind and excessively happy water frightening the silence. The cold and then drying off with the towel that was never quite dry from the day before in the dirty bathroom where everything that couldn't be shown in the little living room was squeezed—the longer she lived the more she accumulated useless things that she couldn't get rid of without pain. After the shower she'd close the windows, shut the kitchen into its old smell of frying, coffee and cockroaches, put on her hat, lock the front door and go out with her red purse in hand—before closing it for good she'd stop for an instant, glance at the already-asleep house, immersed in warm darkness, smile at the things that were already now vacant in a farewell—for a moment she was feeling lightly hesitant and pensive between closing the door and going out gloriously to Vicente's house and going back in, taking off her so high heels, keeping herself in bed and hearing nothing, absolutely nothing. And if frightened Vicente came looking for her—he never would—she'd announce with closed eyes, intense: I died, I died, I died. But that was just a second of swirling error because in an immediate truth she was pulling the door toward herself with a small hard tug, turning the smooth key and entering excessively in contact with things while reproaching herself: why be so rough on the door. In the street she could be discovered by someone's gaze—the secret union she was feeling with people until getting to know them intimately. These encounters could happen to a woman in the city. Someone unexpectedly would understand her most silent substance, going through it with unsurprised eyes; she was afraid to meet that gaze, knew confusedly that this was an intuition that wouldn't last even an instant beyond the instant itself; she'd never even really remembered being understood. Her heart nevertheless was beating faster, in her chest a contraction of freedom and pleasure was being born, so intense and so mundane that she was surrendering herself in truth with a movement, doing something as if for the first time—a secret way of removing a strand of hair, a certain controlled gaze in a shopwindow as if thus closing her hands in order not to scream. She knew nevertheless how to spare Vicente's love: she was pushing with her trembling hand the perception of the things around her and her life was closing around her like the only life—she had barely infiltrated the bus when another breath began, she was forgetting the small dead apartment, her heart was growing rich in difficult movements; a shapeless pain was passing through her and her eyes were opening more anxious and transparent. Even if no one looked at her in the streets and she could walk them indissoluble with her red purse swaying, even if her gestures upon taking the bus divided themselves into various industrious and attentive stages, even if her body suddenly foresaw itself abandoned, aghast, all of that would be a bearable prelude because . . . why? deep down it wasn't because she was going to see him but much lighter, shorter, sillier: because she was going. A pure thrust forward like leaning onto the damp and thin bridge sniffing the rotten wood and looking at the water that was finding its balance beneath the colorless sun—like waking up without any feeling and slowly remembering a bit of hunger mixed with the smell of the neighbor's coffee with milk mixed with the tired and pale sun upon the clothes on the chair—and no memory of the previous day, only the certainty of the day to come. When she was arriving at Vicente's apartment pushing the small door of the side entrance in order not to ring the bell she was waiting for a moment—for an instant it seemed more sensitive for her to guide herself through herself, through Vicente and through her absence from the Farm toward some still-nonexistent thing; the sensation of the present was coming to her so real that she was sliding toward another more solid and more possible feeling: that of delighting, delighting—the moment that was coming was quick and fresh and she was looking at it tired. Suddenly she was gaining more life, acutely, as if she herself were finally beginning. She would manage to spend that new mood better if she had to tidy, sweep, wash—but she couldn't pet and even talk in great tension the way one works, makes the dust fly, and almost sings like the washerwomen. And also because beforehand she needed to know what approach to take with him—sometimes she'd notice that she should keep leaning forward because he was wanting to talk. After seeing him she'd spend hours with her head full of notions already transformed into conversation and of movements born as if out of her own presence in front of herself. Her impression then was that she could only reach things by way of words. It was always a bit of an effort to understand, to understand everything. She would close up and with a small initial exertion make his voice monotonous and cozy as one takes refuge from the rain, even feeling some sensual pleasure in listening to him without hearing him. One day she had almost managed to explain to him that she was with him even when distracted. He'd said—and she'd found out about it later:

"Virgínia, look at that almost red cloud…"

She was smiling:

"Yes, yes…"

He'd stared at her slowly, piercing, never letting her escape, never:

"What exactly did I say?"

She'd tried to speak, got mixed up, blushing.

"I knew you hadn't heard," he'd sighed shrugging.

Confused and eloquent she was explaining:

"I didn't hear the words, I really don't know what they might be but I answered you, didn't I? I felt your mood when you spoke, I felt how the words were ... I know what you meant ... it doesn't matter what you said, I swear ..."

She'd ask questions carefully and never hear the answers. But she preferred to tire herself rather than let distractions happen. Often enough when he'd finish speaking she'd laugh and she shouldn't have laughed. The two would then look at each other for an instant. Thrown suddenly into a horrible sincerity, impossible to disguise. Waiting. And then even whatever was good and cordial would happen very quickly, bring in the background the memory of that undeniable glance, raised like a statue. If she were more intelligent she could have erased the past with new words or even by participating a little more in whatever he was saying. She had however few thoughts in relation to things and feared repeating them over and over; she never used the right expression, always making mistakes even when she was sincere. Sometimes she simply didn't know what to answer and would fall inside herself searching. During the time it took her to respond to him, each moment was noisily lost in the limpid and bottomless field that was her empty attention and she'd catch herself observing them wearing themselves out instead of seeking a convenient reply. Until a light desperation would singe her, she'd look at the things around her, the world was coming up vast, bright, smiling, she would grow so winged and lost that she no longer cared about giving up—she'd retreat pale up to the last instant inside her and take refuge there. And from there she'd say almost without pain from erring so much:

"Yes, Vicente, yes," after all yes added nothing and everything calmed down in its place. And when they turned on the radio and a song rang out he'd murmured:

"An unbearable kind of music ..."

He hadn't said anything extraordinary but his calm demeanor without so much as contempt fit well with the nature of that day—she didn't like it either and traced a movement of repulsion that was perhaps too strong, her lips pressed in disgust. He smiled looking at her and she, animated, living, spoke with disdain through her teeth as if she had triumphed:

"No, I don't like it ... so ... so intrusive ..." her face unmade itself immediately, the expression beneath it emerged engorged, surprised and childish because he was opening his brown eyes behind his glasses, trying to understand her, his shock saying ashamedly, benevolent: but Virgínia ... what's this all about, Virgínia? Yes, she'd gone too far; because really how could music be intrusive? perhaps she'd wanted to say: the music had no dignity in its joy, as she'd heard said once, yes, that was it! but now it had become impossible to explain. And even—no!, she hid hard and alone, so if he wanted to judge her he'd have to judge her in silence. She was unpleasantly surprised when Vicente would interpret her. How other people's understanding would dry one out. She would watch her words with curiosity but afterward couldn't meld her discoveries with herself—how useless it would be to split a branch from a tree, make a chair out of it and give it back to the tree: whatever he'd make of her she'd never take back although she carried it with her. She'd rather he spare her—only from

Daniel could she stand the attempts and the errors because Daniel and she were made of the same hesitant material and never approached things laughing; the maximum joy of both would fit into a little smile of Vicente's. To distance herself thus from Vicente and move toward Daniel scared her and she stuck to Vicente so suddenly that their bodies practically crashed into each other and when she looked at him Vicente smiled. And hadn't that almost been the reason she loved him? because she'd foreseen that Vicente could laugh out loud not barely like Daniel but in a stupid laughter that in the middle of its effort recalled her impossibility to laugh louder—and that would cause a joyful tenderness, a desire to forgive with a laugh and forget. Also in love she'd let him guide her—and the only way in which she thought about it boiled down to seeing herself once again watching him move, speak. Just as she could err by herself: she'd always serenely thought of herself as a great lover until he'd come along, proving her wrong—and thus the months went by. She'd rather Vicente not have embraced her every time punctually. She'd rather not have seen him change his voice and his gaze as if he were finishing one phase and starting a new one. She'd rather he didn't desire her so strongly at times, almost paralyzing her with hurried astonishment—although all that really only happened confusedly, powerless, without provoking even a defense, taking on the only possible form of life. She never had enough time to get used to his phrases because he'd say another as soon as he was finishing the first, she never had enough time to get used to his caresses because he'd immediately move on to the next leaving her still focused on the previous one—so those were the secrets of life. She'd let him guide her ... yes, yes, every once in a while in a surprising bit of news she'd realize what he desired and her poor body would hesitate in mystery, all of her would widen and she'd lose herself receding deaf … —it would be impossible to pass through her being with one of her own thoughts. She'd never try to move ahead of Vicente; she followed him because she couldn't carry by herself, in her damp hand, that quick star that would sometimes lose its shape like a frozen drop that turns into liquid; everything so dangerous, simple, and light … so that was the secret toward which she'd been heading ever since childhood; the center of desire was resplendent and somber, electric and so terribly new and fragile in its contexture that it could destroy itself just by going a bit deeper, just by sparkling an instant more.

They had a little something for dinner at night. Afterward she was going home, the tram cutting the dark. She was feeling that she was going back, that she was going back. If one day he'd think to accompany her home she might experience a deep and stifled satisfaction like the one a married woman must experience every moment. She was jumping from the tram and walking the small stretch on foot. She was opening the door, going up, looking for a moment at the things before flipping the switch—she was connecting herself to everything without touching anything. She'd lie down and pull the white sheets in the darkness—the quiet moment before sleep was coming as if she were falling then into her true state. And that moment was so profoundly quiet that it would dissolve the entire day, tossing her into the night without fear, without joy, looking, looking.

It was finally the natural thing to live alone. They'd barely rented an apartment when Daniel already got a life she no longer fit into. In the first letter to the Farm he'd written that they were enrolled in a language class and that he himself had found a neighbor's piano to practice on. In fact they didn't even know how to get around, find classes or neighbors. They intended above all else to reassure their father and then, since Father was reassured, they themselves calmed down, forgot about taking a class and were just living in the city. And in that way money was growing in power—Daniel would spend almost all of it, soon enough he'd found friends and met them outside the house. Virgínia would stroll, stroll. One day she too had gone out with him—the house was someone's, it was so long ago, Daniel was playing the piano, a lady was playing, her slender arms almost stuck to her hips, her head leaning without strength, people were smoking, there were blonde girls, calm sisters who were also talking politics, Adriano standing between the window and some thing. There she'd met Vicente.

"In any case smile a little," Vicente had said playing, "it's the best stance in the face of life." He'd always loved to talk about the face of life. She was looking at him inexplicable.

"I cannot laugh," she'd said trying to be intelligent and serious, and had spoken about something "deep" or "profound." Vicente's eyes were slightly shining, amused:

"Ah, so whatever is deep is tragic ..."—He had the gift of jolting others people's words by merely repeating them, his lips unhurried, delicate, she'd find out later. "Deep." She'd looked at him, found it difficult and useless to respond, smiled flirting with exhaustion and excitement. She'd never seen him again, as if forever. Deep was neither tragic nor comic, it was a tree, a fish, she herself—that was the impossible and serene sensation. Her life had gone on as if she hadn't met anyone. Then lots of time had passed until the door had opened, she'd interrupted some thought forever, forever, had waited with her sewing in her hands, Daniel had said:

"Virgínia, this is my fiancée."

For long and hollow minutes the room was seeming empty, the house silent and full of wind. But Daniel, Daniel, how could you ... Above all she barely knew Vicente and love seemed to her unfamiliar, so it meant a sudden break with the past. She was a tall body, well-made and compressed, topped by an oval, hard, and limpid face, a feminine ivory laugh. From the sight of her clothes a memory came to her of the smell of a recently printed magazine, some pages still closed. But Daniel ... An air of intimate hygiene, of pureness achieved at the price of antiseptics and amidst the difficult conversation that bright and new phrase, new like a new object, that had left a silence of eyes lowered in the air: I was always busy, I never had time to feel bored. Daniel and Virgínia weren't looking at each other. Perhaps when she grew old, who knows, Virgínia had thought while serving too-strong tea in broken cups, perhaps when she grew old, with some wrinkles and a more concentrated color ... Yes, yes, who knows? for now she was so horribly free from loving herself. Not like Vicente whom she was just now getting to know. No, he wasn't free from loving himself, with him love was like the inside of closed eyes, dragged quickly in incomprehension, in dark satisfaction full of unease, she was realizing this now. And he was beautiful, besides. He wore glasses. There were moments in which his lines would become so full as if about to say something—his body was big and strong but as if made of a single newborn muscle flexible with freshness, he could wrap her up like an octopus and yet his flesh was firm and Virgínia could crash into it. Except his eyes were excessively wide, sometimes silly behind the glasses opening a pause in his face, without merging completely into it. And his lips would come together sometimes distracted and floppy in a horrible expression of fullness and abandon, something like a decomposition—she was turning away, her heart beating quickly, wanting to take refuge in the sight of an inanimate thing, ah go quickly into a perfect region where cold is mixed with light. Certain gestures of his, some words were brutally alive and almost blind, rushed him into a slow center of blood and greed, filled her with nausea and dread—where was that intelligent goodness of his face? She would watch him fascinated, her heart hot after a few instants; yet she could barely manage to free her gaze, she would gain an almost painful coldness, her body would stiffen in its fibers as if wanting to escape as much as it could from that warm life underneath bearing a sincere, almost base perfume.—One day Mother was having lunch, she'd received some sad news and was crying while in her teeth you could see bits of what she'd eaten!—oh everything that happens is innocence, at the same time that's what she was feeling and forgiving. Fullness would stuff her then. If she'd pick up a book she'd find inside it the same viscous movement, souls ingratiating themselves in forgiveness, love seeking love, sacrifices laughing, cowardice and extreme warm pleasure. By God, that was man. Even if she were flipping through an essay on traction machines in a bookstore, in the quality of reasoning she would find feminine and masculine perfume, words falling into line blushing and excited, the path in search of an idea winding around, ascending, living … love, love, piety, remorse, kindness permeating even freshness, sticking it inside the same heat. She was now understanding Daniel's expression, that vaguely terrorized face that he was wearing during the period of nights out from home. Also inside him the tissues would cross in a vegetal structure and he had been thrown into the center of the woman, there where was pulsing the blood of the world. That was the secret of life, then. She was then loving Vicente just as the days run. In fact she was going astray from any desire and her only refuge was the pure thoughts of humanity, the serene dry things, compact—the construction sites near which she would stop short in the streets like a pregnant woman gripped by a weird desire and a new sensibility. At that time she had no sooner eaten than she'd seem repulsed by the food in which still pulsed the memory of a previous life. Without knowing, she'd repeat to herself as in a perfect prayer: whitewash iron sand silence and purify herself in that absence of man and God. Encouraging words, honesty, the need to get close to intelligent and noble people, the need to be happy, almost the need to speak before dying, all of that would seem to lift her through space as if she were bearing a rush of smooth air beneath her body and she herself were a frightened, grateful, tired bubble, "arranging her life in the best possible way." At the moment when the rush would stop—and would it ever stop? she didn't know that she was wondering while moving through disgust and through darkness—she would fall violently in-what, suddenly walking fast after the fall, guiding herself without wasting time to make up for the lost life, guiding herself to-where, eyes open, alive, without cruelty toward herself and without pity or pleasure because she would no longer need to punish herself, without a single word, that was it, without a single one, by God, washed as if after a great rage. To free herself from maternity, from love, from intimate life and in the face of other people's expectations to refuse, to land hard and closed like a rock, a violent rock, who cares about the rest—as she knew how to be Daniel, without even knowing with precision what she was thinking, feeling darkly resentful. Only the first time had she really liked the sea; later she was uneasy so she'd lean against the wall to look at it, forcing herself be moved. She'd feel like a liar, without thoughts but as if she were touching something dirty, her shriveled soul was avoiding, avoiding. Every once in a while, breaking her fear, she was liking it again so strongly that that made her as if forever comprehensible to herself. Amidst these new feelings she'd find herself in some way close to Daniel. But against what? her fake power was waning with disappointment and slowly a troubled sadness was overtaking her, she wanted to rejoin right now the movement shared by everyone, being happy with them, accusing-offended very quickly with humility, without any power so that nobody could refuse her now, quickly, after she in a thoughtless gesture had sought, crazy, to free herself.

Daniel had taken Rute to Upper Marsh and they married there. Virgínia hadn't gone to the wedding; simply, without a fuss, she told Daniel without looking him straight in the face, she'd understood that she didn't need to go and had stayed in the city not like someone saying: I'm staying; she'd remained behind without remembering to go or stay. Father knew she was studying; and who knows? she might find a husband. But she didn't know anyone besides the old cousins, Vicente barely existed, she'd stayed in the city alone, in the bedroom suspended on a third floor. That had been when she'd gone through a period, yes, you certainly could call it very sad. Suddenly like a vein that starts to pulse she'd started living the reality of the apartment abandoned by Daniel and as if empty of herself because her narrow movements and her frayed life weren't enough to fill the quarters with noise and confusion. Until she had the recollection to accept living with the two cousins. On that morning she got ready, washed, packed her suitcases with the dark permission to enter at last the boarding school with which they'd threaten her when she was small. She hired a taxi and blowing her nose cast one more look toward the square, bright, and old building where she and Daniel had for the last time been brother and sister. The car was bouncing, the suitcases were threatening to fall on her and injure her—she was thinking about how she'd taken care of the apartment for Daniel, of how she would wait for him for supper, of how that memory now had strangeness and little familiarity and how she now was rushing into some thing so new like a new body and where she wasn't feeling she would exist for much time. With secret horror, pensive, she was seeing herself more and more similar in a certain way to Esmeralda—imitating the destiny of their mother; the old car was finally entering the dusty street. Morning was rising. Soon she'd see that poor house that she had only visited quickly afraid it was contagious, just twice in all the time she'd been in the city. It was one of those houses where you'd try to sit on the edge of the chair, where you'd catch yourself trying not to touch the flower vases and drinking carefully a glass of water only halfway to the bottom. There was in the somber and by no means extraordinary rooms something that would stand out and alarm because it contained an involving and unfamiliar intimacy—like a strangers' dirty bathtub where you had to strip and abruptly place yourself in contact. Her cousins Arlete and Henriqueta increasingly seemed to her an error and a lie— now that she was getting so close to their reality. Poverty and age. She rang the bell as if arriving from a long journey. Good, now the fun was over—that was her feeling and she was surprised because it had been so long since she'd stopped feeling things as such. Her father should be happy to know that at least part of the family had a house big enough to house his daughter, let her get to know the relatives close up—"and have no reason to be ashamed of them"; how did he know so much about the truth? even without a reason the very beginning of getting closer to relatives was confusedly her shame and dread. Cousin Henriqueta opened the door and seemed to hesitate in the brightness.

"Yes?" she asked with her face tilted in expectation and vague distress, "yes?"

"I ...," Virgínia attempted.

"Yes?"—but suddenly the old lady's eyes lit up and in a little muffled shout she flinched: "come in, come in, your suitcases! ah, the man with the car has to be paid, come in Virgínia, come in, your suitcases, right? Arlete ...," she said turning toward the dark and silent interior, "Arlete, our cousin is here ..."

Her voice had changed imperceptibly and through it Virgínia penetrated into the relationship between the two old maids. Nobody answered from within and the two women were standing for an instant in the doorway waiting. Henriqueta suddenly approved with her head as if she'd heard some answer.

"Come in, my child," she said with more resolve.—And

as Virgínia was moving ahead she seemed to remember in a fright, stopped short, extended an arm halting her with haste and unexpected power, murmured blinking her eyes with difficulty and trying to repeat: "you have to pay the car, you have to pay the car ... the luggage charge too ... the expense was yours ..."

"Yes ...," Virgínia stammered.

Henriqueta was tall, ruddy, and slow. Her face of smooth very silky skin was stained with big, shiny freckles; her neck united itself to her body in curves as on a porcelain doll; she was bald, used a wispy toupee held in place by a ribbon, wore a skirt made of brown cloth turned black, long all the way to her swollen and freckled feet. She was moving slowly hesitating as if her thoughts were always being interrupted by new ideas and she were still mute and confused—but her face was made of surprise and goodness. They entered the long living room with wooden floorboards. In the near-darkness, at a large oval table, Arlete was sitting. She raised her head from her sewing, examined Virgínia with an attention that was trying hard to stay present.

"Good morning, Virgínia," she said at last.

Arlete was small, her face narrowed into an attentive and distracted needle. Her back was broken, her chest was sticking out in a point beneath her tired and sickly eyes. She seemed weak and caustic, she sewed for children. Virgínia dragged her suitcases up the old stairs to the moldy attic. She halted an instant. Her appearance recalled dust that once shaken was slowly returning to its place. Through a single glazed window that couldn't be opened gray and deaf light was entering, without shadows. She lay down for a bit on the hard bed, inhaling that indefinable smell of old age in which she'd been wrapped ever since she'd entered the small dry garden before ringing the bell. Her eyes burning and tired, she was feeling an unchangeable and calm pain in her chest as if she'd swallowed her own heart and could hardly stand it—she was pressing her fingers over the eyes that were stubbornly opening staring and absent, she managed to contain them, scrutinizing the small conquered darkness and as if she were connecting for a few instants to her so-disappeared self, to the secluded and watchful silence, she sighed at last and slowly, looking around wounded and pensive, began to live with the cousins.

The house was so old that its previous inhabitant had moved because he was afraid it would collapse. Below Virgínia's attic, which topped the triangular construction, was a room where the cousins had installed the sewing *atelier*. This dark and dusty chamber seemed even more decayed than the rest of the house. The light came scant through a grated window almost flush to the roof. Because in the attic the wooden floorboards didn't quite come together, Virgínia would crouch down, place one eye on the ground and see in a strange and deep tableau the two old maids sewing, the long naked table, the coffeepot beneath a quilted cosy, the dirt, the scattered cuttings—the sewing machine activated by Henriqueta's sluggish foot would buzz in the air, seem to shake the dust and soft light all around it. Virgínia would get up in a thrust pressing her angry lips with the back of her hand and the room would ring out with the power of her steps. Henriqueta was shouting from downstairs in a voice that always seemed agitated by a constant tremor:

"The house is falling, Virgínia ..."

One morning—the day had begun rainy and the drops of water were flowing behind the windowpane—she went down late for breakfast, pale and inexpressive, with that resigned and haughty look that the days with the cousins had lent her. Arlete looked at her for an instant. And suddenly for no reason as if with effort she'd hardly been able to contain herself, she said to her in a low voice, roughly:

"And why don't you sew with us?"

Henriqueta stopped short, frightened, coffeepot in hand:

"Arlete, Arlete ..."

Virgínia was looking at them mute ... So ... so ... they ..., she was saying to herself dizzy with rage, so they were wanting to drag her, subject her ... wanting ...

"I don't know how to sew!" she shot at them with smothered violence.

Arlete and Henriqueta looked at each other with exaggerated surprise and immediately as if they couldn't disguise how comical it was.

"But teach yourself!" screamed Arlete raising her crippled chest.

Virgínia went pale, narrowed her darkened eyes. My God, where was all that strength coming from, she'd always been calm ... At that moment she was hating the two old ladies with such pleasure that submerged in a dark extraordinary sensation of profundity and sin she answered any old thing, yes, yes ...

And so she was forced to sit and embroider with them. Her clumsy hands would attack the stitches crudely, eyes looking at the window. Henriqueta would tactfully undo her knots and give her the cloth again. Arlete would observe her with narrow eyes, her sickly face enlivened with joy. Even if Virgínia went pale from hunger lunch and dinnertime would not be altered. When the clock would strike one in the afternoon, Henriqueta would stand up, place her sewing on the chair and slowly set out for the tall cupboard that was lost in shadows. She would open its drawers and pull out some small foods, cold and odorless. Coffee was brought from the kitchen and smothered with a strange bonnet that seemed to look and smile, thick with dust. The sewing room itself smelled of wet dust, mold, new fabric, and coffee with cold sweet potato. Virgínia would get up from lunch starving and nauseated, feeling her uncontrollable and young body demanding full of outrage. Yet she was growing older, losing her colors, and was a woman.

On Sunday afternoon they didn't work, the house would stay silent—Henriqueta would sit in the depths of the backyard, hands folded, resting. Virgínia had gone to the little garden. The wilted plants would remind her of the luxuriance of the Farm and she'd breathe deeply, her face turned toward a direction that seemed to her to be the way back. But the city … where was the city? She'd feel inside herself a kind of life that made her disgusted with herself, constant sighs of impatience and all that mixed with a real hunger that was more violence than hunger—she was thinking about food with a power that she would have liked to unleash on Arlete. Arlete … It sometimes seemed to her that Arlete was then her reason for waiting. There was a grudging union between them as if Virgínia too were a renovation for the old maid. Both spoke to each other with small words quick and oblique and were delighted, heads lowered hiding their eyes. Standing in the garden Virgínia would recall her dealings with Arlete and from her pleasure would be born the certainty of a growing decay of a depravation that in the end, beneath the warmth of the sun on her uncovered head and on the grayish plants, would come together in a movement of dismay in which hunger would break out again with a new urging. Bending over to pick up a dry stick she felt with a start that someone was lingering with indecision at the door to the house. She turned around quickly—Arlete. She laughed with triumph. The old maid was staring at her. Arlete!

"Come into the sun," she said to her with a certain rudeness.

Arlete was leaning against the wall, her thin body beneath the black Sunday dress, washed, faded; talc stained her ashen and glum face—her thin hair was tied back in damp braids. And since she didn't answer, her shining eyes looking at Virgínia with coldness, Virgínia didn't hold back and in a voluptuous and daring movement murmured to her:

"You're afraid you can't stand ..."

The other woman wasn't answering. And since the situation had become very strange and a new and sincere reality was coming to the fore Virgínia added a bit frightened:

"It sure is hot out here ..."

"Yes," Arlete finally answered. "The plants got burned."

"Look," whispered Virgínia slow and pale, "I'm leaving, I'm hungry, you know what hungry means. I've paid my rent without fail and I haven't seen food since I don't know how long. That's not right—just for the miserable attic to have to pay almost all the little money I have ... And to top it off that rubbish about having to sew."

Arlete wasn't surprised.

"You came because you wanted to," she said simply.

"And I'm leaving because I want to," screamed Virgínia going up the cracked cement steps, going through the door and feeling on her arm for an instant Arlete's hard body. When she was reaching trembling the middle of the room, near the stairs that would lead her to her room, she heard Arlete moan, turned around and saw her grabbing with both hands the ridiculous bulge in her chest as if she wounded:

"What happened," asked Virgínia suddenly terrorized.

The other woman looked at her with attention and intensity.

"You hit me ... You know that I'm weak and you hit me."

Stupefied Virgínia looked at her. No one who saw them would suspect the ferocious understanding between them. The moment blew into her body a sure and dizzying drive to push her really and she closed her eyes getting a grip on herself. Another second and she'd do it. Her lips white and burning, she held herself back nevertheless because she realized that Daniel wouldn't understand her and she wouldn't know how to explain.

"You hit me," the other was repeating in a rude victory.

"But you ... you ... are a bitch!" she screamed at her, "a lying bitch!"—and that discharge as if faded away her fear and shame, a cold sweat wet her forehead, she felt the brutality of those terms that belonged to the Farm, to the open field but not to the city, she looked at the old lady, yes, the old lady at whom she'd thrown the insult and who was waiting openmouthed with surprise, yellow teeth on display ... Biting her lips she ran up the stairs and the house trembled with her. She spent the night wide awake packing her suitcases, disguising a feeling of horror and fear that was rising in her chest and that was threatening to toss her outside of comprehension. The day had hardly dawned when she went down the staircase asleep, crossed the vacant unreal light of the living room waking up, opened the door, received the fresh morning wind; looked for a taxi as she hurried along, her eyes tired—it felt to her that she'd lied and finally woken up, freeing herself of her feelings. When she returned she found no one in the living room; yet she got the feeling that someone had messed with her things upstairs and that they knew she was leaving. With relief she wouldn't have to say goodbye. She went down the stairs dragging her baggage, reached the front door without running into the old ladies, got into the taxi; when the small door closed and the car started to move she leaned her forehead onto her hands and shaken by a sob of joy kept repeating to herself strangely, she who'd never turned to her family: mother, mother, what has your daughter come to! that was calming her down. She entered a creamery with her suitcases, asked for a coffee, milk, cookies, cakes, she was eating eager and sensitive as after a punishment, eating and suffering stopping sometimes to hold back a kind of pain that was rising through her body up to her throat and that she was disguising with a smile, her eyes burning, dusky.

She'd moved to the boardinghouse; she was going through the dark, dirty, and vague memory of the boardinghouse while leaning against the wall, escaping, running with her heart pale from relief to take refuge in the memory of the apartment where she'd finally ended up. It was a new building, a narrow box of damp cement, thin and tall, with square windows. Yes, it had been a very sad period and without words, without friends, without anyone with whom she could exchange quick and friendly insights. The impression that she was alone in the world was so serious that she was afraid to go beyond her own understanding, to rush into what. It would be easy, with no one beside her and without a model of life and thought by which to guide herself. She discovered that she didn't have good sense, that she wasn't armed with any past and with any event that she could use as a beginning, she who had never been practical and had always lived improvising without a goal. Nothing of what had happened to her until now and not even any previous thought were committing her to a future, her freedom was growing, pensive, by the instant, cold air invading and sweeping an empty room. Her life was made of one day putting on her dress inside out and saying with curious surprise as if when hearing some news: wow, that hasn't happened to me for such a long time, wow. She wanted to stay busy with little things that would fill her days, she was seeking but had lost the lithe charm of childhood, she'd broken with her own secret. Yet she was getting more and more meticulous. Before putting out a cigarette she'd think about whether she should. Then she'd even feel the need to tell someone about it somehow and didn't know how. It would seem to her then that she was swallowing the little fact but that it would never entirely dissolve inside her. She'd work at her day tolerating it deeply. One afternoon, when her money was starting to run out, she took a piece of cheese from a store without paying, without stealing—the cashier noticed nothing, she put the catch as if forgetfully into her red purse, walked out slowly, alone in the world, her heart beating hollow and clean inside her chest, a painful squeezing in her head, almost a thought. She got home, sat down, and remained motionless for a while. She wasn't hungry. And the little money she had would allow for buying some groceries until her allowance came from her father. So why had she stolen? She was unwrapping the piece of cheese, starting by biting it slowly. The cheese was white, full of holes, and old, the kind that's only good for grating and strewing over pasta, ah, the kind you use on pasta ... She started to cry, her lips cold, without innocence. She went to the dresser, looked at herself in the mirror, saw her red face, anxious and sad. She started crying again then without thinking about the cheese, feeling herself profoundly silent, without managing to drag a single thought out of herself. Sitting, she was looking at the kettle. Her small kettle on the windowsill, shining where it met the dusty and opaque blinds; throughout the little room the muffled air was holding back the fire as when it's sunny outside and someone closes himself up in the shade. A dark chair was reflected in the paunch of the kettle, convex, stretched, motionless. Virgínia kept looking at it. The kettle. The kettle. There it was shining, blind. Wanting to expel herself from the mute astonishment into which she'd slid, one of those deep meditations into which she'd sometimes fall, she pushed herself brutally: say something, say it. It seemed to her that she ought to halt now in front of the kettle and figure it out. She was forcing herself to look at it deeply but she'd either cease to see it as in a swoon or she wouldn't see anything but a kettle, a blind kettle shining. Through the numerous closed walls a clock caught in an apartment sounded inside the little room stirring in the air a certain dust—yes, yes, she was thinking in a sudden whirl of joy, relief, and anguished hope as she dangled her crossed leg for an instant and stayed quiet. She would like to connect with the people in the building but by herself was unable to approach strangers; and meanwhile she was starting to look more like a spinster every day; an appearance of good behavior, of serene and dignified withdrawal. But sometimes she'd lose her grip and talk too much, eyes open, mouth full of saliva, surprised, drunk, afflicted, and with a certain vanity about herself that would arrive hot with humiliation. She'd write long letters to Daniel, sometimes in a single vivid and grim burst. She'd reread them with contentment before sending them and it seemed to her that they were truly inspired because though they discussed reality she hadn't noticed it at the time she was dealing with it. She'd doubt whether they were sincere since what she felt had never been as harmonious as what she was telling him, but syncopated and almost fake. No, it wasn't unhappiness that she was feeling, unhappiness was a moist thing on which someone could feed for days and days finding pleasure, unhappiness was the letters. She started taking a base and voluptuous pleasure in writing them and since she'd send them as soon as they were written and try to remember them in vain, she thought of copying them, which would fill her days. She'd reread them and really weep as if weeping over someone who wasn't her. How insufferable was that new sensation that was overtaking her, anxious, petty, luxuriating. Between the letters what she'd feel was suffocating and dusty, unbreathable, in a flurry of sand and strident sounds. But was she being sincere in writing to Daniel? Don't lie, don't lie—she was inventing—accept the thing as it was, dry, pure, daring—she was trying out the feeling; for a while she'd lose the need to be friendly though she really didn't have anyone to be friendly to. And when she'd reach that arid purity she didn't know that she was seeking with seriousness the true things without finding a thing. What would make her despair distantly was in most cases the uselessness of her lucidity; what to do with the fact of listening in the garden to a man refer to his journey and, looking at the ring on his finger, figuring out with a calm clairvoyance—and one that could be mistaken—that he must have visited a place with women and that he kept discussing business and his wife? what to do with that? She wasn't seeing what she needed but what she was seeing. She didn't want to force herself to take a walk, go to movie theaters but without compelling herself her day was dizzyingly aimed at that unknown past and, placid, she'd keep herself in an unhappy silence of acts.—And hadn't it been by compelling herself that she'd gone out once and met Vicente again? rebinding the vague acquaintance perhaps forever. At that time it was already easy to love. Love really was old, the idea had been exhausted at the beginning of her life in the city; she was already feeling experienced and calmed by the long meditation of waiting. She was remembering the first night. Vicente's body leaning on her shoulder was weighing like earth; for him it had never been tragic to live. A bit before she'd tried to joke around, asked him to lend her his glasses; in the middle of everything, she'd thought then not looking at him quickly, in the middle of everything he's afraid I'll break his glasses. And that had given her a certain resignation about the rest.—So who could she hang around with? Who if not the doorman. She'd stop to chat a bit at the main entrance of the building, on the wide street with few trees where the general staircase ascended. Then she'd turn the corner, take a few steps into the little narrow and rustling street, open her own door, with her own almost vertical staircase that ended in the bedroom, the sitting room, the bathroom, and the tiny kitchen. She'd stay at the window observing the long and poorly made street, a hard and bushy tree shivering; she could make out the construction sites rising on the corner. The doorman was a dark and thin man, married and with two children. He told her how he'd got the job. The owner thought that even in a poor building you had to keep up morality. Really families were asking: do proper people live here? And that had been why, he'd repeat as a shy excuse, he'd told Virgínia right at the start—as he did with all the tenants, with all the tenants—that it was forbidden to bring visitors of the opposite sex to the apartments, except brothers or fathers, of course. He wore his belt low and loose, had small eyes, close together. He'd tell her how he lived, how he'd gone to the movies, how he had a little garage at home, of which he'd made an "Office." Only on Sundays did he go home substituted by a hasty and asthmatic old man who wasn't unpleasant but who somehow didn't want anyone's friendliness. Miguel and Virgínia liked each other; since the nights were long for both of them he'd sometimes come up for a cup of coffee. She'd arrange the sitting room with joy as if playing seriously, one day she even bought some flowers. He'd sit and while she was making coffee in the kitchen they'd talk louder without seeing each other, hearing with pleasure and attention their own voices. She'd come in with the tray, both would bring chairs to the table and drink the strong and fresh coffee with a concerned pleasure, exchanging glances of approval. When winter came and rains fell, night in the apartment was good and warm with a young man sitting drinking coffee. She inquired suddenly frightened:

"Sir, you're not avoiding your duty?"

"No," he assured her. "What I have to do is stay in the building. And anyway who's going to need information at this hour ..."

"But the door ..."

"No, the door is already closed. The only people who come in are the tenants and they have the key to come in and out."

She would sigh. She'd tell him a bit about Daniel, about the Farm, about people, like Vicente, that she barely knew.

"Do you think your brother gets along well with his wife ...," he was doubting, seriously, without meaning to offend. "Those rushed marriages. Marriage isn't a game—lots of people think so but it isn't."

He would go to Protestant services; since he was vain and lowly he'd seek out the pastor after the sermons, ask him useless questions, attach himself to him with a proud seriousness. The pastor advised him to read a small section of the Bible every night and meditate. Filled with an unsmiling joy he bought a small used Bible, brought it to the lobby. At home he read nothing, he couldn't manage to be interested in the same things and was sincerely ready to laugh with everyone else at questions of preaching. The isolated life on the lobby stool, the immobility of his arms eventually made him an irritated and ardent man. He'd never wanted to accuse so much, never given alms so full of mindfulness and caution. But with a slow surprise he had discovered his impossibility to concentrate and read the Bible so easily acquired. Every night, forewarned, he would sit on the backless bench, beneath the lamp of the counter. He'd run his finger over his tongue, turn the pages of the book, begin. Eventually his reading would be limited to looking at letters and the Bible made him think of nothing. He'd say to himself: how could I ever study after a day of work, my head still filled with complaints. So often drinking coffee in Virgínia's apartment, he'd imagined reading the Bible with her. He asked her shyly and almost floored by the daring—not exactly because of Virgínia, whose apartment was the smallest in the building but because of himself since he'd never spoken of the new Bible to anyone:

"You understand, ma'am, the Bible is the greatest duty of man. I'm saying that but I mean by that word that woman is also man, you understand?"—during a pause he scrutinized her afraid she could not reach his difficult thought—"We could read a little at night, it wouldn't hurt, anyway, just to study and educate ourselves … What do you think?" he concluded completely disconcerted.

But she couldn't answer right away. The idea of those evenings, calm and full of sanctity, moved her to a point that her face closed up somber and severe. It was as if she were going to have the opportunity to lead a new life—with overstatement she was wondering with a seriousness that was filling her heart with well-being: who knows what is to come. She said with an ordinary mien, a bit dry:

"Well sure, we can read."

"Well right?" he replied getting up agitated and holding in his joyful unease in the face of Virgínia's cold attitude. She however gazed at him for a discreet and sharp instant and he understood that she was wanting them to understand each other inside the falseness. Anyway she had never lived so simply with a person as she did with Miguel—she'd understood him better than any other human being up to that point. With Daniel it was hard, charmed, so steep, renewedly disappointing.

With Miguel it was smooth and simple, he always made so much sense; one day he'd even said:

"I think that deep down all men and women go through life saying: I don't want to think about that. And thinking that they didn't think about it, right? how does that sound to you?"—he had ended up laughing a lot with wisdom, squeezing his eyes. She too was laughing quite a lot shaking her head several times in agreement, swallowing her coffee full of amazement at his insight. And wasn't it true? nobody could stand much of what they felt. And now the Bible …

"Well sure, we can read," she'd said coldly. He looked at her and they understood each other with caution, avoiding any explicitness.

"But drink your coffee before it gets cold!" she cried loudly with intensity. He gazed at her hesitating for a moment with hope and suddenly was overjoyed, rubbed his hands quickly:

"It's true, it's true!"

The next night he knocked on the door, she answered, saw him with the small Bible in his hand; with fury and modesty she retreated, her body rigid, her face indifferent. He wasn't looking at her. He walked to the middle of the living room, stopped indecisive; she was still standing next to the door as if waiting for him to leave. Making an effort upon herself she said after a few instants:

"Do you want coffee before or after?"

He responded hurried:

"Up to you, ma'am …"

She made coffee, they drank it speaking about some unimportant things amidst long moments of silence filled with suspicion and prudence. They finally finished, he said with simplicity:

"Should I read or you, ma'am?"

"You, sir."

"Which part?"

"Any one is fine."

"You don't have a preference?"

"I don't know much about it."

"That's fine."

He opened to the Sermon on the Mount, began to read in a rough and angled voice with hesitations filled up with vague deep murmurs nearly drowsy from the difficulty. All around it was silent; Virgínia propped her head on her hands without effort, with delicateness. On the third evening a sincerity filled with hope had been established between them and she was listening to the reading with parted lips as if to a story. In one part Jesus in the crowd was feeling himself touched by the sick woman and they said to him: but how do you ask who touched you when you are amidst a crowd that presses upon you? and he answered: because I felt a power emerge from me ... This section became a new life for her, she was sighing deeply as in the face of an impossibility; absorbed, her head leaning, she was thinking. Ah, the desire for irony and goodness, like that for travel, that she was feeling; how candid I am! she was astonishing herself then and bathing in faint beatitude. But that wasn't meditating in the way Miguel demanded—in fact she wasn't reflecting and wasn't reaching conclusions—she was thinking about the story itself, repeating it between glances, shadows, permissions and falls. Vaguely she was imagining this: but I too ... Now she was lending meaning to a child-hood memory that without the evenings she would have disregarded perhaps forever: when she was little she knew how to close her eyes and let the light filter in slowly from inside out—but if she remembered to open them suddenly, everything lost its brightness, she would remain tired, yes, without power. Miguel would agree with a certain reluctance that he also felt some similarity to Jesus with himself. One night, a bit disappointed and bored, he told Virgínia that he'd spoken to the pastor telling him about the Bible evenings. With surprise and displeasure he'd heard him say: "my son, these readings of yours lack religion ... from the comments you make and the way you listen ... it's almost a sacrilege to read the Bible like that ... you read it with more seriousness and meditation—I emphasize that word meditation. Go, my son; the difficulty comes from heaven; return and read as one studies. Meditation—I emphasize that word—meditation."

The two sat there, pensive. Eventually, without speaking about it, they broke off the sessions forever. Until one time she invited him to dinner. That day she woke up early, purposeful, calm, and happy. The week before she'd received her allowance—she went out, bought meat, flowers, eggs, wine, jam, rice, vegetables—and for so long her kitchen had been clean, the flies buzzing famished in the sun. Surprised and adopting an attitude of disdain she bought for herself a decorative tortoise comb. She returned home with her face flushed, her arms full of packages—she felt that she was being one of the most truthful people she could be, she was understanding this by the natural and direct gazes of others. These would accompany her with more astonishment when she wasn't carrying anything in her arms. She washed the meat, embarrassed interrupted with a chummy brutality her light humming, her face flushed, salted it, cooked rice with tomato while sighing. She was feeling good, fervently good, as if the deepest part of things were strewing itself in nobility. She made small fried balls of carrot and eggs, rolling the dough with a woman's intimate fingers, her eyebrows furrowed—she would have liked to be small and watching herself envious that she could play around in the kitchen. She prepared a trembling dessert of cream and jam, the kitchen and the sitting room were vividly filled with movements, she seemed to almost be bumping into herself. At two in the afternoon she felt famished and weak; she didn't like to go to restaurants, she still felt a bit ashamed to eat in front of others. But today she was such a busy person, with so much to deal with, having a house that needed to be taken care of, a kitchen where there was stuff to do—it was obvious that this was no time to be sensitive to herself, she thought worried. She got dressed, went to a creamery, had a lunch of eggs and coffee. She returned down the street filled with sun, now discouraged and sluggish, almost apprehensive; went into the house—yes, they were preparations as if for a party, her heart was squeezing pained in a smile. In the afternoon she bathed, washed her hair, put on the tortoiseshell comb, the white dress—beneath the tight bodice she was feeling that physical constraint that gave her at the same time the certainty of being elegant. She went out in the wind with wet and smooth hair to buy bread and a stronger light bulb— and there was no one to offend her ever. She went back home as night was falling, set the table, arranged the silverware, changed the light bulb, cut the meat in steaks atop the frying pan brought from Upper Marsh—she'd stop short from time to time, bend over with a kind of grimace as if feeling a sudden pain; but it was just some feeling of extreme hope and fullness, and since she was alone she could bend over. She powdered her face. She turned off the light and sat by the window to wait and dry her skin, moist and cold with sweat. In the half-light things were shining calm, clean, and fragrant. She sighed. The work on the construction sites had long since stopped, a fragrance of jasmine was coming from the narrow street where a few lovers were already strolling. The moon appeared in the dark sky, a warm summer wind was passing through the city, the neighbors' silverware had stopped clinking. A light numbness took her over deepening her, an unreality full of promise and fatigue was enveloping her weakening her. The moon was rising, a few couples of lovers were saying goodbye. There was a knock at the door. She jumped, got moving, her firm thigh was penetrated by the deaf corner of the table, she breathed getting a grip on herself, the strong pain connected to her own smell of powder and cool sweat; she flipped the switch, light gushed with intensity over her eyes weakened by the darkness, she was surprised because she'd forgotten she'd changed the light bulb. Barely making out the violent outline of things, she opened the door, Miguel was entering drying his forehead with the checkered handkerchief and stopping surprised, looking at Virgínia's silk clothes, the snowy tablecloth, the joyful and rich light, the silverware sparkling. The flowers …

"But you didn't tell me that it was a party, ma'am …"

"Well," she responded red and cold, "come in."

He came in but his demeanor was forced, leery.

"Would you like me to go downstairs and put on my better clothes?" he asked.

"But no!" she was almost shouting covering her ears, hurt, distressed, "but no!"

"It's fine, it's fine," he came to her assistance taken aback, "it's fine, the person who spoke isn't here anymore …"

154

With her eyes shaking with tears, her face swollen, she tried out a happier smile but the light was sparkling in her wet retina and she could see in front of her shining and trembling drops with a certain anxious visual pleasure.

"But what's happening?!" he asked growing horrified.

"Well, nothing! … what could be happening? … a little light in my eyes, I was in the dark, what could be happening? well …"

"In the dark …?" and he was seeming to approach something he would never understand.

"Yes, yes, in the dark, with a headache!" she shouted, lying.

He sat in a chair, his fingers crossed atop his leg. She stopped for an instant; she had nothing to say. He said:

"Sit down."

She brightened:

"Sit? … and who's going to make dinner?"

"Ah, right … Need some help?"

"No, no, thanks," she declined almost offended. But she couldn't move without knowing how to leave him sitting there and go to the kitchen.

"What time is it?" he inquired.

"How should I know?" she retorted, remorseful.

"That's true …"—he pulled out his copper watch, looked at it: "it's … it's … it's … nine o'clock! three … three … three … to nine!" he said laughing without her knowing why.

"Do you want dinner now?"

He looked suddenly frightened, he shrunk his neck into his shoulders in a gesture of desperate ignorance.

"I don't know, I don't know … it's up to you, ma'am …"

They looked at each other an instant longer. She went to the kitchen to make the steaks. Every once in a while she'd stop and hazard a movement toward the living room—she couldn't hear anything. Little delicate drops of sweat were being reborn atop her upper lip, her body seemed to have thickened, the malaise of the dress that was growing old upon her body. A bit worried she fried two eggs, warmed up the small fried balls, the rice—listened to the living room, silence—took the tray to the table. She had prepared herself to say something lively but whatever she was going to say escaped her palely when she saw him sitting in the same position with his fingers crossed. Yet upon seeing the steaming plates, Miguel's dry lips parted in a weak smile of hope and despondency. She gave herself a little jolt and said smiling, attentive:

"To the table, to the table!"

Miguel sat down, rolled up his pants with a hurried sigh, started looking all around, under the table.

"What is it?" inquired Virgínia interrupting herself sharply.

"Napkin ..."

Ah she'd forgotten! the flush heated her face and neck. He showed he was timid:

"No need ... I only asked because, you know, at those fancier dinners they always have them, isn't that right?"

Yes, yes, yes! She almost running to the kitchen, took the bottle of wine from the ice, grasped it with her inert hands, felt herself reanimated by the cold, touched it quickly to her hot lips. But he'd showed up at the kitchen door and was saying with a suddenly masculine air:

"No ma'am! I won't let you ..."

She was looking at him terrified ... He stepped back surprised looking at her with the wine in her hand.

"Ah," he said, "I thought you'd gone to get a napkin ... Because there was no need, any old scrap works ..."

156

They remained unmoving for an instant intent on each other.

"The food's getting cold," he finally said as if removing the blame from himself, "the food's getting cold."

She laughed:

"But isn't it? come on … And you still need to open that bottle, work a little," she added flatteringly.

"But you spent a ton of money, I can tell."

"Well, it doesn't matter."

"That's true enough. Money was made to be spent."—They fell silent. But why wouldn't he take the wine bottle that was freezing her hands?

"Don't hesitate to split the expenses … if you want, ma'am."

"No, thank you."

"Fine, fine, my motto is: don't insist."

They started to eat silently; the food was good though the steaks had some gristle; the wine was hot and smooth and he drank almost all of it—by dessert his eyes were shining moist and suffering. She remained silent serving the dishes with ardor and a concentrated calm; she seemed impossible to be deterred. Then she made coffee and when they drank it, again his eyes looked full of mischief: what coffee! he exclaimed and she assented smiling deeply. He said to her at last, looking at the ground while lighting a cigar:

"The dinner was very good."

She was looking at him quizzical, concerned. He quickly raised his eyes to her, lowered them fast but suddenly faced her with despair:

"The thing is my wife found out that I come here!"

Virgínia stared at him at first without understanding, asked almost stupid while her head was refusing to work and switch directions:

"Why?"

"They told her! what the devil can I do! people are talking ..."

At that she'd already understood, her face pale with surprise; several instants rushed by vacant, countless ... and she was feeling a beginning of wrath that actually did her good, in some strange way it symbolized the dinner.

"So why'd you come?" she finally flung at him hard and exasperated.

"Sorry," he murmured as if in a leap, abruptly mannered and with caution, "sorry, I always called you 'ma'am' and to hear this tone now ... I never took that liberty, the world is my witness"—and suddenly some idea popped into his head, he opened his mouth with terror and stupefaction.—"Don't you even think about getting me in trouble now! damn it, I'm a married man! I told you from the beginning, I never called you by your first name, I never touched your hand, don't deny it, ok? don't deny it!"

Very white beneath the lamp that was now sparkling in an increase of mute energy, she was looking at him, her lips calm and colorless.

"Forgive me, ma'am," Miguel was going on frightened and already at the beginning of an awkwardness, "the dinner was good but just because I came here doesn't mean anything, right? I myself offered right at the beginning to split the costs, right?" he was asking anxious and suddenly full of hope.

"Right."

"Well then, well then!" he screamed less asphyxiated, "I

knew you were reasonable, ma'am ..."—he became more polite speaking with difficulty.—"You understand, ma'am, a married man isn't free, it's that old story of making a commitment ..."—he laughed in a pale and disconcerted grimace. Both were still standing, each at one end of the table beside the places they had occupied at dinner. The silence was growing between them like an empty balloon filling more and more dangerously with air and strangely could not be interrupted, each attempted word would die empty in the face of its power. She remembered with a hard pleasure the ugly names she'd learned at the Farm—but something like modesty or already indifference was keeping her from pronouncing them and she waited for an instant watchful, scrutinizing herself imperceptible, blinking with speed. She thought once again that such a strong light was strange, her little sitting room so enriched and mute. But how to use such facts as a way of life? they weren't plausible, they seemed to lack the first reality; so what to attach them to? those were the true events themselves and she wasn't getting any explanation from what was happening, no overview except the simple repetition of what was happening. Miguel was waiting with purposely inexpressive eyes, trying to maintain his earlier strength and not lose ground; some extraordinary thing was slowly happening in the room.

"You are the lowest thing in the world, sir," she said loud and simple as if singing.

"But ... what ...," the man murmured flinching surprised, immediately attempting an offended expression.

She sighed deeply.

"Therefore would you please leave forever,"—she was speaking calmly and hearing with pleasure and attention her own words coming out long and exact; the fatigue from the dinner preparations was weighing on her body.

"But ... but I didn't offend you, ma'am, did I?" he murmured.

She looked at him without strength, absorbed:

"Yes, yes ..."

"I did?" he was screaming extremely perturbed.

"Oh no, you didn't. I'm just tired. Farewell, farewell."

"I'd like to explain that I didn't ..."

"No, farewell, farewell," she replied.

Surprised and already filled with displeasure he was departing while staring at Virgínia with martyred and humble eyes.

"Listen, what's this all about?" she suddenly screamed at him, taken by a light fever when he was already at the door, "you don't have to leave upset with people!"

"But isn't that right? isn't that right?" he was screaming hurriedly with his moist eyes blinking.

"That's right."

And since a moment of empty and pensive silence followed she concluded:

"Farewell, farewell," — and almost pushed him down the stairs as she closed the door.

She'd spend the mornings sitting at the table looking at her fingers, her nails smooth and pink. Could everyone know what I know? would occur to her deeply. She was trying to distract herself by drawing straight lines without the aid of a ruler — but where was the charm of the work? unable to say quite why it seemed to her that she was failing at every instant. Sometimes she'd say a few words out loud and while she was hearing herself it seemed to her in an uneasy and delicious astonishment that she wasn't herself and would surprise herself in a fright that was a lie too. And then in another weak and drunken astonishment, she was herself. She'd say in a small bored voice, shaking her head: well I'm not happy, I'm not happy at all. Or she'd come to live in an intimate exaltation, in an ardent purity whose beginning was an imperceptible fakeness. She also knew how to close her eyes and shut herself off with a brute power. She'd then crack open her eyelids with delicacy as if letting that power slowly drain—and make things out under a certain golden dusk light, wafting in a tremulous fire, brightened and filmy; the air between them was tense and cold, noises would sharpen into swift needles. Tired, she'd suddenly open her eyes all the way, set the power loose—in a mute bang things would dry out ashen, hard and calm, the world after all. Or she'd be reborn like someone trembling, a jolt of surprise. She'd dress with as much care as if about to find a crowd waiting at the door. She'd go out into the street, walk slowly down the sidewalk showing herself, her eyes watchful, the feeling that she was glowing ardent, serious. She was a hard insect, a scarab, flying in sudden lines, beating against windowpanes singing with stridency. And really, despite her modest appearance and her pale cheeks, some people would look at her with curiosity, often with more than a moment of attention. She'd get excited with secret brutality; suddenly it was so much the only truth that people would get ready, dress up, take on the attitude of their clothes, go into the street, mingle luminous and turn themselves off again at home—she was understanding the city with sureness and ardor. She'd feel proud of not being Esmeralda. For an instant here and there she was looked at as if she'd have a great destiny. Suddenly at a glance she'd think: this man knows something about me! but what did she care really? for something existing didn't need to be known—that was the feeling, her eyebrows furrowed and then a quick calm would follow hesitant after whatever it was that had not quite become a thought. She'd go home tired as if leaving the party where she'd been crowned. She'd spend days reading; she read like a painted prostitute, full of keenness and of a boredom that burned her soul and quickly dried her out. What worried her most then was being able to go to bed so early. From the moment she woke up she'd start thinking about the instant of going to bed. The way the hours passed seemed to have trans- formed irremediably and she was living among them pushed by the duty they'd suggest. Nobody would stop her from going to bed at seven at night. The only reason she still ate dinner was because then she'd go to bed at five in the afternoon. She'd get herself completely together with calculation and care and then stay on the lookout breathing. In the afternoon she'd gone by tram to a pretty and calm street and met with horror the worst old lady from Upper Marsh, who had been in the city for a few months with her sick sister. The tram was going fast and she couldn't see anything. The old lady had hardly started speaking, however, instead of the irritation she expected to feel some thing reduced her simply to herself in a quick weakening of desires. With humility she spoke with the old lady, easy with herself, almost giddy, even exchanging impressions about mat- ters of apartments and shopping, censurable ways of leading life. Inexplicable already she then cozied up to the woman as if she were a girlfriend, suddenly showing herself to be femi- nine and busy feeling without displeasure on her bare legs the scratching of that long skirt; she was obscurely trying with sensual pleasure to win her friendship and sympathy. The old lady was withdrawing her thin face, somehow offended and dominated because she'd barely managed to open her mouth and speak, she who always had leaned over others with narrowed eyes, asphyxiating them with news.

"You can well imagine what a big city is," Virgínia was shouting surpassing the noise of the tram on the tracks, "it simply wears a person out! And apartments are so expensive, right? And sometimes so small! And I live in a relatively cheap building, thank God, but the others are a horror. I'm telling you: a horror! you can't hear me because of the tram." — The vehicle was halting for an instant at the stop and the old lady again attempting with dryness to take charge of the conversation was asking her if she lived alone. — "Yes, yes, but the building is of the best possible morality," Virgínia was saying to her frightened. "Just think that in the city, from what I heard said in a boardinghouse where I lived, the girls with the best appearance are actually the worst possible — horrible, isn't it?" she was laughing. "You really only learn stuff like that by living here."

When the old woman said goodbye with haste and coldness, frustrated in her own news, Virgínia squeezed her hand, effusive as if she were abandoned:

"Best wishes, you hear? best wishes, ma'am, to you and your sister!" — the old lady went off with surprise, now charmed and smiling and Virgínia sat an instant with open eyes, watchful, thoughtful. Daniel … How Daniel would look at her judging; but judging what? she wondered. And whatever had happened was reducing itself thus to just a silence and a sensation that she understood she hardly could transmit to Daniel; therefore she didn't want him beside her, she preferred to be alone — she huddled in the corner of the tram; alone was the way she could wear herself out; the most alive things didn't have so much as a movement to dress them, it was impossible to fulfill them; if you tried not only could you not do it but they themselves would die confounded. And two people no matter how quiet would end up talking. When however three days a week would come she would rise with joy because at last she was caught.

Sometimes a sharp desire wrapped in a wave of fresh and propelling happiness, a sharp desire to sculpt would give a small shout of surprise in her heart. She'd open the small suitcase of the clay things, without hesitation plunge them into hot water in order to dissolve them and obtain material for new figurines. She would work in a happy concentration that lent her face the old nervous transparency. The figures however were in the same line as the ones erected back in childhood. Grotesque, serious and motionless, with a delicate and independent touch, Virgínia would obstinately keep saying the same thing without understanding it. She would bend her head and seem to continue to grow.

With the passing of time a secret watchful life had been born in her; she would communicate silently with the objects around her in a certain tenacious and unnoticed mania that nonetheless was being her most interior and truthful way of existing. Before carrying out any act she would "know" that "something" would go against it or that a light wave would allow it; she had so much desire to live that she had become superstitious. She had entered her own reign. The rooms that smelled like tunnels, the things lightly dislocated from themselves as if they had just been alive. Superstition was the most delicate thing she had known; through the slipping of a second she could surpass that warm and mysteriously vehement affirmation that the thing, understand? is there, right there and therefore is like that, objects, that small pitcher for example, knows itself profoundly; and even that half-open window, the little table perched on the points of three legs beneath the roof, understand? knows itself profoundly; and then there's also whatever isn't present (and which helps, which helps, and everything moves forward) (even that (power)) (an instant that follows itself and from it is born the yes and the no) (but if you linger a bit longer you end up "knowing" that the instant is an instant and then it is mutely shredded) (you have to start over) (winding, rewinding, winding powers) (without letting certain things of the world get too close) (above all what's past is past and is exactly just of that small instant we're talking about and also that one, and also that one, and also that one) (but every one for itself)—and before you know it without a single word she'd already achieved. Anyway her whole being was propped up by a few words. But used with such meaning, with such a kind of blind and strange nature that, when she used them out loud or in thought or when she heard them, she didn't tremble, didn't recognize, didn't realize; in her busy and detailed intimacy she was living without memory. Before falling asleep, concentrated and magical, she would say farewell to things in a last instant of lightly illuminated consciousness. She knew that in the half-light "her things" were better living their own essence. "Her things"—she was thinking without words, sly inside her own darkness—"her things" like "her animals." She would feel profoundly that she was surrounded by things living and dead and that the dead ones had been alive—she was feeling them with careful eyes. Slowly she'd go sub-understanding, living with caution and consideration;

without knowing she was admitting her desire to see in the extinguished and dusty light bulb more than a light bulb. She didn't know that she was thinking that if she saw just the light bulb she'd be on the wrong side of it and wouldn't grasp its reality—mysteriously if she went beyond things she would grasp her center. Though she thought "her things" as if saying "her animals," feeling that their effort wasn't in having a human nucleus but in staying on a pure extra-human plane. She was barely understanding them and her life was of reserve, enchantment and relative happiness; she'd sometimes feel curled up into herself—wasn't most of her existence thing? that was the feeling; most of her constellation was living with its own unknown force, following an imponderable path. And in truth if there were any possibility of her not being intimately quiet, by virtue of that inexpressible impression she would be. Seated at the table, looking at her fingers alone in the world, she was thinking confusedly with a precision without words that was like light and delicate movements, like a buzzing of thought: thoughts about things exist in things themselves without attaching to whoever observes them; thoughts about things come out of them as perfume frees itself from the flower, even if nobody smells it, even if nobody even knows that that flower exists …; the thought of the thing exists as much as the thing itself, not in words of explanation but as another order of facts; quick facts, subtle, visible exactly through some sense, as only the sense of smell perceives the flower's perfume—she was resounding. The quality of her thought was merely a circular movement. She was noticing a scratch on her finger and attentive to life forgetting everything as through slumber is forgotten whatever was thought an instant before sleep. Like someone whose body needed salt as an essential substance and then ate it with thirsty pleasure—she'd always felt a simple and avid pleasure in making an effort and saying to herself clearly: I see a chair, a box of powder, an open pair of scissors, a black drawer … The great still-life in which she was living. Nevertheless she felt she was mixing things up, arranging them at her pleasure and bothering them. Ah, if I had time, just a little time, she seemed to be saying to herself with her head bent and confused. Anyway she'd noticed: when she'd open her eyes wide she'd see nothing. Except the words, thoughts made of words. When she'd stare with gaping eyes at her seated grandmother she'd lose the notion of the grandmother and see nothing, not even a little old lady. The truth was so fast. You had to squint. It was occurring to her in strange and swift seconds of vision that her communication with the world, that secret atmosphere that she was cultivating around herself like a darkness, was her final existence—beyond that border she herself was silent like a thing. And it was that final interior life that was carrying forth without lacuna the thread of her most elf-like existence in childhood. The rest would stretch out horribly new, had created itself as if out of itself—that body of hers now and its habits. And that religion was so little rich and potent that it didn't have ritual—its greatest gesture would exhaust itself in a quick and unnoticed glance, full of "I know, I know," of a promise of fidelity and of mutual support in a closed and almost evil union; united and simple, no movement would symbolize it, it was the accepted mystery. Really however she didn't know what was happening to her and her only way of knowing it was living it.

Only thus could she connect herself to the past of which

she lacked the memory. Stripped of memory she was living her life simply without ecstasy; yet a strange attention would sometimes overtake her, vaguely she was trying to think how she had emerged from childhood toward the ground, she was trying to orient herself to no avail; in an odd moment it would seem to her that she'd lived the same instant in another age, in another color and in another sound—her rhythm would suddenly break off, she would halt and with a calm made of shock and caution fumble in her interior, try to discover. As soon however as she became aware of this nebulous and dark examination she would rush into a confused sweetness, in the understanding of the impossibility and bewildered for a second she would lose her daring footsteps. She would seek with patience to remember more clearly her girlhood without events; some fact would arise in her memory like pillars spread out in a lucidity without foundation. As soon as she got close to them she would feel them dissolve at her touch. What had she lived off back then? she was gathering some poor facts that weren't really dug up on her own but by the remembered word of others or by the recollection of already having managed to remember, she was assembling them, organizing them but she lacked a fluid that might solder their extremities into a single principle of life. Events were aligning spaced out, solid, hard; while the way of living was always imponderable. A certain effort would cause the memory to return, a certain attitude that she couldn't quite figure out as if not finding a good sleeping position on a night of insomnia. Ah, if only I had time, she'd shake her head in reproach and pity. She knew she'd never quite have it. The place where she had been born—she was vaguely surprised that it still existed as if it too belonged to what is lost. She herself was now living on her feet like a raised column—what was left behind was the world before the column, a warm and intimate time, yet if she'd think about it trying to revive it, suddenly an impersonal time, fresh air coming from an abyss of sluggish clouds. She was trying to feel her past like a paralytic who uselessly gropes the unfeeling flesh of a limb, but naturally she knew her history as all people do. She was seeing herself separate from her own birth and yet was feeling diffusely that she must be somehow prolonging childhood in a single uninterrupted line and that without knowing herself developing something initiated in forgetting. The Society of Shadows …—she was all of a sudden smiling palely while her eyes were shining for an instant and were extinguished in the effort of reconstruction. The Society of Shadows … She was remembering that she and Daniel lived in little secrets, frightened; little secrets … was that it? no, no. Above all she had always possessed an extraordinary memory for inventing facts. Yes, and that they would meet in the clearing, yes, in the clearing. How they must have experienced fear … one is so courageous as a child; is that it? after they'd agreed to tell Father about Esmeralda's meetings in the garden. Poor Esmeralda, but why? she didn't know, the truth is that she'd told, Father had shouted, she herself had pretended to faint or really had fainted … so sly! life had changed then, she was sure of that, certainly because she was no longer a girl at all; then she'd sew, go on walks, visit some houses in Upper Marsh, serious, silent, Daniel would help their father at the stationer's. Though she didn't remember that period with clarity—she was living so much each day—she now felt she was being impatient with herself. Except what she didn't forget—she was

smiling—was that someone had drowned himself in the river
… it might have just been a hat but they'd been frightened. In
any case she was keeping the secret. Ah, she'd gone into the
basement, the basement! and was that important? her memory
was dissolving into shadow, the splendor going out in sweet
and poor silence. A profound fatigue, a certain befuddlement
was taking her over, anyway nothing had ever happened to
her … and so why that awareness of a mystery to preserve,
that gaze that meant having existed ineffably. She was vaguely
aware that she'd already once lived going beyond the moments
in a happy blindness that was giving her the power to follow
the shadow of a thought over the course of a day, a week, a
year. And that mysteriously was living perfecting oneself in
the darkness without obtaining so much as a reward for that
imponderable perfection. Later she'd try to tell Vicente things
about her childhood and about Daniel and surprised would
hear him say laughing: I already know more or less what you
two were like, but what did you actually do? So she hadn't
told him anything? she'd stay quiet and scared. You could wear
yourself out just being; every minute that had passed she had
been, she had been. She couldn't tolerate talking about herself,
she gathered herself up insoluble, anguished—in short the essential thing would escape words spoken and that was in the
end the feeling of having lived whatever she'd recounted; the
delicate incessant indecision of a life seemed to be in its relationship with whoever was living it, in the intimate awareness
of its contact. Sometimes she'd manage some thing similar to
herself. It was however an easy and almost skilled freedom, a
process of freedom—a power being used and not something
moving forward while still creating itself; the difference that

might exist between something that had been flung into the air and something that could fly on its own. Every once in a while however the imitation would manage to be more truthful than the thing imitated and would almost reveal it for an instant. What she was reaching was a form of memory.

Ah yes, she would have liked to move into the future so that the present might already be past and she again might try to understand it as if this game of losing were summoning her to a vice or a mystery. She was trying to be sincere as if that were the way of seeing reality; never could she then sum up her current life without joining facts to facts and not reaching the feelings themselves. Three times a week she could go to Vicente's house and love him because three times a week he would hand in to the magazines whatever he was working on three times a week. The other days were a great white pause. She would wake up, drink water, sit down in the living room deposited in the flowery robe that stretched across her breasts and behind—Mother, Mother arising through her. She'd pace back and forth without knowing what to do with herself as if she had more body than she needed. She'd hardly feed herself. But suddenly something in her would break down and her being would eat with great gusto, violently, miserly, bonbons, sweets, very spicy dishes—she who had always been frugal like a plant. After thinking for an entire day about a food that was for sale very far away, she'd decide to go out and buy it and gained in life. She'd bring it home shuddering with impatience and devour it. With empty, tired, slightly dumbfounded eyes, she'd fall asleep heavily. After Vicente she'd grown fatter, and since she was somewhat tall, her body was now existing with twice the power, more firm. Her waist had grown more pronounced, her skin had lost its dryness and the gilding of the sun and stretched out smooth and white—her hips had broadened and now she was a woman. But her face had lost its vague fire. She'd keep calm with a slightly outmoded appearance like a recent arrival. Only in white did she acquire an urbane tone and as if she felt it she chose that color for her best attire. But without the outings, without space for a broad life, she was always tired. Her hands playing distractedly on the table, she'd even imagine that it wouldn't be long now before she died because a constant force was attracting her toward the earth and sleep was useless, inside it she did not find repose. She was getting the impression that she'd already lived everything despite not being able to say in which moments. And at the same time her whole life appeared able to be summed up in a small gesture forward, a light daring and then in a soft wince without pain, and no path then to head down—without landing straight on the ground, suspended in the atmosphere almost without comfort, almost comfortable, with the tired languor that precedes sleep. Yet around her things were living so violently sometimes. The sun was fire, the earth solid and possible, plants were sprouting alive, trembling, whimsical, houses were made so that in them bodies could be sheltered, arms would wrap around waists, for every being and for every thing there was another being and another thing in a union that was a burning end with nothing beyond. In reality however she possessed a harmony of her own, yes, yes, yes, like a flower that makes up a whole from its petals. Which didn't stop the despair of the things that she was not from at times being born from her heart and stopping her from getting too filled with whatever she had never possessed, so ambitious and envious she had always been.

She'd returned from Vicente's house feeling ill, her body was aching, she'd vomited with wide, sad eyes. On the second day of illness the fever rose. She was no longer feeling especially envious. She looked at herself in the mirror, saw her sparkling and motionless eyes, her parted lips. Her breathing was burning her chest, it was wheezing and superficial. She was going to go back to the table and sit but in a sudden movement of almost unexpected rage entered her bedroom, got dressed and went out, the gestures united in one single push by the fever that didn't let her pay attention to the time that was elapsing. The fresh wind was pacifying the heat of her body and her face—and that was connecting itself almost immediately to the instant of rage. She felt so weak that her limbs were giving out at times; then she would lean on a tram post pretending to await transport. She finally sat on a garden bench and lost for long and hollow minutes the awareness of herself and of the place where she found herself. When understanding returned like a heart that starts beating again with power, she was in the middle of a thought whose beginning she couldn't remember: so it's preferable to give … so it's preferable to give … Children were playing ring-around-the-rosy, their shouts sparkling in the garden, resplendent drops of the water from the fountain filling the air with fine glitter. She couldn't look at it, lowering her injured eyes and fixing them to the dark earth, to the grass pacifying and tender as in a cold balm. The clean children with bows in their hair were now playing badminton living extraordinarily. The cries were piercing her with effort and one of the stranger ones was freezing inside her, she was gnawing on it astonished still hearing it almost as if touching it with her fingers, crystallized in dark scarlet, running with a vacant shimmering along a sinuous ribbon … she was growling it without understanding it, without understanding the world, horrified and calm. The birdie crashed at her feet. One of the children shouted at her:

"Throw it!"

She looked at them in silence without a movement. They came near, peered at her with attention and curiosity, the little intelligent eyes examining her face, approaching like trusting rats. They formed a semicircle of waiting and silence. The skinny girl who was waiting for the birdie howled from far off with the veins of her neck bulging:

"Come back!"

Since nobody was answering, she herself came over, put her hands on her waist, her body hitched up, extended her neck forward. She furrowed her face as if the sun were out and set to looking at Virgínia. She was staring at the children mute; suddenly an onset of rage overtook her while in the interior of her body a wave of more ardent breathing was moving:

"What is it?"

A few girls put their hands on their mouths hiding little laughs.

"What, so we're not allowed to look!" said the most daring one, with a cunning and cynical face, launching the attack. They all laughed aroused, ready for some new thing. Terror overtook Virgínia, she pursed her lips, felt lost. She looked at them helpless and cautious while her empty head was throbbing like a heart. With swift, feverish thinking that was almost painfully intense, she was needing to please them—she spoke with a humble demeanor, afflicted and hard, observing them:

"You know, I'm not feeling well. Can you believe I haven't eaten for two days, I only drink tea!"—she stared at them dismayed, they were backing off surprised by the change, seeming to doubt her sincerity and scrutinizing her as if it might be some story invented for children.

"You're lying"—said one girl with watchful, black eyes, short braids, a dark-skinned and decided face.

"No, I'm not, that's how it is, I swear!"—her hot breath was spreading close to her face—in a sudden inspiration she said to the one who must be the most important: "touch here"—and extended her hand placing it on the girl's arm, waiting for some sign in her face that she felt the heat of her fever. Soon she saw with enormous pleasure several little hurried hands reaching toward her, touching with curiosity and caution her arm, her fingers, her hand. A boy who was running by halted, came over, and without understanding what he was doing, advanced, touched with care and astonishment Virgínia's arm, hesitated, lifted his hand to her shoulder.

"She really is hot!" the children were saying looking at one another stunned, moving busy and excited.

"You don't have a father or a mother?" asked one blonde wearing white linen chambray, her face delicate, exact, and fine. Virgínia seemed profoundly surprised.

"I do, I do," she said to the young creature, assenting feverish, running her tongue across her dry lips.

"And why aren't they taking care of you?" inquired the strong little dark-skinned girl in surprise.

"You know, they live far away, that's because ..."

"Oh I know," said the boy with a sudden intelligent look, "I know, you don't have money to go back!"

"Why to go back? how do you know about these things?" asked Virgínia.

"Just yesterday the maid at home didn't have money to go back," said the boy with a certain pride.

"Ah yes, ah yes," — Virgínia was seeming to meditate.

"So? did you figure it out?" asked the oldest girl, the skinny one.

"Yes, I figured it out, I'll go back ..." said Virgínia looking them with fury, disguising it. "I'll go back, I'll go back. And now can I go?" she inquired with an indecisive, almost timid air. They looked surprised, glanced at one another quickly without answering. The dark one shook her braids:

"Who was keeping you?"

The others said — "yeah, right!" They laughed a bit wrinkling their noses at the sudden sun that had appeared. Virgínia got up, the children now with their heads raised, hands on their foreheads protecting themselves against the glare, they were retreating watching. She said:

"Fine, goodbye," she was hesitating as if it were dangerous to withdraw. A few answered goodbye, the little blonde pressed her hand one last time with force on Virgínia's arm. Virgínia had taken a few steps when the boy ran up shouting:

"Miss! miss! the maid said that when she'd go back she'd buy a ticket in that yellow station, you know, that big one ..."

Virgínia was stopping listening to him in silence. The boy had nothing else to say, he was waiting. He seemed annoyed:

"So, that's what I wanted to say ..."

"Yes, yes, thanks a lot *really, really* ..."

When she passed a nearby bench a lady dressed in blue, without a hat, with a big purse, was seeming to say something to her. She stopped, bent her head: ah, yes, the woman had watched the scene, hadn't heard anything and was asking her out of pure curiosity, with a certain overfamiliar and malicious eagerness, what had happened.

"The world is full of naughty children," she said showing that she'd be understanding about any fact that Virgínia might tell.

"Yes," said Virgínia and moved away. The garden was spread in long horizontal lines, the grass was swaying in the fluctuating shadows of the branches, the air was stretching out bright, softly electric. And suddenly warm drops of water started to fall. She took shelter in the gazebo along with a fat old man, with a heart condition, who was slowly gasping with fright and pity, his eyes staring at the rain as at hopeless disaster. A sluggish, thick, and noiseless rain was falling, filling the space with long shining streaks.

The next day, yes it had been at that time, she'd visited the young doctor. He was laughing imitating her. With a falsely paternal demeanor he would brush his body against hers, brush against her cheek that face with two days of beard growth while on the other cheek he was giving her little slaps . . . while she surprised and confused was feeling almost good, very good—he was tall and pale and women were worthless to him. He had a wedding ring; how could you ever guess his relations with his wife? He was getting closer in that calm, white office and she was still sitting on the table where he'd examined her quickly. He'd had two nights of childbirth in a row, he'd said at the beginning with tact and ceremony, hadn't even been able to shave, he was saying as she was taking off her hat while carefully storing the hairpins. And after he examined her they sat talking, he was losing his coldness, joking so intimately, so distantly . . . in the white, clean office seeing her as just anyone, desiring her without sadness, not even waiting for her to let him try something, just wanting to make himself desired, cheerful, mischievous, and distracted, having fun with his own virility. Yet serious, his eyes watchful and mobile.

"But doctor …"

He had moved off for a second looking at her with a severe appearance, imitating her solemn and hoarse voice: "—but doctor! …" A weight was lightly squeezing her neck, her arms, she was feeling a shapeless taste of blood in her throat and in her mouth as always when she'd feel fear and hope—she could overturn some idea and accept the adventure, yes, the adventure that he wasn't offering her. From a new center in her body, from her stomach, from her reborn breasts a sharp thought, desperate and profoundly happy, was radiating outward, without words she was wanting him, in an instant he was becoming some thing prior to Vicente. Without sadness, as if on holiday, to rush into the future! and since he was coming even closer, she awkwardly, quick, brushed her mouth against that cheek rough like a man, near the ear … He looked at her fast shocked and odd! she was wavering with open eyes, the office was spinning around red, a heavy and grave blushing rose to her neck and face while she was trying to make excuses with a difficult and foolish smile. He looked at her attentively for an instant, with wisdom touched upon certain common words and suddenly everything was dissolving into a simple joke. She looked at him dry and ardent, extended her hand to him, he said leading her: don't get mad, nausea means nothing, you can tell your boyfriend …, she exited the office entered the dark, crimson, somber, luxurious and so cool elevator. When she received the dusty, luminous, and strident air of the street she walked fast, free. Little by little she went more slowly through the afternoon, choosing broad streets. A certain indifferent and opaque serenity was making her movements easy and the rest of the day simple—she'd forget, Virgínia, she'd forget. But she'd passed a woman beside her with a perfume of lemon, water, and grass, frightened and penetrating, a smell of lemon and grass—like a horse her legs gained a nervous, happy, and lucid power. Quiet Farm. She was inhaling the mysterious perfume that nonetheless was emerging. Because it was so ... so alive ... so ..., she gave up, pulled back her head feeling herself lacking the courage to go on so strong was her hope. The sun shone pale on the sidewalk, a cold wind pierced the whole afternoon, she hurried her body clenched with power, her heart trembling as if a pure feeling had passed through it ... a great fatigue that was made of ecstasy, bemusement, permission, and perfume seized her and without being bothered, softened, she felt that her eyes were filling with tears because of the doctor and that they were starting to run warm and radiant down her cheek. She went onto a staircase and blew her nose; she was wanting to alight on the same fluctuating, iridescent, and hard feeling but didn't know which thought to focus the sensation on, so incomprehensible and fleeting was the world.

She later understood that the doctor had assured her that she wasn't pregnant ... How Vicente would laugh. She herself thought she'd never have children. She'd never even feared them as if through some quiet understanding of her most secret nature she knew that her body was the end of her body, that her life was her last life. Ah she liked children; life with them was so rich ... so ...—the rest was being lost in a gesture without force, almost inexpressive. But how to watch a life weaker than her own? she'd avoid children with care and when faced with them a desire would quickly possess her, the desire to escape, to seek out people to whom she could give nothing. Above all she wasn't one of those women who have children. And if someday she made them be born, she'd still be one of those women who don't have children. And if all the life she'd live should diverge from the one she ought to have lived, she would be as she ought to have been—what she could have been was herself profoundly, ineffably, not out of courage, not out of joy, and not out of awareness but out of the inevitability of the power of existence. Nothing would rob her of the unity of her origin and the quality of her first breath, though these might be entombed beneath their own opposite. In reality she knew little about whatever was hiding beneath her undeniable life. But not dissolving herself, not giving herself, denying her own errors and even never erring, to keep herself intimately glorious—all that was the fragile initial and immortal inspiration of her life. She'd touched her neighbor's child one day; the child lay its little hand in hers, looking out the window. Little by little, with a hard and playful gaze, with light emotion in her body, she grasped his small flesh full of little sightless and soft fingers, squeezed it between her hands, the child didn't notice, he was looking out the window. Virgínia would stop for an instant so that she wouldn't get overconfident and go too far. She was getting progressively more excited, telling a story, made up something funny, but really funny, the child laughed a little, his own face reflected in a windowpane broadened shining, flushed, unaware of itself, moving around living and shy. Afterward the child left as if nothing had happened. A fertile woman was so vulnerable, her fragility came from her being fruitful. She herself would sometimes feel an ecstasy made of weakness, fatigue, of a deep smile and of a difficult and superficial breathing; it was a deep, blind possibility that would finally conclude with a sigh and in a quick well-being, in a pale sleep full of exhaustion and scrambled dreams in which she'd seem to want to scream freeing herself from the sheets: my fruitfulness suffocates me. If she had a child she'd always be in panic. Every second she'd expect to see him put beans in his ears with mischief and wisdom, put his little finger in the electric socket. And every second she'd be thankful, skinny, and nervous, for the miracle of nothing happening—because she'd be skinny and nervous. Until, accustomed to the gentleness of events, she would find peace, drinking tea with cakes and embroidering. And then the child would head straight for the electric socket. Only her fear would prevent tragedies, only her fear. She put on her gray wool cloak, went to the zoo. The monkeys weren't doing anything, grooming themselves, watching, hanging from the bars blinking, making signs, watching like sweet prostitutes. She was approaching the tiger breathing in the heat and the vice of the smell of the cage; conquering her own destiny she was forcing herself to look alone in the world into the eyes of the tiger, at its rolling walk, raising herself above the terror, until from it a kind of truth was emerging, something that was pacifying her like a thing, she was sighing while wrinkling her eyes. That repugnant smell of fatigue was doing her good, she was closing her woman's teeth. The head guard said to her:

"Some people I have to kick out or arrest. Imagine, madam, that some men light a cigarette, take a drag, and stick it in the animal's snout."

She said: how horrible, but her body stirred quietly inside, hurried and dark. The rheas were laughing silent, full of joy and silliness but there was a sign warning that they were dangerous. They didn't look it, the thin and sinuous neck directly stuck to the voluminous hips, full of calm movements. She was walking slowly, sinking the heels of her shoes into the mud, it was winter, the hush of the empty garden, only the occasional murmur of the animals, the slight cry of a bird. Her steps in the wide squares surrounded by cages, were cautious. She would pass the immobile and cold cobra with her heart dry with courage. One day it started to rain, she was looking, wet, at the animals pacing worried in the cages, the puddles of water were singing. The black velvet jaguar was moving its legs, its paws were touching and leaving the ground in a soft, fast, and silent step. The female, with her face raised above her reclined body, was panting rapt with satiation, her green eyes wild. The guard showed her the open cut in the palm of his hand, the jaguar had made it. But there was a docile tiger, he'd show you, madam.

"I'm going to wash my hand because I touched meat, otherwise with the smell she'll attack."

He told her that he always went into the cage with a knife, don't tell the director, okay? That secret made her slightly dizzy, she closed her eyes for an instant. He held out the knife for some reason she didn't understand: touch it! But why? she wondered scared, she touched the cold and shining blade that the raindrops were seeming to avoid and that was leaving the taste of blood in her mouth, while with her open eyes, her face almost in a grimace of nausea and horror, she was smiling. Water was running down the umbrella. And if she told Vicente … She was feeling the need to tell him. But what could she say about that, she was learning as much as she could learn in herself about sensations while looking at length at a clear glass of water; the sensation would seem to be in the glass of water itself. Thus was the need to confess the only feeling that existed, the only restless reality. What to tell? She was also remembering, as if right on time, that Vicente's sympathy was almost a disappointment. No, she wouldn't tell him anything, not even about the Farm. And as she was thinking: the Farm, like bells chiming in the distance, she was feeling that near the mansion in that same instant the meadow was stretching out dead and flat and that atop it were living long unstable abandoned weeds. He wouldn't have sympathy for that but that was exactly what she couldn't tell him either. She hadn't yet managed to tell him how her life had lost its intimate nobility, how now she was acting according to a destiny. The presence of a man in her blood or the city had dissolved her power of directing her own search. Where, where was the power that she possessed when she was a virgin. She'd lost her indifference. Sometimes on the way back from the movies, grasping Vicente's arm, she'd see the night pale with moon, the trees in the darkness of a faint, feel that some thing was approaching inside of her and want then to attain it, have a moment of engrossed sadness. She knew however that the man would keep her from suffering, dragging her to the fluctuating and balanced half-sensation of their bodies. He'd force her not to despair, summon her insistent and inaccessible toward a demotion, who knows why. There was a struggle between them that wouldn't be resolved either by words or by gazes—and she was also feeling, surprised and stubborn, that she was trying to destroy him, that she was afraid of the man's moments of pureness, she couldn't stand his instants of solitude as if there were something unpleasant and dangerous to her in them. It was an unnoticed struggle that nevertheless connected them in a same instrument of attraction, misunderstanding, repulsion, and complicity. Despite everything he'd taught her a lot. Listening to him marvel at the path men had taken until discovering the transformation of the moist, sweet coffee bean into a bitter infusion—yes, she was learning a new way of being surprised. The way he had of grabbing common words and making a thought out of them. She'd say: it was raining so much, Vicente, it seemed like the world was going to end; he'd answer playing: and if it ended would you suffer? she was tossed into a greater and deeper world, or could she be mistaken? from everything he'd head off some place. He'd say of someone: what a way to waste your life ... And she'd scream to herself: but no, you could never waste your life, you just couldn't ... he'd hastened things to a strange and irremediable level. I wasn't happy, I was missing some thing that could satisfy me—he'd say and another time would discover for her almost a way of thinking, so new that it would pain her as if she were ripping the course of a river from its bed. He would without words let her know about things that she had never seen. She told him:

"Sometimes I spend my days with a hope so ... you know ... and suddenly I have no hope at all ..."

"Hope for what?" he asked interested.

"Not quite for something ..."

"But what do you mean?" he'd insist, "you must know ..."

She didn't know how to explain and was surprised by Vicente's incomprehension. Later she learned that he'd understand if she said; I spent half the day in a good mood and the other half in a bad mood. She started to change into Vicente's words and sometimes would feel that it was more than words that were transforming. That same afternoon she'd finally met Vicente's sister, who lived with their aunt and uncle. The big breasts, the pure face without makeup where the nose was fine, pale, and curved; the bare arms, the dark and calm eyes—but she'd be impure when it was her turn. She read mystery novels and her voice was slightly hoarse. Virgínia looking at her was feeling an intolerable envy, staring at her with avidity and cold. Rosita was despising her with eyes without curiosity. Virgínia refused the cigarette pleasing her with nausea and baseness. She sat with them in the tea house but Rosita wasn't even an eater; she was staring at Vicente's "friend" with naked eyes while Virgínia was trying to smile into the cup while holding in a difficult pang of fear, thinking about her own nose that was shining, her unkempt and frightened hair reflected in the fancy black-framed mirror. She had a few dresses of indefinable color, light hazel, cream, bluish, the neckline somewhere between round and oval swimming at her neck, made of a silk that neither plunged nor protected, wrinkled as if just taken out of a suitcase—she would wear old clothes, as if in order not to exist, feel good in them, not betraying Upper Marsh. Because whenever she'd wear them "she ran into someone of circumstance"—and the fact seemed to her to have some extraordinary and invincible inevitability, some thing that would almost demand a respectful deference—there wasn't even any point in no longer wearing those clothes, such was the force of things. And that added to the unease that she and Vicente would experience when they ran into each other on the street. As if one were surprising the other. She was drinking the tea in little gulps, she'd refused toast secretly in order still to please Rosita and as a sacrifice. She was feeling guilty alongside Vicente—in front of both of them was the virgin dressed in white linen and with bare arms, her big and well-made nose, her pale gardenia skin. How dare I live. She'd always been envious, the truth had to be told. They got up, accompanied Rosita to the aunt's car where the driver was waiting. They said goodbye, Virgínia sighed out of relief and sadness, the street suddenly had so few people, it was quickly looking like an empty and calm Sunday. She walked with Vicente through the streets without looking at him until they reached the apartment. He too seemed somehow touched, was addressing her with an excitement interrupted at intervals—in the elevator he touched her waist with his hand and she ducked almost rudely. But in the bedroom she became sad, looked peaceful, resigned, loved him with a strange and wistful tone that she herself didn't know, loving in him the inaccessible sister, the dead father and mother. As the end of the three days a week closed the door behind them, the heat of Vicente's apartment brusquely isolated itself behind its walls, soon in front of her the ground, quiet and fragrant in its coolness, would stretch. The lights were blinking in trembling halos and that's how a golden lamppost was communicating with another across the distance. She was crossing the dry street, the walls in darkness, taking the bus and the wind was light whipping her cheek. In the bright, warm, and shaking interior of the vehicle the faces beneath the hats were condensing in the silence of the journey through the night and behind each one life for an instant would seem tossed to the back of the stage, the theater seats empty in the half-light—the bus was moving forward. The driver kept his hand on the steering wheel, almost still, slow, the illuminated cabin was apparently moving all by itself. Virgínia was getting off, walking with large useless rain boots squeezing her feet. On the deserted street her footsteps were slapping sonorous and expectant on the sidewalk. The moonlight was pouring over the construction sites. The Farm livid and sleepless was coming to her in a wave amidst the fog, she was hurrying her dark pace, going forward. She was placing the key in the lock, sweetly the door was giving way and the tall and pale staircase was popping out for an instant before her eyes quite clearly; it would immediately shift its position when she'd advance her foot. Her own figure was moving ahead filling the narrow hall-way—slowly going up seeing the steps half dark half light un-til getting lost in the confusing height of the house. She was finally reaching the landing, the staircase and the street would stay behind immobilized in the quiet for an entire night until dawn emerged and someone once again would move their air. In the illuminated bedroom she was taking off her rain boots, examining her toes pressed together like small smashed birds. She was separating them with slow hands, smoothing them out. How she liked her bedroom; she'd smell its tunnel odor when she was getting close and it was nice, nice inside it when she'd go in. She'd notice that before going out she'd forgotten to open the windows and a smell of herself was coming from all over—as if when returning from the street she was finding herself at home waiting. She'd open the windows and an air cold from the sky and from fresh water would rustle limpid over the things renewing them. She was hesitating a bit trying to connect herself to her things, to see a sign in the objects, but soon felt right away that it was no use, that she was free and among calm outlines. She was leaning out of the window for an instant, her face offered to the night with anxiety and delight, her eyes half-closed: the nocturnal, cold, perfumed, and tranquil world was made of her weak and disorganized sensations. Oh how strange, strange it was. She was feeling good and knew that before she was suffocating, it seemed to her that at night the water of the world would start to live— she was breathing and the relief was almost violent, maybe the strongest moment of the day; always an instant had saved her, a gesture wouldn't let her be lost and was making her lean toward the next day. She was changing her clothes serene and careful. She was getting into bed with deep self-love. She was concentrating for an instant until discovering a faraway, clear, and fragile chirping, the cricket shining. Her own spirit was taking her over. She was sighing. Oh God, it was strange how she didn't feel any hurry. Deep down she was terrifyingly quiet. She was lightly thinking about the next morning. In the city, even if silence were the closest air, behind it always some sound was lurking. You'd wake up, hear that continuous, soft paper bruise that was silence ... notice a little flute and a small drum set loose who knows where in the air, resounding remotely, limpid and good-humored—and know that in the square of a barracks soldiers were doing exercises in the sun. But now it was night, she'd just finished taking the last, hollow steps on the shady sidewalk. Submerging in fatigue, looking for it. Her fatigue had something flowerlike about it, a winged and unconquerable perfume of fresh melon, that ecstasy of exhaustion and flight ... weakness was getting mixed up with the sheerest exultation. Before closing her eyes she was remembering in a final vision the staircase placed on the earth, dark white, dark white, dark white, running motionless among the walls up to the closed door. Closed, dark, compact, serious, smooth, large, tall, impassable—how good it was, how happy.

The next day she received the letter from her father notifying her of her grandmother's death. She'd died unattended, during the night. The next morning the maid hadn't heard the difficult knocking of the cane on the wooden floorboards and with relief had only gone to bring her milk later. There was the old lady sitting in bed, her shirt open atop her dry and rough chest, her eyes deeply surprised, her mouth open. Father had cried for days and nights. The burial took place in the rain, the relatives from the south already dressed in black and with bad colds. A day later they were taking the train back home each one taking a souvenir of the grandmother and a basket of provisions for the train journey—her father didn't overlook anything, it was his family. He'd inherited the mansion and the surrounding lands. The other children got nothing because they'd abandoned the old woman when her desire would have been to live with everyone under the same roof; that roof dusty in its thick crusts, so vast that it could shelter dozens of men and women and that had always remained empty in the meadow full of wind. Her father was asking Virgínia to come spend a few weeks at the Farm, if she could break off her studies and her life in the city. Even her mother was under the weather with some trouble in her teeth.

So she was going back. She stopped in front of the window in deep meditation. She wasn't sad, she wasn't happy, but pensive. To break off life in the city now that it was becoming a bit intelligible. Vicente. Ah but to see Daniel again … but Vicente. She knew that she'd already made up her mind to go yet was reasoning, doubting, doing the math with a certain vanity and with some satisfaction. At last she understood how clear the journey was inside her. So she gave in. For two days she didn't go see Vicente, readying her suitcases, arranging coldly with Miguel to sell her furniture at a low price, explaining to him that of course she'd be back soon but would live in a boardinghouse, maybe in her cousins' house—she was so busy! After a few interrupted thoughts she seemed to have decided to say nothing to Vicente about the departure. She was imagining how hard it would be to tell him and see in his face—ah she was guessing it—not surprise, disgust, yearning but that empty and delicate expression that he'd put on when he wanted to make his thoughts indecipherable. And there was also a cunning and extraordinarily feminine calculation—she was smiling almost voluptuous—in keeping the secret: a bit later he'd be bound to feel her absence, come look for her and Miguel would tell him ... And then she'd show up! I like you, he'd said one day with a kind of stubbornness in his voice. She'd almost protested without strength: yes. I do, yes, he was repeating, you know, and his tone of voice kept going stubbornly as if he were fleeing something; his eyes absorbed and focused seemed to limit and not give in. Without knowing how to explain herself, the phrase almost offended her. Amidst her preparations she was stopping for an instant. Suddenly the journey was taking on a new meaning, she had very much wanted to go back to lay eyes on Quiet Farm ... In a few instants her desire was growing acute almost with pain and she was feeling a laughing joy. Yes, to say see you later, mother, and go out into the fields, go out early into the wind, erase herself upon meeting the morning—that was what it meant to see Quiet Farm.

Thus arrived the day before the day set for the departure and she was supposed to see Vicente for the last time. She'd woken up very early in the morning, got up but couldn't do anything, stayed thoughtful and calm. Sometimes a long trembling would awaken her, she'd look around without understanding. The clock struck ten. But the time wasn't hurrying as it did on other occasions. Now everything was peaceful, clean, arranged. She barely ate lunch, serious and somber. In the afternoon however, when she was supposed go out, her strange state grew more marked, she scrutinized herself almost annoyed without understanding herself and in light of that vagueness difficult to surpass like a void and that was holding back her movements. So it was missing Vicente ... the city ... what? almost irritated she sat on the edge of the bed with her mind made up to understand herself harshly. A long, calm sadness seized her. So! so ... what's this? she wanted to say to herself congenially, slap her own face delicately and end up with a smile. She was however so far from having that strength as she was whenever she tried to grasp it. As if she kept pushing herself and creating in herself fake urgings to wake herself up, an afflicted and tired unease took over her body like a slow nausea, her nerves sharpening anxious, in vain. Fast and vacant thoughts, almost feverish were occurring to her and she was vacillating without making up her mind. What then? what was happening? it vaguely seemed to her that she was going to Upper Marsh forever and that made her happy scaring her. What then? she was asking herself somber and enraged. The confusion was taming her but suddenly awakening almost in a scream: I have to go ... Vicente ... She was turning to the window, looking at the distant clock: yes, she should tell Vicente that she was leaving, that she loved him, that was it! how could

she not have known, my God, that was it! the thought however
hurt her terribly, she understood that the confession would
leave her weak and that she only could depart with the vigor
of her own secret and if she didn't have to confront Vicente's
face. And why leave? she could still tell her father that she
couldn't interrupt her studies now ... yes, why not give it up?
she was telling herself filled with a trapped and crazy joy, she'd
always created intolerable states for herself, she herself, she
herself ... yet she could break them off, now she could ... Some
thing had however been mutely decided and she could never
take it back.—When she'd head to the table at the Farm and
was going down the stairs one by one inevitably, she'd wonder: if I wanted to with all my strength could I break off the
descent, go up and lock myself in my room? and she knew it
wasn't possible, that it wasn't possible, that it wasn't possible
step by step and there she was perplexedly seated at the table
with everyone. Now motionless without making up her mind,
she suddenly remembered that she could make coffee to get
herself moving and then drink it. And then drink it, and then
drink it! she thought abruptly alive. But she wasn't even getting up. She held back tired of herself, distractedly nauseated
by her hot life, by so many moist, slow gestures, by her benevolence, by pleasure and by shelter in suffering—severity
and dryness were what she now would vaguely desire, terrified
by so many feelings, but she wasn't managing anything, limp
and watchful. The thought of making coffee shook her again
with more vigor, my God, that would be rebirth, to drink clear,
black, hot, perfumed coffee—world, world, her body was saying smiling mutely in pain. With a certain timidity she was
observing how she was by herself. She could cry from joy, yes,

because by drinking coffee she'd have the strength for everything. She pressed her face to the cold bed and warm tears, warm and happy ran, slowly they were growing into sobs, now in little sad sobs she was crying feeling the cold bed warming up beneath her cheek. In a movement of abandonment she no longer wanted coffee as if the still unmade coffee had gone cold while she was crying. She was opening her eyes, her face crumpled and aged, her eyelashes divided in sheaves by the water and the brightness was so white, so open, mild … buzzing in the air … the leaves waving … a wind drying her lips, stretching her damp skin. She was hesitating. She was feeling a long pleasure that was laziness, weakness, cravenness …—that sensation ah, while living one lives eternally, an almost queasiness in the blood as if she were fast giving in … Something curious and furrowed was occurring to her and disappearing, a feeling of irritated levity. And as if suddenly reacting in a jerk, she decided with a shudder of energy and confused hope to not have coffee but to go to Vicente and love him as she'd never loved him—closing her smiling and tired eyes she foresaw that her sensation had been so strong and high that it must have wounded her lover on some point of his body.

Vicente stood and walked to the window. What was he waiting for anyway? for her to come. She'd disappeared several days ago without warning and that was somehow irritating and was bothering him; she was making herself remembered—and that was new. He was worn out, he thought while stroking like a blind man the cold marble windowsill. He had worked a lot and grown tired, he completed while blinking his eyes in understanding. He had a long and elastic movement with his body, felt comfortable, almost consoled for the day he'd spent working alone. He saw reborn that intimate satisfaction that was the irresistible desire to be amidst others, to talk, to say goodbye with a laugh, a desire to hear the latest political news and to have lunch with a friend afterwards talking about fast women, to get a message to rush to meet in some place, a pleasure to walk while moving his legs and read the newspapers awaiting events—and at the same time that comfort that many people were awaiting events. Above all he'd organized deep within himself a strong and severe feeling, a permanent and not excessive concern for his health, a certain upright approach that would reemerge at the necessary moments. He looked for his cigarettes tapping his hands on his pockets, fumbling. He remembered Vera in white and he furrowed his thick eyebrows—yes, he saw her again while hoping to find his cigarettes as he himself then and now was repeating with pleasure that familiar gesture. He was clasping her arm squeezing her, bruising her: you're so skinny! he was saying with raving and contented eyes. He surprised himself a little when he realized how he'd been livelier and more boyish then, felt a quick disgust that his concern with lighting the cigarette interrupted. Her well-made skinniness seemed to him like a stubborn malevolence and he was taking it like a loving offense. Whose punishment was love—he smiled with mischief and disguised his slightly queasy smile. You're so skinny! he was saying angry and the two secretly, with a touch of hate and of awe, were understanding each other. The first time he'd talked, talked, she was listening, smiling, agreeing but not looking at him head-on perhaps uncomfortable? distraught? what was actually wrong? he wondered and again all his uneasiness was summed up in a blinking behind his glasses: could I have been too intelligent?

Every time he'd slept with women they resurfaced in his mind gathered into one single spot beating with quick open life, a watchful, curious, mischievous, amusing, extremely tired, and hopeful spot. He wanted to hold on to the sensation but saw himself in the void, sitting in the armchair, his long legs spread, his feet, his hands, the living room, some flies. Vaguely what had been left over was the room with the flies and him almost waiting for Virgínia. He confusedly asked himself if he'd been tactful with all of them, thought with quick irony about how really they were the ones who would often hurt him, even Virgínia with certain ... One day he'd said to her shy but irresistible: don't pinch me. He blushed a little. As for Irene, he hadn't been able to stand her anymore, connected her to her smiling and distraught husband once and for all, was nauseated with himself, feeling sorry for her and hating to run into the child, that uneasy and elegant family. How rude they were, how they cheated, how they burned, yes, how they burned and they wore themselves out. There was some thing in women that bothered him. Except Maria Clara. They end up wearing me out, they like me so much, he thought smiling at the anecdote. The courtesy, the strength with which I embrace them, the little prostitutes, simply delights them, he concluded curious and fatigued. His own acrid sensuality brought him a movement of dense drive inside his chest and a sharp repulsion. And that gesture of rejection wasn't coming from his vigilance over himself but was his sensuality itself. He stood, the palm of his hand smoothed the rough skin just shaved, he glanced at himself quickly in the mirror—the sly gaze he had when he was alone; he almost grimaced with disgust at himself so sudden was the lack of relation between the face and the thought, he once more felt extremely annoyed at being alone. He went to the small terrace, leaned on the parapet looking at the distant street, the calm sea, the little people walking and stopping to look at the sea, the cars rushing by. Three girls were walking and stopping, laughing. He lingered fixedly upon them, his twisted face seeking the laughter from far off. To see so many girls so cheerful; if he fell in love with one of them, he'd detach her from the others and greet her as something odd and offended. Because more than seeing joyful girls joy itself was too much. That was annoying him. How well I know life, he thought with an avid satisfaction. He smiled. You cannot imagine how curious I am to know what's going to happen to me, he said to Adriano. What was going to happen to him was in a way limited because wherever he found women he'd look at them. He was missing certain sensations that he'd never managed to grasp. But something kept not going well twirling around—almost as if that day were the anniversary of something that he with a certain pain and effort couldn't quite recall—a defect? someone was waiting while laughing softly for him to remember, laughing in hot murmurs ... Vera. Vera in white. In a thrust as if without roots he threw the cigarette off the balcony and looked somberly at the inaccessible street, thought then that Virgínia hadn't come and said with rage that that was why the day seemed startlingly long, calm, and curving. It was a lie. Adriano would ask him from time to time about Virgínia, he who hadn't asked about Maria Clara, about Vera and would laugh with a shaking pleasure about how Vicente deceived Irene's whole family, including the child. Including the child—Vicente was astounded by Adriano with disapproval and hesitation. He felt once again that his friend had some thought about Virgínia, that he was giving her more importance than she deserved. But how to explain to Adriano that Virgínia was … wasn't much? she had something stagnant and always dry, as if covered with leaves. Was that it? no, that wasn't it, since he didn't even know how to think let alone transmit his impression of vague disgust with that woman who seemed to be growing little by little in his hands and who wouldn't make any man proud. Uncomfortable, uncomfortable, without giving pleasure … She'd so often greet him distracted, without concentration. He wouldn't interrupt himself, fallen into an open-eyed astonishment, the curious sensation and almost laughing with surprise at squeezing in his arms some heavy, serious thing, without movements and without a trace of loveliness. Occasionally he'd say ironically, a little shy out of fear of hurting her: why don't you hold me? she'd be taken aback: don't I hold you? You don't, he'd answer bemused, you let yourself be held. She'd restrain herself, strangely seeming to have thought the idea was funny. And one day he'd even told her baffled: don't pinch me. Like blind people they'd find each other every once in a while with bashfulness, grace, and almost rage at the shame. Though he'd sometimes vaguely feel her trying to transform her own rhythm of looking and living in order to please him but he knew that for her this would be as hard as opening her eyes in the middle of a nightmare and sliding into a gentler dream. In short—he furrowed his eyebrows thinking it was comical, desperate, and awkward—in short, she was uncomfortable. What a nuisance! he thought trembling almost on purpose, shaking and freeing himself from the difficult sensation. Again he felt calm and severe. Once more he was trying to remember slowly, from the beginning, in the hope of striking upon the spot that was beating inside him without managing to open. He remembered when he'd met Virgínia—her body full and peaceful, her wispy bangs, pale neck and, above all, while on the piano her beautiful and arrogant brother was playing by heart an anxious and ardent waltz—she looked like a child withered, withered between the pages of a thick book like a flower. Her brother was playing filling the room. He remembered how the waltz had a rhythm full of slowness, he thought with a bit of warmth, a smile that looked good on him, on that fellow over there playing the piano with black, straight, well-combed hair, dressed for summer. Looking at Virgínia he hadn't even felt a present despair but something like a recollection of a past despair, long since lost and therefore now forever without solution. He finished the thought with speed in order to carry on with another one that had crossed his mind—yes, Daniel had played the Merry Widow very well, by ear and with variations, exploring it in ways he'd never heard before, with ardor and power. The memory of the music, so rounded and calm, was what he was wanting and he started to whistle with sadness and pleasure. That way Virgínia had of lightly pressing her fingers to her lips, loving pathetically their softness. He'd asked her later to get rid of the bangs as if bothered by the nice and simple look that her appearance would take. Without bangs she was at least something like a big, cold woman, close to a type. At the same time how much she seemed to know about herself. He'd never remember to notice in all his life that he'd once loved a yellow flower in a cup of water. Yet after she'd speak, he'd think: but yes, but yes ... I'd like that too or once did ... She'd always be ready to take out with controlled deliberation a tattered souvenir from childhood like a moldy treasure with depths of smoke. And she'd fill the space with her small and secret silly chattering. Somehow whatever she was living was being added to her childhood and not to the present, never maturing her. Because of the way she was you could expect anything from her, even for her to die from one moment to the next without pain, without anything, leaving him baffled, almost guilty. With a certain surprise he realized that this thought had already occurred to him before and he connected it to the fact that she'd told him that someone, maybe a gypsy back where she was from who would err horribly in her prophecies, had predicted for her and Daniel a sudden death. He didn't feel … He didn't feel safe by her side, was always dreading whatever she might announce, had grown used to expecting from her placidity some uncomfortable word. Sometimes when he'd embrace her, she'd inquire with a sweet and tired voice and that inquiry was what he could recall as the most feminine part of her: and what if I died right now? There was in the inquiry a tone that left him, more than the question itself, devastated. Just like going full of enjoyment to take a drag from his cigarette and feeling it extinguished, cold, — cigarettes seemed to be his starting point, cigarettes and glasses. He laughed with a certain roughness: and it wasn't that he didn't think about death. If he could tell her: let's forget it, let's forget it. But he wouldn't even know how to go on: let's forget what? She was some thing to look at and then say to yourself: by God …, with a bit of rage. She wasn't even pretentious like the brother. She wasn't even beautiful like the brother. In fact, with surprise, she was nothing. And she must have changed exactly because he'd loved her that way. How sneaky she seemed. Yes, sneaky and virtuous. That light way of walking, those curled-up positions she'd come up with for her body, the way of talking with the person while having her gaze absorbed, all that made him bend toward her, her inaction would stimulate as Vera's perfect thinness had stimulated him—he'd almost need to be provoked to anger and disdain in order to start to love and thus would feel extremely virile. But by now he was already wanting to see her differently. And he'd even ended up discovering that there was nothing underneath those lovely habits, just distraction and a certain fatigue which she never quite got over—that woman who'd never take up a sport. He'd thought there was a bit of posturing in her attitudes and that had attracted him. Her simplicity however would leave him with lifeless arms, her sincerity. Oh, please free yourself more from me, since a life so attached to mine weighs on me—he'd said to her one day during a fight; he noticed that he was always fighting by himself. But she had looked at him in such a weird, such a limpid and strange way that he'd fallen silent for an instant, surprised and pensive reduced to himself with a kind of pleasure and gratitude. In a low and serene tone of voice he'd then murmured some little thing that would guide them back into the flow of the days. No, it wasn't their fault, it hadn't been Vera's: why is the person you live with the person you should flee? he was lying exactly to those women. He felt against Virgínia the rage of their loving each other, inexplicably, like a whim, the hard hatred of being stuck to a woman who'd do everything for them to be happy. The drive that was burning him was keen, making him breathe the most pure and sufficient part of revolt. He even made a gesture with his hand through her hair just to enhance her and also make her live outside herself. He detested her for making both of them live in a certain way calmly, hating her because she hadn't even been the one who'd reduced him. But the same instant of hardness brought inside it a melancholy thought of peacefulness. Running and rerunning stubborn fingers over the delicate edge of the cigarette case, he closed his eyes a bit and imagined himself free from Virgínia, pursed his lips with fake toughness and fake joy such was the sincere power that he was experiencing—but to be free was to love again. Why would she demand less than he could give? he inquired being reborn and fleeing. And so uselessly mysterious. He'd happened to mention a man who worked in the pharmacy and she'd said: he's my friend. How do you know him? he'd asked surprised, maybe a bit jealous. She hadn't answered, making a reluctant movement with her head looking at a random spot on the floor with firmness and disgust. If he kept asking, she'd always answer: he's my friend. After a while he'd found out in passing that she'd met him right there in the pharmacy, where they'd chatted a little while she was waiting for a prescription. So you couldn't say they were friends: and why hide all that? she couldn't have a reason to disguise such a simple fact. Just because she always liked not to say things, he'd guessed with disapproval and surprise. When he'd met her he'd tried to set up an intelligent courtship, thinking at first that she was that type:

"One has the impression that one has known someone for quite some time upon seeing them for the first time, when one manages at a glance to perceive the harmony of their features with their soul"—that had been more or less what he'd said explaining to her the reason he'd felt attracted *to her person*. But something didn't let him carry on in that tone. And a few minutes later, at the first opportunity he'd transformed himself, trying another approach, asking smiling about some phrase:

"and you? how much do you know? ..." expecting the smiling, mischievous answer of someone who gets it. With a clumsy and quickly disguised start he watched her respond with mystery and seriousness, almost ridiculous, making him blush and not know which direction to impress upon his bothered eyes: "I myself don't know."

And when he'd decided that everything was impossible and resigned himself without the least pain, the situation much later figured itself out with ease, and this time more serious he watched her, simple, surrendering to him with little emotion. He himself still didn't know how everything had slid into that state. One day he'd run into her on the street, they'd walked together a little way without having much to say, the beginning of the mischief that they'd started off more than a year before seemed very much to have ended. The conversation had been spinning, spinning, they'd said goodbye without regret as if forever, with a certain unease. And two days after that meeting, they, who before hadn't seen each other for so long, ran into each other again with surprise as they were crossing the street, he was grabbing her arm avoiding a car, whisking her away pulling her by the elbow as if hoisted onto the sidewalk, she was looking like a scared chicken whose wing someone was trying to tear off, they were laughing a little at the coincidence and looking at each other attentively while laughing. He'd walked with her through the streets, they'd sat down in a garden. With a certain irony toward himself and with a daring lacking great pleasure he'd invited her back to his apartment, she'd accepted, came quickly, returned another day without his having invited her, the conversation was spinning on, spinning without much point. And afterward when he'd think about her his eyebrows would furrow, his eyes would drift amused, comfortable, and cheerful. The way she'd say while looking out the window: there's a smell of swimming in the sea, at first didn't make him lose patience. He'd try to correct her: swimming in the sea doesn't smell, if you really want to say sea smell instead of salt air, which would be correct. But she, though she didn't answer back, took on a silent and impenetrable expression. And now, for example, why wasn't she coming? He thought that actually he'd never come looking for her, that he could have gone to her building, asked the doorman; he shrugged with a curious gaze. He wanted to see her face again and since before he'd thought of Adriano, he saw a mixture of Adriano with others and in the background just a vacant fleeting face of Virgínia's, a plea whisked off by memory. Could it be that for me she's a "person"? How glum and untidy she was at Irene's dinner. With Vera, everything so brief, yet she wasn't even "she" inside him when he'd remember her. He'd think about Vera with a small internal signal, with something that pointed her out without wounding her with a word. And when he'd speak of her with someone he'd do so with difficulty and repugnance, pronouncing: Vera, with hardness, coldness. Virgínia was always Virgínia—he felt as if they'd robbed her, saw her then with clarity, her brown eyes, her delicate nose, that indecision in her face as if she might be frightened; almost with emotion as if he were staring at an old portrait. He felt sympathy for Virgínia, that feeling that was making him a bit ashamed of himself, that same sympathy that made his sister say to him: you're so good, Vicente! When she'd come today with big open eyes, smiling without power, he'd have to get up very quickly and—not stretch out his arms, of course—but say: darling, you took forever! which was true. Yes, yes, it was true. He was already seeing her looking right at him pleased. Pleased? would she be pleased? or surprised ... or what? Virgínia ... she'd laugh. No. Right now he was wanting her to come in also to see her reacting, living. He paced a little excited: why didn't she just come? That was when an instant of astonishment and raw solitude attacked him, ah, he squeezed his flank bending over, the feeling of amazed tang when biting into an unripe fruit—ah, that side, for an instant life was losing its careful everyday meaning, his singed face was spinning showing a fresh, new, terribly incomprehensible surface—he clenched with one of his hands and with his whole life his right side where the pain had developed into a moving arrow; he tolerated it with closed eyes, his pale mouth shut: that's where death would come from one day: his grandmother had died from the same side, his father had died from the same side, he'd die from the same, something shrinking into an unknown liver. Gradually the pang faded. He slackened his lips, cracked his eyes; took off his glasses, his whole physiognomy transformed without them, he acquired an innocent and silly look like a child's; blinking he wiped his wet forehead with a handkerchief, gave a sigh of relief that recalled a gasp; in that instant father, mother, siblings, and women were lost, he was looking around his naked body at the nascent world. A few moments more and a calm and inexplicable power would overtake him again; he was lighting another cigarette, his replaced glasses giving him with the familiar sensation the old train of thought. He vaguely noted it, thought: what would I be without them. But why wasn't she coming—the longer she took the harder it would be because he would have lost the urge. The reborn impatience tired his heart—once again that sharp certainty that today was the anniversary of something difficult and heavy. He was astonished that he'd agreed to spend the day so alone … When he was small he'd answer: I am too lazy to be alone. So if she wasn't coming yet also demanding … yet also expecting him to say … Oh yes, he drove her off quickly. That was it. No, no, not quite that either … He smiled inexplicable, lighting another cigarette.

Later then she came in the white party dress … the hat with the wide brim atop her long face … she was halting for an instant with pleasure trying watchfully to arise in a vision … for what? as if commemorating the day … Vera popped up in his memory dressed in white. Something bristled inside his body. And when he looked at Virgínia's pale cheeks, her as if childlike lips, that calm manner, he felt that it would be absurd to say anything in a different tone. Despite everything, wanting to try he said out of sympathy:

"That sure took a long time, Virgínia!"

She replied in a delicate tone, almost flowery:

"You know how those buses are."

Smiling. For what? then as if that were more than he could stand, almost the most understandable moment of the day, he sketched a gesture of loss and despair that at first vague immediately became conscious and excessive. And since she was looking at him with open eyes, he thought: but my God! really it was more than he could stand after that day and he could almost say it was setting off a kind of sob, not tears, by God, helping himself with the memory of his dead mother to whom he still felt so bound by a certain forgotten yearning, of the women he'd slept with gathered in a single exclamation, of that day when by working he'd kept busy and let himself stay alone, of the now renewed pleasure of waiting for the future, of his feeling for Virgínia, desperate, enraged, childish the way a man cries, Virgínia noticed. And right after the observation, suddenly stunned, she concluded: he was crying! Unable to come closer, unable to speak, she was looking at him. But what was happening? since everything was so good between them until now ... they liked each other so much and suddenly ... She was looking at him. He didn't know where to turn, his face still disconcerted in the middle of the room, astonished with himself; if he were to interrupt the expression of pain he'd have to transform his physiognomy then and there while Virgínia would observe him silently; if he kept looking bitter he'd be in the middle of the room as if crying, as if naked; why hadn't he leaned beforehand on a window or sat down hiding his face? but the strongest sensation of that moment was relief: if any woman besides Virgínia saw him in the middle of the room ... for Virgínia, he was guessing, it was natural to cry and maybe that's why, with rage at himself and at her, he'd given in to the easy opportunity. A certain peace came rising from some place in his body, maybe from his side; it was a peace with an onset of a good mood, of a light joy, he was feeling like laughing a little and joking about his own stupidity but didn't know how to tack the laughter onto the previous movement and kept his contrite face on. Virgínia could speak:

"Vicente, what's this all about?"

He detested her for a new, quick, and sparkling second; he saw all the defects of that pale face where the different eyes would always seem indecisive. But once again the warm and dark wave was rising through his chest and since Virgínia was moving a bit closer he clasped her hands and since she gave in, he pulled her close to him, made them both sit down. That still meant: darling, you took so long!, even without reaching out his arms. But there was something light and comical in that scene—he thought of it as if already telling it to someone, to Adriano, and getting from him the vivifying vacancy of his smile; but wondered whether that type of scene wouldn't be depressing for himself. Right then, with furrowed eyebrows, he'd give quite a lot for an instant of true tragedy because that way he'd rid himself of the weight of that day. Clasping Virgínia's hands, he realized that for some time he'd been feeling two pieces of cold and rigid flesh between his own hands and looking at her quickly saw a bright face, frigid, luminous and tense, with frozen lips. So he'd scared her that much? so everything really had been that serious? the discovery was worth a proud smile, interested. He immediately felt a more protective inclination than the "he finally exploded" one. But she, with a slight touch—a gesture of holding him back—in a subtle and sudden display of will, showed him that she was still wanting him to stay as he was. And he, surprised to be led exactly by Virgínia, thinking about somehow telling it to Adriano, Adriano who just then was seeming to him to be his hidden power and the only ardent connection in his life, surrendered, kept the same tone in his face, desperate, abandoned. At the same time he wasn't pretending, on the contrary; something in him was still aching in expectation and his body was burning in a nice desire for nobility, for exaltation, yes, for exalted nobility.

"Why were you crying?" asked Virgínia and since just then she was moved she wasn't trying to put it politely, she was vulgar and ferocious. The silence of the living room floated for a long while without alighting upon them.

"I don't know," he said.

"Yes, yes."

He disguised a look of profound surprise.

"Yes ... my little darling."

He looked at her taken aback ... Adriano would smile—but why did he see him smiling with sadness, which was impossible in Adriano? he looked at her taken aback ... and there was nothing for it, the ache on his right side was lightly reborn, from that point he would start to leave, the room was brightening with the sea breeze, the salt air filling his lungs like a fisherman's, the walls like erect mummies, unmoving image: he fell to his knees at Virgínia's feet and mindful of the deep ache in his side and which nevertheless was hesitating to define itself, leaned his head on her legs, on her calm and warm thighs and was silently breathing and receiving back his breath mixed with Virgínia's smell, with the smell of Virgínia's white silk—Vera. But what was she understanding? he was still wondering almost amused; it was as if she wanted to surpass him, he who had no idea what was going on and was shrugging.

Kneeling beside her with his face buried in her body. She was looking straight ahead, dry, almost severe. Almost without understanding herself she turned her head a bit brusquely toward outside the window making the brim of the hat that she hadn't had time to take off vibrate. With her eyes hard and unmoving, her face was hiding from itself a slowly difficult expression that was taking shape with effort and attention, an expression of wildness and brightness struggling with that flesh used to waiting with patience, haughtiness and coldness for a moment that wouldn't arrive. And that now was bursting in her heart with such inevitability. The minutes were going by. She suddenly felt pain commingle with flesh, intolerable as if each cell were being stirred and shredded, divided in a mortal birth. Her mouth abruptly bitter and burning, she was horrified, tough and contrite as if in the face of spilled blood, a victory, a terror. So that was happiness. The wounded splendor was bumping in her chest, insufferable; a sack of light had burst in her poor heart. She never could have gone ahead; weak and terrified, she'd reached the limp and fecund point of her being itself. She was waiting. Then with difficulty she moved her sweet hands through the hair of the redeemed man, gave him everything through her trembling fingers, she who'd never managed to introduce the contact of her life into the clay figurines. She spoke the first word of her new experience:

"Vicente."

He raised his head, looked at her, was astonished, she existed above Adriano. And since she was strong in that moment, calm and full like a woman he surrendered as he'd already surrendered to the other women. She clasped the man's head with her hands; in a precious and fresh gesture she kissed his light eyelids. The pleasure in the man was luminous and intense; he raised his eyes wanting with a silence to give both of them the certainty that he was a man and she a woman. And flinched in an irresistible movement pressing his right eye with the palm of his hand.

"But you stuck your finger in my eye," he was saying lost from himself, drying the tears that were pouring out.

A joyful and deaf drum had been attacked in the middle of the room, an empty pavilion. Some thing had been concluded with sun and brightness! the drum was rolling in the middle of the room; and then never had a silence been so mute, calm, final in the hollow precinct. Vicente removed his hand from his eye, seemed to awaken for a slight instant; he saw her peaceful and erect beneath the tough hat, looked at her almost with curiosity; thought indistinctly: my God, if I were the world I'd regret having hurt a woman so much. Vera; could he have wounded her so much. But Virgínia strangely already seemed cured and simple, not having stopped more than the instant itself in that instant; she'd put down her hands, placed them on her lap, led them to the book atop the little table, rested them on her lap once more. Suddenly she brought them to her head and finally took off the hat, placed it on the table, smoothed her hair that was damp. She was remembering that she'd once had a classmate and that she'd simply loved her, as much as she could love Maria Clara. The girl—how could she ever remember her name? the girl had long golden hair and blue eyes, small, wicked. As long as Virgínia stayed inside her fear and shyness everything was light and delicate between them; afterward she started gaining confidence and one day amid the laughter of a game—everything was so loose, so natural, and so happy ... really, how could she ever have guessed ...? she'd grasped her friend's treasure, her long hair and a few shaking and frightened strands broke, stayed in her hands; the other had screamed in pain, turned to Virgínia who was still bearing the excessive smile of joy on her already alarmed lips, and to her guilty, closed, and dumbfounded hand in the air; had screamed: big brute! Yes, yes, it had been exactly that. And one day she'd grabbed the neighbor woman's daughter and held her in her arms until between them there was only intimacy; the whole child smelled like her own mouth, like the bedroom of a little girl sleeping. She wanted to hug her and the girl cried, the mother came with watchful eyes, the little girl said: she gave me a booboo, the mother had taken her daughter back saying that it was nothing. Yes, that had all happened.

"Are we going out?" said Vicente with tact.

He had stopped wrinkling his eyes, he was running his refined and masculine hand across his face as if needing to feel the hardness of his own features; he was disturbed; and on his cheek a certain smooth line was highlighted that was revealing so well that brand of attentive kindness of which he was capable. She stared at him as if awakening, as if she shouldn't forget him ever.

"No," she said.

No, she didn't want to go out, she didn't want to erase anything and was looking peacefully out the window. Just then she really was lovely—Vicente looked at her while lighting a cigarette, offering her one. She accepted; and then truly there had never been anything to erase and forget; the stretch of life was mixing with all of life and in a single current everything was moving along incomprehensible, essential, without fear and without courage. Carried by the imponderable power of the minutes that followed one another in time united to the instants that blood itself was beating. The afternoon was fine and calm. Virgínia was remembering that she was going on a journey, saying nothing and intensifying her contact with the existence around her. He himself went so far as to speak with great freedom and his mood was brightening, he was showing himself to be likable and cheerful. She was easily focusing and even told him how much she'd liked and understood what he'd said one day, maybe at the dinner at Irene's. He was astonished that she'd recalled the phrase, understood above all, and almost extended his hand to her not out of vanity but in a kind of apology mixed with a confused premonition that they could have lived better, that he could have lived better with Vera, could have been nicer to Irene. She was feeling so peaceful that she even said: Maria Clara was so pretty at that dinner of Irene's! But the simple way that he replied: she's one of the most attractive women I know—depressed her; she smiled yet had imperceptibly changed the level on which she was existing as if the living room had darkened in its brightness. She was constantly remembering the journey, remembering her grandmother, surprised to be thinking so much about her. Confusedly, because death was seeming to her an act of life, death in old age was a fresh extemporaneous fruit and a sudden revivification. For her practically only now was her grandmother starting to exist. She was seeing again her fixed and moist eyes, her eyelids blinking in a powerless indecency, that rumpled brown farm skin, so much greater than her hard, blind, childlike body. She imagined her cunning and funereal saying: while I existed I ate a lot. How old, heavy, and dead was that thin grandmother who was suddenly remembering to die. She shuddered lightly at that thought that had blossomed in her cruel and free, shrugged with disregard yet a vague anguish that was mingling also with that final afternoon with Vicente contracted her eyes in fright, made her heart squeeze in well-spaced and empty beats; she moved away from the thought in a run. She'd usually slip past the old woman at a run, giving her a quick kiss and going on. Sometimes she'd open her eyes really wide while looking at her grandmother as if truly to notice her and couldn't manage to see her as if it were a first time— her grandmother wasn't existing with the difference that her not existing was incomplete; just a face you'd kiss the way you kissed a paper package; and suddenly this woman was dying like someone who says: I lived. She was surprised to spend her last afternoon with Vicente thinking about the dead woman, but out of some dark and stubborn desire was still stuck to the horrible old lady—which in some strange way was meaning the farewell she was giving Vicente without his realizing it. No, she wasn't going to speak of the journey to the Farm. But in an attraction that was mysteriously giving her a taste of a forbidden, low, exciting thing she was trying to speak of her grandmother, yes, and not even say she'd died ... Her excitement was growing, she was telling details, recounting facts that were almost becoming revealing, almost, yes, but still secret— and the vileness, some irremediably nasty and clever thing was spreading through the clear and salty air of the room. Vicente was interested in her grandmother! He was joking: it must be nice to live in an old lady's shadow. But like a suddenly rung bell, echoing violent through a city, he added:

"MAYBE I'LL MEET HER SOME DAY?"

And suddenly all her mad desire to mistake life and subjugate it at the price of the wickedness she was inventing, all her desire that was making her just then in some avid way happy was cut with a slow and cold knife and the world fell into reality with a pale sigh. She felt the fatigue of her whole game. Why not be simple, nice, understanding, attentive, and natural? she was wondering full of reproach; anyway, with another sigh, she was thinking she was scared. He went to the refrigerator and brought meat, milk, pudding; she made coffee, they sat for a little dinner. She'd never felt so good with Vicente. Even when he'd embraced her she'd understood that he was blinking, ready to forgive in the future the misfortunes that would overcome him. Even if she hadn't been able to understand him, she'd greet him as a woman knows how to greet a man, as a mother. And while they were eating, the light on, she was despising all the happiness she'd had with Miguel. Vicente was speaking of someone so witty, so ... In a daring move she was saying to him: "it sure is easy to say funny things; you close your eyes and don't think ... and are stunned by what you say ..." He smiled:

"Well darling, then close your eyes whenever you want ..."

She laughed too, closed her eyelids courageous and simple, her heart fluttering; she wavered a bit:

"World ... great world, I don't know you but I've already heard and that bothers you ... bothers me like a rock in my shoe!"

He gave a frank and happy guffaw and while laughing was looking at her attentive, surprised:

"Keep going, baby ..."

She was gaining confidence like a dog grooming itself; she closed her radiant eyes, went on with her blushing and hot face:

"The body ... from back then died ... beneath the windows that ... were opening ... opening onto the pink, Vicente!"—she herself was laughing. Should she stop? she was wondering, because she'd end up saying something excessive, good morning, so-and-so, ruining even the past. But he was laughing extremely amused and she couldn't help it, so fascinating it was to feel herself loved. He was laughing without embarrassment, getting uglier, his face open—suddenly like brother and sister, like from the same family, like people who expect nothing from each other, my God. If she'd only known that to win him over she had to close her eyes and speak, if she'd only known. It was with a bit of sadness in eyes sparkling with laughter that she went on:

"Darling—darling, little green flower in the white guitar. Boy—boy, little green flower in the moonlight … in the moonlight … in the moonlight …"

"No," Vicente was saying excited and speaking seriously— "what you should do to get it right is not think, exactly not think …"—He smiled—"You're a little like the improvisers of serenades, you know?"—he was suddenly looking confused— "Adriano must like to know you have that gift."

"Why?" she asked less cheerful.

"Well, he thinks you're interesting. I think he really likes you," he was answering almost exchanging a look with her about the oddity of the fact.

Yes, it was like a night of glory. She laughed quietly, soft, her eyes full of overwhelmed and dreamy moisture. Staring at her, Vicente felt his heart surrender, a sweet, warm, and suffocating foam enveloped him, his eyes were tamed, smiling. She was looking—he'd never been so beautiful. With a kind and simple voice he said blowing lightly on her face:

"I love you, girl."

He'd hardly said it however, without transforming the power of his face and even trying to keep it in order to follow the new feeling with freedom, he realized imperceptibly that he didn't love her, that he'd loved her maybe precisely before saying: I love you. Enraged with himself, he wanted to take back what he'd said while observing Virgínia's face so frightened and translucent. Could that be the first time he'd said it? he wondered with surprise and reproach. He'd said too much, he'd said too much, he was thinking looking at her with fatigue and pity.

"Your hair's falling in your face," he said with a disguised rudeness. And that's how he was saying again that it wasn't love. But almost impatient he was feeling that it would be impossible now to rob her of the "I love you," and she was smiling with a joy that was making her unlikable, such a bore.

"Let's go out, take a stroll," he said annihilated.

With a frightened movement she grabbed his hand saying: no, no ..., because going out would make the day end. Without understanding her he looked straight at her, asked: why? Since she couldn't explain, she smiled at him with a droll, extremely friendly and attractive look, lost. He can't help laughing, she said with certain pride and surprise: what a woman ..., and leaning over to kiss her hair felt the dizzying and serious perfume of her body, some thing that couldn't be cheated, kissed her eyes that could hardly close so full were they of life; he leaned his face almost with sadness against that cheek fresh and bright like a gaze.

"Virgínia."

Then, when she felt that she should go in a little while, the fuse was blown, the sea wind was puffing through the dark rooms ... He lit candles while saying:

"You know, I have to translate this last page now because I broke off before you came: I was very tired. And I have to go out very early tomorrow."

She'd been idle wandering around the living room that was seeming to fly with the wind. She was taking a close look at things while furrowing false eyebrows, touching them with delicate hands, living intimately. She smoothed with her fingers the curtain, her body was giving itself over to a vague movement accompanying the sigh of the sea, raising her arm and suddenly she felt her own shape cut out of the air. She was aware that if Vicente caught sight of her he'd have the same quiver. She looked at him but he was distracted. Another minute in the same lightly alive position and he might notice her … She realized however that stiffness was gradually substituting the grace of the pose, her own sensation aged and in a pensive and painless gesture she drew back her body to its own proportions. She abandoned the living room, crossed the winged bedroom, reached the glazed doors and looked at the street below. The sea couldn't be seen except in a flash like a dark and profound movement—she trembled. It was raining, the street was shining black and sweet, the cars were running. An inspiration pierced her so sharp and sudden that she closed her eyes shaken, captured. Stumbling over the undefined furniture, breathing in that reserved darkness, she reached the door of the living room where he was working, his myopic eyes seeking the letters in the fickle twilight.

"Vicente," she said smiling, anguished. "Let me sleep here."

He lifted his head surprised and soon through the flame of the candle a smile was flickering.

"You want to?"

"Very much," she asked laughing, her hoarse voice heavy with loveliness.

It had been such a happy night, the rooms were fluttering with the fragile flames of the candles. They had drunk a cup of milk and also a glass of clear and gentle wine. Then she'd changed clothes looking with intimate passion at the nightgown she'd leave with Vicente, while hearing him close the doors and walk in the kitchen, in the bathroom. Her face, after she'd taken off the dress, was reflected shining and blushing in the surprising light of the candle; her shoulders were being covered in red and dark shadows. Vicente was closing the front door checking the locks once more; there were thieves in the area, they'd come in even through front doors. The world was feeling big to her, throbbing and dark, so full of fear and expectant joy! while the parlor window was knocking dryly in the wind and Vicente was rushing to close it. Then they lay down together, serene; Vicente was pinching with his fingers the lit wick of the candle. Rain was breaking out again and the distant trams were singing on the tracks vanishing in distance and silence. He stroked her a little with attentiveness, said in a quiet, almost severe voice, which fit well in the dark room: "Sleep, baby."

She realized seconds later that he'd fallen asleep. A silence of fire extinguishing itself in ashes. She still kept her eyes open. For a moment she missed the cricket. Having a cricket lodging in your bedroom wasn't having a pet, it didn't mean much but you'd always remember; it was an insoluble memory, hard and shining like the cricket itself singing—she'd miss it when she went back to the Farm. And because she'd thought about the journey she reached out her hand in the dark for a caress and with a start, her eyes suddenly flung into the air, she found his belly cold, limp, and throbbing like a toad's. Vicente. She waited a bit, tense, sharp; then gave herself over to an almost joyful resignation. He was breathing peacefully. Indistinctly snoring. She smiled while sinking her head into the pillow with secret mischief and new courage for the coming days. One day ..., she was thinking pursing her lips in an incomprehensible threat directed at Vicente, one day ... He kept breathing loudly almost snoring, unconscious. And she in a movement of retreat and self-reproach ended up avoiding her own future, with a sigh. She could no longer disguise the broad well-being that was sinking her into her own body, thoughtful, her whole being bent toward one same, difficult and delicate sensation. She was blinking her eyes in the darkness with pleasure. And a new hope. But not for the future, more like a hope for living that very instant. Then, amidst the vast space of the world in which her body was wavering content, she remembered her father, of whom she'd once been ashamed not wanting to be seen in his company in front of her classmates. She remembered her mother, sometimes sweet like a grazing animal and from whom she'd separated forever at birth with a glance, a reproach, and an unforgivable watchfulness. She remembered the center of her own heart that seemed made of fear, vanity, ambition, and cowardice—that had been her past life. She felt isolated amidst her sin; and from her extreme humility, her eyes moist, suddenly with ardor she'd be better just to please God. But from her own awareness of her evil was also coming a dark and lively pleasure, a deaf and innocent sensation of having won, of having with inevitability and depravity lived heroically. She was on guard, lost in a half dream where reality was arising deformed and smooth, without thoughts, in visions. Sometimes she'd sink further into a sensation and that was sleeping. Then she'd be startled, an instant on the level of the room hearing Vicente breathe in a warm and wound-up sleep. She'd get closer to him, nestle her body against that tepid and serene spring from which a very pleasant smell of tired skin was coming. Again she'd get lost in sweet and extraordinary mists, pursuing an intimate pleasure that wouldn't be defined. She halted brusquely upon hearing him speak.

"...because I didn't turn off the light ... but I ... that my pain ... my pain ..."—his voice was thick and slow.

"What, baby?" Virgínia asked with her heart trembling in fear. She was feeling like she was talking to someone who didn't exist and her own voice had frightened her sounding hoarse and curt in the darkness. Above all something was a lie. What, Vicente? she forced herself to ask again and remained attentive; the silence was thick as if the question had fallen into the sea itself, she felt that no reply would come. Though she didn't expect it, the air between them was however barely a pause and only slowly melted into silence and disappeared with effort into the night. He had squeezed his right side and said: my pain. Could he be sick? she shivered with a certain repugnance and pride; even with Daniel she'd experienced disgust for illness, feeling alone and cold beside someone suffering. The rain was falling softly. He was calm and whispering, she finally gave herself over to the pillows with a sigh. It seemed horrible to her to ask a question and not receive an answer; the person would connect to some invisible thing that would cling to the voice; she sighed again. She was trying to reconstruct the little life whose threads he had broken with his voice. She turned her head toward Vicente. How to blame them both? everything was so hard, there were so many forms of offenses between people who loved each other and so many forms of not understanding each other; nothing essential had been reached with their love; she was breathing slowly, sweating sweetly, her hand resting on her chest where a heart was beating that was made of surprise, fatigue, and wine. Slowly she started seeing herself awake as if she'd drunk fresh water. It seemed strange to her to be watching the darkness; she remembered with certain fear her own apartment in that night abandoned to the dark, the suitcases open to the wind—a vague fervor was lifting her for an instant above herself and powerless letting her impalpably fall into her own destiny. She remembered the afternoon with Vicente; the happiness was so violent, shaking her so; those horrible instants had taken her outside herself, unfamiliar, odd and broken off from her interior; so you could perish of happiness, she'd felt so abandoned; another minute of joy and she'd have been tossed out of her world because of her daring desires, full of an intolerable hope. No, she wasn't desiring happiness, she was weak when faced with herself, weak, drunk, tired; she quickly found out that exaltation wore her out, that she preferred to be hidden in herself without ever trembling, without ever rising; for the first time she realized how she really seemed inferior to several people she knew, that brought a sensation of indisposition and searching to her mouth, a certain anxiety without pain as if she'd imperceptibly dislocated herself from her own figure; in a vague suicide she sighed slowly, changed the position of her legs, gathered herself while turning herself off; her unfolding was like something that moved in every direction; her chest was squeezing shapeless, slowly Vicente's breathing was giving her a rhythm and she slid toward a peaceful fatigue. In the silence of the first drowsiness a tone of inquiry was rising and with numb eyes she was feeling a movement inside herself, milky, vague, almost restless as an absurd reply. She told herself almost like "no" and thereby was replying to "something" that agreed and was satisfied cringing and she not only was learning what it would be but also admitting peacefully with some ardor that that's how it was, this was the only kind of experience she had, this was her only life without sin. In the stillness of the room the wood of the floorboards cracked. Things were starting to live by themselves. She fell asleep.

She opened her heavy eyelids an instant—the brightest

breeze was starting off the dawn, weak and luminous sounds were spreading afar while the room was still keeping a nocturnal, warm silence—she closed her eyelids.

Then she opened her eyes in a start—great clouds of brightness were approaching, after the night of rain a hard and aroused cold was arriving, the air shining fresh, damp, and full of sounds ... Still unconscious she was getting frightened, the day frightening her—her eyes open ... Then the idea sliced her in a wail: begin the farewell, the farewell! it was tonight! the journey! She looked to the side: with an almost ridiculous and victorious surprise Vicente wasn't there, the tangled sheets, the dent in the pillow ... The nightgown slipping from her shoulder, sitting on the bed, and that cheerful breeze blowing her hair, making her skin shiver—she was coming to a halt breathless. Vicente wasn't there, she got up quickly, crossed the dry and cold floor with bare feet, the wide nightgown undone at the pleats that had been carefully invented in order to please. On the little table in the living room she saw Vicente's note; Virgínia: I had to leave early to turn in the assignment, sweetheart, we'll certainly talk tomorrow, I'm working all day today, be sure to come tomorrow, sweetheart did you sleep well? your Vicente, Vicente, Vicente. She dressed quickly with large mute eyes, stopping to say anguished, deeply surprised and rushed: arrh!, full of pain, combing her hair, leaving through the back door locking it, tossing the key onto the doorstep. She didn't wait for the elevator, went down the stairs quickly, found herself on the street. The light of day was invading her eyes, the morning smell of the sea, of gasoline, she was hunched over as she walked, almost running but her body was making her uncomfortable loaded down with the days she'd already lived—

she'd looked to the side and Vicente had left while she was sleeping—she was almost running with difficulty suddenly pressing her mouth with one of her hands. So, so wounded ... her chest dilated, burned, empty, the air was scratching her eyes and she was hurrying down the street protecting herself as if walking against wind and storm, her widened gaze; she was going on but stopped short with her hand on her breast, the hat! oh my hat! she'd forgotten it ... and that stabbed her with brutality ... she was opening her mouth aghast, squeezing her bust with her fingers: my hat. The feeling of the structure of her body like a fragile and electric limit containing nothing more than air, wild and tense air; only wounded, her body pushed a ways back pale and boundless—so that's how she'd return to the Farm! suddenly that was the truth, the only one after awaking and not finding Vicente! tricked, not finding Vicente, having overslept! and my hat?! ... She'd lost it forever. With her body heavy once again almost running, almost crying she took the taxi wondering if spending like that she'd have enough money for the journey, sinking in the smoothness of the car, speaking muffled and dark to the driver who was smiling kindly with a thin face, freshly shaven, skin taut and happy, ready to begin his day. He pressed the accelerator with his foot, a hot sound filled the vehicle, he pursed his lips with firmness thinking vaguely how he could make a good living making the car neigh in preparation for a fare, then earning money, keeping it safe in his pocket, opening the door to let the passenger out, putting back up the sign acquired at City Hall: Free. Yes, Free, Free, Free. He closed his lips furrowing eyebrows full of responsibility and severity while honking the horn, looking at the traffic light and thinking with a certain benevolence, feeling the car seat already warm and familiar in a promise of a full day, of a nice interruption for a nice lunch, of lots of fares through which places?: this first passenger was friendly.

She'd take the night train that would leave around six in the afternoon. And this day that was preparing her departure, she went through it with calm eyes, dry and surprised, flung into the empty time that was the unknown future. What would come? what if Vicente showed up? the journey, waking up at dawn already in the train ... and maybe never again to smell the quiet odor of the morning awakening with dust in the city: how violated she'd be. Each gesture she attempted to express that luminous opening that was squeezing itself in her chest, each gesture in that direction was wearing itself out without involving for so much as an instant the true meaning of her pain. It was pain that dry thing suddenly tearing her apart. Wearing only that short slip, her fat arms naked, she was standing with a nightgown in her hands before stowing it in the suitcase, almost saying to herself: but I am crazy against myself, against reality! because all she'd have to do is want to and she'd be convinced that the reality of the journey was something else, of the train, of having a snack on the train, of seeing her house again, and not the mad one. But some fantastic feeling was blowing her toward a slow and supernatural atmosphere, almost impersonal and with terrified eyes she was forced to see and transform. No, don't think, let yourself roll along with the events. But she was remembering Vicente and leaning forward, her hand squeezing her body, her eyes closed, full of nausea and emotion, in unexpected and well-spaced cries like the pains that announce birth. Then a relief and a cold sweat were running through her with tiredness, she was opening her eyes, pale. She was stowing the night-gown, fluffing it in the suitcase with the tips of her fingers, the most futile thing she could do to interrupt that voracity of her heart for tragedy. So she was going away! It was only that. Today she'd be on the train and ... She couldn't complete her thoughts, she was loath to trace them out so definitely that they'd appear bright in their poverty; and then, once they were independent, she'd have the pain without the understanding and the tolerance that she'd give herself before realizing what she was really thinking. Farewell, my dear children, she was saying quietly in the untidy bedroom to provoke in herself at last the crisis of that state. She was dejected, old, her long face yellowed. She was sleepy too: if she slept she'd be saved, she thought with fear and ardor.

She lay down and right away the fatigue of the poorly slept night weighed upon her. Ah, how horribly happy she was to be exhausted. A vague lament took shape in her entrails and she told herself feeling agitated and painfully contrite: it's fatigue, nothing more. She fell asleep falling falling falling through the darkness. She halted: the metallic city. The metallic city. The Metallic City. Everything was sparkling excessively clean and inside her was the fear of being unable to reach the same great sparkle and of extinguishing herself humble and dirty. The women were blonde and with a movement of the head would get new hairdos; fine, straight, and silky, almost fleeting and irritating hair flowing like rivers from their round heads. Someone could reach the city's highest dome, see the metals shining below and shout: I want to die, I want to die—she interrupted herself: it was the first time she'd wanted to die since she'd been alive. And some thing was also saying: my

God, with infinite tenderness, almost with shame, almost with mischief: my little God. At that point the pillow was a heap in which you'd sink your head and find warmth, warmth of feathers smelling of your own body that was inhaling the perfume; a warm and persistent power was slowly sucking the person toward the center of the bed and of sleep, and you were falling, falling, no use to try to free yourself from the dream and head toward the whitish and sickly sunlight that was existing atop the eyelids like a wobbly weight. Escape the dream, escape the dream. But the director of the city, with eyeglasses and a smile, how painful it was to stand before her, she was coming and forcing her to eat eggs cracked in frying pans hot with lard, to eat them one after the other, dozens, Vicente, dozens, feeling her stomach crying with disgust. Then the "I want to die" was coming again—it was the first time since she'd been alive—but now so strong and serious that she was thinking that up till then it had just been a rehearsal. With a sigh she was finding a job as a washerwoman of the tubs of the blonde women of the city of the director—how quick and whirling it was. They were great smooth bathtubs and the women were so beautiful, their thighs so big that she was ending up being one of them. They were seeking eggs in vain; how rare they were, how rare they were! When they'd find them they'd eat them raw and naked, thin as silk, entering the bath. Then the thing she feared most—brown, shining, and agonizing—was growing slowly, growing growing growing until simply somebody was forced to laugh to belie the tragedy; it was increasing until being too much for the ears and for the eyes and for the taste in the mouth and to annihilate any idea of grandeur you could have, the oceans invading and covering the earth; then at last diminished. But how much? tell me how much? enough, enough! she was arguing with her hand outstretched—tapering in such a way that one thread was penetrating the other as the thread pierces the needle and the sensitive fabric. You could understand that one more little effort and it would be possible to wake up. With an extra-human thrust she lifted her body from the shifting mud with the panting power of her own desire alone and was violently flung into the void of the yellow day that was buzzing; the smell of the room erected by the heat revived her consciousness and she realized with a light sigh that she'd awoken—a light hand was surfacing upon the water and the dream was growing clouded. In a powerful migraine her stomach was writhing, her head pulsing. With the slip hitched up she sat almost unconscious upon the bed and as in the first surges of sleep gave herself over for a long time. She'd sometimes open her eyes still wider, lightly peek out, then cringe horrified. She finally awoke. A clock was striking closed in a faraway apartment, shadow and dust. She half-stood. From the awakened and newly anxious fatigue, like that of agitated matter, a tenuous urging was seeming to exude, disoriented at first, then sharp, almost shouting with the contained power of blooms—she stood. But am I mad? but no, she kept repeating radiant and weak, but no …, she kept repeating unawares, what does it matter what's to come … it was so simple … a shudder of life ran through her fast, intolerable, she almost vomited. In a bewildered impression she was feeling that there was no wretchedness too great for her body … yes, that she could stand anything, no, not out of courage but because vaguely, vaguely, because the initial thrust had already been given and she'd been born; she was thinking the very sensation of inevitability that after all was her final certainty of being alive, the impossibility of in the deepest part of her flesh admitting that in that same instant she could be killed. Yes, and afterward she kept seeming to have reached her own limits, there where joy, innocence, and death commingled, there where in a blind transubstantiation sensations were tumbling into the same pitch ... and since she'd reached her own limit, she sat again, quiet and white and lightly glanced at the things without waiting, without memory; she smoothed the strap of her slip, one of her big pale breasts, suddenly reduced to the beginning. From the construction sites the voices were coming. She'd reached a rare instant of solitude in which even the body's most truthful existence was seeming to waver. She didn't know which would be the next instant—as for the first time life was faltering thinking about itself, reaching a certain point and awaiting its own order; destiny had worn itself out and what she was still seeking was the primary sensation of living—the theme interrupted and the rhythm throbbing dry. The moments were resounding free from her existence and her being detached from the time atop which it was gliding. She pressed her hand to her chest—actually what she was feeling was just a difficult taste, a hard and persistent sensation like that of insoluble tears too quickly swallowed. From the construction sites voices were coming. She seemed to reflect an instant and set to listening.

"The little girl answered: go on, that's right!"

"But did she?"

"Well then, man! ..."

The ending was rounded out with a mean, low guffaw penetrated by another brighter laugh mixed with a deep long one;

in a higher tone a young man laughed so calm and virile that she perked up her ears and before he finished they all started back up together dissonant and violent. They stopped and the scraping of the shovel on the ground could be heard, followed by resounding thumps upon hollow wood. She quickly sighed, lowered her head looking at the dusty floor. The idea came to her fatigued that things were awaiting continuation, that she should move and set them in motion. The train, the suitcases, Vicente. And since she was quite removed from herself and from her own power, she tried, without even knowing the nature of her urge, to connect herself to a more sensitive and more possible pain, the kind that might set off a solution; she got up confusedly thinking that she was going to separate from everything and cried fakely. But there was no sadness, there was fatigue and indifference while she was looking at the dark floorboards with resignation. After this she could at last live as far as the suitcases and the train were concerned, as far as her daily destination and the future days that seemed to need her to exist. Behind everything, almost undetected, there was horrible like a yellow and desperate light the danger of herself, the fear of repeating yet again that sensation she'd just had, a foreboding of beginning in which she was suspecting the approach of death, dizzying and calm. She lived a rude day and without light. In a single burst she arrived at the time of departure; the sun was still illuminating the city full of trams and people.

With her two suitcases already placed in the baggage car, she was watching other people's farewells. The brown hat was trimmed with blue matching the dress beneath the gray mantle. She was especially dreading the moment when the train would give the first start, the first whistle and the first pain.

She entered the narrow toilet that was stinking, took off the small hat, started to wash her face pointlessly, to put on her make-up, to comb her hair, arranging her clothes, fooling the instant. She was applying lipstick when the train got moving, jostled her arm, left a violent mark of lipstick on her pale and glum face, farewell! Her heart squeezed breathing only on the surface, her face darkened and dead. The worst had passed. She went amidst bumps, sat brusquely among those strange people. She was looking around the train, dust in her eyes, her lips dried out from water and soap. A blondish child was crying in the lap of a young, fat lady. The final cutting brightness of the windowpane was shuddering amidst deaf noises; her heart was hardening small and blackened. She got up to have coffee smoothing her already wrinkled skirt; her chest was contracting rough like an eye reddened and dry from dust. A hoarse and frightened retching was pushing her with jerking movements in the train toward the back of the car while she was forcing her body forward trying to reach the buffet car — the whistle rang out sudden and long, the locomotive shook even faster, no, my God, no, she was saying to herself in a whole and stubborn despair looking coldly ahead and reaching with difficulty the stages of the train that was running; while near her heart it was as if she'd swallowed a black and immobile object. A skinny child was crying in the restaurant in front of a glass of milk, always, always. When she'd come to the city, with her wide-awake body distanced from the back of the seat, her heart dizzy with curiosity and youth, a child was crying too; and an aroused smell of food, perfume, coal, and cigarettes lending her eyes a mysterious and hushed respite; her serious and sensitive face beneath the long ribbons of that hat excessively childish for the advanced girl she was, a few fine wrinkles. But now it was as if she'd swallowed some resistant spark, her eyes burning. She was remembering the journey to the city—on that day a momentum was coming from the hot coal breath and damp grass and from that continuous noise that seemed to push her toward adventure, toward adventure, adventure; beneath the old hat ribbons she was swallowing the dust happily and observing the aroused fatigue of the travelers bouncing benevolent, the women's bright large eyes; it seemed like a picnic. The noise of the wheels was then preventing conversation and the passengers were looking at one another isolated by the atmosphere gray with noises; and it was good as in a home, she herself sitting with Daniel who was reading newspapers hiding his heart. It was good as in a home. People were eating sandwiches without getting too close to the backs of the seats, as she herself was doing, and chewing busily assessing the distance. And now ... Now came the coffee, a little bread with butter and she was alone. She wasn't feeling unhappy. Especially she was feeling a haughty and cold sensation that nobody could take from her everything she'd lived; she was paying a certain intimate and dark attention to whatever was happening and that later, perhaps impossible to remember, would nonetheless be part of her history. She looked out the window: an isolated bar amidst the scraggly bush, built of brick and whitewash, was foreshadowing a village; it was just two doors, a dog lying down chasing away flies and everything passed swiftly, the settlement itself in shadows, in quick strokes, long, unfinished. The train was moving along the clearing in the dark bush, wet from the last rain; the smell of sugary water, the tracks were shining sinuously, disappearing beneath the train. She started to think about how in reality she could have not left; and the idea that she'd be at that very moment in the city waiting for the next day in order to see Vicente awoke a new muffled scream in her heart. She'd never had a more precise and strange notion of two places existing at the same time, of one same hour unfolding all over the world, and that instantaneous feeling brought her closer than ever before to everything she didn't know. How I know how to make things up all the way to the end—she was leading herself through an unwitting stubbornness to a point where in fact she was reaching whatever she'd wanted and yet couldn't stand the thing she herself had created. It would be so much easier to be better for herself; people took care to have company during every moment of life, even Daniel; and she, mysteriously detached, had managed to end up alone. She was remembering how shortly before going to live in the city with Daniel she'd agreed to spend a month on a ranch far from the Farm, even when she'd feel boredom and wariness because of what was about to happen; remembering how she couldn't eat dinner on that ranch of old ladies and offended servants, her chest seized in tears, her body burning in silence; and how she hadn't been able to sleep, lying in the strange low bed, hearing big rats passing by; and how she wouldn't have been surprised then if the door had opened and a being had come in and branded her with sweet purple fingers, without anyone to save her, far from her lax-limbed family but who would circle around her and prevent fatal things from approaching; how had she been able to forget that month of fear and meditation? only now had the memory returned. And then, her eyes staring at the darkness through the window of the train, she remembered how she hadn't gone to the Farm with Daniel when he'd been engaged and how nevertheless it would have been easy not to end up alone; then she'd lived with the cousins ... and yes, before she found an apartment she'd stayed at the boardinghouse. With a sigh she finally approached the memory of the boarding-house. It was a religious holiday; when she'd come in for dinner for the first time—the little tables covered with red checkered tablecloths, a little jar of wilting roses, nobody was looking at her, she'd already acquired a distinct and calm demeanor— once again she couldn't eat anything, her throat constricted by a disturbed and nervous solitude. Her hands were trembling and she was looking at them astounded. Then she'd gone up to the bedroom with its grimy partition screen; put on her nightgown and with a single movement discovered herself in the long mirror, her thick body appearing in a sad voluptuous-ness through the fine fabric—those horrible spinster night-gowns before Vicente. She was seeing her face red with tears, her hair arranged in a discreet bun of a woman who's alone; a misshapen and odd child who would arouse looks of curiosity. Ah yes, God didn't exist, that was becoming so clear, the cheer-ful fresh wind was saying so as it entered the bedroom, the red flowers in the jar were repeating it and everything was con-tented with secrecy and terror. Without knowing what to do with the long night she'd taken off the nightgown, got dressed once again. She didn't dare think foreseeing that thought would isolate her even more. A light on in the neighborhood was giving a slight dimness to her bedroom; the screen was seeming to shift and breathe. The flowers were trembling in the narrow jar. The little table covered with a dusty tablecloth was hovering extraordinarily still as if not making contact with the floor. She had half-leaned on the covered bed, lain on the pillow and was staring at the air of the warm night; buzzing was filling the stifled summer silence. Suddenly, in the heart of the old house a vein burst in splinters and blood, in congested joy—she sat up with a start in the bed, suppressed a scream of horror. A little band was playing in the hall below. The saxophone was piercing the meager instruments dislocating them. Motionless, clasping her blouse to her chest, she was hearing as if in a dream the hoarse and disjointed foxtrot. Someone turned on a light in the house across the way and her room lightly struck opened into vacant brightness. The music halted, moist, short claps followed one after the next in broken lines, broke off. That day with its sanctified date, businesses closed, finding men in pajamas in the hallways and in the coed bathrooms of the boardinghouse; now they were getting a band ... Tomorrow! leave tomorrow and find somebody once and for all! she was promising herself. And that idea—how powerful she sometimes was—and that idea which she knew was a lie was calming her down, making her able to wait with a more uniform heart, consoled like a child, feeling around carefully so as not to get hurt. How necessary it was to be delicate with herself—she'd learn this ever more, with each moment she was fulfilling; to live as if she had heart problems—feeling her way around, giving herself nice good news, saying yes, yes, you're right. Because there was an instant in the permission one gave oneself that could reach a dry and tense awe, a thing whose purpose one simply couldn't quite say. A state in which having power would be death itself perhaps, and the only solution would be in the quick surrender of being, quick, eyes closed, without resistance. She'd spend her days in the room. While the husbands were working, the wives would wander through the boardinghouse in light and flowery bathrobes, getting together in the living room to chat, one would paint another's nails, giving one another new hairdos and lending one another lipstick, sewing clothes, looking at magazines, like the monkeys in the zoo. Just one couple hardly ever turned up. He had low eyebrows over shifty eyes, a tiny face and wide ears like a bat's. She was small, with little neck, a slightly protruding chest, docile, odd, and ugly. The two seemed connected through secret things, as through a sexual crime; but he'd protect her and she felt protected. She also remembered how she'd thanked almost ardently one of them who had lent her a magazine and how then she'd backed off with coldness thinking that she'd been ridiculous; she'd gone to her room and sat wondering whether she'd thanked her too little or humiliated herself too much; and then she'd tried to punish herself by not reading the magazine right away, thereby seeking perfection? yes, my God, but yes, that was what she'd sought, her big, rough child's body, that was what she'd sought with seriousness: the perfection of herself. A child's wide and mysterious life—that was what she'd always seemed to experience with big cold eyes. She also remembered how in the silence of the new apartment whatever it was she didn't lack would so often arrive every month and how in that way life would follow life inside her body, impassible, following a rhythm that she would watch proud and restless, cautious. She remembered how she'd sit after dinner at the table, sweetly watchful, her heart pierced by fear and by waiting; a light wind would run across the surface of her body, chilling the air, the new curtain snapping blindly. A presence with frightened white lips was languishing in the air, the silence was inhaled in a dizziness, she'd lower her brow, a sound was coming from afar in the street, born of movements and words: yes, yes …, her breath was panting weakly, her eyelids blinking. Yes, yes …, in a surprised fatigue some thing was not being carried out, sliding like the wind and disappearing forever; a cold apprehension was making her shudder; the long and tense silence was uselessly sharpening her senses … She'd spend her days understanding herself. She finally remembered how one afternoon, scratching the tablecloth with her nail, she thought she heard someone knocking on the door. She got up and opened it onto the empty hallway. Finding no one had frightened her so that she'd cringed, closed the door quickly without noise and pressed herself to the wall feeling her heart beat dizzy and brusque, that feeling of error that never would explain itself, an inevitability chiming in the clock with courtesy and precision. The solution was in the quick surrender of her being, yes, yes, with eyes closed, without resistance. That really was existence. So that was existence—she'd always need to repeat it to herself and thus could live with a certain absorbed happiness, amazed. How to seek the joy in the center of things? no matter that on some remote and nearly invented occasion she'd found and lived in that very center. Now she was possessing the responsibility of an adult and unknown body. But the future would come, would come, would come.

Her berth was above a blind lady's. A smiling and scrutinizing face that would seem extraordinarily lively, intelligent. She offered her help with lukewarmness without managing to suffer with the woman. The blind woman responded with a firm voice, clear and polite:

"If I need anything I'll call."

She went up with effort, closed the curtains and in the narrowness of the compartment lay down. The rolling of the train was vibrating in her brain and lulling it to sleep; she closed her eyes deeply.

Maybe she opened them with slowness much later, but they unclosed as if in the same instant ... It was dark night, the train was fleeing. The curtain over the window was moving sluggish and soft to a mild wind. And she thought or saw a shadow that was that of an extraordinary woman, slim and peaceful, mobile and lively as the air itself, looking at her like someone bending over in silence. Virgínia really opened the eyes she'd closed so long ago and in a fright rose slightly on the narrow and shadowy berth that the curtain was veiling. The train was running without obstacles through the calm and perfumed night. How much time had elapsed around the rueful woman? she smiled without knowing why, her head pensive; she was having a foreboding with a serene and absorbed pleasure of how new, naive, and undecipherable existing was, how she herself could one day be figured out by a stranger on a railway without saying a word. She closed the windows, the curtain, lay her heavy and pale head upon the pillow that was shaking along with the whole sleeping car. She lost consciousness and only every once in a while would feel the weak and nauseating light that was on without really shining above her head, within reach. She'd turn over and forget once again. Then she opened her eyes and without understanding herself sat staring, heard the snoring of a man near her body, behind the curtain rough with dust, in the contiguous compartment. Now the whole car was wheezing darkly, the lights had been turned off, the rolling of the train was intimate, fantastic. A compact darkness was pressing on her open eyes. She removed the curtain that was covering the outside window of the berth and a bluish moonlight sliced her body with surprise … The train was running violently through the night and the meadows were stretching wan, bloodless … behind in the past, never managing to reach the moment in which she was living. Her eyes were passing in a run over a tree and the tree was motionless, without a breeze to threaten its leaves. Yet it was cold. The green of the silent cornfields was stretching out purplish blue and shimmering in the mysteriously bright landscape; but the depths of the vision were hiding, black and reserved, an arm hiding eyes with the secret. She could make out a telegraph pole in the distance and the train was nearing it in the same rhythm of watchful puffing; when her window was reaching it and both were the present, the post was flung back all at once with violence and the train was moving off forgetting it brusquely. She sought a feeling in herself and was just bright, sleeplessly bright. She didn't try to sleep, the decision calmed her face—with her head on the raised pillow she was watching the plains go by one after the next, hearing the train's alert whistle lift itself toward the sky; the odd spark would whirl by the window, a small painless scream, dragged along. Water would sometimes shine quietly out there and immediately disappear forever, until the end of her life. She was floating in the deep vacancies of sleep with her senses lax and lost. Rarely, like the silent scratching of a comet, she'd emerge quiet from the waves to the surface, lifted by a simple urge, by the same absence of power that would inspire an unclosing of eyelids. Slightly awake she was hovering far from the world, wavering atop her own dormancy, surrounded by the dark past moment and by the one that was already be-

ing drawn up; being awake was at that point of the same matter as sleeping, but purified in a single veil and she was seeing through it sleepwalking and meek. As long as the long
second lasted she was thinking and her lucidity was the raw
brightness of the moonlight itself; but she didn't know what
she was thinking; she was thinking as a line departs from one
point prolonging it, thinking like a bird that just flies, simple
pure direction; if she looked at the colorless void she couldn't
make anything out because there was nothing to make out,
but she would have looked and seen. In that way she'd have
another kind of sleep on days of confusion and martyrdom;
she'd then gather herself into sleep as if she'd been poked with
a lance and she shriveled up her existence leaving the waking life empty. Much of her past hadn't been carried out on
the surface of day but in the slow movements of dreaming,
though she could rarely remember them. She heard muffled
sounds of suitcases and footsteps, understood that she'd slept.
It was dawn, night was evaporating; a foggy light was hovering
in halos above the things. Through the lowered window she
could see that the sun had still not risen but was noticing the
freshness and the new life trembling delicately in every leaf.
She sat on the bed, raised the thick glass and a sudden cheerful cold surrounded her; she hadn't suspected that the night
had ended so completely. She combed her tangled hair, went
down to drink something. To her relief the blind woman had
disappeared. She drank coffee with dust, tried dark and greasy
sweets. A fat man was looking at her from inside eyes with his
chin parked on his chest. She was drinking the warm liquid;
maybe she was sad but had just then the firm feeling that she
couldn't live off her own sadness, off her joy, or even off whatever was going on; off what then? she was spinning around

worried and watchful as if seeking a position in order to live. It finally occurred to her for the first time that she'd see everyone from home, that she'd go back to her room. That Daniel would be at the Farm, his wife ... no, his wife was spending six months with her own parents ... Daniel tending to the stationer's with their father? Since later she'd find the landscape lovely she started to notice it in a slightly distracted perception. After her coffee she smoked and while she was smoking she tried to focus, understand her life in that instant. She was seeking while observing herself—but was seeing nothing but the ashen sky as always happened whenever she tried to think with profundity. She was apparently seeking the connection that must exist between the elfin thing she'd been until her teens and the woman of reasonable, solid, and cautious body that she was now. She was going to see again the place where she was from and feared, a little nervous, impatient, and shy, her own judgment. I had my chance in adolescence, she wasn't aware that she was thinking while blowing the smoke with the kind of prudence and awkwardness that she was deploying toward the cigarette. I lost my chance in childhood. Though her current body had a daily destiny. She remembered Vicente with a frightened yearning that was also surprise at the strange calm and joy of relief. She might not even return, she came to imagine. She observed at last that this had been her impression ever since she'd received the letter from her father. But she didn't want to think and pushed away the thought closing her eyes quickly, moving her head and expelling the smoke with decisiveness. She was a little hungry and that promised to erase something. When I get to eat ..., she was saying to herself in a vague threat, her lips dry, as if addressing a new day. It occurred to her in a first stirring joy that she'd see Daniel,

240

that he'd repeat "your type is becoming more and more material ..." and she'd blush at her lack of children. She felt pacified, expectant; even in a not very happy and comprehensible life the continuity of moments would result in some floating and nonetheless stable thing, which ended up meaning a balanced life. A little girl with a flannel tied around her neck, broken, brown teeth in a round face, serious and pale—was standing beside her. Looking at her. Virgínia gave her a quick smile. Her last experience with children had been tragic.

"You staying?" asked the girl.

Surprised, almost scared, Virgínia looked at her with more attention.

"You staying?" the other continued with patience and politeness.

"What ..."

"*You staying?*" demanded the girl screaming.

"I'm staying, yes, I'm staying," Virgínia hastened in alarm while looking at her with confusion. The girl was still standing, observing. The mother, sitting with her back turned, realizing that something was happening, turned around, looked quickly with her yellowish eyes, asked: were you chatting? Virgínia assented. "She doesn't have her words straight yet," said the woman in a strange tongue, smiling and turning back around. She seemed happy to see the child occupied. The girl was watching them while waiting with docility.

"You staying?" she asked after a pause.

"I'm staying. And are you staying?"

She seemed to fall into a great astonishment at that question; she drew back frightened without taking her eyes off Virgínia. Suddenly she went up to her mother:

"Am I staying?"

"Yes, yes," said the woman with her back still turned, her expression impossible to guess.

She walked up to Virgínia, stopped a little ways off.

"I'm staying."

"Ah, yes, great, great."

"And you staying?"

"Staying where?"

Again the question terrified the child, she gazed in anguish, her face bright and round. Could she be an idiot? Her runny nose was shining damp in the sun, soft and short. Virgínia took advantage of her retreat to disappear. When she'd already arrived at the end of the car with horror she was reached by the girl.

"This is Conceição," she said showing a rag doll. She was holding up the little face with anxiety and politeness, her dirty nose seeming to wait as if she were blind. Virgínia pursed her lips, her eyes suddenly hard to hide: My God, what did that little animal want?

"Ah she's pretty, your Conceição is pretty," she told her almost in a sob.

"You staying?"

Maybe she'd come back for good but nobody knew it and around her the instants weren't connecting themselves to the future, just temporary and unattached—they were saying all the things to her and she was understanding. Her grandmother had died and her father was going up the stairs upright, the steps were creaking. Virgínia was putting off to the next day keeping the promise to find out if he was suffering and to help him. Her mother had dealt with a slight indisposition, her teeth were starting to look old and unwell. And as soon as she got out of bed everything could be ready for Virgínia to return. That period at Quiet Farm was so placid and unconquerable that she was allowing without surprise the possibility of going back without even walking through the fields a single time, without sitting for a moment peacefully beside the river.

She was looking. In vain she was seeking clues to her childhood, to the vague air of complicity and fear that she'd breathed. Now the mansion seemed to get more sun. The limestone chippings from the gnawed-at walls had lost their sad sweetness and were only showing a tired and happy old age. Her father, though still the same, had now inexplicably become a type, his own type. And her mother had transformed. Her skin had dried up, acquired a peevish tone; she was still well-preserved from her forehead to the beginning of her mouth, but after that old age was rushing in as if it had been hard to hold itself back. She'd wake up with a rested, swollen face, eat well, embroider, her chin double and firm, her head half-erect with satisfaction and dignity, making a perfect story of her life. The features of her face and body had become distinguished and domestic; a pale fatness was spun around her figure that now, so aged and rigid, would acquire for the first time a kind of beauty, a familiarity and a pleasantness, a certain air of fidelity and power like that of a big dog raised inside the home. She seemed to have discovered a new secret from which to live; she was interrupting herself for a second, running her tongue over her teeth:

"When I'd go to Upper Marsh …," she was saying …

Because for fifteen days her husband had driven her every day in the buggy to town until her new dentures were ready. It had even been necessary to sew in a hurry a blue linen dress with several rows of buttons. All she'd have to do was run her tongue across her teeth and the small, calm town would come back to her in a disturbance that would make her blink, her tongue forgotten on her upper teeth, her lip curled. It had become a habit to seek her teeth for a quick contact. And by now the caress would be unwittingly followed by an irresistible tic that no longer seemed to bring her the clear memory of Upper Marsh but just a certain rushed and anguished taste, a muttering of approval. Looking at her Virginia would feel clenched and disgusted wondering how that woman could still live; and how the form of love that her mother now felt was made of gluttony, of total surrender, gasping fatigue, and hope, by God, hope. Her own thoughts were frightening her, Virginia was stifling her body, turning her head to the side as if diverting it from herself. She was regarding them fixedly but kept making them out as at the moment of jumping from the train: faces slightly twisted and unfamiliar as if she were seeing them in a mirror. On the Farm now a simple truth was being breathed, almost wholesome and airy. In each bedroom would a different color light up as soon as the doors were closed? In the clean and bright lives into which no moist angel would ever slide, the miracle had dried into stalks of fragile grasses in the wind— where, where was whatever she had lived? Quiet Farm had lost any cloister-like characteristics. Only for an instant was she picking up in the air that old vibration, that shaky life of the things in the mansion that she'd known so well to hear when she was small. The Farm had risen to the surface in her absence and was shining in the sun; its inhabitants seemed resuscitated but, without awareness of their own death, were going along calmly upon the flat ground. What had happened? she was feeling there each thing free of her presence and her touch—in a revolt life was refusing to repeat itself and to be subjugated. Now the house was useful enough for her big and timid body—she was observing with slight bitterness in a smile that wanted to mean lived experience but that was just sad and pensive. Even in the park of Upper Marsh—she stopped short clasping the shawl she'd started wearing again—the fountain had stopped underneath the little statue of the naked boy and without the shine of the water the child god had vanished. A living child was playing in the dry fountain. The yellow dress. Two new hotels had set up in the center, some lads and girls crossed the streets with whips and riding clothes, observing.

Esmeralda's clothes had the same pleasant smell of freshness and salt. That's how she'd dress up, take care of herself and burn perfumes in her room—and her preparation was so active that time would pile up while she thought she was living minutes. She'd wear feminine clothes with voluptuousness; her breasts would hide like jewels among frills and pleats, her thick pale legs sprouting from long skirts. She'd look with surprise at Virgínia's nude dresses, smooth silks, and short hair.

"You didn't learn much in the city, Virgínia," she'd tell her.

With age she seemed to have rushed into her true body and Virgínia could imagine how men might want her. Vicente, yes, Vicente would turn around to look at her with attention, unaware that his face was suddenly becoming masculine and hard …—she'd come across that expression in him so many times on the street. So why hadn't Esmeralda married anyway?

she was shrugging with indifference. The round face on top was coming together in a deliciously feminine point, almost repugnant to another woman, so attractive it was and so destined for men alone. And she had still other marks. A tiny mouth, arched and hard, almost in her chin like an unused toy, a pale always lively mouth, slightly protruding eyes, black. Some thing about her inspired the desire to walk all over her and abuse her even without rage. Around her eyes fine wrinkles, skin of a fearful color despite being matured and almost cooked. And that power pulsating with a haughtiness of a unique woman. Daniel did almost nothing, letting their father take care of the store. Sunburned, he went hunting, swimming in the river, had earned strong and shining muscles, living with ferocity and calm off his own body. She would look at him from afar; how to get closer? With sloth and fatigue she'd say little useless things to him, they'd barely run into each other. He didn't seem to miss Rute, nobody ever mentioned her, actually. Yet in four months she'd return to spend six months with Daniel. Virgínia managed a few moments with her brother; they went to the balcony, leaned against it silent, distant.

"Daniel," she said.

She wanted to talk about Vicente.

"Hmm?" he asked.

He'd never known how to ask or to listen, that was true. She was thinking: we have nothing in common, nothing. And in a calm apathy she was looking at the transparent air. It was almost the end of the afternoon.

"You've been well?" she asked him at last.

He looked at her quickly and answered nothing. She filled up with a difficult and cold feeling, saw his white suit so starched and narrow at the shoulders, his hair nice and straight, kept at him just to be obnoxious:

"You've been well?"

"All you managed to do was get fat but you're still the same Virgínia: so vulgar and clueless that I feel sorry for you. Screw you, kid."

They stood pensive for a moment. He finally said:

"I'm going."

She stayed bent over the balcony; she saw him leave, shrugged. He was walking hard and clean. Walking, walking, one footstep following the next in the silence of the road stepping on damp, thick leaves. He went into the side trails; unhurried he went on, went on. The mansion had been lost, he was walking. He took a shortcut, crossed the new road, went into the first streets of Upper Marsh. On the narrow lane covered in grass a few hens were scratching in the twilight. He walked on stepping on the dry stone. The dark sloped street opened onto a luminous, colorless, and cold slice of the river; all the garbage of Upper Marsh was piled up black upon its bank; he put his hands in his pockets, wrinkled his eyes as if affronted by the evidence of things. He was now in a square with high walls, calm and full of clear air like the courtyard of a convent. At that hour the windows were closing, the odd open one revealed on the parapet an uncollected cushion. Upper Marsh seemed constructed of pale stone, wrought iron and damp wood. The houses were stooping old and blackened as after a fire, weeds were growing in tufts on the sloping roofs—he went on, smoothed his black hair, fine and combed went into the business district; from the shops that were still open was coming a suffocating smell of a gloomy place where old cockroaches, ashen and sluggish, are walking, a barn smell. From the telegraph wires dirty rags and papers were hanging. He saw the church. With a quick movement he took his hands out of his pockets; entered the shadowy humidity stepping with careful and peaceful feet on the brick slabs. A lit candle was burning on the altar of St. Louis, thin and delicate. He read: Do Not Put Paper on the Floor and then left, hands in his pockets; the air was still bright; he walked on. Suddenly he saw: there were five people approaching. He stopped short, pressed against the wall. The woman was dry, her neckline excessively wide, a shoulder peeping through a rip; she was wearing blue slippers and her hair was disheveled in an enormous design around her dark, thin face. She was clasping the hand of a little kid who was shuffling along with a piece of bread in her closed fist, whimpering. In front of the mother a girl of about twelve was coming, tall and serious inside a large black dress, the face of a widow. A skinny, lively girl was skipping all around her mother, grabbing a stone, gnawing at a piece of bread wiping with her forearm her broad runny nose. And behind them all a boy of about nine, cap pressed halfway down his forehead, a bag threaded through his arm at shoulder height. Five people, he said in a low voice. The group stopped in front of the row of identical houses. The little girl stopped crying, licked the butter from her fingers. The boy approached, took off his cap with fatigue. He, the girl in black, and the mother were looking at the houses with faces creased by the remains of the foggy brightness. The mother, holding the hand of the little girl who had sat on the ground, was hesitating. The houses painted pink. She pointed her eyes to a terrace, examining. A fat white woman was knitting while swaying. The boy with the cap and the girl in black were looking at the mother waiting. She ran her eyes over the houses one more time, over the swaying woman. Then she pulled the little kid by the arm and said low, her voice coarse:

"Not here."

But why not? wondered Daniel disturbed, almost enraged. The girl in black started walking again. The mother dragged the little girl who was rubbing her sleepy eyes. The boy adjusted the bag on his shoulders, put the cap back on, straightening it. The skinny, lively girl was skipping along in a run and waiting to gnaw on the roll or lingering beside some gate. The group got smaller and smaller and disappeared. He'd seen, he'd seen. He sighed deeply as if waking up and his eyes really had the blind luminosity of eyes that returned from sleep. A weak lamp started blinking in the colorless and sharp air of dusk. Before he averted his gaze he heard a noise at the top of the street. He turned around and saw nothing at first because another group was approaching against the light. Gradually he started making things out and with a muffled exclamation recognized two soldiers leading a prisoner, pushing him, halting every once in a while to beat him up. The group was getting closer, he stitched himself to the wall. A feeling of nausea filled his mouth with a saliva redolent of blood. The prisoner kept going between the two soldiers with his red eyes blinking, his mouth open, his face marked by the hands of the policemen. Daniel shrank back: they were passing right beside him, the prisoner let out a groan and one of the soldiers pushed him with a punch in his back. Daniel closed his eyes deeply, gritted his teeth with pallor. A delicious amazement was overtaking him giving him loathing and strength, an extraordinary feeling of closeness. It occurred to him to knock down the soldiers and free the man—but with motionless eyes he was feeling more capable of knocking down the man and injuring him with his feet, with his feet. He suddenly smiled caressing his upper lip as if smoothing an imaginary mustache. The prisoner and the soldiers plunged into a corner … With a start he observed the street empty once again and holding back a curse he headed almost at a run in the direction where he'd seen the woman and the four children disappear. He went ahead sticking close to the walls … he turned a corner, yes, there they were moving off at the end of the street … He was hurrying, his footsteps were booming, and the fear of not getting to them made him shout calling them. The woman turned around, hesitated for an instant in the deserted street, the group stopped. Daniel was getting closer, getting to them fast with wheezy breath, shining eyes. Now he was seeing the woman up close, making out her dark and dirty skin, those worried, tired eyes. Frightened he stuck his hand in his pocket, took out a coin … He extended it to the woman with harshness. Without unclosing her lips she looked at him in shock, was about to touch the handout but with a sudden suspicion drew back, answered him:

"No, thank you."

A movement of wrath and surprise overtook him. The two looked at each other silent; he was roughly brutalizing her with his raw gaze. A second later Daniel finally said almost with courtesy because he knew he'd dominated her:

"Take it."

The woman hesitated. All at once she extended her hand, took the coin, threw him a gruff and difficult look without murmuring a word. He saw her go off, looking at her with decisiveness and pleasure, with penetrating strength and deep internal laughter—flinging a scream of triumph flapping his wings over the victim. Night was gradually falling. On the narrow, closed door the sign was almost sparkling: Sete & Snabb—Forwarding Agents. A skinny girl appeared on a corner and like a flash disappeared into the black interior of a house. He stared indecisively at the deserted street. Rute, Rute, he murmured in a dry sob. The shadows of closed warehouses were crossing the pale ground, stretching along the road, reaching the other sidewalk. He was hesitating. And then kept walking setting out in the twilight like a vampire.

It wasn't just from Daniel that she was finding herself distanced. In her absence the little daily facts that she knew nothing about went erecting themselves into a barrier and she was feeling excluded from the family's mystery. In between the conversations the instants of silence kept filling with reserve and vague disapproval. They were seeming to blame her for not staying gone, for having lived with them her childhood and youth. As if defending themselves from an accusation that in reality she wouldn't know how to make.

"What good things happened?" she'd ask smiling fakely.

It was so hard to tell what had happened during the separation ... everything escaping words.

"Well, everything went along just the same as always," they'd finally say annoyed.

They were feeling stuck to one another and their eyes would shine irritated when they'd then speak. Really what had happened: they'd experienced a certain day-to-day calm pleasure in having lunch and dinner together, meeting in the hallways running into one another, communicating through small odd words. They went on living together as if in order to be to-gether still at the moment of death—together, if one of them died, all would be less afraid to die. The friction in every min-ute, the breathing of the same air would give rise to whatever in them was fastest and they'd exchange brief words. Conver-sation would shed light on objects, questions of household management and the stationer's. Habit would allow them to swap impressions with a quick glance, with a half-smile that would never penetrate the depths of the day. Maybe each of them knew that they could only free themselves through soli-tude, creating their own intimate and renovated thoughts; yet that individual salvation would be everyone's perdition. As now they were avoiding a more awakened sensation because they couldn't transmit it. And to keep possessing that scared security, which they didn't realize they didn't need, they would come together sullen, unaware.

Virgínia was trying to speak with Esmeralda; she wanted to tell her what Vicente—a boy—had said to her. Since it was hard to repeat a compliment and since she'd been ashamed in the face of her sister's keen, hard gaze, she added hurriedly with displeasure: well, I'm just repeating what was said ... Esmeralda agreed quickly, impatient and curious: of course, you're just be-ing sincere ... Despite her heightened awareness of her own movements, Virgínia agreed with a humble gesture of modesty that immediately squeezed her astonished heart with the cold fingers of irony. Later it wasn't possible to keep talking because, while her words were stumbling forward, she was still rigidly bad to herself, still attached to the ridiculousness of that inti-mate and servile movement. As if it were Esmeralda's fault, she avoided her for the rest of the day with repugnance and unease.

At night she was awakened by strange noises coming from the kitchen. She got up, went down the stairs. Esmeralda was boiling water, with a hot-water bottle in her hand.

"Mama?" asked Virgínia buttoning her robe.

"No."

"So you're the one feeling something?"

Esmeralda didn't answer right away, she puckered her mouth in a repressed cringe of irritation as if Virgínia were forcing her to respond.

"It's nothing, a trifling pain," she said grudgingly, dry.

Virgínia was looking at her with coldness. She wanted to ask again but was reluctant. Esmeralda had always liked to seem pushed around by others. She was already leaving when she saw her sister, almost in a cry for help, twist her head, purse her lips averting her eyes—and thereby giving Virgínia the chance to see how she was suffering.

"But what's going on?" Virgínia inquired.

Esmeralda opened her eyes, stared at her with sullen rage: "To hell with it, it's nothing."

Thus Virgínia felt she'd entered the family. She sighed.

"Well if you're practically crying …," she said.

"What do you want? for me to laugh? Fine life I've got, don't you think? it really does make you want to laugh"—with a hard smile she added—"Or do you want me to go listen to little idiot Vicentes? Fine life I've got …"

Virgínia blushed surprised, hesitated an instant.

"But who has a better life?" she said with unease, slightly vexed and suddenly sleepy.

"The bishop. Leave me alone, damn you."

"And damn you too. You spend all your time eating yourself

alive, you think I don't know? that I'm blind? torturing poor Mama, other people, accusing, gnawing at yourself like a maggot ... So you leave me alone too. I never had anything to do with your life. Nor you with mine."

"Poor Mama ... So you feel sorry for her?"

They exchanged a wordless glance, without translatable meaning. Of cold curiosity, of imminent hatred, of mutual support and pleasure.

"So much so that I sacrificed myself, this is my reward," said Esmeralda.

"You sacrificed yourself because it's your nature to sacrifice yourself, just like it's mine and Daniel's not to suffer. I never suffered because I didn't want to. Because you want an excuse for your fear, that's why ..."

"And if it was how would that be my fault?" gushed Esmeralda's voice violent and muffled.

"Please don't scream and wake everybody up," said Virgínia.

She left the kitchen: the clock in the little dark hallway was striking two. Yes, how would it be her fault? A slow and meditative feeling was seeming to overtake her for all time. How had she not foreseen everything that was creeping around the mansion? how could she have left the city? The weak light in the kitchen was still on; and Daniel still hadn't returned. She was slowly climbing the stairs grasping the hem of her robe, stepping barefoot on the sleeping and silent velvet. At the top of the staircase she stopped and looked at the darkness of the room below. She waited an instant. Then she remembered: she used to cross the shadowy corridor feeling the carpet on her bare feet, her neck rigid with fear ... with each step, the hand could grab her clothes, her hair; when she'd see from the top of the staircase the sultry brightness of the living room she'd fling herself uncontrollably down the black steps, her eyes scratched and dry; in the faltering and secluded light of the oil lamp she'd breathe softly, her heart beating wide, hollow, livid; she'd touch objects with light hands, seeking deeply their intimacy; Mother was sewing, Father was reading, Esmeralda sweeter back then was looking out the window at the half-brightness of the courtyard, Daniel was scratching in a notebook; the un-oppressed living room; nobody was looking at her and that was the protection they could give; unnoticed, she was walking slowly among them, inhaling again the familiar and strange fluid, feeling that she was safe from the empty, black, and whispering countryside, from the hallway closed with darkness; behind the window the violet fireflies were lighting up and leaving no traces.

In an inexplicable desire she now wanted to go back down the staircase. She stretched out her hand in the dark and in contact with the cold banister almost took leave of whatever was natural in her decision; she hesitated for an instant as if awakened by the freezing marble; finally beneath her hot hand the banister was seeming to come to life, she gathered with her other hand the skirt of her long dress; as she was going down the steps, she was unconsciously straightening her ample bosom in a majestic, slow posture, feeling inexpressibly like another person, someone indefinable yet extremely familiar like an old desire that no longer needs words in order to be renewed. A diffuse and vivid memory. She stopped for an instant. Then she clutched her robe, walked to her room.

The next day first thing in the morning she opened with seriousness and leisure the photo album. There were relatives with hats all the way down to their foreheads, deep dark eyes, affected poses, so difficult. And again ridiculousness would touch her, make her fall into a confused and sweet feeling that had perhaps always been the strongest one of her life. You couldn't be ashamed to like family—that was the inexplicable sensation. She felt she was touching portraits of the dead and yet she was seeing her mother as a girl, her father with tense whiskers and a man's face, her aunts still alive even now; her heart closed in an anxious and sad yearning. My loves, she was thinking with damp eyes, aware of the fakeness of the expression, deepening it still more with pleasure. A real love, painful and broad, was escaping her chest and she was smiling moved and benevolent with the power of her own feelings. Anyway life, she thought in a cheerful and shy burst, in a sigh. Now she was gazing without focus at the pictures where her mother in old, elegant clothes was revealing the dark rings under her eyes—she was feeling mixed and hopeful, her heart so bristling and tender as if the season had changed, as if suddenly she had begun to love for the first time a man.

When she sat for lunch with everyone, she who still hadn't grown unused to eating alone, carefully with Vicente or with courteous strangers in restaurants—with a repressed shock saw, repeating the impression she'd had during the first lunch after her journey, the way they ate, chewing with open mouths, a look of undisguised pleasure; swallowing with gluttony, pushing away the empty plate with indifference and satiation. Esmeralda was leaning her arms halfway across the table; when something on their mother's plate appealed to her she'd charge ahead without a word with her fork; their mother would consent with a quick grumble. With a certain revulsion she felt sharply moved, unable to swallow the food, tears in her eyes—she was so weak and aged by her recent time in the city, it was so horrible to see the family gathered having lunch silently and voraciously. That same night even she gave in and at the dinner table everyone looked alike. She looked at them and was now feeling united with them, knowing how to love them—so strong was the spirit of the house. There were times when the room and the bodies leaning toward the plates, that silence that came from the fields, the atmosphere that no particular feeling could designate, was by her intensely understood—she'd stop short with her fork in the air, looking at them contrite and happy. She was experiencing a kind of resignation that was like a slow step forward, noting with a gentle surprise that she could marry, get pregnant, deal with the children, cheerfully fail, move around a house embroidering linen towels, repeat, yes, repeat her mother's own destiny.

And as if everyone understood that she'd finally come back, the dinners became calm and cheerful; they'd stay at the table talking, laughing, taking their leave late heading slowly to the bedrooms, faces still smiling and thoughtful. Only Daniel would leave earlier or even stop turning up at meals. The next day everyone would meet, laugh, live as if on shipboard. They'd ask her what she'd seen in the city; she and Esmeralda would chat crossing words that didn't contradict one another. Esmeralda would lean her big breasts on the table and smile shaking them with kindness and sparkle; Father would chew without looking at them and yet would listen. The food was more abundant than in the past, there was talk of closing the stationer's, of turning the Farm into a ranch for guests. Mother would listen while eating with pleasure, her eyes thinking about the idea; Daniel was cutting the meat with precision and indifference, Virgínia listening to their father in a silent distaste. All at once she'd looked at Esmeralda. Without realizing she was being observed, Esmeralda had broken off her meal, teeth closed, chin rudely pointed in a forced smile while her narrowed eyes were looking at no particular place, hard with hope, almost with revenge. Yes, guests, guests, guests—her full and excited bosom seemed to be saying. What can you tell us about the city? she was still asking. The two were still at table after everybody else had retired; they looked a bit alike, both were almost tall and large. What could she tell?—Virgínia was leaning her face on the back of another chair, remembering when she'd felt fever and nausea, the bedroom getting rough and her solitude growing with pain while she was leaning off the bed toward the ground looking vaguely at the scratches and dust on the floorboards, asking God to let her vomit at last. And if she spoke of love, what could she tell her? the sensation was that of having been abandoned while sleeping, she'd looked to the side, Vicente wasn't there and still now her heart would clench in fright, regret, and astonishment: she'd overslept. Yes, she could tell about a woman she'd seen one day; she described to Esmeralda her clothes, just that, how luxurious she was. But she could never forget that woman she'd met on a bus—a true lady, Esmeralda—almost the strongest thing in the city. How lovely she was—Esmeralda was listening with an embittered face, her youth lost—how lovely she was. But she didn't know how to say the rest. How to explain to her those lively and worried eyes, her keen mouth, her neck bent forward introducing a face that was horribly selfish and distracted from others. She'd come from the street—you could tell—was taking the bus home, lips hard with disappointment, but she didn't want help, nobody could help her, she was despising everyone else with alarm. She had clearly come from a place important to her life. The hat covered with little black and soft feathers was ridiculously elegant. In her large, slender ears, of a very washed brown color, were luxurious earrings surrounded by instantaneous rays of luster, and lending her whole face a harsh and menacing life. On her fingers the rich rings and the wedding band; she was sitting on the bus, shaking along with it, her hand firm on the back of the seat in front, her memory faraway, her face proud, serious, hard, and ardent but that would be brutally humble, violent, and disheveled for someone — for someone she was still looking for now. She was extending the hand with the wedding band and the rings thinking with her face that would know so well how to humiliate and that was in love; she was married and wounded, you could tell, you could tell. Esmeralda was listening, her eyes wandering while imagining, an acrid and intolerable envy drying out her lips. Virgínia was observing her, with surprise guessing to what extent both were made of something ingratiating, fearful, and low, how both in the end were sisters. With distaste and dismay she was changing the subject, telling her that her small apartment had its own staircase, that the general stairs also passed by her door, that all day long she'd hear the steps of people going up and down. She told her that one day, returning from somewhere at the hour when the city lights were going out ... — Esmeralda interrupted her:

"How?"

Virgínia didn't understand:

"How what?"

Esmeralda was saying almost upset and timid as if afraid to touch:

"What you said just now."

Virgínia took a while to understand and finally disguising her surprise repeated:

"The city lights go out ..."

"Yes, yes," said Esmeralda with coldness, "go on."

"You didn't go to theaters?" she was asking her still.

"Not one," Virgínia was saying.

She'd gone one night to a concert in the company of Vicente and Adriano; they'd had a light dinner at a small restaurant and she was feeling comfortable, simple, and cheerful. In the lobby of the theater she'd stopped short in the presence of the sultry furs, the noses silken with powder, a cold made of light, clean and frozen movements. The women were sparkling calmly amidst whispers. She herself was feeling grotesquely human with her blue woolen dress and her cream shoes, her hair parted at the side and loose. In a small pocket mirror she was furtively observing her serious face, long, pale and large— a failed nun with hard and martyred eyes. The stuffy concert hall was panting and the piano notes were stumbling solitary amidst the hand-held fans. She couldn't quite take pleasure in the music but was sheltering in the sound with a certain anguish, her white face leaning toward the distant stage, her body contained and still. While Adriano was losing himself in the depths of the loge, while Vicente was running his natural eyes over that superior world; of which nobody knew that she and Esmeralda could be raised to serve, with joy and curiosity.

"No, to almost none."

"What did you talk about with people?"

"Oh, I don't know … Of course I didn't talk to them the way I'm talking to you … You try to say pleasant things, show that you're well-educated, that you know how things are done, the customs of other lands … Show that you're not just anyone" — she was getting excited with moving eyes, the foam of saliva appearing in the corners of her mouth — "There in the city if you don't stand up for yourself you get left behind … You think with all those people I'd speak the way I'm speaking now? No! try not to make mistakes, to say things …"

Esmeralda was agreeing. Whereas she, with her eyes still steady, was remembering herself threatening with a finger: if I ask for a cigarette don't give it to me, okay? and then she'd ask, the person would decline, she'd ask, the person would decline, just like that, just like that — she glanced around slightly oppressed. Gradually however she reclaimed a smiling strength. Esmeralda was agreeing examining her with more interest.

"Did you date?"

"No," said Virgínia — the two women looked at each other firmly in the eyes.

"Did you take walks by the sea?"

She told her about the sea, really thinking about Vicente, about his apartment. She might have been cold to men but how sensitive she was to the sea. Waves would form on the surface of the water without altering the hushed, thick mass — and that would stir in her a serious urge, dangerous. The bigger waves would burst salty smells of foam into the air. After the water would strike the rocks and return in a rapid reflux, a desert resonance would linger in her ears, a silence made of small words scratched and short, made of sands.

"And did you go swimming?"

Vicente had often invited her but she'd been ashamed. Wavering, hesitating in her lack of direction, she seemed to fear the pleasure she would feel. The idea that the sea could surround her made her eyesight darken while in a deep sigh she'd show herself how much she'd like to feel it and Esmeralda stayed back thoughtful, hearing her silence without understanding. Finally she'd decline because she was afraid of the sea, afraid of drowning. And that's what she told Esmeralda and that was almost the only thing that she herself knew.

"No, I didn't. One is afraid."

"I know," said Esmeralda.

She was asking again and asking like someone fumbling around distressed, without ever finding the question she really wants to ask. Virgínia was understanding her without words while they were looking at each other sincerely deep and speaking of various things. She knew that Esmeralda would like to hear that one day she was sitting on a bus distracted and tired; suddenly the unmoving faces atop the bodies, the heat of the wheels, the dust shining dry as it met the sun, all of a sudden a movement of her own arm grazing the seat or her breast awoke in her the understanding of the lust that was vibrating in soft uninterrupted sounds in the air and connecting creatures with fragile and quavering threads. Over there the mouth of a woman was quavering, almost in a wail or almost laughing perhaps; and another woman's neck, smooth and thick, immobilized by repressed and closed movements; and that white man's hand leaning as if at last on the railing of the seat, full of rings that were imprisoning his broad old fingers … another instant and the moment would come together in a muffled scream, in fury, fury and mire. But gradually the bus had started moving again, everyone had penetrated with it a shadowy and silent street, the branches of the trees swaying serenely. Virgínia was vaguely aware that this was what Esmeralda was hoping to hear, aware that she should tell her what had happened on a certain bus; but she kept seeing without understanding the faces traveling and could only think and say: it was so hot! everyone was so tired, it was two in the afternoon—just that. And Esmeralda wouldn't understand.

"Are there a lot of no-good women over there?" Esmeralda was asking morosely drawing close to the question.

"Yes there are."

"Ah ..."

The two were holding back thoughtfully, waiting.

"How do they do it?" she asked Virgínia again.

"One day I was sitting in a café and one of them was drinking a soft drink while looking all around her. She was skinny, little, her eyes made-up, missing a tooth on one side. An enormous man was sitting at one of the nearby tables, laughed, asked in a low voice but I heard it clearly: what kind of drink is that? She said: orange and it's sour."

"Just that?" Esmeralda interrupted.

"Just that: orange and it's sour." They stopped for a moment looking at each other—"They kept looking at each other, then she said: you're fat! He laughed narrowing his eyes, said nothing, but then said: yes, yes ... They both then started laughing. I was scared they'd see me and left."

"Ah ..."—Esmeralda was observing her and adding in a smile in which there was some pleasure—"I would've stayed."

Virgínia shrugged tired and distracted. The boardinghouse where she'd lived was close to a street with some suspicious vacant houses. One Sunday afternoon a few women, two thin ones with dark rings under their eyes and two more or less fat ones, ruddy, with intense eyes—came to stroll down the good street, passing the boardinghouse where, on the sidewalk chairs, a few wives were choking: the thought of looking for man here! ... They weren't saying "looking for a man" or "looking for men," but "looking for man." But no, Virgínia was confusedly understanding, they weren't looking for man. Their hair was wet from the shower, in bright and calm dresses, and arm in arm they were coming toward the decent street to take a walk on other people's Sunday. If a man recognized them and spoke to them, they'd have to give in because they'd no longer allow their own desire, they might give in immediately, surprised and thoughtful, with melancholy and brutality, laughing and having fun. Virgínia was understanding them so well that she amazed herself, suddenly reserved and severe; she was avoiding Esmeralda's questions with irritation and reproach. Esmeralda was peering at her watchfully, her eyes focused. She was allowing slowly and with difficulty Virgínia's existence and couldn't quite accept that her sister really was another woman. She was leaning toward her, listening with a certain disdain and a bit of irony, despite her interest. As for Virgínia, for the first time she was experiencing a conversation between women. Even without love or understanding it was good to talk to Esmeralda. Between women you didn't have to talk about certain things, the main thing was already spoken as if before they were born and all that was left to tell were gentle, fresh intimate notions, little variations and coincidences. It was a familiar and silly conversation, somehow a lament, somehow a defense; a hope mixed with advice full of a long experience while eyes would dive into eyes with depth, rapt and almost distracted, heavy with distant thoughts; her voice was growing softer, slower and lower. Virgínia was ending up leaning on the chair with vacant eyes, in silence, while the other woman was propping her cheek on the hand that her elbow was supporting atop the table. Not among the women of Vicente's group; they seemed to be specialized in men; they'd feel superior and cheerful about having them as just friends, forming a heroic and vaguely perverted group, astonished at itself.

"Is there a lot of noise when you're trying to sleep?" asked Esmeralda. "And the cinemas? And that guy, that Vicente, where'd you meet him? what's he like?"

"Daniel took me one day and introduced me at a party ... He ... he ... he's just a normal person ... I don't know, there's nothing really special about him. He wears glasses." — She wouldn't be able to tell anyone and not even herself what he was like. Yet how well she knew him inside herself, engraved in the reactions of her own body. She was feeling him clearly, refreshing by an effort of desire and memory the slight aversion that her flesh would experience in his presence; like the quick and immediately fleeting perception of a perfume: a light tightening beneath her skin; less than repulsion, a deep certainty of the man inside her blood as if he were connected to her in an excessively intimate way, almost wretched. Through Esmeralda who knew nothing, she got a different and more intense liking for the city. And looking at that beautiful woman who'd never known a man she felt insultingly rich, straightening her body with pride, surprise, and disillusionment. She was remembering Vicente clearly just then ... seeing him walking as if inside of her. And her feeling was so real that she was discerning him walking through a shadowy and smooth atmosphere because her own interior must be shadowy and smooth—that had always been the air of her thoughts and dreams. But if deliberately she wanted to remember his face, surprised she'd see emerge before her eyes an outline of Adriano. And one night she had a dream with Adriano—a dream that filled her with surprises, shame, and mystery; she deeply forbade herself any joy and dreamed nothing more. With disdain she however could not refuse herself, confused: yes, certainly Adriano was a person, yes; the little man; after being with him she'd sometimes want to fill the vacant urge of power that would be born with a clear and lively exclamation: yes! even if no. She pushed him off with a wave of her head; yet he lived on holding himself in at her brink. She was forcing some memory that by blossoming would bring Vicente into her presence. What she'd most recall about him however was some thing you couldn't say or think; a certain condition that would arise between them as soon as she thought of him, establishing the connection … and that would solidify in the vision of Virgínia herself watching Vicente's serious taste for walking around the room knowing that she was present, in some thing that would fill the air of both of them, a watchful reserve of both—an atmosphere of slight difference of sexes like a muffled smell of face powder—while he with small gestures of his eyelids, teeth, lips, kept affirming his free discreet masculinity that, though it truly existed, had something fake and excessive about it—Virgínia and the walls were watching. She was remembering in a second how he'd change clothes in front of her. It was one of the inner events of their shared life. When he was going to change clothes, as if somebody pressed a button, life would fall into a familiar framework and they'd

carefully repeat their gestures in every detail: she'd freeze with
big eyes as in a classroom, her lips touching each other in innocent watchfulness of herself because she really was interested;
he'd seem to interrupt his thoughts while changing clothes, his
eyes focusing on a spot on the ceiling or the wall according to
whatever movements were imposed on him. In the moment of
transition between one article to the next, his body unwrapped
in the cool air of the bedroom, she would stare at him quickly
but without harshness, smile at him with her eyes while lightly
squeezing her mouth. Right as a new piece dressed him, the
event ended and the moments were carrying on scarring all
around him. The fact was so tenuous that she'd remember all of
him in a slight second, in a movement of the eyelids — the recollection would actually reduce itself to the throwing of a shirt on
the chair, while seeing that movement again she'd stay for an
instant in the air listening, her body living in its own insides as
in the velvety, shady, and fresh insides of a fruit. He'd been terribly well-disposed lately; in such clear health that it depressed
her; how naturalness would shock; she only felt good among
shy people and nothing bothered her as much as self-assurance.
Watching Esmeralda's life now it seemed to her so frightening
and wide to have a man as if he'd been born from her desire.
And sometimes even that desire would seem extraordinarily
wrong. To have a man who could die from one instant to the
next but who high, high, in a tension of balance, seemed to live
eternally. She was leaning on the column of the balcony, looking
at the full stars, so shining and without blinking, wrapped in a
vague sheet of fog, milky way! she was looking as if she and Vicente were seeing together. Without remembering that when
they were together she wanted almost outraged to be by herself

in order to look better. She was seeing the hard, calm stars, thoughtful before going to sleep—reflecting things so high that not even by living every life could she accomplish her thought: Vicente was a man; he was living far away. I feel you somewhere and I don't know where you are—she was managing to think in words. Her love was so delicate that she smiled uncomfortable, pierced by a frigid sensation of existing. It seemed to her extremely strange that in that same night he was living in that same world, that they weren't together and that she wasn't seeing what he was doing, so much stronger than the distance was her thought of love. Love was like that, separation couldn't be understood—she was concluding with docility. But she also didn't know whether she wanted to have at her side on that night that pale unshaven doctor, the only man from whom she'd felt the inexplicable, anguished, and voluptuous need to have a child; she felt her life press down with love for him, her heart was thinking with strength, with shyness and blood, come to me, come to me, for a long swift instant. How she'd passed through whatever could be without managing to touch it ... What she loved in him couldn't be accomplished like a star in the chest—she'd so often felt her own heart like a hard ball of air, like an untranslatable crystal. Above all what she loved in him, so pale and mischievous, had an impossible quality, pungent like a sharp ridiculous desire; she was feeling sweetly able to belong to both. And Vicente was perfect, he was a calm man. She thought with surprising clarity, using for herself nearly words: I love him as I love something that's good for us, that gives well-being but not like something outside of the body and that will never pacify it and that we want to reach even with disillusionment; my heart isn't inflamed by that love, my most intimate tenderness isn't worn out; her love was almost a conjugal dedication. It hurt her however to think that way, it was so tender, keen, and full of bristling life for him to exist inside her, to breathe, eat, sleep and not know that she could think that way of him. She was forcing herself severely to a fidelity whose secret species only she understood. My love, my love—she was saying and with a certain effort love was finally trembling so much in her interior that for the first time it was rising to an unreality and an unconquest, seeming not to exist melding with the most ravishing part of the dream. And to get still closer to Vicente she was reflecting that the doctor, along with Arlete and the guard at the zoo, was still out there waiting and that she, out of impatience and lack of time, hadn't absorbed him. She was also feeling unhappy, leaning on the balcony, on the lookout for the noise of a distant carriage—and suddenly, out of pure volatility, she was desiring something perfect, something like whatever would kill her. A certain ardor overtook her, Vicente, not even he knew how he could be almost perfect, not even he knew how hungry he was and would ask to go to a restaurant and hesitate between the dishes on offer and suddenly calling the waiter with a loose gesture to impress her and impress himself. And at the same time the world was existing around us without menace. Especially all those thoughts were also the lie. Leaning on the balcony, she was wanting some thing with more vehemence than she'd ever wanted—and she didn't have the nerve; it's just nerve, that's it. But it was also sweet to fail—she leaned forward, rested her face on the column, smiled because it was strange and exciting to smile by yourself in the darkness—deep down she was confusing the vanity of feeling new desires with the taste for possessing the things that they represented and was mixing with everything the faraway despair of ignorance. Yet it was perfect to live alongside that instant as if both were forming some thing that ought to be looked at by someone who was a stranger to the moment and to her—she was taking for a second the shape of the stranger and thinking it was perfect to live in that moment. She went to bed, it was a cozy cold. She'd still experience the best things in sleep. She liked more than anything when it was raining and she'd feel the warmth of the bed and the windowpane shining; she'd try not to fall asleep in order to live the wait for sleep while she was blinking with comfort, with sweet and panting mischief—it was so good, so much more sensual than moving, than breathing, even than breathing, than loving a man. She'd have so much hope for what she might dream. You didn't even have to think about it, going to sleep happened all by itself, smooth like smooth falling, like the body's insides living without awareness, without purpose.

"With a steady job a woman who has a brain manages to put off her husband, not live with him all the time, oh you can," their mother was saying as she came to embroider with the two of them.

"What do you mean 'put off'?" Virgínia was asking confused.

"Oh, honey, every woman knows that a man is a big bother."

Virgínia was mutely astonished.

"I don't think it's right to meddle much in my daughters' lives. Apparently only Daniel wanted to get married: the girl's very nice, a little quiet, but seems to be a good match for him, at least that's my impression, and you know, everybody makes mistakes. Even we should be happy with whatever happens. I actually think you two are right not to marry"—she was stopping the embroidery, looking ahead with squeezed eyelids.

"Basically things are inconvenient," she was saying with wisdom, blinking her eyes a bit and that, she was confusedly feeling, was the highest point she'd reached in her understanding of whatever was surrounding her.

Hearing her, Esmeralda's eyes were sparkling in her hardened face. Just now she ought to blame her mother. Virgínia asked her, in the half-intimacy that was floating between them:

"When I was small I heard hints about something that happened to you ... some boy, I'm not sure ... Papa mentioned it again when I did that foolishness of telling about your other affair in the garden."

Esmeralda was blushing, her face was being disturbed in a delicate smile.

"Just nonsense," she was trying to look unconcerned. "You know how 'he' is, from a bit of nonsense he makes a world and invokes God. I hadn't wanted it to be nonsense, I wanted it to be a serious sin and now at least I'd be free," she concluded with a muffled violence as if this were an old thought she'd decided to surrender out of fatigue.

"But you can start to be free now or whenever you like."

"I don't know," she said with her face tight and red.

"Why not?"

"Why?" she mimicked with rage. "You think it's simple for people to get rid of everything they have, end up without a home, without anything ... just to be free?"—she stopped for an instant, face suspended, understanding vaguely that she was blundering against herself ...—"Just to be free?" she repeated hearing with growing despair the sound of her voice. "Why speak of those things? the hell with you!" she screamed irate.—In a delicate slightly astonished pleasure she felt the hardness of the very heart of life, her reborn body breathing with a vibrant warmth, in legitimate rage; a sharp urge to movement rose up through her legs, spread hot and painful through her chest, found its balance in her face, held back and then freed itself through her suddenly shining and tender eyes. Her figure slightly extinguished in a shadow of uncertainty and melancholy. So, then she was living just off herself, off herself … off her own solitude … off her anger … so … No, what happened? she was getting mixed up.

Virgínia shrugged.

"Either it's worth it or it's not," she said without pleasure. But she was also feeling that she couldn't fight, even if her path forward could only be chosen by fighting. Something above fighting was making its way slowly and reaching a goal. She was feeling, they were just two women. She stayed quiet for an instant looking out the window at the bright and exasperated air of two o'clock. When she turned her head, Esmeralda was observing her. She looked at her too, thought about how the other woman was pretty and calm with her thoughtful, wide eyes, her whole body abandoned and pale, that tired strength.

"You didn't learn much in the city, Virgínia," Esmeralda said to her again.

"Yes …"

Again they fell silent without waiting, without fright. The living room was large and deep, the table was stretching out darkly with one of Mother's small embroideries in the center.

"I found everything so changed …," said Virgínia as if in a sigh.

Esmeralda looked around slowly. Virgínia got up, went to the window.

"I'm going upstairs," said Esmeralda and Virgínia didn't turn around.

Esmeralda pushed her bedroom door, inhaled distractedly its sultry perfume. In the shadowy room the snowy bedsheet was popping out fresh, embroidered, surprising. She sat with care and lightness on its edge looking around in the twilight. A long woolen shawl was wrapping her round shoulders and her bosom, making her look sensitive to the cold. She suddenly stood, walked to the window, opened it, the brightness entered. No, for her Quiet Farm hadn't changed. She could close her eyes and she'd see the hard violence of the naked trunks, the sweetness of the light clusters of acacia in the wind; so often she'd already sought with her gaze that same stopping-place cut out by the windowpanes, which she herself cleaned, she herself—like jabs of confession and redemption in her chest, she herself!—so often she'd made out the landscape broadened all the way to infinity when her gaze would free itself beyond the heavy curtains that she herself, she herself had embroidered. She bent forward for an instant as if to try on reality one more time—yes, after the garden the countryside was being disclosed. Grasping with one of her hands the thick cord of the curtain she was pulling herself together with haughtiness and with her back turned to the interior of the mansion she was watching over it on the lookout, coldly. In the distant kitchen the wild cat that she herself, she herself had tamed, was eating the ground beef while the black woman was talking to herself and washing the dishes. The rooms empty of guests; just a day ago she'd gone over them carefully, checked that everything was silent and in order. The hallway stretching out full of shadows, the deep staircase, the carpets extending to the bedrooms. She sighed. No, she was seeing everything as she'd seen it all these years. In the garden the figure of Virgínia was moving—Esmeralda bent over slightly, followed her with her gaze. It was a simple body, tall and well-fed, Virgínia's; she was leaning down picking up something off the ground and looking at it closely, her hair falling in her eyes, while even from afar you could feel that strange defect in her face, a watchful inconsistency, a bit cross-eyed. With interest Esmeralda was observing her, with a certain benevolence, which she had never been able to feel toward Daniel. But Virgínia had brought nothing from the city. She, Esmeralda, could live better and bigger than Daniel, Virgínia, their father or their mother, she, she was the one who possessed an exceptional and bitter strength, a concentration of life that had given her that inaccessible patience down through the years. She was really bigger than all of them and hadn't hurried toward life and toward the city because she'd been scared. Her fear was as proud as her strength. She set out almost quickly, froze. Outside Virgínia had sat on the rock in the garden looking at her light legs with determination. Esmeralda made a rough, firm movement with her hand and the cord of the curtain burst, fell with a small cheerful noise on the dark wooden floorboards. She looked at it a little, perplexed, hard, bad. Suddenly she sighed closing her eyes quickly; more calm she picked up the fringed cord, opened the sewing drawer and sat down to fix it.

She was holding herself back however within her final degree of strength. And that same night she got lost. She was looking at herself in the mirror; she was still quite pretty with her virgin wrinkles of hope. In her motionless face the yellowish color was sweet as on an almost-decomposing fruit; her movements were still lively at a tense height that only daily despair and menace could manage to create. Virgínia's arrival had introduced to the mansion a bit of the invisible life of the city; without feeling Esmeralda was shining with more asperity in her bedroom; waiting with new reserves. And as if she'd gone too far in this new gulp of danger she couldn't stop the urge of her own body and jumped over the abyss, grew old as if she'd already loved. That same night she'd dined with a troubled appetite and laughed agitated showing her white and pointy teeth, Virgínia had appreciated her, Daniel unexpectedly had also been friendly, Mother was leaning into the back of the chair with contentment, while she was explaining to them with a penetrating and ironic wit little unimportant facts. They were laughing benevolently, drinking small sips of an old wine that Father had brought from Upper Marsh. And though that was never what she could expect—no, by God!—she gained in life almost violently, lived hours of somber glory, heavy with promises. Her radiant eyes were shining moistly at her own body, so much at herself, her movements easy and rough—what was happening to her? she was giving in. They said good night, she went to sleep so tired that her body stumbled deadened onto the big smooth bed. She was asking slowly wondering almost for no reason: anyway why? for what? As if suffocating, her face feverish, she took off her clothes and for the first time lay down naked. She fell asleep with a childlike pleasure, awaking in quick and vague moments almost frightened, her heart beating without rhythm, her being swollen. She'd curl up then beneath the sheets in a cold that seemed to come from her own innards, beneath the furious clinking of an indecipherable memory. At the sound of the beings and things may God open her heart, allow her to see inside herself and, fear expelled, at last say to death, I lived. Ah, ah, she was groaning almost awake. The moonlight was whitening the lowered windowpane, cutting the room in deep shadow and blue brightness. Almost unconsciously she was running her fingers over the fine embroidery of the pillowcase that she herself, she herself, she herself had made. Ah, ah, she was groaning staring like a madwoman at the frozen and motionless air of the bedroom. She was falling asleep aching, sinking into the pleasure of sleeping with her mouth dry from sleep. She woke up later the next morning—suddenly an old and quiet woman. She was listening to herself while she dressed, wounding herself out of habit with the same words from the night before but without hurting. She'd slipped toward a dark calm made of solitude and the lack of martyrdom. She went down for breakfast. Her breasts were looking modest under the blouse that just yesterday had squeezed them with anguish. Her legs were peaceful in their stride, her heart had distended. Did I oversleep? she was wondering without understanding. She was trying in vain to open wider her eyes with their swollen and deadened eyelids. With horror she had already lived her life.

She sat benumbed for breakfast at the deserted table. Everyone had already left. She interrupted herself with difficulty—the gate was creaking, somebody was crossing the garden. Virgínia entered the room with a bright and shining face. She was carrying enormous dry branches for the hearth.

"I broke everything … I scratched myself, look!" she almost shouted in a laugh, wounding the other woman's fatigue.

"You're cheerful," said Esmeralda.

Yes, she was cheerful. She laughed while sighing: cheerfulness was lending an unfamiliar and awkward appearance to her long face. While she was depositing the branches in a corner of the room it seemed to her that that night she'd truly slept at the Farm. They'd laughed so much, Esmeralda, even Daniel had listened smiling, Mother chewing while blinking her eyes with love for Esmeralda. And then the wine ... she was drinking it and remembering Irene's dinner party—how happy she'd been then! she thought, dizzy. She'd said goodbye at the foot of the staircase but her desire was to go out and start walking until exhausting the power of the wine. She'd lain down sleepless, bright and light on the bed as if she'd never slept, as if she'd never sleep. Our family can be so happy! she was thinking. The world was spinning inside her chest gently and she couldn't say whether sweet joy or smooth sadness was now circulating in her blood with the wine. They'd laughed so much ... even Daniel had listened smiling ..., she was going over the scene one, two, multiple times. Even Daniel had smiled, even he had smiled. She was tossing and turning in the bed. Ah, how she'd already lived ..., she was burying her head in the pillow with an absurd feeling of happiness and disturbance, smiling without surprise. One more instant though and the sensation was vanishing, in its place an expectant darkness was lingering inside the pillow as if she were expecting to remember from one moment to the next some unusual and fleeting thing. She lifted her forehead, her big body leaning on her elbows, watchful like a dog that senses a stranger. Her tired head fell over again and she sat thinking for a long while about nothing. When she'd reopen her eyes she'd notice that she really had been thinking, thinking and rethinking with stubbornness, lightly and without noise, about this strange scene: a man walking and meeting another man, both stopping in the darkness, looking at each other peacefully and saying goodbye beside a white, tall wall; the men meeting, exchanging a glance, saying goodbye beside the white wall, the men meeting ... An underlying tone was emerging and with it she was accentuating little meanings without words, dotting herself with emphasis or doubt and that after all was her attitude and "her way of being." She was almost always feeling well. Water was running trembling in the interior of the house, vibrating in the air. Bit by bit distant and dry despair came from motionless well-being itself and from the void of the night without future, she was seeming to feel that she could never mix it with the following days, even with new insomnias. A useless clearing was opening, she was stopping in the middle of the journey without meaning to, perhaps forever. But the night was long like a life that falters. She fell asleep because some thing never would be reached with open eyes. She dreamed that she was lying in the field, her skin beneath the wind feeling a prolonged, high, rosy, deeply diffuse pleasure, a leisurely enjoyment in the powerless body as if she were living exactly the instant that was forming and fading away, that was forming ... fading, that was forming ... fading, breathing in and breathing out, marking time with the bright, full, and fresh beating of her heart. In the dream she possessed with abundance something that, when awake, would be an elongated and imponderable sensation, needing to vanquish so many impossibilities that it would only arise as a foreboding, in some forgetfulness, in a silence, almost the air all around her. What she'd dream so large at night, would be during the day just the flutter of an ant in the field. She was sleeping, her head sunken in the pillow; and from her pale-lipped abandon the face of a girl was emerging, the vacant and sharp features like the sound of a small bugle in the limpid distance.

At dawn she opened her eyes as if waking up were slowly taking shape inside her without her knowledge and then blossoming ripe, perfect, and incomprehensible. She saw around her the bedroom being born from the darkness in silence. A cold breeze was blowing. She pushed away the sheets with her legs, without impatience, in a movement so full and balanced that it was exhausting the limbs' reason for being. The chamber was floating in the half-light and the frozen shadows were deepening their edges, distancing the white walls veiling them in a confusion that was promising a foggy abyss beyond it. She walked barefoot to the window, lifted it, and a rested freshness touched all her body as if the short, thick nightshirt wasn't even there. Below, in the vacant and sleeping garden, each stalk was emerging from a halo of cold, whitish smoke. She was paying heed in the silence of the morning as if listening inside herself to the resurrection of a symbol.

"You went out early," murmured Esmeralda pulling over the coffeepot with a sigh.

"I didn't even have breakfast!" Virgínia was saying with a piercing and unpleasant voice.

"Keep your voice down, for the love of God!"—Esmeralda was furrowing her eyebrows and face as if she'd been scratched. She was gradually undoing her wrinkles, smoothed her face into a tired expression, reopened her eyes slowly.—"Well I no longer have the nerve to wander through those swamps," she said, rapt, pouring the coffee into Virgínia's cup.

And then everything had been easier. Daniel was lying on the ground and the tree above was the being closest by, dominating the sky. Virgínia had sat on a rock and with a dry branch was tormenting the ants. He sneezed and the sneeze cut the air in every direction into small arrows that gleamed under the sun and broke with a delicate noise. Virgínia sought with her eyes something she was feeling glowing uninterrupted all around, singing somewhere. It was a quavering thread of water from the tap flowing toward the earth. She turned around, tried to forget. But she knew that the glow was going on and the uncomfortable and vivid certainty was seeming to hurt her eyes. She got up to turn off the faucet. When she returned, Daniel's face was peaceful in the shade, his muscles relaxed, maybe thinking deeply. But he wasn't saying anything and she too stayed silent pursing her lips because they'd agreed as children never to rush each other. Then, since long empty moments were passing, the instant almost arrived when it wouldn't hurt to start talking. She chose and murmured little easy things, quick questions, with furrowed brows and an indifferent air; the answer was coming dry and ready. And suddenly she almost made a mistake because she wandered off excessively from the beach into the sea by asking him:

"And old Cecília? have you seen her?"

He looked at her quickly in an almost rasping surprise, in an anguished smile she looked at him so he'd understand that the memory was possible, Daniel; it was possible, it was their own, the question didn't simply mean "how's old Cecília doing," think about it, Daniel … He hesitated for an instant, swayed his head in understanding, almost smiling. Virgínia breathed with hope, remembered herself the visit they'd paid Cecília on an afternoon that had been lost to memory. My house! this is the house! …, the woman was saying with a strident voice, the blinds were flapping dryly three quick times and the air was getting so cool, it was so nice and excited living-all-of-a-sudden, the air had a strange sharpness, frozen and pure, they were feeling cold and stimulating, quite odd, able to make with irony and the most delicate intelligence someone notice little eccentric matters unobserved by anybody else—they were hardly holding in some thing with balance, flashing, and laughter. She herself was wearing a thick, dark woolen shirt. They were wanting to get along well with the old lady, seeking common ground, speaking only of things all three would like and the woman with an aroused pleasure was nodding her head a lot, listening, agreeing while they were speaking, she was laughing allowing them to see her broken teeth—but by God, quick, quick, about a mother, about a daughter, about a sister, about someone who'd been born and was going to die. The curtain was flying halfway across the poor living room, rushing life into a rhythm of abundance and pleasure, Virgínia had felt the desire to travel, a sharp will, almost cheerful and piercing, already desperate. But darkly she was needing not to distance herself from Daniel for a solitary dream and got to thinking about how the journey was something with stages and days, with time, with many observations and not just a single sensation, a single flight and a single satisfaction in response to a single desire.

"Poor Cecília must be fine," said Daniel in a vague smile.

"And Rute?" asked Virgínia quickly without looking, twisting her lips with indifference.

"She's with her mother," said Daniel with simplicity.

"She doesn't want children?" inquired Virgínia catching a luckless and raving ant under the dry branch.

He was silent and she without looking at him felt he'd become even more mute. She blushed, didn't push, was thinking: but I didn't want to pry ..., horrified, hurt, with a touch of burning hatred. But he said suddenly:

"When I ask her that, she laughs and just says: you still don't want to"—he waited a bit and then continued with a certain surprise that seemed to be renewing itself right then— "that's all she says, I can't get anything else out of her."

Virgínia agreed several times with her head:

"I know, I know."

Daniel looked at her with interest:

"What?"

But exactly what she'd understood had been lost in an instant, she searched with attention, only managed to say with a shrug:

"I don't know, I think women when they're not rivals understand one another."

Love isn't everything that produces children, Vicente had said one day with brutality at the beginning of a fight whose cause she'd forgotten, so upset and sad she'd get because she forgot them. But why wouldn't Rute want children? the reason she'd just grasped had entirely escaped her. She pictured Rute again—that was someone who knew how to keep a secret. She didn't seem to have any need to talk about her life. And that would almost offend people. She was smooth and fresh and would look quite like a picture of a saint if not for the intelligence of her imperceptibly watchful eyes, keeping her impressions to herself. She'd say good-morning like a postcard, smiling full of cold life. Was that it? She was picturing Rute again and thought strangely that she was calm and good—yes, that had been the sensation in the Grand Hotel, in the city, there where Daniel's fiancée, her parents, and her two sisters were staying for a while and where Daniel had met her. But she'd hidden the sensation from herself and was then thinking lying to herself: she'll make Daniel's life something with lunchtime, dinnertime, bedtime, with sexual regularization, healthy, clean and almost noble, like in a sanitarium. Daniel had brought Virgínia to introduce her to the girl's parents. In the vast hotel room they'd gathered for a great perplexing visit, without having anything to say. Rute was wearing a pearl-gray silk dress, her face without makeup, pale and peaceful. Yes, from that point on there was something in her that Daniel wouldn't understand. And that she never would show him—smiling, looking at him, loving him, her head raised without any support. How had she not confessed to herself from that point on what she was seeing? Virgínia was thinking; maybe out of stinginess. She'd talked with Daniel's future mother-in-law, a short little woman, lively, squeezed into a girdle, her tight breasts suffocating her neck; her grayish hair done by a hairdresser. Between frightened and almost pensive smiles and glances, they were gradually disclosing the family. Rute had always been a clean, careful, and studious child who lacked the courage to caress and please. And suddenly she'd chosen a boy and would have to live far away! that seemed to be what she'd always plotted against the family—her defenseless mother was looking at her from afar while the daughter was serving tea while smiling at what her father and Daniel were saying—but at the same time how to feel sorry for herself, the mother was saying still following her with her eyes, how could she feel sorry for herself if she also seemed to have plotted against Daniel? With surprise and almost disdain for her decision, so unfeminine—the mother was seeming to fear for her future as a woman—with surprise and almost disdain, with joy and emotion they heard her decide to live for six months at the

Farm with her husband and six months with her parents and those sisters she seemed to love with proprietorship, severity, and tenderness. The sisters, dressed like rich girls, were getting bored beneath their curled hair enduring with almost comic eyes the visit of Virgínia and the "fiancé"; of such fast matter the girls were made.—She looked at Daniel, the fluctuating shadow of the branch darkening and lightening his face, she guessed without surprise that he had fallen in love with Rute. Love isn't everything that produces children! The phrase came back to her again without meaning, nagging and tiresome. And then not just the phrase but moving itself, her own feelings, Rute's smiling silence, difficulty, peace, everything mingling in the same slow and thick matter and she breathed the air, pure existence, with a vanquished sigh, almost enraged.

"Why didn't you hold me back?" he said.

But ... What? ... what was he saying?! He hadn't asked anything ... what was he saying? what was he accusing her of ... she hadn't asked anything ... Suddenly she understood, didn't look, keeping in check her hard and tense face.

"Why didn't you hold me back ... you should have known that it was out of a kind of desperation. I'm so lost"—he was narrowing his eyes, his face calm, his hands on the back of his neck; his dark teeth inlaid in nearly white gums, because he was seeming to smile—"I'm so lost. Why did you let me make a mistake ..."

The brazenness, that brutality in confessing. She found him truculent and voluptuous, that man to whom only ever happened things that he could understand. So that's why I came, to face down an animal, she almost hated him, oh those friends of Irene's were right to laugh at him, she looked at him with crudity feeling her own face red with perturbation. How old he was, his face sunburned, the wrinkles ... she looked at him in desperation, gritted her teeth: but no, if he grows old what do *I* do? he can't grow old, he can't, he can't.

"Why did you let me make a mistake?" he repeated suddenly, his monotonous voice frightened her.

Desperation? no, she didn't know it. I swear, Daniel, I swear, how could that fool and egoist that I am ever guess—she saw herself once more in the apartment doing nothing, looking out the window, basely desiring some men, waiting, she hated herself profoundly surprised at having forgotten that Daniel was the most important thing. But at the same time how to forget that since they were small ... her wanting to call out to him and not being able to, him not hearing ... the hat ... He'd never know how hard it was to give him a word to ask for assistance or to help him, how alone he was all along. Her heart hurting, she said:

"You make mistakes with a power that cannot be held back ... I really think that making a mistake with that violence is lovelier than getting it right, Daniel, it's like being a hero ..."— Yes, she'd finally said it. As if hearing herself, she repeated with sweetness and tranquility—"You are a hero."

He said nothing, he knew, was closing his eyes enduring his own life. She remembered how he'd say: I don't want to be a boy. She looked at him with delicacy. He was a man. Boys and girls would have to change their names so much when they grew up. If somebody were named Daniel, now, he should have been Círil one day. Virgínia—she leaned into her own interior thoughtfully, while Daniel seemed to be falling asleep under the tree—Virgínia was a name full of watchful peace like that of an alcove behind a wall, there where thin weeds grew like hair and where nobody existed to hear the wind. But after losing that perfect, skinny figure, as small and delicate as the mechanism of a watch, after losing transparency and gaining a color, she could be called Maria Madalena or Hermínia or even any other name except Virgínia, of such fresh and somber antiquity. Yes, and when she was small she also could have easily been Sibila, Sibila, Sibila. Virgínia ... She sighed with a movement of her head. As if she couldn't stand Virgínia's and Daniel's past. Sitting on her legs, she looked at him—there had been a time when he'd thought it was essential to possess a magnet. Certain people to whom it seemed to have been given the destiny to live life over again. He stirred, divined his sister's presence, she flapped her hands, they looked so alike in that moment, they'd always been the same. A long path had brought them to that instant. They felt so sincere that they looked at each other quickly with apprehension. He closed his eyes; she stared at the distant air, so painful was her tense breathing, they were feeling so much brother and sister, so ready to look at the world together, with interest and mockery as on a journey or something, with little chatting and absorbed silences, yes, making everything a joke, everything, the journey was so impossible, they were so full of love forever, forever ... And which would be buried in seconds beneath the passing of the instants greater than eternity. Oh, grant him an instant of true life, his beautiful face expanded in color and hope! She leaned against the tree with staring eyes. She was urgently needing to say something with rage, with joy, for violence to smash the air into fire, to revolt, understand herself!, for a galloping horse to emerge running through the meadow, for a bird to shriek. As if a stone started to speak, he said and she heard him with a surprised heart—had it been a foreboding?—beating hollowly already in a beginning of tranquility, he said calm, eyes still closed, in such a vulgar tone:

"What devil makes me want to resemble myself."

Never would he say "we." She sat looking at the ground, the hard and brittle stick was leaving gray pieces of rotten wood in her hands. The sun was opening pale over the garden, the ants running without noise, almost without touching with their thin legs the resistant ground. A low and insinuating wind was blowing the dry leaves around the tree. She said, the stick lightly scratching the ground:

"If you only knew how delicate life can be."

They stayed with inexpressive and suspended faces in an indecisive and watchful tranquility. The light feet of a little bird stepped on some leaf that stirred, the shadows were taming and deepening the old garden. She penetrated into a good silence until Daniel asked, suddenly pushing an icy tack into her heart:

"What about you?"

"I am Vicente's lover," she heard herself answer.

"Happy?"

She waited a bit.

"You know, always the same, I couldn't be happier than I am, I couldn't be unhappier than I am."

He nodded in agreement. And since she couldn't stand it a second longer, she stood with a small harrowing shout:

"Let's walk!?"

He said:

"No, I'm going in"—he got up and walked away from her

and as on the day of the drowned man, once again she wouldn't know how to call out to him, how to cry for him not to leave her alone right then—she sat on the little patch of grass under the tree with open eyes, her heart beating calm, dry, bloodless. Yes, maybe it was better that way. From the dirty earth a smell of dust was coming, a breath that was not born of whatever was always alive but of whatever was seeming continually to die. There was an extremely pleasant, gray, and cold silence beneath the weak sun. But the trees were rustling, green, dark, and leafy. She closed her eyes letting herself almost waver. The day long like an arrow heading nowhere. Gradually, under lowered eyelids, some thing was running ahead like a hare, but sluggish, it kept running and getting lost like a wounded hare losing blood and running until weakly reaching the end of blood. She could say while acknowledging—that's it, that's it, with assurance. How sweet it was to run along and get lost in weakness, but it hurt and frightened; she could dread the dark room from outside in yet it was horrible to be the dark room and she was the dark room itself. It was so sweet because you couldn't understand it; in the middle of everything she sighed and that sigh had been a sensation that the instants were going forward. When she'd possessed a watch she wouldn't sigh; she'd look at it; but it had broken. It was just that she was feeling tired, leaning against the tree, women tired more easily than men, tired as if from an invisible wound blood were flowing uninterruptedly like air, like thought, like things existing without respite, the hare running. How perturbing lightness was. She was so happy. To live one time was always, always. Except she wasn't proud and that was as good as being solitary, without sharing oneself with the world—you had to be proud, establish victory and piety. How incomplete it was to live! she shouted at herself sharply in a clarion that suddenly snapped. She slid down the tree, lay atop the sparse grass, covered her eyes with her bare forearm. How incomplete it was to live. What was she fighting against? because in the deepest part of her being, beneath the forearm darkening her, she was feeling a slight tension, her open eyes guarding against. That was destiny—she seemed to notice—because without that she'd be freed to let herself penetrate into so many possibilities ... she, who was keeping herself inside good sense with a stubbornness that strangely didn't seem to be born of a deep desire but from something like a nervous whim, from a foreboding. Open eyes guarding and a slight tension preventing ... what? behind those eyes there might not be anything dear and alive to protect so faithfully, maybe just the void connecting itself to the infinite, she was feeling confusedly almost in a doze— connecting her own depth to the infinite without so much as awareness, without ecstasy, just a thing living without being seen or felt, dry like an unknown truth. How horrible, pure, and irrevocable it was to live. There was some silent and inexpressible thing beneath her darkening forearm. Atop each day she'd balance on the tips of her toes, atop each fragile day that from one instant to the next could snap and fall into darkness. But she miraculously would cross it and exhausted from joy and fatigue reach sleep in order on the next day to begin again surprised. That was the reality of her life, she was thinking so distantly that the idea was getting lost in her body like a sensation and now she was already sleeping. This was the secret and daily event, which was still beneath her forearm, even if she shut herself in a cell and spent all her hours there, that was the reality of her life: to escape daily. And exhausted from living, to exult in the darkness.

She got up, took off her shoes, tossed them behind the tree, went off walking, walked, walked, walked. She crossed the meadow beyond the Farm, walked, walked. She entered the narrow, long road and her gaze got used to the green shadows, the solid and claylike earth. Now she was wandering distractedly, her bare feet creaking in the warm dust of the late afternoon. She walked, walked. Once she raised her eyes and then they opened and filled with sweet moist surprise ... Because from the twilight where they found themselves they were sprouting toward the blue-green of an enormous meadow with open arms and from the sad confusion of the intertwined branches on the road, they were now floating in extensive lines of light, long, peaceful, almost cold ... joyful. It was a plateau of free, green land, open beyond what her gaze could contain. From the low road where she was stopping, Virgínia was seeing at the beginning of the ravine the odd tall weed flutter in the wind where it met the sky, almost getting mixed up with its colorless luminosity. And those vertical, pale strokes were so thin and their rhythm under the wind was so fast and light that her eyes clenched by the light would occasionally stop making them out, just feeling them like a delicate tingle in the air. How could she have forgotten the plateau, how could she have forgotten ..., she was reproaching herself shaking her head. She abandoned the vine that her fingers were torturing and waited with her eyes vacant, anxious. Slowly silence fell over the murmur of her final steps and a hushed stillness rose. She didn't know what she was doing standing waiting and hesitated. She also wasn't familiar with that soft prostration in her heart, smooth and successive drops down to something like a calm weakening like that of the afternoon. Thus she stayed counting with astonishment the seconds by the smooth beating of the arteries somewhere in her body. Until slowly but then in a single instant she understood, she had to go up. She drew back for a moment intimidated by the discovery that wasn't connected to the whole day, that wasn't united to old desires and that was arising free like an inspiration. She hesitated, it was getting so late. But in a light urge she leapt over the plain and her body was moving ahead of her thought. A single golden and pale color was covering the grass weightlessly. Yes … somewhere a doe was softly opening and closing its eyelids licking a smiling and still tired newborn, her hair was trembling finely like fragile weeds while with half-opened senses opened she with difficulty and attention was conquering the land. No tree, no rock, nakedness up to the horizon of erased mountains; her heart was beating superficially and she was hardly breathing as if in order to live it was enough to look.

It was then that she experienced all the way to the end whatever it was whose foreboding had already worried her at the edge of the plateau. With a contained joy, flashing and fine, she felt almost ignorantly that, but yes, but yes, somehow there she was in the meadow … you understand? she was asking herself confused, her dark eye watching to the rescue of the whitened mountains. With her lips parted, dried by the wind that was blowing ceaselessly she continued her hard and humble glory with lighter feet, her body sharpened in movements. Smiling she imagined that behind her, while she was climbing and never reaching, terrified eyes of many men were following her as if she were an escaped vision … yes, yes, that's how it was getting easier and easier to move her big white body forward … she smiled coyly behind her and then, as if she'd really believed in what she'd imagined, saw that she was alone. But a man, a man, she implored frightened … who understood her just then in the field, who surprised her almost with pain. But nobody could see her and the wind was blowing almost cold. She was feeling so pretty, she furrowed her eyebrows, grab it, grab it in order to be seen, loved, love! Nothing would make use of her though, beauty seemed so lost to itself, it remained somehow intact and thoughtful like a flower with an unconquerable nature; nobody, nobody could see her—silence and solitude were reaching her from afar in a limpid breath. The light instant would flee without touching the memory of any man of the earth and she could never entrust it to anyone because it would escape gestures and gaze. Only she herself would keep it like a violent spot, a hot, white star in the center of her body. And other human eyes would be useless because only she herself could comprehend that in reality, beneath the final sun, in the long green meadow, in the deepest reality she was almost moving toward the distant light a finally naked being, her legs erasing themselves at the root of her body, her breasts advancing high, translucent, cold—that was the pure urge that was nonetheless false. Only she herself would understand. And because she was creating inside herself, that was where the grace with which she was stepping just then was coming from. She tried to laugh by herself since she was wanting to hear herself and right then might still be able to invent a new laugh. Her light laughter scared her with strange mischief, she shuddered in the air like rosebuds that open in silence, the singularity of cold air atop the flesh of her face. She turned around, the wind covered her cheek with her rough hair, she saw that the road had moved off in a red thread lost forever, her heart took fright, watchful, prudent. The mountains ahead were still unreal and she would never reach them. At large in the field she then felt a slow and serious fear mingled with the joyful event, fear of leaping over the line of pleasure and suddenly sinking into the breadth, deep, dark like the sea … and atop that sea was float-ing the cold pleasure that was sharpening into needles of ice and that would break like a gleam that goes out—then she closed her lips that with great difficulty were ceasing to smile, dry and limpid. She lowered her eyes for a second. When she raised them she wanted to look at the field with solemnity and sadness to hold back the excess of fullness so hard to en-dure and that's how she looked at it because she was solemn and sad.

The way back was hard going, without momentum and without ecstasy. She felt like she was crawling along in the dust, night was falling, she was halting with hurting feet, des-perate. She was sitting for a while on the side of the road, the clouds were darkening, the branches were swaying in calm murmuring; she was squinting afraid to start crying. She was thirsty, saw a little stream flowing nearby but the liquid was tired and warm, giving in her thirsty mouth a harsh impres-sion instead of prickling her with cold shudders. Everything was starting to refuse itself, everything was putting away its qualities of being, night was closing. It was seeming more and more impossible for her to reach the Farm, she was hoisting her heavy, sweaty body and seeing nothing but the road going round and round, shutting itself up like a goal that she was trying to reach hopefully but that wasn't a goal, that was opening onto a new already-dark road, slow and staggering like a nightmare. Darkness was falling bluish over the mountains; in the twilight the fireflies were existing in a colorless instant of flight, the shrill and fearless song of a bird was penetrating like a sidelong flight far away. Did I go the wrong way? she was wondering extremely disturbed ... Arrh, she was saying deafly, going ahead inexpressible and at large, arrh! Her bare feet were burning and her little toe was bleeding black with dust. She was stumbling out of dismay and fright, stopping at times for a second, just to listen—nothing could be heard, the crickets were buzzing unsteady, hard, incessant, the dizzy twilight, so vacant, it seemed to be some error of vision, she was running her hand over her eyes but again finding the gray and cold air, full of the new rumblings of the forest, the trees creaking. Intimately she was still the one who had dared lift herself beyond what she could do, again she had been the one who had created the moment of pain, dreading herself surprised by the coldness with which she was directing herself to live, and how she was regretting it, how she was regretting it! don't dare, don't dare, have less courage and even less strength than she did, that's it, that's it! She was thinking softly encouraging herself, her eyes open with difficulty in the half-dark of the night, her body moving ahead unsteady at a speed that kept on giving out. It seemed to her that with every moment a pause was being born in which she was fleeing backward, backward, having to travel back over the road already traveled. Invisible branches were catching on her clothes, thorns tearing apart the fabric, scratching her skin with sharp violence and blood was blossoming like drops of sweat. She wasn't groaning, no, she wasn't groaning, she was saying with rage and mettle like a beast of burden whose steps falter: ah! ah!, her voice was coming out hoarse and intense, she was getting excited, almost running, never, never had her body existed so much, never had living weighed so heavy upon her—her spirit was breathing a fragile and hesitant breath, enraptured she was inhaling the cold air with violence but wasn't bringing it beyond the surface of her being, suffocated. I promise, I promise not to go back to Vicente, my God! Carried by a veiled foreboding, expending the new sensation as the memory of the past unfurls, she was thinking of the sin and telling herself disturbed: later, later I'll think it over, later, I promise to stop everything, not to go back to the city, yes, that's what they were wanting, they, "they" were wanting her not to return to the city, to stay here. She remembered that when she was small she'd walk around the cemetery in Upper Marsh, where thick fruit trees arose, heavy, calm, and she'd say to herself wounded like an instrument that frees a sound, she'd say to herself: don't eat those fruits, don't eat! she'd say it to herself as if something had previously inspired her: eat, steal, eat—and she could only manage to say frightened: don't eat the fruits!, she was distracting herself by thinking, distracted herself by walking … There! there was the end of the road! all she had to do was run and reach the field, then the fence … the gate … home. She started to murmur words in a low voice in a deep prayer, speaking to herself intensely, maddened, hurting herself with hard words of purification while with eyes shining with extraordinary firmness she was gradually reaching the meadow … the gate was creaking. She was on the grounds of the Farm, started running while raving tears were flowing from her eyes and she was sobbing without even trying to understand herself, running ahead, surrendered to the stream of life.

Still crying, fumbling, she was seeking her shoes behind the tree. She grabbed them with dirt in her nails, sat on the great rock in the garden lifting her skirt and blowing her nose on the cotton slip. She looked at the old construction half-covered by the tree beside which she had sat: weak light was shining yellowish and somber in the tall windows, nothing could be heard, noises were being born and getting lost even inside the mansion. The house seemed to her hushed, supernatural, distant—as if she'd died and was trying to remember, as if the house could vanish a few seconds from now and the ground would stay behind smooth, empty, dark. Who would know if death really was reality—as if her entire life had been a nightmare and she finally woke up dead. But moments later a kind of calm buzzing started coming from the center of the house as if noises, movements, and conversations crushed together in a single sound. It was her house, her house—she possessed a place that wasn't the forest or the dark road, nor tiredness and tears, that wasn't even joy, that wasn't raving and pointless fear, a place that belonged to her without anyone ever having said so, a place where people would accept without surprise that she was coming in, sleeping and eating, a place where nobody would ask her if she'd been afraid but where they'd greet her while continuing to eat beneath the lamp, a place where in the most serious instants people could wake up and maybe suffer too, a place you could run to frightened after rapture, where you could return after the experience of laughter, after having tried to surpass the limit of the possible world—it was her, her, her house. She wiped her eyes, sought with trembling and such weak hands to clean the dirt from her feet, put on her shoes, got up. Standing on her tall heels she found herself in a slightly familiar sensation, felt some assurance, ran her dirty hands over her face trying to erase the expression of the tears, lifted her skirt, once again blowing her swollen nose. Nearing the mansion she was wanting to have a thought that thanked the vague salvation she was feeling in her chest, she halted looking at the white old walls immersed in shadow and silence, the windows blinking all lit up. She'd live at the Farm, she then thought in a beginning and it seemed to her that she might have lived her whole life in search of that thought, just as some would live leaning through confusion toward love, glory, or themselves. She smiled biting her lips with shame and pride in already laughing — to live her whole life at the Farm — for an instant she herself vibrating inside her smile with an unmixed joy, for a quick instant. She went straight to the staircase without looking at the family already sitting at the table.

"I'll be back in a minute …"

She washed her face, her feet, her hands, put iodine on the scratches on her body. She wet her hair, combed it trying to smooth it, every once in a while a kind of little sob as a reminiscence. She looked at herself in the mirror — in the dark and dizzy light her face was seeming big, fresh, blossoming and shining, her dark eyes were moist and intense, she was looking like a monstrous flower open in the water — she went down the stairs feeling extraordinarily young and shaky. They were eating, nobody asked her anything; after all night had hardly fallen and she'd come back on time. She served herself black beans, peas, meat, rice, and cornbread, started eating slowly, eating everything painstakingly, guilty and happy, holding back the odd sob. The black countryside seemed impotent to her, she was sometimes remembering the almost mad pleasure she'd felt in the meadow, but recalling with nausea and fear, with hatred and flight, like a thing that hurt so, so badly, like a vice, she who had been expelled from pleasure, she who had been expelled from paradise. Mother said:

"Potatoes?"

She handed over her plate with docility and got potatoes. Her mother looked at her with approval and harshness:

"When you were a girl you got in a lot of trouble with your father for eating potatoes."

Virgínia laughed feeling her eyes shining wet and flickering in front of her own vision.

"You have a cold," the old woman asked.

"I don't know, Mama ..."

"Take some cough syrup before going to sleep ... Esmeralda has it in her room" — she looked at Esmeralda with politeness and leisure, she'd always be her favorite daughter.

"Come by my room before you go to sleep," said Esmeralda. She looked tired and sluggish.

"And what's wrong with you?" asked Virgínia.

"Nothing ..." the other responded. "I just woke up like this. I actually slept well last night."

"But how do you feel?"

"I don't know, I told you!" Esmeralda got irritated, "leave me alone."

Father was eating, his glasses on his forehead, staring at the plate. Daniel was cutting the meat, putting it in his mouth and leaning toward the folded newspaper.

"I don't know how you can read in this light," said Virgínia — she was wanting to touch each person with a word.

He quickly lifted his head, annoyed, distracted. He said: "yes …," went back to his reading, his face lowered, chewing.

"Papa, do you want more corn?" she asked blushing. Because she remembered right away how he couldn't stand being uncomfortable, that he was the boss at the table, the one who would invite and force others to eat. The old man didn't reply, didn't hand over his plate. Without knowing how to proceed, she said one more time, darkly offering herself as a daughter, disturbed to keep pushing but not knowing what course to take:

"And rice?"

"Nobody has to order me to eat," he said at last, "I know all by myself what's good for me," he concluded resistant.

Surprised, but that was Father—she looked timidly at her family … Papa, Papa, that's how you are, don't ever die … How dumb she was, she said to herself a bit suddenly, straightened up and set to eating with resolve. At the end of the dinner some thing seemed to diminish like disappearing mists and reality was emerging almost like the reality before her walk. The scene had already been seen, it was that of the daily dinner—she felt calmer, more indifferent. She was remembering the walk through the night, feeling it inside her like a still aching and tender spot, like an inexplicable place to which you could return; she was pushing away the thought immediately with a gesture but already reflecting: maybe I overdid it, maybe I'm sick. Yet suddenly the electric power started to fade rapidly, the lamp was almost going out and in the half-shadow full of wind they all halted with their forks in hand, their eyes looking up. The interrupted dinner. Later, in a single surge, the light rekindled with power a shining brightness spread over the long table and over the faces … reality emerged whole, some thing was coming to an end—the family was starting dinner again. Contrite, angry with herself, Virgínia couldn't help noticing how calm and emotionless she was. But she'd stay at the Farm forever! she thought with ardor and harshness, wounding herself. It was strange that she loved them so much, that she couldn't stand the pain of imagining them dead and nevertheless wanted, yes, she wanted to leave. Then they got up, the old people went upstairs, Daniel went out, Esmeralda and she sat in the rocking chairs in the parlor without speaking. That room that was at the end of the dining room would only get a bit of the brightness of the other room and was growing quiet almost in shadow; it was the mansion's hottest room, the smallest and most comfortable. Virgínia saw Esmeralda close her eyes and huddle clasping the corners of the dark shawl on her chest. She herself began to rock herself gently, her hands on the curved arms of the chair, her eyes fixed on the ceiling unconsciously watching the back-and-forth movement. She was loving and understanding people more and more and nevertheless more and more was realizing that she ought to isolate herself from them. But she needed to stay, stay … Esmeralda looked so old to her … how hadn't she noticed it before? the wide eyelids closed in an abandon that was bothersome, the legs curled atop the chair, all of her nestled as if she were cold or had a fever, so wilted, so much smaller than she really was. But if she called her she'd hear an irritated exclamation. Yes, stay, watch the end of those lives with which she'd been born, reconstruct her forgotten childhood with the help of the memory of the place, live at the Farm where she'd had her greatest instants, take back, take back. She was rocking herself quickly, quickly, gently. But with the stubbornness of a world that warns with impotent eyes of the danger, she was feeling without even comprehending that the place where one was happy is not the place where one can live. She was closing her eyes while rocking herself quick and smooth and intimately she had to go on, deeply she was wrapping herself in anxiety and sweetness, deeply she had to go on in that ineffable perfecting that never would go to a higher point but was in the continuation of instants itself. What would be the intimate understanding of that slow succession without hope? why wasn't it living off a single time ...? She was lulling herself in search—obscurely whatever it was that always remained exactly equal to itself, through the instants was already imponderably something else—in a confused way it was from there that her most pent-up hope was coming. Deeply hidden and discreet she was rocking herself—and that was the meaning of living second by second breathing in and out; you couldn't breathe right away everything you had to breathe, you couldn't live all at once, time was slow, unfamiliar to the body, you could live off time. And it would be an instant just like the lost instant that would bring an end. That's what she was experiencing extraordinarily entangled, with open and thoughtful eyes; without feeling cold beneath the shirt ripped by thorns she was saying to herself surprised and distraught as in the face of a nausea, beneath a muffled worried joy, in a fatigue with shudders of intense exhaustion: but what's wrong with me? my God, so I'm leaving, yes! She was also suffering and wondering sweetly now, submissive to herself: but for what? why after all do I wish to go? How uniform her story was, she was now feeling without words. That she was living in agreement with something; diffusion had been the most serious thing she'd experienced—chrysanthemums, chrysanthemums, she had always desired them. She was feeling that she'd recovered a lost meaning and was telling herself apprehensively and rocking herself quickly and gently deceiving herself: and now? and now? Leave, suffer, and be alone; how to touch on all the rest? Esmeralda had fallen asleep huddled up, her cheek dead; a distant inexplicable expression was fluttering in some indefinable feature of her face as in the murky bottom of a well. And now? and now? All the Farm asleep and dark was seeming to be wrapped up with the chair above the countryside.

She sat in the steaming train with her brown hat now trimmed with red—she sought in her purse the pack of cigarettes abandoned since she'd entered Upper Marsh. She was feeling cheerful, as if cold and fresh inside her body. Alone again, she was starting to experience "the things," to allow them. She was thinking about Vicente, with a bothered sigh taking out a cigarette and lighting it. What had happened anyway? that was the sudden question to which she was desiring secretly but firmly to reach a certain impossible-to-define answer; she was sighing intolerantly in the face of her impotence that nonetheless was making her better possess the very state in which she was finding herself. What had happened? she wasn't sure what she was trying to learn with that question. She was smoking. The vague notion of what she'd always wanted seemed to have been constantly thrashing around inside her without ever taking shape. She was guessing however, by a mysterious assent to her own lie, that having lived so continually, with patience and perseverance as in a daily job, guessing that amidst all the lost gestures the true one must have escaped—though she could never get to know it. And that she'd resolved at some indistinct minute of her life, in some glance or a brief sensation, a bodily movement or a merely curious and unnoticed thought, who would ever know. A chain of confused and indecipherable instants seemed to have served as the ritual for a consummation. And whatever might be too delicate to be accomplished through the brightness of facts, had worn out the thick defense of an entire daily existence. She herself, against herself, might have secretly agreed to the sacrifice of the mass of her life, heaping upon herself lies, false love, ambitions and pleasures—just as she'd protect somebody's silent escape by capturing everyone's attention with uproar and confusion. She was feeling complete and a bit tired, smoking, but her eyes were shining calm and inexpressive. Before that indeterminable instant she had been imperceptibly stronger as if held up by a clouded thrust from an unknown direction; now she was just a weak and watchful woman, yes, starting secretly an old age that someone would call maturity. There was some clearer word that almost brought her closer to her true thought and then, without understanding herself, she looked at herself in the glass of the window, examining herself. Her own face had lost its importance. She sat better adjusting her position. She was smoking and thinking inexplicably, without reaching herself. And really how could she ever foresee whatever was happening without interruption inside the most being of her body? ... Sensations had always held her up with a light continuous strength and that's how she'd arrived at the present moment. Even at that instant, if she stopped deeply, she could still discover primal impressions flowing like delicate noises pure words ringing out, the sea bestowing foam upon the deserted beach, maybe in memory, maybe in foreboding, being itself, through the guile of its distraction, murmuring essential, disintegrating gathering getting up: wash, place in the sun, the damp thing loses its dampness, new skin shining smooth in the shade, wash, place in the sun, the damp thing loses its dampness, new skin shining smooth in the sun, wash, put in the sun, let it lose its dampness, skin brightens up, wash, put in the sun, let it lose its dampness, wash ... Clouded by the cigarette she was refusing to go ahead. Maybe she was referring to some serious and deep thing that was worrying her; or that might not be worrying her, that was just carrying on its natural life as the heart that beats now simply continues the past moment. The meaning of that junk of sensations was obscure and carrying on with perfect mystery; her unfurling wasn't giving her pleasure, wasn't giving her fatigue, wasn't making her happy or unhappy, it was the person herself living and she was looking out the train window calculating how long it would take to arrive at the next station, wanting at last to stand and move around a bit her legs tired by motionlessness. Ah, the chandelier. She'd forgotten to look at the chandelier. It seemed to her that they'd put it away or otherwise that she hadn't had time to seek it with her eyes. Especially also she hadn't seen many other things. She thought she'd lost it forever. And without understanding herself, feeling a certain void in her heart, it also seemed to her that in fact she'd lost one of *her things*. What a shame, she said surprised. What a shame, she repeated to herself with regret. The chandelier ... She was looking through the window and in the lowered and dark glass was seeing mixed with the reflection of the seats and the people the chandelier. She smiled contrite and timid. The featherless chandelier. Like a great and quavering cup of water. Capturing in itself the luminous raving transparency the chandelier for the first time all alight in its pale and frigid orgy—motionless in the night that was running with the train behind the glass. The chandelier. The chandelier. Without understanding herself, gingerly putting out the cigarette with the hard heel of her shoe, as if through it she were feeling the heat of the ash on her heel, the confused impression was returning. From which she after all had lived, even intact through the events, from which she'd had the occasional instant full of meaning—the pure sensation was coming and going with a touch of wonder and really she'd never know how to think whatever she was experiencing. As if for no reason, she remembered that when she was little she would play at trying not to move, like all children who'd already forgotten it; she'd stay quiet, enduring; the instants would pulse in her tense body, one more, one more, one more. And suddenly movement was irresistible, some thing impossible to hold back like a birth, and she'd carry it out electric, harsh, and brief. Confusedly there was in everything she knew that same moment of indomitable attainment. And for all she knew, the uncontrolled gesture would secretly escape in every life. Without knowing why, she thought of her dead grandmother. She'd always observed in old people something that couldn't be summed up, that wasn't exactly lack of desire, or satisfaction, or experience, ah, never experience—something that only the imponderable living of all the incomprehensible instants of sleep and wakefulness seemed to grant.

So strange and imperceptible were the power and fecundity of the rhythm. Nothing would seem to escape the continuous sequence, the intimate spherical movement, inhaling, exhaling, inhaling, exhaling, death and resurrection, death and resurrection. Anyway everything was the way it was, she thought almost brightly, almost cheerful—and that was meaning her deepest sensation of existence as if things were made of the impossibility of not being what they were. She seemed suddenly to understand, without however explaining herself, because lately her unease had grown like a girl's body that, suffocated, foresees puberty.

She got up, walked along with the noise of the wheels, her movements leaning against the direction of the train; somehow was thinking that the effort she was making was funny and maybe that's why she smiled as if carrying out some purpose; she entered the dining car, ordered coffee while arranging her dusty hat, vaguely taking on the attitude of a tall, large, and good-humored person. She was feeling a bright peace open like a disregarded and tranquil field; eventually she forgot about herself and started observing with docile interest the things on the train, a woman chewing. The odd spark would cross the windows with fast violence, that now-now-now of the wheels that seemed like an internal murmuring. The sun was setting, the train was running through the already colorless fields. The restaurant was almost empty, atop the stained tablecloths flies were landing, everything was rough and dry with dust. It was with a jolt that she noticed her own abandonment. She scrutinized herself with slight anxiety. Some imperceptible thing had nonetheless already transformed itself. With a bit of concern she was listening to herself, the awakened being, deeply uneasy. She was slightly paying attention; the naturalness of things around her had vanished, like the final trace of warm sleepy pleasure when you wash your face, now existence itself was shaken, hard and broken several times. She herself was feeling intimately without comfort, her entrails awake as if her shoes were wet or her sweaty clothes stuck to her back—in a disquieted distaste she moved away from the back of the seat. She was understanding in a powerless and stupefied disappointment, already a beginning of deep fatigue flickering in her eyes, understanding that she hadn't reached any ownership, that the departure for the city wasn't symbolic. And the sensation she'd experienced a few minutes ago? she was searching hopefully. But no, no—and she wasn't up to understanding her own thoughts—in fact whatever there was that was untouched, awake, and confused inside her still had enough strength to cause to be born a time of waiting longer than that from childhood up to the present day, so little had she arrived at any point, dissolved while still living—that was frightening her tired and desperate from her own unstable flowing and that was something horribly undeniable, and that nonetheless was soothing her in a strange way, like the sensation every morning of not having died during the night. With an unnoticed movement of discouragement she was confusedly wondering whether she'd forget forever what she'd felt in the end that was so firm and serene and whose kind she could no longer quite pinpoint with clarity, in a beginning of forgetting. No, she wouldn't forget, she was clinging to herself without realizing it, but how to use it? how to live from that? she could never wear it out and that was also something undeniable, the train was carrying her forward as if losing her from herself, the

wheels were wheezing, the fellow from the restaurant was leaning his body along with the movement of the car, finding his
balance, losing his balance, the coffee was hot, yes, certainly the
first time in the world that in a dining car somebody was managing to drink hot coffee, which was a thing to slightly shake
your head about, surprised, as she was doing now wagging the
red ribbon of the brown hat.

With her suitcase resting on the ground she waited for a moment on the corner. Yes, take now a taxi, find Miguel, ask for
the money from the sale of the furniture, yes, yes. But she
sighed motionless and alert. The dusty face beneath the hat
slightly out of place on her head was looking dark and oppressed by a vague fear. What was happening! because all of
her past was fading and a new time was horribly beginning?
Suddenly she began to sweat, her stomach clenched in a single wave of nausea, she was breathing terribly oppressed and
panting—what was happening to her? or what was going to
happen? In an effort in which her chest seemed to endure a
viscous weight, with an unsurpassed malaise, she crossed the
street pale and the car turned the corner, she took a step back,
the car hesitated, she advanced and the car came into light, she
perceived it with a shock of heat over her body and a fall without pain while her heart was looking astonished at nothing in
particular and a man's shout was coming from somewhere—it
was speedily the same day three years ago when she'd halted
ahead avoiding by a hair's breadth stepping on a rigid and dead

kitten and her heart had retreated while, with her eyes for an instant deeply closed out of disgust, all her body was saying toward the inside of itself in a dark and concave moment, deep in the sonorous hollow of a silent church: arrh! in deep vivifying nausea, her heart retreating white and solid in a dry fall, arrh! And since she was thinking darkly about Vicente she saw Adriano, Vicente, Miguel, Daniel—Daniel, Daniel! in a bright and dizzying race through the streets of the city like a wind through flowing hair, she entered the Farm for an instant, she rocked herself quick, quick in the chair and with absolute amazement looked at herself white and with dark eyes in a mirror—long corridors were taking shape inside her, long tired corridors, difficult and dark, doors closing one after the next without noise with fright and care while a moment of Daniel's rage was thought by her and the instants were brightly following one after the next—she and Daniel chewed the last of the fruit that was running down their chins and were looking at each other with shining and intelligent eyes, almost one of them enjoying what the other was eating, it was cold, her red and painful nose in the courtyard of the Farm; she directed a shiver at Daniel. She who'd never wasted time—confused, deaf, fast, bright, dissonant, the noise that comes from the orchestra tuning and tuning itself for the concert and a movement of well-being seeking comfort, the unaccustomed heart. What was happening was so simple that she didn't know from where to understand. In the frozen twilight black corridors, narrow, empty and damp, a dormant and numb substance: and suddenly! suddenly! suddenly! the white butterfly fluttering in the shadowy corridors, getting lost at the end of the darkness. She was obscurely wanting to cut herself off, she was obscurely wanting to cut herself off. The street was steaming cold and sleepy, her own heart was being taken by surprise, her head heavy, heavy with stunning grace—while the streets of Upper Marsh were heading fast and flickering inside their smell of apple, sawdust, import and export, that lack of sea. And suddenly ravished by her own spirit. It was an extremely intimate and strange moment—she was recognizing all of this, how often, how often had she rehearsed it without realizing it; and now, extraordinarily hushed, purified of her own sources of energy, surrendering even future possibilities—ah, not to have recognized then that type of gesture, almost a position of thought, the head leaning to one side, like that, like that … not to have paid attention to it then … how frightened she would have been if she'd understood it—but now she wasn't frightened, the urge was inferior to the most secret quality of being, in the frozen twilight a new exactness being born; no! no! it wasn't a decaying sensation! but wanting obscurely, obscurely to cut herself off, the difficulty, the difficulty that was coming from the sky, that was coming. The first real event, the only fact that could serve as a beginning to her life, free like throwing a crystal glass through the window, the irresistible movement that could no longer hold itself back. She'd also tried to rehearse when she would seek to distinguish the smell in the construction sites, had rehearsed the smell in the half-twilight, whitewash, wood, cold iron, fallen dust watching. - - - how could she have forgotten: yes - - - , - - - . The field empty of weeds in the wind without her, entirely without her, without any sensation, just the wind, unreality approaching in iridescent colors, at high, light, penetrating speed. Mists fraying and uncovering firm shapes, a mute sound bursting from the divined intimacy of things, silence pressing down on particles of earth in darkness and black ants slow and tall walking atop thick grains of earth, the wind running high far ahead, a limpid cube dangling in the air and the light running parallel to every point, was present, thus it had been, thus it would be, and the wind, the wind, she who had been so steady.

The people then gathered around the woman while the car sped off.

"But I really saw how the car arrived just then, but just then, and ran her over!"

"Those drivers are crazy, my son almost got hit one day but luckily …"

"He said that just then, but really just then …"

"Nobody's calling the paramedics?"

"Why don't you call then, sir? what a crazy …"

"Step aside because I'm going to check that woman's pulse, I'm a medical student …"

"I'm not calling because I'm not from here, could you, sir …"

"Ah, he's a medical student, he said he's going to check the woman's pulse …"

"The driver sure was clever and got out of here, didn't he …"

"Get the paramedics, nobody move … I'm not from here, I don't have experience with those things! call the paramedics!"

"But I'm a medical student and even a child can see that the woman's dead! call the police if you want, do that!"

"Poor thing, but it doesn't hurt to call the paramedics, maybe it …"

"Here comes the guard …"

"He said he was a medical student and that even a child could see …"

"Will you look at that, will you look at that!" a fat woman shouted astonished and victorious, "I can't believe I'm seeing that I know this ... that ... I was just about to say a name the dead no longer deserve!" she slapped her mouth shut.

"But what? how?" various interested people were asking.

"God forgive me, but that woman was carrying on with my husband—and there's the punishment! My husband is the doorman of the building where she was living and that ... that ... started seeing my man in her room! just imagine! shameless! I warned my husband to cut it out and I almost strangled this ... But will you look at that, of all people to see die ...," the poor woman was suffocating, choking.

"Ma'am, are you sure?" an old woman in black asked quietly and interested shaking the hard rose on her hat.

"And how!" screamed the woman opening her arms.

A few people were laughing, others murmuring something about the inappropriateness of the conversation.

"Poor thing, but if she's dead like that man says there's no paramedic can save a dead woman, call somebody at the morgue, I'm not from here, I don't know ..."

"Since nobody's moving I'll call, I'll call! But there's no need to push, madam, there's no hurry now, right? I'll call ... Ah, no need, it's all right, here's the guard!"

A pallid and shaky brightness reeled in his chest, he saw her lying on the ground with white and peaceful lips, the bun in her hair undone, the brown straw hat smashed. So it really was her.

"And who are you, sir?" the guard was shouting at him taking up his duties and seeing him standing, pale, calm, small. He hesitated for an instant. Then slowly he looked at the guard and with courtesy responded:

"I'm ..."

"Don't tell me, don't tell me, I know! Wait ... wait. Ah, of course, from the Edifício São Tomás! How could I forget?! I gave you a ticket for going the wrong way down a one-way street a long time ago, right?" laughed the guard remembering—all the wrinkles in his face were stretching out kind and innocent.

He laughed too, dabbed the handkerchief on his lips politely.

"So she's dead?" he asked.

"She sure is and the damn driver got away from me. I already sent someone to call for an ambulance to the morgue. Anyway so glad, really, so glad to see you again!"

So she'd see men in her room. And so she'd see men in her room! Prostitute, he sighed. Death had unfinished forever anything that could be known about her. The impossibility and the mystery tired his heart with strength. Adriano sat on a garden bench, barely leaning on the backrest. His squinting eyes were looking into the distance, he was breathing with difficulty out of surprise and rage. With his handkerchief he slowly smoothed his hard, cold forehead. And all of a sudden he wasn't sure if it was out of frozen ecstasy or intolerable suffering—because in that single instant he'd won her and lost her forever—all of a sudden, in a first experience of the shame, he felt inside him a horribly free and painful movement, a vague urge to shout or cry, some mortal thing opening in his chest a violent clearing that might have been a new birth.

RIO, MARCH 1943
NAPLES, NOVEMBER 1944

313